SHATTERED BY THE SEA LORD

LORDS OF ATLANTIS

USA TODAY BESTSELLING AUTHOR

STARLA NIGHT

Cover by Earthly Charms
Editing by Linda Edits

For inquiries:

Starla Night
starla@starlanight.com
https://starlanight.com

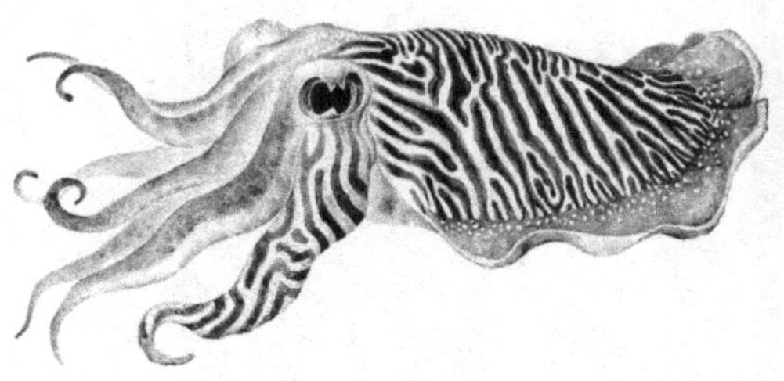

ONE

The day of the plane crash started out completely ordinary.

Sunlight kissed the palm trees outside Dannika's guest cottage, the owner's peacocks began squawking for their breakfast in the back garden, and four nude warriors broke down Dannika's bedroom door.

Dannika jolted up in bed and flung off her lavender-scented sleep mask. "Wha—? Is it?"

The warriors raced around her suite, peeking in the bathroom, closet, and the attached kitchen. Intricate iridescent tattoos covered their bulging muscles, and their hands patted their bare biceps for missing daggers and tridents.

One warrior with bright orange tattoos swirling across his lightly bluish-tinted skin—his name was Gailen—leaned out her open kitchen window. "There! She cries for help in the grass!"

The warriors raced out the way they had come. Dannika's front door hung open, swinging on its hinges.

The peacocks squawked louder with surprise. *Heeeemeee. Heeemeee.*

Gailen called, "Where are you? We hear your cry for help. We are coming!"

Heeeemeee. Heeemeee.

Oh, goodness.

They'd misheard the peacocks.

"Again?" Dannika collapsed, noodle spined, against the carved hardwood headboard and yawned. If she closed her eyes or squinted... No, she'd never mistake the call of a peacock for a human. They sounded like birds with a throaty squeal.

She yawned, then pushed the sheets off her long satin nightgown, tugged on a fluffy bathrobe, and belted it as she wandered to the front door. "Gentlemen? You can relax. It's just the peacocks. Again."

The morning sunlight warmed her front step. A pleasant breeze carried in the scent of ocean salt, sweet grasses, and fresh banana bread made with some of the ripe dwarf Cavendish bananas hanging in the garden.

Gailen strode around the side of her white cottage. An all-seafood diet with plenty of exercise grew the marine warriors into big, hard, gorgeous males intent on claiming and fiercely protecting their soul mates. And performing the occasional peacock rescue, fully nude.

Dannika forced her gaze to his muscular pectorals and face. Above the waist. Definitely above the waist to ignore the bounty that nature had endowed him with. "Please call the other warriors to come out of my back garden."

Worry wrinkled Gailen's brow. "Someone cries for help. A woman, or a child."

"And I applaud your responsiveness." She rested a comforting hand on his beefy shoulder. "You must have run all the way from the beach. But it's a bird, I promise you."

He peered around the far side of the waist-high hibiscus hedge. "Are you sure?"

"I grew up with peacocks. And they made the same sound yesterday morning when Tial broke into my cottage, and the day before, when Zoan did."

The other warriors rejoined them, and Dannika greeted them individually, focusing on their serious, tattooed faces and not on their hard, toned, endowed lower bodies.

Gailen's frown deepened. "Land creatures are so strange. Do you not think so? Why would a bird make such a cry or carry such a tail? It is too strange."

"The world is a strange place." She patted his bulging bicep. "Just think of how shocked we humans were when mermen appeared on our shores."

On the land, they looked like any other muscular, warlike, nude tribe. But under the water, gills sprouted in their lower backs and their feet elongated into fins. Dannika had seen it a few times. It was fascinating to watch.

And five years ago, it had been unthinkable. Mermen were the stuff of legends.

Who would have believed they were living beneath the ocean all along?

For centuries, the warriors had arisen only to unite with brides on isolated, sacred islands. Modernization had emptied those islands and caused a population crash. Five years ago, one warrior had defied his rulers and sought his bride on the mainland. His quest had revealed the mer to the shocked modern world—and launched Dannika's mission.

That first modern bride had envisioned a dating site for warriors to find their soul mates. With the help of good friends, she'd made her vision a reality, and for the past year, Dannika had been running it.

The mer were still a critically endangered species. Dannika's work had never been so necessary, and she awoke every day excited to do it.

She just usually awoke a little later and better rested.

"Why don't you return to the beach?" Dannika suppressed a yawn. "I'll join you as soon as I've dressed."

"We disturbed you. I apologize."

"Oh, no. I wanted to get up early today." She guided him to the white stone path and released him next to the still-open front door. "As always, I'm honored that the warriors of Atlantis care so much about my well-being that you feel the need to break down my door."

"Yes, that was also strange. During your welcome speech, you said that you have an open-door policy, and yet, when we came to investigate the cries for help, we had to break open your door."

Ah.

She looked into their innocent, sweet, but also very capable faces. "I should have said, 'Please ask any questions.' Let's not break any more doors."

"What if you are behind a door when we have a question?" Warrior Nilun demanded.

"You can wait." Dannika stood at her door. "Knock, at the very least. Or you could ask another warrior, or—"

"Your leader." Their leader sauntered up the cottage path. "Me."

Her heart stumbled. *He's back.* She suddenly couldn't breathe. "Ciran?"

Unlike the nude warriors, Ciran wore dark blue Bermuda shorts and an unbuttoned shirt that showed off his well-defined six-pack and belly button. He had a relentless rhythm to his stride, an obdurate resistance that could withstand a hurricane.

He fixed his unusual two-tone eyes on her. His irises were coffee brown mixed with leaf green, like his tattoos. The marks curled across his skin, but their colors never quite touched. "Dannika."

Her heart picked itself up and started beating faster and faster.

I turned you down, but I never stopped thinking of you, and now you've come back.

She took a half step off the porch to run to him, throw her arms around his broad shoulders, and do something crazy like sob with relief.

The bright, interested stares of the other warriors brought her up sharply.

She forced herself up onto the porch again, smoothed her sleep-wrinkled robe, and brushed down her wild black hair. "Well...uh...when did you arrive?"

"Last night." He returned the other warriors' salutes—pressing their pinched fingers together at chest level—and surveyed the gathering. "Where is your guard?"

"Oh, Zoan?" She tried to lean casually against the doorframe, almost slid off, and straightened abruptly. "I, um, let him go."

His gaze bore into her. "You let him go?"

"Yes, I..." She waved in the direction of the hibiscus hedge. "Zoan met his soul mate. She came by last night to take him to meet her family. They'll be back after breakfast."

"He left his post?"

"I told him to."

"That is—"

"Ordered. I ordered him to."

His eyes narrowed.

You should have told me you were coming. Someone

should have told me. Why don't mermen have personal assistants? If they had put you on my calendar, then I wouldn't be a mess right now.

Gailen spoke up. "Then we did cause a problem, Dannika?"

"Yes," Ciran said.

"No, no." She peered over Ciran's looming shoulder. "You didn't know. It's fine."

Ciran turned to the warriors. "Go to Lotar."

They saluted uneasily and hurried down the beach path.

"They didn't mean it," she told Ciran. "I hope you're not mad."

"Mad? No." He swung back to Dannika. "You live on the surface. You are the expert in human affairs."

"Yes, thank you. I am."

"And therefore, you know whether or not you need a guard."

"Yes, well...I don't think it hurts to have a guard. But my mission is to match warriors with their soul mates, and I won't stop, even if it puts me in danger."

He stepped closer. "Then you are in danger?"

She held her ground. "No more than anyone else at MerMatch.com."

"You are its leader."

"And that's why I need us to get along. If you have a problem"—she made a sweeping gesture at herself—"tell me now."

His gaze followed the path of her hand down her body, trailing over her breasts, caressing below the navel, down bare legs and all the way back up. "Hmm."

Oh. God.

Her throat went dry.

She coughed. "What? You have a problem?"

"Yes." He rested a forearm on the doorjamb above her cottage and leaned in, scanning her bedroom and then back to her. Protective, but sensual. "Do not sacrifice your safety for our happiness."

"My mission—"

"Is honorable. Our warriors do need mates, and we desperately need young fry. But Dannika, you also must be safe."

"If I don't support your warriors once they find their soul mates, I'm not a very good matchmaker, am I?"

"You are an excellent matchmaker."

Her heart throbbed. "Oh?"

"Yes." Ciran's true belief blazed into her. "You have brought happiness to many warriors, and you shine like a beacon of hope to those who are still searching. But Zoan would never forgive himself if you were hurt in his absence. Please value yourself as we do."

"Oh." She swallowed hard. "You're so sweet."

He tilted his head. "And you will value yourself?"

"I hear what you're saying. But when you've met your special someone and you're falling in love, every moment is precious. You need to spend it together."

"Warriors can endure a separation. Once a warrior has found his soul mate, he will not stop until she accepts his claim."

A thousand silent signals passed between them. This gorgeous, protective warrior focused on her with his huge, intellectual heart, and a hot current in her blood pounded to his rhythms. She wanted him now just as badly as when they'd first met. Worse now, because the craving to taste his love had only increased.

You must be safe. Please value yourself as we do.

These pure-hearted warriors deserved all she could give and more. Ciran especially. She needed him to be happy.

She needed him to have a wonderful life.

And that was why she had to put aside her shallow lust and focus on his future. "I'm so happy you've come back. Are you finally ready to open your heart?"

"Dannika." His dark gaze stole her breath. "My heart has always been open to you."

"No, I meant..." She cleared her dry throat. "You're ready to find the bride you truly deserve?"

"More than ready."

"I'll be so happy to guide you to your soul mate."

"She is right here."

Her heart throbbed again.

Focus on his happiness. His future. His bride.

"You know..." She cleared her throat again. "You know that I can't accept."

"Do I?"

"You should. I've told you before." Dannika rested her hand on the doorknob and inched away from the hard wall of muscle she just wanted to cling to and squeeze. "It's common for a client to fixate on his first point of contact at a dating agency."

"I do not fixate on a contact." His gaze dropped to her chest. A slight smile curved his firm lips. "Your soul glows with my presence."

Dannika pressed one palm to her chest. "I've heard my soul is bright."

"My warriors see your affinity with the sea. But your soul shines even brighter in my presence."

"Well...ah, that's because...uh...you should focus on yourself, not on me."

"Our souls resonate, Dannika. That is how a warrior recognizes his bride. How I recognized *my* bride."

His voice lowered, and the husky tone made her heart squeeze. Rivulets of desire flooded her feminine channel, and need pinched her breasts.

"I will not descend again until she is mine."

Heat soaked her.

His hard gaze said that he knew everything. Her reactions, her arousal, his effect on her.

Magnetic desire urged her to pull his rock-hard body into her arms, straddle him, meld their lips, and kiss him senseless. His hands would clamp her waist and press her against his demanding erection. She'd murmur wild promises to turn him on—that of course she was his bride, and he was always right—and she would throw her head back as he took her the way she'd dreamed—literally dreamed, naked and sweaty in tangled silk, gasping awake with shock and then promising herself never to remember. She'd seen his cock, full and gorgeous, the day he'd first emerged from the water in New York and strode to her with unwavering certainty. She knew exactly what she was missing by keeping her hands to herself.

"That is...one person's opinion," she finally said, the doorknob digging into her back.

"Actually, all the warriors agree you are my bride."

Wait.

What?

"You've talked about this to the other warriors?"

"They expect you to accept my claim, leave the surface world behind, and journey to Atlantis. Tonight."

"Tonight?" She released the door and forced him back a step. "Well, reassure your warriors that I'm not going anywhere. Running MerMatch is my top priority."

"Your destiny is—"

"My destiny is to find your warriors their soul mates. Everyone deserves true love, and yours, Ciran, is still out there."

He sighed in frustration. "She is standing in front of me."

"Do this exercise with me, Ciran. Envision your future bride, believe she'll come to you, and manifest her."

"I see *your* desire."

"Close your eyes." She stepped back, around the door, and put it between them. "And don't worry. I'm perfectly resolved to put your happiness above mine."

He shifted his weight onto his heels. "I am not."

"That's why I have to be strong for the both of us."

"Dannika—"

"I'll see you on the beach." She closed the door on him and rested her back against the warm wood.

Last time, after days of fighting her unexpected attraction to the two-tone warrior, she'd finally sat him down and formally rejected him. He'd taken it hard, refusing her offer to meet any other matches, and stormed to the docks. Instead of the relief she'd expected to feel, her heart had come loose in her chest and felt strangely bereft. Almost... well, not devastated, but she'd spent the next two weeks fighting back tears when she misplaced a paperclip.

And now he was back.

She peeked out the window.

Ciran stared at the closed door. His jaw flexed. He wasn't angry this time. Not bitter.

No.

The emotion reflected in those fierce eyes was determination.

Uh-oh.

He tipped his head as if to say that this round had gone to her, but he was far from beaten. He turned on a heel and strode decisively down the beach path to his warriors.

She rested her head on the wood and let out a huge sigh, then rotated the small, loose silver wedding band on her ring finger.

Just because she had a feeling didn't mean she had to act on it.

Dannika had fielded interest from plenty of good, kind men. Had she acted? No. Because she'd already met her soul mate. Met and married him.

Everyone deserved that bliss.

Ciran would just have to move on to a better woman. One who made his face light up with happiness.

Dannika had to keep him at arm's length until he got it.

He'd get over his infatuation.

Any minute now.

TWO

Dannika could not deny her soul's desire forever.

Ciran stormed down the white stone path, through scrubby brush, and descended to the pink sand beach. Energy pulsed in his veins. Excitement flushed his pores.

He had given up on her once.

You're a sweet warrior, Ciran, but I just can't return your feelings. I'm sorry. You'll soon understand. She'd rejected him kindly, and he'd believed that she could sense more in their souls than he could.

But her glowing reaction to him just now had confirmed the truth.

She *was* his bride.

He would never give up on her again.

His second-in-command, Lotar, waited in the clear, sandy shallows. His iridescent gray tattoos glistened with droplets of seawater, and his dark hair was slicked back against his skull. He wore red Bermuda shorts, tight against his trim body.

The other warriors clustered behind him, nude and waist-deep in the gently rolling waves.

"Where is Dannika?" Gailen asked.

"Dressing." Ciran nodded at the pile of sand-strewn shorts and shirts. "Wear the human coverings."

They slogged to the beach and obeyed. Gailen struggled with the unusual fastenings, and the other warriors helped him.

"Does this mean we will make the dating profile videos for Dannika?" Gailen asked. "Or will she go with you to Atlantis now?"

"You will make the videos."

"Will she share it with mainland brides?" Tial, a smaller warrior with large eyes and evergreen tattoos, asked. "Will there be time?"

"She will share it."

"When is she leaving as your bride?" Nilun demanded.

Ciran hesitated.

Lotar met his gaze. He was a silent, introspective warrior with excellent instincts, but given the choice, he preferred to swim alone. He'd led this unit of warriors to Bermuda without complaint, but anticipated relinquishing his responsibilities.

"She has not accepted my claim," Ciran said finally.

Lotar tipped his head in silent relief.

The other warriors stared at Ciran.

"Why not?" Tial asked. "When she saw you, she glowed brighter than the sun."

"Her soul was blinding," Gailen agreed.

"Is she frightened?" Nilun asked, his sharp tone and gestures turning even the simplest question into an urgent query. "Does she think you will fail to protect her? Does she not know you are a second lieutenant, and you would die before she came to harm?"

Ah.

Nilun's high opinion of him soothed Ciran's taut brow like a balm. He rolled his shoulders, trying to release muscles that carried too much tension. "Dannika does not have unworthy thoughts. She will fulfill her promises to the mer before she allows any personal desire to intrude."

"Can she not do that as your bride?" Gailen asked.

"She can."

"Then..."

The distant cawing of seabirds sounded lonely on the rustling wind.

Tial's already large eyes grew wider. He asked softly, "Are you okay?"

Of course Ciran was not okay.

He'd surfaced to claim his soul mate, and she denied him. All the warriors had surfaced for the same reason. His failure shook the very foundation of Atlantis.

Long ago, mer and humans had lived in harmony, but a mysterious Great Catastrophe had plunged the two races into war. The mer had retreated to the undersea world and faded into human legend.

But then their females had died out, and their race had faced extinction.

The ruling All-Council had forged an ancient covenant with human brides on sacred islands who promised to keep the mer's secret. Each bride would descend, give birth to a young fry—always male—and then return to her island community. In that way, the undersea world once more thrived.

But in recent generations, the sacred islands had

emptied and modernized. Few brides remained; fewer young fry were born. The mer once more faced extinction.

Then a new voice arose. Kadir urged the warriors to break the ancient covenant, reveal their existence to humans, and seek mainland brides. Across the ocean, rebels had joined his ranks, and Kadir had founded a new city in the wreckage of the ancient Atlantis.

Ciran was one of the first warriors to join his rebellion. He was one of the first warriors to seek a mainland bride.

And he was one of the first warriors to fail.

What barrier prevented Dannika from accepting his claim?

The obvious answer was that she did not value herself. She sacrificed her safety, her happiness, her future for others. That was too much. She needed a warrior to protect, honor, and treasure her.

That warrior was Ciran.

But there was something else. Something deeper she refused to share. He sensed the barrier, submerged beneath her easy rejections, perhaps hiding even from her own consciousness.

Eventually, he would dismantle her easy rejections and then, together, they would face her real objection.

In the meantime, he needed to explain her refusal in a way his impulsive, loyal, too-helpful warriors could understand.

"I will not ask Dannika to be less honorable than she is. She must meld modern dating with the sacred bride ceremonies. When warriors can find their brides without her intervention, then she and I will, of course, descend and marry before the Atlantis Life Tree."

Another long silence followed.

"Perhaps she is not the only one who is too honorable," one of his warriors muttered.

Ciran crossed his arms. "Who said that?"

They shuffled uncomfortably.

Gailen finally spoke to ease the tension. "You are from Undine, so you can devise a strategy to meld these systems for Dannika."

"I am from Atlantis now."

"Ah, yes... But she knows you were from Undine, right?"

"We have not discussed my origin."

"Forget this human dating. I have the answer." Nilun jabbed his finger at the pink coral sand. "Willing brides come to this beach, here. They drink the elixir and enter the ocean. Warriors swim among them as a predator swims among prey. Then, when a warrior finds the bride who resonates with his soul, he cuts her from the rest of the humans, and it is done. She is his. There are no surface words or meaningless delays. She must accept our claim, no choice, and we descend directly to Atlantis."

"That is not the human way." Lotar's voice was soft but sharp.

"The human way takes too long. Why so much conversation and argument? And even the brightest humans cannot see soul lights as the mer do."

"It is strange." Gailen squinted at the path to the human sleeping areas. "Why must Second Lieutenant Ciran, a serious and honorable warrior, labor to convince Dannika of his worth when Zoan, a much lesser warrior, easily convinced his bride to accept his claim?"

"Are you talking about me again?" Zoan called from the top of the beach.

"When am I not?" Gailen saluted the jolly warrior

striding down the white stone path. Gailen's thumbs did not align properly, so he could never make the proper form. "Where is your bride? Did she escape you already?"

"Do not insult Zoan!" Nilun quested for the daggers that were not on his bare biceps and thighs, and then clenched his fists. "He is a warrior a hundred times your worth."

"I do not know if I am one hundred times the worth of Gailen." Zoan's shirt was buttoned improperly, and his dark hair stuck up askew as if a loving bride had ruffled it. He lifted his hands and wiggled his thumbs. "Perhaps just two thumbs' worth."

Nilun frowned.

Gailen gave him a wry grin. "She did run away from you, then?"

"To gather her family. They are having something called an 'engagement party,' and she is buying a dress. But her family will come here later. Perhaps one of her three sisters is a match for you."

The warriors straightened.

"Brides should come to us." Nilun flexed his arms. "Mine will know I am a capable warrior, and although I am not a second lieutenant, she will not hesitate to accept my claim."

Everyone looked at Ciran and then swiftly away.

Zoan's gaze followed. "You have found your bride?"

"It is Dannika," Gailen answered for Ciran, chatty as usual. "She glows brighter than the sun in his presence but refuses his claim. Answer me this, Zoan. Why should a bright female deny an honorable warrior like Ciran when another easily accepts a warrior like you?"

"I know." Zoan tapped his forehead. "Second Lieutenant Ciran, did you show her your size?"

The warriors hooted.

A mer hardened only when his bride teased him seductively, which usually happened in the privacy of his castle, so despite constant nudity, the warriors rarely saw each other aroused. But, apparently, arousal size held some importance to humans. It had become a topic of recent discussion.

"My bride became quite excited," Zoan continued. "We talked for hours about large houses, metal cars, and engagement dresses. Perhaps Dannika has a problem with your size?"

The other warriors burst out laughing at his daring.

Ciran lifted a brow. "My size?"

"Of your mating gemstone." Zoan's face betrayed no hint of the comedy he'd set up. "Of course."

Mm-hm. Sure.

Ciran let out a long, harassed sigh and shook his head.

His warriors almost fell down with hysteria. Even Lotar, who never smiled, rubbed his lips.

Ciran let them laugh. Zoan's lighthearted question distracted from his very real problem.

And anyway, Zoan's teasing illuminated the strength of Atlantis.

Their warriors came from so many cities that misunderstandings happened every day. King Kadir listened to the lowest-ranked warriors, accepted being wrong, and solicited their experience to change his rulings. His officers did the same. These moments of camaraderie formed the connections that bound the warriors together into a cohesive unit that Ciran was proud to lead.

When their laughter subsided, Ciran divided the warriors into patrols, automatically systematizing their work according to their preferences and talents. Some shucked their human clothing to sweep the reef. Others looked for hidden dangers threatening their small, isolated beach.

Zoan lingered nearby.

Ciran saluted him. "Congratulations on claiming your bride. May your castle overflow with young fry."

Zoan saluted back. Then he glanced around as if to check that no one was listening and sidled closer to Ciran. "Is Dannika your bride? Truly? She is a bright female like Queen Aya. It can be difficult to sense which warrior makes her shine brightest."

A hot shard embedded in Ciran's chest. "It is me."

"Then how can she reject you? It must pain her as much as it pains you."

"She has a long-standing tolerance to her own suffering."

"That cannot be healthy."

Ciran tipped his head. Zoan's easy acceptance made the shard fade to a throb. "But her responsibilities at MerMatch overpower her soul's desire." *For now*.

"Really?" Zoan gave a rare frown. "Is that what she says?"

"Yes." Ciran changed the subject before Zoan got too close to his own conclusion. "I have a unit ready to escort your bride to Atlantis."

"My bride wishes to remain on Bermuda and acclimate slowly to the mer life."

"How slowly?"

"A month, a year. Perhaps five years."

"You would leave Atlantis for five years?"

Zoan shrugged. "The time is up to my bride."

He rotated to face Zoan head-on. "Atlantis is always under attack. The All-Council plots to destroy our city.

Will you avoid your duty to your fellow warriors? To your king?"

"King Kadir does not mind."

"You just found your bride. How can he know?"

"Dannika called the mid-Atlantic platform last night. They conveyed the message down their electrical wires into the city. It is so convenient, this human communication, is it not? Much faster than echo points and ocean currents."

Then it was true, and Ciran had made an improper assumption. "I overstepped. Forgive me."

Zoan choked. "Do my ears lie? Did a second lieutenant actually admit his mistake?"

"I can repeat myself."

"No, no. We live in an age of wonders." Zoan sobered. "I must get used to trusting my ears. We rely on souls to convey feelings. If I have learned one thing from watching the queens at the Atlantis Life Tree, it is that they value their words more highly than warriors do."

Hmm.

When Dannika talked, he only heard her disvaluing herself. Another bride would be better than her. Another bride would be more capable.

Had he missed something? What else did she reveal?

Gailen sloshed up to Zoan and threw an arm around the warrior's shoulders. "Listen to this expert. He has had a bride for one day. Now he knows everything about brides."

Zoan lifted his nose. "I already knew everything. My bride simply affirms my expertise."

"Expertise? How did you find such an innocent female?"

Zoan elbowed him. "Good luck finding one who dislikes thumbs."

Gailen tripped Zoan over his knee and doused him in

the shallows. Zoan splashed, thrashed, and then grappled Gailen. He toppled in after. The warriors wrestled good-naturedly under the waves.

Lotar looked over at them, alert to break up the altercation, then saw Ciran and hesitated.

Nilun shouted and raced across the beach.

Ciran stepped in front of Nilun. "Control yourself."

"Control myself?" The hotheaded warrior gestured at the shallow-water wrestlers. "Gailen attacked Zoan!"

"Use your eyes. Are those warriors angry?"

"They are fighting!"

"Are they?"

"Yes!"

"Nilun." Ciran pushed him back on his heels, forcing him up onto the wet sand. "If you cannot sense the difference between a friendly test of strength and a bloody duel, you will never rise in the ranks."

Nilun's chin jerked back, and he stood ramrod straight. Rage contracted his features, but he quickly controlled it.

"I know you can observe your surroundings," Ciran said. "You are an excellent patroller and swift to defend your friends. Take a deep breath."

He inhaled through gritted teeth.

"Tell me how you know it is a friendly test of strength."

"I do not," he snarled.

"Then tell me how *I* know. What signs do I see? Recite them."

The warrior glared at the wrestlers just like a recalcitrant trainee, even though he was a fully grown adult, but by degrees, his shoulders lowered and his brows lifted. "They do not seek their weapons. And Zoan did not crush Gailen as he could have."

Nilun shared a few more observations. Gailen and Zoan

stopped wrestling on their own and clambered out, sopping wet from the surf, clapping each other on the back.

"Practice honing these observations," Ciran ordered. "Stop, observe, and then act."

Nilun frowned. "If I hesitate, someone could get hurt."

"If you do not hesitate, you will make a mistake."

"But—"

"A mistake will hurt an innocent warrior. Do not let your fierce loyalty become your greatest flaw."

He lowered his gaze, nodded, and, at Ciran's order, returned to his patrol.

Ciran mentally shuffled patrols to schedule Nilun with any warrior except Gailen. He needed a long time to cool.

Across the sand, Lotar nodded at Ciran in silent respect. The grim set of his gray-tattooed jaw conveyed just how much he had not wanted to lead these warriors alone.

At least one warrior was glad that Ciran had not already united with Dannika.

He did not think he was unobservant. But if Zoan was right, he must hone his observations of Dannika, or he would rush to the wrong conclusion like Nilun.

She would reveal her secrets, and he would overcome every barrier until they united.

The future of Atlantis depended on it.

THREE

Ciran just had to realize he was wrong.

Dannika slipped into a lavender caftan dress with an aqua scroll pattern down the front and along the split sleeves, then examined herself in the mirror.

Was this dress blockier than the gold maxi she'd just rejected? Or less flattering than the scoop-neck green wrap she'd tried on before that?

Dannika tugged at the bodice.

Maybe she should wear the green wrap. It was lower cut, and—

Ugh, no, she needed to get down to the beach and start filming.

Dannika resolutely closed the closet, then spread her makeup across the long bathroom counter. Hmm. Subdued daytime coverage, or dramatic film-ready flare? She tapped her smallest brush against her tub of iridescent green eyeshadow. That had been an impulse purchase a few months ago. Funny she hadn't realized how closely it matched Ciran's tattoos...

She shoved it back into her makeup clutch, selected

muted colors for a mature, natural look, and set about smoothing, shaping, and shading.

Yes, Ciran was like a dream, and he made her want to take a shower—with him in it—every time he glanced her way. Virility seeped from his tattooed, ripped, capable pores. Any woman would fan herself after encountering him.

Dannika's mission came first.

She would put on a good smile when she found him the kind of young woman he deserved.

Dannika practiced the smile.

Hmm. A little flat.

She dropped the false smile and examined her scalp.

Three gray hairs intermixed with her long locks. Forty years in and she now had three gray hairs.

She grouped them together so her hair would get the idea and sprout a fabulous single gray streak, grabbed her woven beach tote, and flounced out of her guest cottage.

"Miss Dannika!" The owner of the cottage, an affable black Jamaican in his fifties who'd emigrated years ago, lifted his portable receiver. "Your assistant called. Is there a problem with your cell phone?"

"Oh, thank you so much." She embraced him. "I forgot to turn it on again."

"Yes, I thought so." He returned her hug with one big arm. "And don't worry. The repairman is coming to fix your door. I heard the noise this morning when I fed the peahens."

"That's so kind. Please add it to the bill like the others. You're so understanding."

He surveyed the property. "They have brought my good friends some happiness. And I know how hard it is to understand the ways of a new land."

"Don't we all." She hugged him again.

He patted her and ambled to the back garden.

She rummaged in her woven tote, found her cell phone, and turned it on. Twenty missed calls in five minutes, plus a plethora of unread messages.

Oh, dear.

Dannika dialed MerMatch directly.

"MerMatch, this is Hazel." The calm, organized voice of her assistant sounded efficient and helpful.

"Hi, Hazel. I'm sorry I missed your—"

"Oh. My. God. Dannika! Are you okay? Where were you? I called you a hundred times."

"I know, I saw. What was the—"

"I thought those anti-mer Sons of Hercules got you. Found out your location and, I don't know, sniped or bombed you."

It was so sad that only a short time after the warriors had dared to reveal their existence to the modern world, a human terrorist organization had popped up to drive them back into the ocean.

"I was perfectly safe," Dannika said.

But Hazel continued her litany of fears. "Or worse, that Ciran showed up and finally bossed you back to Atlantis."

Dannika laughed awkwardly in front of a shrub that smelled heavenly, like allspice. "Is being in charge really so bad?"

"Yes!"

"Hazel, you're doing fabulous."

"No, no, no. I'm surviving. The water is up to my neck."

"Hazel."

"I can't talk to important people like you do and make them see that *we* are the good guys. When are you coming back?"

"The final group arrived last night. We'll finish filming today, and then I'll go over the women's profiles and see where they can meet."

"And then you'll be back?"

"Yes, more or less."

"Thank. God. I cannot survive without you."

"Hazel, you give me too much credit. You run the whole office even when I'm there. I stride in, pick up your files, and stride out. You're capable of more than you think."

Hazel laughed hysterically, which was her way of disagreeing.

Dannika could just picture her assistant combing nail-bitten fingers through her adorable chestnut-brown hair, draining any drops from her third hazelnut latte, and polishing her cell phone screen on the lapel of her splotched cream suit. She only got manicures when Dannika made her, but it was an excellent way to feel nice, and it rescued her cuticles.

"But why are you really calling?" Dannika asked.

"Oh. Yes." Hazel sucked in a huge breath and released it. "Starr sent over more audio files of the Sons of Hercules planning an anti-mer attack. She tried processing them with different voice software to get rid of the distortion. I forwarded the file. I don't know if it'll make any difference, but maybe you'll be able to recognize the leader now."

"I'll review it. Anything else?"

"Oh, yes. Your friend called about the dinner party tonight. He has big news."

Her heart lifted again. "Yes?"

"He didn't tell me. He said he'll call back."

"I'll keep my phone close. Thank you so much, Hazel."

"God, I hope you convince the senator to let mermen

onto US soil again. Then you can meet the warriors where God intended: right here in New York."

Dannika chuckled and hung up.

The Sons of Hercules had bombed, shot, poisoned, kidnapped, and committed biological warfare against the warriors. Some attacks had succeeded, and others had failed. But their most vivid success had been in lobbying. For an organization that had started out radicalizing isolated, socially maladapted young men on college campuses, they'd grown into a lobbying machine that had driven fear into the hearts of politicians. The US had recently become the first nation to close its borders to new merman applicants.

Which meant that only a few warriors—Ciran, Lotar, and the others who'd already surfaced and claimed their mates—could enter the country. New warriors such as Gailen and Tial could not.

Not that the government could police a hundred thousand miles of shoreline. But it meant that Dannika would not invite all of her single warriors to a big speed-dating event in Central Park either.

Bermuda was just two hours by plane from New York. But the fishhook-shaped cluster of islands, fifteen miles in length and only three miles wide, were a British Territory. They didn't care what the US did or didn't allow.

Of course, Dannika didn't want to test their goodwill. The Sons of Hercules had attacked across the globe.

But so long as they were still willing, what better location to meet with mermen than in paradise?

The diverse islands enjoyed milder tropical weather because it was so far north of the Caribbean. Yesterday, she'd had to stop filming due to howling winds, thunderous rain, and screaming birds. Such storms, along with the treacherous coral ringing the islands, had once given Bermuda the nickname of "the Devil's Isle." But more days were like today. Balmy wind combed through the squat, pineapple-shaped palmetto trees. Fragrant loquat fruits ripened beside bushes of allspice and island cedar.

She followed the path to the shoreline. Sunrise colors lingered on the foamy waves sifting the pink morsels of the beach.

Twelve warriors clustered in the shallows around Zoan. His new bride, lovely Indigo, must have just arrived, because they were still doing introductions.

When Dannika imagined brides for the warriors, she pictured confident young women like Indigo. Long, wavy black hair flowed down her open back to robust curves. Stylish beads adorned her beach wrap, and delicate blue and white flowers crowned her head. Her excited smile, bright white in her dark brown skin, lit the beach.

The warriors mostly stared in awe.

Zoan, by contrast, looked relaxed. He'd always had a twinkle in his eye, but the lines of hardship had smoothed.

Ciran focused on Indigo with his usual intensity. "Zoan says he will descend to Atlantis when you are ready. When will you be ready?"

"Yeah, after the wedding." Her cheerful Bermy accent was mildly British. "My family is flying in from all over. They're so excited. We never dreamed of this day, getting a Sea Opal the size of a boulder. That's a proper rock."

"And when will you descend?"

"Yeah, after the wedding and the honeymoon, and then Zoan'll teach me how to swim, and we'll come down. Say hi on our way somewhere really exotic, like Paris or Brazil."

Steely-eyed Lotar lowered his chin. "You will cross the ocean alone?"

"Yeah, I don't know. Depends on how we feel, right?"

"Right." Zoan grinned.

"That is..." Lotar trailed off and stared with intent at Zoan. "Brave."

Zoan grinned more broadly. "We will see how we feel."

Ciran's gaze flicked to Dannika, then back to Zoan, and his eyes narrowed. "Are you claiming Indigo as your bride, or do you intend to make her a queen?"

"Ah, you keep saying those two things." Indigo patted Zoan's arm excitedly. "What's the difference?"

Ciran answered. "A bride stays beneath the water with her warrior only long enough to produce his young fry. A queen pledges herself to our city, defends our Life Tree, and stays underwater with her warrior forever. With her dedication, she can channel the energy of the Life Tree and wield life-saving powers."

"Well, I'm thinking the queen one, because magical powers would be really great, but I have to be able to see my family."

"You will. The queens surface frequently." Zoan ticked off the visits on his fingers. "Queen Elyssa hosts Thanksgiving at her father's house, Queen Lucy surfaces with her young fry to visit her parents regularly, and Queen Aya has spent more time on land before the human 'United Nations' than she has under the water."

"The queen one, then."

"I knew you would say that." He kissed her cheek, and she glowed.

Ciran frowned.

"Ciran, you look into clear water and see mud. Brides are all around us. Atlantis is no longer a few warriors huddled inside one tiny castle fretting over our newly sprouted Life Tree." Zoan rested his arm around Indigo's waist, and she leaned against him in solidarity. "Relax."

The young couple's happiness brought tears to Dannika's eyes. That was why she did this work. That right there.

Ciran's hard gaze inevitably found hers. He always sensed her emotions, and if she went to him, he would undoubtedly wrap her in a comforting hug.

But she couldn't let herself yield to temptation.

She sniffed and veered to the camera crew, dropped her tote beside a stool, and fixed her best smile for the employees she'd flown over for this shoot. "Did you sleep well?"

"Better than you, I heard." The lead videographer, Stevie, grinned up at her. "I see you got some new additions. Four warriors and another leader?"

"These are the last. How are we doing? My assistant can't wait to see me in the office."

"The weather should cooperate to finish filming today. And I have a rough cut of another promotional video for you to review."

"Perfect." The sooner they turned the tide of public opinion to reopen the borders, the sooner she could return to her usual environment, where she did not get tempted by gorgeous, inflexible warriors. "We need all the positive press we can get."

FOUR

Her first interviewee today, Gailen, sat stiffly on the camera crew's stool and endured a local makeup artist's touch. The artist emphasized his vibrant pepper-orange tattoos that matched the vivid threads in his irises.

Dannika sat across from him. "Stay calm and answer my questions as fully as possible. Okay?"

He glanced at Stevie holding the camera behind her and then at the two assistants positioning shiny reflectors. "Okay."

"Speak into the camera as if you're speaking to your future soul mate, because you are. She will see you, hear your story, and come to find you."

A nervous but hopeful smile broke across his face. "How?"

"She'll tell me that she wants to meet you."

"But how will she know? Our souls cannot resonate until we are in each other's presence."

"Um, she'll just know. Trust me."

He nodded slowly.

"And then you'll meet and get to know each other over a few dates..." Dannika leaned forward and patted his damp shorts-clad knee. "And it will be perfect."

"Why?"

"Why what?"

"If she knows I am her soul mate from watching a video, why must we get to know each other over a few dates?"

"Ah... Because sometimes you have to make sure your first instinct is right."

"Is that why you have not accepted Second Lieutenant Ciran's claim?"

Embarrassed heat made her armpits prickle. "No. That's completely different."

"Because your first instinct is very right. He is a thoughtful and honorable warrior. Consider this. He is the only patrol leader who has always assigned me tasks I can accomplish. Everyone else forgets because of my thumbs."

"That sounds like the sort of thing Ciran would do." Dannika kept her smile fixed in place. "Let's focus on you. Why don't you introduce yourself?"

"You know that Ciran has also waited many years to meet his bride and produce a young fry. If you worry about his mating gemstone, he will show you its size, and you can plan your future with large cars and houses."

"Gailen." Ciran appeared at her right like an angel of mercy. Stern, flaming mercy. "Answer Dannika's question."

The pepper-orange warrior straightened.

"I am Gailen of Atlantis." He pressed his fingertips together in the salute. His thumbs pointed downward, permanently bent out of position. "Pleased to meet you."

"Yes..." She glanced at Stevie. If his recording was going well, he would splice Gailen's interview to make a smooth clip.

Stevie gave a thumbs-up.

Dannika returned to Gailen. "What do you want your future bride to know about you? Your past, your goals, your interests."

"My interests?"

"The sort of thing a bride should know before she descends to the bottom of the sea."

"Ah." Gailen leaned forward. "She should know that long ago, the mer and humans lived together in harmony, but then a Great Catastrophe caused the floating mer-human city of Atlantis to sink—"

"Oh..."

"—and the humans hunted us, and all the mer queens died out—"

"I, ah..."

"—so the All-Council forged an ancient covenant with sacred brides, but then they all disappeared—"

"I meant..."

Gailen recited King Kadir's rise, the founding of Atlantis, the first mainland women who descended to become their brides, and the All-Council's subsequent attempt to wipe out the city.

"—but our modern brides channeled their queen powers to save Atlantis and bring a new light of hope to all warriors." Gailen took a huge breath. "It is hard to tell a story in the air. How do humans remember to breathe?"

"Some don't." She uncrossed and recrossed her legs. "Thank you for that enlightening short history of the mer. How about a little personal history? Something that might interest your bride."

"Yes." His expression was so open, so eager. "What is she interested in?"

"You. She's interested in you. Why don't you introduce yourself?"

"I have already introduced myself." He straightened proudly. "I am Gailen of Atlantis."

Perhaps today's interviews would take longer than she anticipated.

"Gailen." Ciran drew the other warrior's attention. "What is your role in Atlantis?"

"I tend the Life Tree and propagate the best-tasting foods."

"What is your city of origin?"

"Aiycaya."

"Which is where? In human terms."

"On the bottom of the ocean, east of the Caribbean island of Haiti."

"And why did you leave?"

"For the same reason all warriors leave their home cities, abandon their fathers, and betray their kings."

"Describe yours."

"A hurricane destroyed Aiycaya's sacred island, but the All-Council refused to let us find a new one. For a generation, no young fry were born. Our elders died out. When King Kadir summoned warriors to Atlantis to join with modern brides, I tried to escape. Three times, Aiycaya warriors caught me. The last time, they broke my thumbs."

Gailen tapped his fingers together, then tried and failed to do the same with his thumbs.

"They said if they caught me again, they would kill me." He gave a heartbreakingly sweet smile. "So they did not catch me again."

A lump formed in Dannika's throat.

All the warriors had a similar history. Their cities had

come to the brink of extinction, no warriors found brides, and the All-Council stuck by its inflexible ancient covenant.

She had to help them. Dannika cleared her throat. "Thank you, Gailen."

Gailen tossed a cheery smile her way, bobbed to his feet, and swaggered to the other warriors.

Okay.

Dannika marked some notes. "Ciran, could you tell the other warriors the kind of interview answers that will be the most powerful at reaching their future brides?"

He tipped his head and prepared the next warriors.

In the middle of the preparations, Indigo's family arrived with joy. They carried baskets of fresh fruit, snacks, and the island's famous fried fish with raisin bread sandwiches.

Dannika welcomed them with hugs all around. "My assistant, Hazel, should have sent you the information packet for new brides and their families. You're also welcome to watch these interviews to learn what Indigo can expect in her role."

Her mother, father, and three sisters settled onto their comfy picnic blankets. They watched with expectant, eager eyes.

Nilun sat with a determined glare.

He might not be Dannika's first choice to introduce to the new family...but it would probably be fine. "Go ahead and introduce yourself."

"I am Nilun of Atlantis, originally of Djullanar, and my bride will have no fears under the water. I will protect her from all dangers."

"Great. That's perfect. How—"

"Raiders, exiles, and All-Council armies." He slammed his fist into his chest. "Beware."

"Very good. Can—"

"When a shark bites and mauls and tears into her flesh, I will fend it off."

Dannika held up her hand. "Okay. Let's—"

"When a megalodon rises from the depths and inhales the very city itself, crushing and destroying, I will fly to its eyes and blind it with my trident."

"Nilun." She subtly coughed. Indigo and her family stared at Nilun in terror. "Acknowledging risks can be healthy, but focusing on them exclusively might discourage a future bride."

"But I will protect her."

"Right, and emphasizing risks that are unlikely—"

"These risks are very likely. I have encountered all myself."

"Mm. Recently?"

"Yes. In this very year." He puffed out his chest proudly. "And I defeated them all. I am a worthy, capable warrior with two thumbs. My bride should not fear."

"So...okay, and why not share the wonderful things your bride can enjoy while you're there taking care of any danger?"

"I do not understand."

"What's empowering and beautiful about being a mer?"

He pondered the question. "We do not breathe air..."

"Yes, and?"

"We can see the souls of our enemies from a vast distance. Thus we are more able to prepare. Unless they are hiding in an ambush. Then"—he slashed his hand—"we must fight. With trident and dagger. Yah!"

Okay.

She looked back at Stevie. "Is that enough to make a profile? Do you think?"

He shrugged. "I'll cut something together. Want to take a break?"

She checked with Indigo's family. They had set aside their picnic food and side-eyed the surrounding warriors.

Indigo rested her left hand, with a sparkly engagement diamond, on Zoan's bare knee. "Did you go through all that? Raiders and sharks? Megalodons?"

His eyes twinkled. "Well..."

"Not on the first day," Dannika assured her. "And as a bride, you have an advantage over the warriors in that you'll eventually develop queen powers."

"Yeah, I'm so curious about those," Indigo said. "Channeling energy? From the Atlantis Life Tree? How does it work?"

"There are three main powers: pushing, shielding, and healing. One will emerge as you strengthen your soul-mate bond. Zoan won't let you get into a dangerous situation until you're ready."

Indigo nodded, eyes wide.

"Sure." Zoan's eyes twinkled with suppressed mischief. "You can believe that if it helps you sleep at night."

Indigo bumped his shoulder. "That does, actually."

His twinkle disappeared. He nuzzled her with genuine kindness. "Good."

Whew.

Dannika's phone rang.

Her call.

She yanked it from her tote, stood, and answered as she walked to a quieter region of the small beach. "This is Dannika."

"Dannika, my dear, I've been trying to reach you." Her elderly friend, Frederik, crackled on the weak connection. "How happy I am to finally get through."

"Yes, I'm all ready for tonight. I've arranged an afternoon flight." She checked her wristwatch. "Thank you so much for scheduling with the senator. I just know we can lift the restrictions on mermen if we can show him they only mean peace."

"My dear, I'm so sorry to be the bearer of bad news. The senator's office called. He can't leave Washington."

The sandy shore tilted beneath Dannika's sandals. A seabird's melancholy cry echoed in her pounding ears.

No. It wasn't true.

A hard lump formed in her throat. Tears pricked her eyes.

"Oh, gosh. Oh, goodness." She turned away and fanned herself with a jerky motion. "Can we change the hour? Or the date?"

"You know what it means when a politician gives that answer. It's just like when a Hollywood producer tells you he loves your script and he'll be in touch. If I had a penny for every time I heard that, I'd be producing the next blockbuster myself."

The sun slipped behind a cloud, and the tableau of warriors and camera crew took on a gray cast. Only Ciran gazed her way like a splash of color in a world of sepia.

She couldn't face him right now.

"How disappointing." She hurried down the beach away from the warriors. "I thought the senator was sympathetic. What happened?"

"He has a college-age daughter."

"So?"

"Your office has produced lovely informational ads, but your opponents have struck right in the man's ugly heart. 'These monsters kidnap, assault, enslave our innocent girls. Don't let yours become the next victim.'"

"Those are all lies."

"Yes, well... In the old legends, mermen *were* monsters. And the Sons of Hercules are happy to remind us."

"Yes, but in the old legends, Hercules was an insane, violent murderer." Dannika rubbed her clammy hands, one after the other, on her caftan. "You know his twelve labors? He performed them in penance."

"Yes, for offing his innocent wife and children. I attended Oxford, my dear."

"Yet our mermen are the ones who attack innocents?"

"The modern education system has murdered the classics," Frederik agreed. "Yet the message packs a punch. When it comes to love, fear always wins."

That contradicted everything Dannika stood for.

She shook her whole body, rejecting it with everything she had. "I can't believe that."

"Rom coms are fine, but horror will never die. I sell the stories. I know."

"No, I mean, I'm sure you're right, but..." She scrubbed her burning eyes. "Where do we go from here?"

"Why don't you come down tonight anyway?" Frederik suggested. "We'll have a little powwow and figure it out. You have the connections."

Dannika did have the connections, but her best one had just declined her dinner invitation.

Again.

Gailen and the others were counting on her.

She was failing her warriors.

"We can open a bottle of sherry and reminisce about old times," he continued.

"Mm." She cleared her throat. "Well..."

"I am sorry for missing Eliot's annual memorial. Can you believe it's been eighteen years since he died? What an awful, awful day. Worse for you, I'm sure. The only blessing is that you weren't there to see it, although that's also sad, in a way."

She rotated her slightly loose wedding ring. Guilt was a familiar companion. It was the cost of having found true love. "I may come down..."

Ciran's voice punctured the air behind her. "You are leaving Bermuda?"

She whirled.

His dark eyes mesmerized her. "Where you go, I go."

The tingle started in her belly.

She sucked in a breath and let it out. Then she moved the phone away from her ear to answer him. "Your warriors must need you here."

"Lotar is a capable leader." His fingers encircled her wrist. "You need me."

"I don't..."

But he saw the truth.

And so did she.

I don't want to need you.

Dannika closed her lips and rubbed her tongue across the nude gloss. She didn't want to need Ciran, but when the world broke down around her, all she wanted to do was lean into his unbending support.

But no.

She pulled her spine straight and took a deep, calming breath. "Yes, I am returning to the mainland. And you are welcome to come as well. We can look at bios together on the plane, and by the time we land, I'll help you pick out the perfect bride."

FIVE

As she listed her requirements, Ciran's eyes narrowed in refusal. "I will look at anything with you, Dannika, but you know you are my bride. Accept my claim."

Which meant to share a kiss.

Heat waved through her veins and twisted in a hot ache between her thighs. Her nipples tightened. Desire flooded into all her nooks and crannies, the sensual pieces of herself that she'd long ignored.

Her body yearned to envelop him, lick the salt off his abdomen, delve beneath the rim of his shorts, and encircle the cock she found within.

Ciran would be a passionate and sensual lover. If she let him have the tiniest taste—if she let herself indulge—she would wreck his life and ruin herself forever.

"I will claim you, Dannika." His low voice was so possessive, it made the hairs on the back of her neck stand up. "You are mine."

But if she gave in...

Luckily, she didn't have to.

Shouts erupted from the other warriors. Pushing, shoving, and a scream.

———

Just when Dannika's soul was finally starting to glow, his warriors had to start a fight.

Ciran released Dannika, pivoted, and raced down the sand.

Gailen fought with Nilun.

Lotar forced the grappling warriors back from Indigo's family. Her young sisters clung to her parents. Indigo stood behind a somber Zoan.

Gailen rammed Nilun into the sand, landed on top of him, and continued the struggle.

Ciran yanked Gailen off.

Gailen fought with surprising strength, but Ciran finally contained the enraged warrior. "Calm. Breathe. *Breathe*, Gailen. Inhale the air."

Nilun rolled to his knees.

Lotar stood in front of him and gestured silently for him to remain down. Nilun grimaced but obeyed.

Gailen finally took a deep breath and let it out, his limbs trembling. "Curse you, Nilun. Spiky pufferfish have more brains."

"You dare insult me?" Nilun surged to his feet.

Gailen swiped at him.

Lotar's arm flashed, barely seeming to touch Nilun, but the hotheaded warrior went down and stayed flat.

Ciran forced Gailen back. He never attacked without reason. "You struck first. Explain."

"He was scaring them." Gailen jabbed his misshapen hand at Indigo's sisters. "Their souls blackened with fear."

Even now, the young girls looked dimmer than when they'd arrived.

"Because you lied," Nilun groaned. "The ocean is not a big, empty room. Every mer is not a friend."

"Enough," Ciran growled at Nilun. "Remember the lesson of the morning. What do you observe?"

"Gailen will lead them into danger."

"Nilun. Look at the humans. Their souls."

"And? The ocean *is* dangerous." Nilun rose to his knees, gave Lotar a wary eye, and rubbed his abdomen. "Especially near this island. All the mer know that. And yet he urges these defenseless females to go into the water and play."

The girls hugged their mother. Their souls all dimmed.

Dannika encompassed the humans in a big hug. "Oh, it's not like that. Indigo will be perfectly safe with the warriors of Atlantis, I promise you."

"What did he mean, 'especially near this island'?" Indigo's mother asked. "We're in danger near here?"

"Yeah, I want to know about that too," Stevie, Dannika's videographer, chimed in.

Lotar frowned blackly, and the warriors who'd surfaced before Ciran shuffled with unease.

There was no special danger near Bermuda.

Unless...

Nilun rested his hands on his thighs. "Everyone knows what I mean."

Unfortunately, Ciran did.

The hairs on the back of his neck stood up.

And he wasn't the only one. The other warriors subtly edged away from the sea and rubbed their necks.

Ciran held his ground. "This island is outside of their territory, Nilun."

"Is it? Are you sure?" He glared at the blue shallows. "Would you let your young fry play in these waters alone?"

Dannika looked from one tense warrior to the next and finally sought Ciran's gaze. "Why not? You've been swimming here for days."

"We are adults," Nilun said. "Warriors. We can fight back."

"Nilun." Lotar's warning was soft but sharp.

He subsided.

"Ciran?" She put her hands on her hips. Her coverings flowed in the gentle breeze like an anemone's tendrils, graceful but with a fierce sting. "What's he talking about?"

He hesitated. There was no need to frighten Indigo's family further. No need to speak the name even warriors refused to whisper.

"Lusca," Stevie said with grim certainty. "He's talking about Lusca."

The warriors jumped. Nilun snarled, Lotar tensed, and Gailen jolted.

A ripple of forbidden fear surfaced on Ciran's skin.

He rubbed his forearm. "How do you know that name?"

"So it does exist." Stevie jerked his chin at the warriors closest to him. "I've been asking around, off and on, ever since you guys emerged five years ago. But nobody would confirm it."

"What is it?" Dannika asked. "Lusca?"

Another ripple bumped on his skin, and the other warriors tightened their defensive formation.

"It's a city full of very angry mermen." Stevie bounced his camera off his thigh. "Around 1492, conquistadors emptied their sacred islands, so they go around sinking ships with giant squids."

The warriors murmured in shock.

Dannika blinked. "What?"

Clearly, Ciran had not paid enough attention to the human recording their images. "How did you know of this?"

"Whoa, whoa, whoa." Dannika held out both hands. "Are you saying it's true? There's a city of mermen going around *sinking ships with giant squids,* and this is the first I've heard of it?"

Stevie gestured at Ciran to explain.

His heart sped as if he was being studied by a quick, deadly predator. "Do you need to know this?"

"Yes, I need to know this." She crossed her arms, her tote bouncing against her waist. "The Sons of Hercules have been claiming for years that the mer mean us harm, and if a city has declared war on humans, I need to know. I need to know it right now."

THIS WAS INSANE.

War? Squids? Angry mermen?

No.

Ciran eyed the other warriors, clenched his jaw, and focused his intensity on Dannika as he unveiled the news she least wanted to hear. "It is all true."

The other warriors freaked out.

"Second Lieutenant! Speaking of it is forbidden. You will summon *them* with your loose talk."

He withstood their shouts with his usual resolute, unbending firmness.

Lotar gazed at the sea as though preparing for an actual invasion.

The Sons of Hercules would have a field day with this.

What a PR nightmare.

And the warriors knew it.

"Dannika represents us to her people. Our future brides," Ciran told his agitated warriors. "She has asked for the truth. I will not lie."

"She cannot tell the brides," Nilun protested. "They will fear us."

"Oh, *now* you worry about scaring brides?" Gailen asked dryly.

"Of course I am concerned. Who would not be?"

"We may never surface again," Tial said, wide-eyed. "Bermuda will ask us to leave. We will never find acceptance on land to meet our brides."

"Dannika will not let that happen," Gailen said encouragingly.

They all looked at Dannika. The desperate eyes of her warriors pleaded silently for her help.

"Of course I won't," she promised, because they *would* find their brides. "But, um, why don't you tell me what we're dealing with here? So I can prepare a proper statement. Like, why has no one talked about this before?"

"I would also like to know," Stevie said.

"We do not speak of the city because the All-Council labeled it anathema."

"So is Atlantis," she said.

"But there is universal agreement. They sink ships indiscriminately. Break apart families. Steal young fry. All mer cities shun Lusca."

The warriors shuddered as if him saying the name summoned the devil.

Wow. Okay. What a nightmare. Dannika steeled herself. "Tell me everything."

"I do not know the word Stevie used, but long, long ago, humans invaded this city's sacred islands. They took, enslaved, or killed the sacred brides. Enraged by the loss, the city declared war on all surface humans. They sank many, many ships."

A deep unease settled over the warriors as if Ciran were opening an umbrella indoors while walking under a ladder and breaking a mirror. They clapped their biceps and thighs, quietly questing for the absent daggers.

"The All-Council gathered its largest army, filled with willing volunteers from all the cities, to end the attacks. They failed. Lusca controls what you call giant squid and an even larger animal known as the kraken. They are formidable."

Kraken?

What could that even be?

"Ever since, we have avoided their territory," Ciran continued. "Lusca has been cut off from the rest of the mer —from resources, knowledge, trade—and so they are reduced to raiding. They attack anyone who ventures too close, and some careful travelers who are simply unlucky."

"Why hasn't it come up before now?" Dannika rubbed her elbow. "Mermen were discovered because of the GoPro. We know more than ever about the ocean. But giant squids are attacking innocent boats and nobody has a clue?"

"The squids mess with electronics," Stevie said. "They turn the ocean red and cause a nasty fog. You can't power engines, can't use the radio."

Again, all the warriors turned to the videographer.

"It is not the squids," Ciran corrected, frowning, "but the red mirror stones the warriors use to control them. How *do* you know this?"

"My stepmom ran into them south of here. They operate out of the Bermuda Triangle."

The Bermuda Triangle.

Thousands of disappearances, unsolved mysteries, rumors of ghost ships, sudden fog, monsters.

It all fit.

She didn't want to believe it.

Dannika said flatly, "Are you serious?"

"Serious as the grave," Stevie said.

"Oh, for goodness' sake. Please be joking."

"I wish. I've been searching for Bex ever since..." Stevie calculated. "It's been almost twenty years. And I asked around *a lot* after the mermen emerged. It's why I took this job. I was always hoping to find something." He jerked his thumb at the warriors he'd filmed the previous days. "These guys know."

They averted their gazes.

He again tapped his camera against his thigh. "As soon as I finish editing, I'm chartering a boat and seeing what I can find."

"It will not be much," Ciran warned.

"My stepmom's a survivor."

"The Lusca do not leave survivors."

"She escaped once. They sank her sailboat, and she later got picked up by a yacht with a satellite phone. Red fog closed in and cut us off. I give it decent odds she escaped again."

"The Lusca destroy all humans. This stepmom could not live on the ocean for twenty years. It is impossible. And if you search those waters, you place yourself in danger."

"I know. But we *are* in the age of the GoPro, and I have an advantage Bex didn't."

"Which is?"

"I know they're out there." Stevie made a fist. "And I've had twenty years to prepare my anti-squid devices for combat."

SIX

Dannika finished the interviews with a darker soul than the one she had started with.

Whenever Stevie's camera turned away from her, she studied her cell phone or worried the chunky, colorful rings adorning her slender fingers.

"You are in no danger from Lusca on the land," Ciran assured her at the end of the interviews when they boarded the car to the airport. "And our warriors are skilled at avoiding them beneath the ocean."

"It's just another thing." She blew air between her soft, dewy lips. "The Sons of Hercules don't need any help to make the mer look bad. But if they're right about this...no. I can't let fear win."

He rested an arm on the seat behind her. "I will protect you."

"In a physical fight, I know you would." She buckled him in as the car began driving across the island. "But in the land of public opinion and politics, this is just another unfortunate setback."

"Tell me your resources. I will conceive a strategy."

"I need to convince a senator to reconvene his committee and open visa applications for the mer."

"Show him our size."

"I'm sorry. I know you guys are muscular, but I'm trying to be as nonthreatening as possible. The concern is—"

"Of our mating gemstones."

"Oh!"

"Humans value these Sea Opals, yes? Show him our largest sizes. We give these to our brides, and our brides enrich their land. Perhaps envisioning, touching, manifesting the potential bounty may change his mind."

"As they say, money talks." Her lips curved. "I feel like you've worked in politics before."

"Undine youths train first in strategy and second in the skills of a warrior." He leaned closer. "Tell me all your problems, Dannika. I will solve them."

Her soul flared, and her gaze dropped to his lips as though tasting him. Her tongue grazed her lower lip.

She was hungry.

Hungry for him.

And then she shook herself and oriented her knees away. "You know what? I'll turn you over to our public relations expert as soon as we land." She stared intently into her cell phone and gave a heavy sigh. "We can use all the help we can get."

Ciran leaned back.

He could be patient.

The landscape passed in a blur. So many humans populated the land. Some had bright souls, some dim, all colors and sizes, in growling cars or strolling along the gray pathways in front of the pastel, square, and glass shelters.

At the airport, they transferred to a small open car and crossed to the sharp-nosed plane. Their driver met with other humans and loaded cases of Sea Opal elixir into the underside baggage compartment. It glimmered with an unearthly shine.

Normally, elixir took centuries of steeping mating gemstones in the ancient sacred churches. Drinking the liqueur gave brides the ability to transform long enough to return to a warrior's city and sip the nectar of the Life Tree, which would make the ability permanent. But since many sacred churches had been destroyed, and Atlantis had never had its own sacred islands, healer Balim had discovered a method to steep the mating gemstones in only a few hours using a human technology called an Instant Pot.

Indigo had drunk one bottle when she'd accepted Zoan's claim. Ciran had left a case of elixir with Lotar for any more brides discovered on Bermuda. The rest would return to MerMatch.

Dannika ascended the narrow stairs, then pivoted. "Oh, that's right. I wanted to—oh!"

Her heel slid on the hot metal, and she teetered.

He caught her easily.

"Ciran, I..." She slid into his arms, fitting perfectly against the crook of his elbow. Her breasts brushed his rib cage. She rested a hand on his chest. "Oh."

The gentle dip of her waist, the fertile flare of her hip, the rounded cushion of her buttocks pressed to his side. She was female and perfect. A sharp, hard need pierced him. *Mine.*

His silent claim seemed to cross the air.

Time hung suspended.

Her lashes fluttered, lowering, and her chin tilted up.

Dannika offered her soft lips? He would claim them.

And her.

Heat pounded into his cock.

Ciran lowered his head.

"Yoo-hoo!" A cheery woman in a button-up uniform waved from the top of the steps.

Dannika sucked in a huge breath and turned her head at the last moment. Ciran's mouth grazed her cheek. She paused there, so close, yet so far.

Need coiled around his cock like a vise.

He no longer felt so very patient.

Dannika pulled back and looked up the stairs. "Hm? Val?"

"Are you coming?"

"Yes! Oh, goodness. I got a little...ah... I tripped, and Ciran caught me." Dannika disentangled herself from him and avoided Ciran's gaze. She ascended the steps, gripping the railing on both sides, and ducked to enter the metal tube. "Val, it's a pleasure, as always."

"You too. And this is Ciran? So nice to see you all." The woman tipped her head. Her soul was a dark shade, showing that she had no affinity for the sea, but her manner was friendly and welcoming. "I'll be your pilot this afternoon. As always, no cell signals during flight. Don't want to spook the instruments."

"Of course." Dannika embraced the woman. "Tell Mr. Ryerson thank you so much for lending us a company plane on such short notice."

Val patted Dannika's elbow. "I sure will do that. Howdy, Ciran, and welcome aboard. You're my first merman. I guess after this, you can call yourself a flying fish! Say, how often do you mermen fly?"

"Never."

"There have been a few flights," Dannika said, "but most were emergencies."

"Well, I'm going to take care of you. No emergencies on this twin prop today. Have yourself a seat, and we'll mosey."

Dannika walked down the aisle between seats. Her hips swung back and forth, feminine grace with a powerful promise of undulating fertility.

He wanted to clamp her hips and grind his cock into her arousing buttocks.

Which he had just felt. His body throbbed with the memory of her imprint.

Patience.

The first row was reversed. Dannika selected a forward-facing seat and rested her woven shoulder bag on the small table.

He dropped into the seat facing her.

She would not evade him.

Not in this small metal tube where he had her trapped.

She glanced over the other seats, then shook her head. "You're sitting there?"

"Because a warrior does not part from his bride."

"Right." She bit her lip. "I admit I have a tendency to let you get a little closer to me than I should. It's not fair to you. It sends mixed signals."

"Because the truth is in your soul. Your body responds."

"Well, it's...it's a little more complicated than that."

"Only because you resist."

"Right! That's it exactly." She smiled as if he'd agreed with her. "And so I'm sorry, but there will be no more almost kissing, no more near misses or anything like that. Agreed?"

"Yes. If you offer your lips to me again, I will not miss."

She blinked.

And then her chest glowed with acceptance.

She enjoyed remembering their kiss. She wanted him to claim her.

He knew it. He saw it, sensed it, felt it like a ray of warmth lifting his own heart.

She splayed her hands across her chest as though to shield the truth from him. "You're driven. Your future bride is going to love that trait. Oh, that reminds me." Dannika pulled a sheaf of papers from her bag and set it on his lap. "Look at these bride photos. I'll set up a meeting with anyone you like. Go ahead. Take a peek."

"Dannika." He rested his hands on the sheaf. "I will wait for you to accept me. I will accompany you and meet any human you wish. But know this. I will never select another bride."

Her soul flared and then dimmed. "You have to."

"Our souls resonate."

"Then I'll figure out a way to make it stop." She forced a smile to her lips as she settled into her seat. "Just you watch me."

A sliver of fear speared him.

Could Dannika do that?

Was it possible?

Queens were powerful. They could do anything.

Could Dannika end their resonance through sheer will?

———

CIRAN'S EYES BUGGED.

Dannika had to look away before she burst out laughing.

As if she could stop their resonance with her mind.

If she could have stopped this unearthly attraction, filling her veins with pinging desire and making her squeeze her thighs together because she ached for his cock, she would have done it months ago and saved them both a lot of heartache.

But since she had to deal with it all the time, it was fun to watch him squirm.

He was just so irritatingly certain. So impressively logical.

So deliciously attractive.

She clicked her seat belt and took off all her rings—except her wedding band—tucking the loose jewelry into her caftan. Her fingers always swelled when she flew. But the wedding band never left her ring finger, swelling or no.

It was her protective talisman.

Look what happens when you love someone.

Ciran had never been devastated by love. He felt frustrated now. That was nothing.

If only he'd choose someone else...

Val walked through and stopped at his seat. "Hey, there, hon. Call me overly cautious, but I'm going to have you switch sides." Val patted the seat across the aisle from Dannika. "You can move back once we're in the air."

He changed to the opposite side and followed Val's instructions to fasten the seat belt. The sheaf of binder-clipped bride profiles rested on the seat where he'd left it.

Oh, he wasn't getting out of it so easily.

Dannika unbuckled to hand the sheaf to him. "If you won't look for yourself, why not look for your warriors?"

He took it reluctantly. "I receive no useful information from these flat images."

"You can picture which of your warriors might look good with one of these brides."

"Their looks do not matter. Only souls." He fixed his hot, gorgeous gaze on her. "Only resonance."

Want hummed beneath her skin. He plucked her desire like a string. And it took all her will not to tear off the seat belt, clamber into his lap, and plaster herself to every square masculine inch.

Whew. A hot shiver traveled up her spine. Mm, licking his skin and feeling the teasing bite of his kiss on her neck...

No, no.

No.

Dannika sat back in her seat and opened her own folder of notes while Val completed the preflight checks with a cheery monologue. "Suit yourself."

This was going to be a long flight to Miami.

———

DANNIKA FLIPPED THROUGH HER PAPERS.

Ciran flexed his fingers over the bride papers.

If she could make herself no longer be his soul mate...

What a nightmare.

An abyss of blackness.

"Look at the bios," Dannika said, without looking up from her papers.

Ciran opened the folder.

Squiggly patterns—human letters—lined the white papers. Small, glossy square papers captured female torsos and heads. Faces froze in...what? Smiles? Hard to know for sure without seeing a soul light.

And humans saw this every day.

Knowing no one's true feelings, how did humans mate? How did their race survive?

And yet humans had survived. Blind, confused, and guessing, they had even thrived.

No wonder Dannika could not respond to him.

He must not let her cut off their resonance. He must reach her another way.

Zoan said to focus on Dannika's words. She expected him to hear her meaning and ignore the fluctuations of her soul light.

How?

The airplane doors closed. Val strode through for one last check and then disappeared into the front of the plane. The engines revved. The metal body of the plane reverberated with discomforting fragility, and they rolled forward. Bumps jostled him in the seat.

He gripped the armrests.

Dannika glanced over. "Don't worry. The plane is like a large car."

He raised his voice over the engines. "But more isolated. You avoid all attacks from rivals."

"Right." She knitted her fingers together and pressed them against her chest. "If someone attacks up here, you crash."

The silver ornament of her husband glistened. Once, she had accepted the claim of a male. She had believed that male's words. And she had loved him.

Ciran needed to become as worthy as that warrior.

Patience.

He would have all the time together on the mainland to convince her.

They had all the time in the world.

SEVEN

Their plane bumped along the long, flat ground at the human airport. The gray-and-green land-scape outside the windows moved faster and faster. Then a gust of wind whooshed and Ciran's stomach dropped. The ground fell away. They were flying.

How strange.

The cluster of islands shrank into the turquoise ocean. Low clouds puffed outside his window. The engine made a new sound, both low and unsettling, like the current across a particularly depthless cavern. It numbed his chest.

But the isolation was a key point. Warriors always had to calculate their safest route between points in the ocean to avoid meeting rivals. No wonder humans were always taking airplanes.

"Hello and good afternoon, you all." The pilot's voice sounded tinny from overhead. "Flight time to Miami today is four and a half hours. The weather doesn't get any better, and we refueled in Bermuda. You are free to move around the cabin and help yourselves to drinks and snacks. This trip was brought to you by your friendly host, Cal Ryerson of Ryerson Enterprises."

Ryerson Enterprises constructed things known as oil platforms on the coastline of the United States. The sea platform over Atlantis, in the middle of the Atlantic, was one of the largest projects in the world. It anchored over the deepest water humans had ever attempted.

But after it was complete, the warriors would have their floating island, and they would be able to once more meet with sacred brides.

How had the ancient warriors built the original city? It could rise to the surface or sink beneath the waves with the push of a lever. Ciran had helped excavate several stages of the ruin. The mer no longer possessed the skill to build up—or that knowledge was locked in the archives of the hostile All-Council.

"Hey." Dannika leaned across the aisle to Ciran. "This flight plan goes directly over the Bermuda Triangle, and I know we only talked about squids attacking ships, but planes run off electricity and quite a few have gone missing in the region. Are we in danger?"

"No. A squid attack begins with red fog."

Dannika glanced out the window at the clear blue sky.

Yes, they should be safe today.

She nestled something in her ears and traced the wire back to her cell phone.

He unbuckled and dropped into his original seat across from her. "Do not spook the instruments, Dannika."

She removed the plug from one ear. "It's in airplane mode. At the moment, it's a self-contained audio player."

"There is no risk?"

"None." Then she twisted her lips to the side. "Well, not to the instruments. Our security expert, Starr, sent more recordings of the Sons of Hercules leader. His voice is distorted, but the rhythm and word choice are so familiar...I know it's someone I've met."

"That makes identification easy."

Her eyes widened. "Easy?"

"Set meetings with everyone you have ever met. You will find the leader."

"Everyone!" She laughed, and her soul light brightened with a cheer that warmed him. "Do you know how many people I've met?"

"Even if the list is a hundred names long, the importance of the task means you must do it."

Her laughter subsided. "Is that how many mermen you've met in your life?"

"If you do not count the warriors I have faced in battle, then yes."

"I can't believe we're in the middle of a war now, but it seems like it... To answer your original question, I've probably met with a hundred people this week. Once you count everyone I see regularly, my friends, my parents' friends... yes, easily. And when you go back to past months, for example, when I volunteered at the Winter Art Charity Auction, we had nearly a hundred volunteers and over a thousand guests. Plus journalists, the board of directors, employees of the museum, and so forth."

Ah. Yes.

The surface world was unfathomably vast.

"But I shouldn't laugh. Your idea isn't bad." Dannika poked at her phone. "It's funny that we're in a Ryerson Enterprises plane right now. My mind keeps going back to a Winter Art Charity Auction six years ago. I was monitoring the silent auction, and Preston Ryerson kept erasing names. We knew his reputation—he couldn't just bid enough to win, he had to win on his terms—and when my assistant caught him, he treated her with such contempt. It really put me off. Of course, he's been dead five years at least. But I have to think...what is it about that scene that triggers my memory? Someone standing behind him? Someone he was with? I really should request the guest list. A few thousand will take some time to get through, but it's better than the nonprogress I've been making on my own."

"Tell me your problems, Dannika, and I will solve them."

"Yes, you said that." Her smile faded, and she worried the ring around her knuckle. "I wish everything was that easy. You really felt nothing for those photos?"

"Do humans?"

"Yes. Especially men. They're so visual. And once you become willing to open yourself to the possibility of a new life, a new partner, and you can really see it, your true love just manifests. I've seen it time and again."

"Manifests meaning you become aware that someone is your soul mate?"

She nodded.

All from seeing flat images... It was unfathomable. "Did you see a flat image before you met your husband?"

"Oh. Eliot?" She relaxed and considered the ring for a long moment. "No. But the first time I met him, I knew he was the man I would spend the rest of my life with."

"Why did you think this?"

"I don't know. It just hit me, an overwhelming feeling that couldn't be stopped. Like when you and I..." She jolted upright. "I mean, not like *our* first meeting. Not at all. It was totally different with Eliot."

"How?"

"Uh...well...I was so young. I never realized anything could go wrong."

Something was missing. He was missing it. "And you always knew your husband was your soul mate?"

"Almost immediately. I was playing in a harp trio, and he was repairing the church's pipe organ where we practiced. One thing led to another and..." She shrugged, a small smile on her face, a steady glow in her heart. "He brought peach roses to our first performance."

"And these roses caused your knowing?"

"No, that was just nice."

"You knew Eliot was your soul mate because he was nice?"

"Oh, the feeling had been building long before the roses. But I finally said yes to our first date."

"So you knew before? How did you know?"

She frowned. Her soul light fluctuated like crazy, burning bright and then darkening to black before creeping back to near normal again. "I just...I was a different person back then. When I fell in love, it was with my heart wide open, fully embracing my bliss. And now...well. That girl died with Eliot. Sadly."

Frustration curled beneath his impatient fingers.

How did you know, with your limited human senses, that your husband was your soul mate?

Her answers did not fit the question.

When Gailen could not properly introduce himself for the dating video, Ciran had stepped in to bridge the gap of understanding. Who could step in for him?

"I was so young," she continued, as if age mattered at all. "So carefree and easy. I had no driving mission, no idea of what the world needed from me. No idea of what could happen when you make another person your whole world."

Dannika leaned forward and rested her hand on his knee. "And that's why I want you to meet a woman who will love you like I loved Eliot."

Frustration seethed. "You are that same woman."

"I'm not, though." She patted his knee, then rested her palm more completely on the hard muscle. "That's what this all comes down to. I want you to be effortlessly happy with a woman who will love you wholeheartedly. A woman who is unburdened by life's tragedies. If I could give you anything, Ciran, I'd give you effortless, wholehearted true love."

She leaned back. Her hand slipped away again.

He caught her hand. "I do not want an effortless love."

"You don't know that." She twisted and switched so she was holding his hand in both of hers and traced the lines of his palm. "Your heart line is long. That means you can't see the future."

"But I can see our souls."

"Other warriors have made mistakes."

"And other warriors have been overwhelmed by the surface world. They've sought to anchor themselves to any bright-souled human."

"So I might anchor you—"

"You"—he pressed her palm to his chest—"are my anchor. You are also my star, my love, and the female I want in my life."

Her chest glowed and her cheeks flushed. Her eyes watered, and she licked her lips. "Don't."

"I want you as the mother of our young fry."

"Ciran."

"Only you, Dannika. This is not a sudden declaration. I have watched you. You are loving, kind, and wise. You will be a great mother to our young fry."

"My life is flashing before my eyes..." She hardened herself and pulled away. "And so are many other things. Whew!" She fanned herself. "Hot flashes. I'm probably entering early menopause. Then I couldn't even have kids, and you would be so sorry."

"If you cannot have young fry, the Life Tree will heal you as it has healed others."

She shook her head at him, then tried again. "I want you to have a happy life. Just not with me. Because no matter what you say, Eliot was my soul mate, and now he's gone. And that's it for me. I had my greatest love, and it's over. Forever."

This was the crux for her.

"Dannika." He rested both palms on top of hers. The hard metal band pressed into his hand. "Your husband was a good man. I do not doubt you were soul mates. If he were still here, I would not be. Your soul would resonate for him and him only."

Moisture shimmered in her eyes. She swallowed hard and sniffed. "I don't know why I'm so affected. You're only repeating what I've been saying."

"Because it is validating for another to affirm you are right. And you are. I do not argue with your love."

She sniffed. "But?"

"Yes. But." He squeezed her hands. "Eliot has passed into the blacknight sea, where the males gone before him eternally sing of his honors. And you are here. On the surface." He pressed both palms to his chest again. "Your soul resonates with mine. It does not matter what you or I want. This is what is."

She swallowed again. "But why?"

"I do not know."

She choked and sniffed. "You seem to know everything else."

"No. But I do know that every moment you deny our connection, your soul darkens. Every time you declare that you are undeserving, you weaken your inner self."

"Because this is impossible..."

"When the sacred islands were full across the ocean, and each city had its own customs, large families were normal. If a warrior's soul mate died, no laws prevented a warrior from seeking a second."

"But did they? Your records are incomplete."

"I cannot be the first warrior in all the millennia to claim a bride who has once loved a human." He tilted his head in concession. "But if I am, then I hope to make the right decisions now to bring our races into closer alignment."

She sniffed again. "I just don't know."

"You doubt our connection. But I do not. Trust in me." He vowed upon his own soul. "Until all your doubts fade, I will have confidence for both of us. And when you fully accept my claim, you will never doubt again."

She took a deep, shuddery breath and let it out. "So I have to embrace those fears and they'll melt away?"

"Embrace your strength. Embrace your destiny. Embrace me."

Her gaze traveled over his face, from his hairline to his dark brows, across his nose, and centered on his lips. Hers parted, and her breath had a catch.

Her soul glowed with power.

She wanted him. He wanted her. She cared about his warriors and the future of the mer, and so did he. She listened and thought and worried. And so did he.

The moment stretched.

He would follow her to Florida, he would follow her to New York, he would follow her to every land in the world.

But perhaps he would not have to.

All she had to do was yield.

Give in to what her own soul knew that it wanted—needed—and embrace him with a kiss.

Maybe, just maybe, their souls would connect in a vibrating metal tube that numbed his chest and soared in the clear sky unbelievably high over the vast oceanic blue.

And then she would leave the surface world and join with him in Atlantis, where she belonged.

The engines abruptly made a new coughing sound, sputtered, growled, and then quit. A strange stillness filled the tube, and his chest pinged from the sudden silence.

Dannika's eyes widened and face blanched in fear. "Val?"

"Hey there." Their pilot's voice sounded tight. A second later the intercom kicked on. "You're going to want to buckle in and assume the crash position."

Dannika pushed Ciran to buckle in and connected her own straps, tightening them down. Her shout sharpened with dark-souled fear. "What's going wrong?"

"A slight problem with the fuel."

"But you refueled in Bermuda!"

"Yes, and I watched it, and I smelled it, and I tested it. And I need all my concentration now because there's a slight problem."

They coasted over the waves like a bird coming in for a landing.

This did not seem bad.

Dannika's face turned green. She manacled the seat armrests and stared out the window. "Oh, no. Ohhhh, no."

"What is wrong?"

She blinked and tore her gaze back to him. Her soul was dark, black with fear, like a hole in her chest. "We're going to die."

Hmm. The flight did not seem substantially different from before aside from the slowly approaching surface. It was infinitely more pleasant without the engine burr. "Is Val unskilled?"

"No, she has to land with no controls. Or pontoons." Dannika stared out the window again. "We're going to hit that water like a concrete wall. It's going to tear off the bottom. Tear off the tail. Tear us apart."

"Dannika." He reached out his hand. Because of the restraints, he couldn't reach far or take her hand. All he could do was offer. She had to cross the last distance to him.

She swallowed, and her face turned less green, more pale. They could just reach their fingertips over the table.

He clasped her cold knuckles in his. "Nothing will tear us apart."

She frowned, and then her brows wrinkled and she snorted. A smile crossed her lips. "You are unbelievable."

He squeezed her fingers. "But true."

And then they veered toward the water.

EIGHT

She was going to die.
She was going to die.
She was going to die.
And she'd brought Ciran with her.

Why?

Dannika clenched his fingertips with one hand and the armrest with the other.

The Sons of Hercules knew she was on this plane. They knew. That was the only explanation. Sabotage.

Why hadn't she taken the threats seriously?

Why had she thought nothing would happen to her?

The air whistled, ominous as an oncoming train, and the sea loomed. Her vision tunneled on the reflected water.

Then...

Rumble-rumble-rumble.

Chaos.

The plane bounced across the leaping waves like a stone skipping across a river. Every bounce, the metal shuddered. Pens and plastic cups levitated, and the profile papers fluttered across the interior. The plane dipped left.

"I do not fear the water," Ciran said.

"But, uh, right now, I do." She wrapped her fingers around the slender rod. It was so small. So skinny. How could it cause so much resistance?

"We're going to get you out, Dannika." Val panted. "As the plane sinks, it'll fall apart. Are you one of these mer? Can you breathe?"

"No."

"Right. Okay. Let's try again." Val positioned herself around the opposite side of the metal rib to push while Ciran pulled. "Now or never. Really put your legs into it. Ready? Now!"

She and Ciran strained. Dannika pushed. Sweat dripped down Ciran's face. His muscles bulged and trembled.

Water gurgled up to the back of Dannika's knees. It was a pleasantly cool temperature. Just like a morgue.

Panic shot through her. Dannika whacked the bar. Her hands ached.

It didn't move.

Val and Ciran both let go.

Val bent over, panting, and then straightened. "This isn't working."

"But it has to," Dannika gasped.

"Wait here." Val sloshed up the angled aisle to the tail where it was still dry, and forced open drawers. "Not here. Not good. What about...also not here. Did they get the whole emergency kit? I am going to fill their shorts with fire ants and hang them by their short hairs... We have a raft! Must not have expected me to land it, the spittoon-swilling sons of mustard. How about...yes. Ciran!" Val handed him a crowbar.

Ciran wedged it between the seat and her ribs and pushed.

The chair rattled.

"The bolts," Val said. "Underneath. Pop the whole seat free."

He forced it under the seat. Something popped.

Yes!

The seat did not swing free.

"I need to get out before the water rises." Val gripped the emergency door handle. Fear, anger, anguish crossed her face. "If I can help, Ciran..."

"Go." His biceps strained to bend tons of metal against the trauma forces that had caused them to collide. "I can only rescue one human. It will be Dannika."

"Are you sure?"

"He's sure," Dannika promised wildly. "I'll be right behind you."

"I'll inflate the raft." Val forced the door.

It creaked and then popped away, carried by the force of the waves and current. She stepped to the rim. The plane tilted. She splashed out with a shriek.

The plane abruptly lurched, and waves flooded in.

The current swirled over Dannika's lap as the plane continued to sink.

"Did she make it?" Dannika's limbs trembled. Maybe from cold, but maybe also from shock. Her teeth chattered, and her bones vibrated against their sinews. "Did she get free?"

"I cannot concentrate on two humans." He strained and then gave up, shaking out his limbs and staring at the chair as though trying to see a new problem.

"I know, I know. But did she?"

Ciran ducked under the water.

Water gurgled and bubbled. Waves slapped her window, engulfing the plane like an aqua snake. The light dimmed and changed to blue. Salt water sprayed from the cracks.

Water splashed up to Dannika's chest.

She gasped.

Ciran surfaced again. A dangerous knowing filled his gaze.

Uh-oh. "She didn't make it?"

"Val is on the raft." Ciran stared at her very hard. "I cannot remove the metal rib."

"What about the seat?"

He shook his head.

"You got most of the screws. I bet a strong push with the crowbar, you could pop them."

"Another piece of metal has twisted around the plate, securing your chair to the floor. It is as though the plane is holding on to you with metal tentacles."

Oh.

Wow.

That was...

Huh.

How could she survive a crash and drown when everyone was trying to save her?

With Ciran trying. Desperately. To save her.

"Dannika." He threaded his fingers through her wet hair. His thumb stroked her cheek. "I am sorry."

"No." She swallowed. "You did your best. I mean, you'll think of something. You always do."

"I have." He dove beneath the water again. Subtle waves brushed her ankles. He struggled to free the seat from the twisted wreckage of the plane. She sensed him deep within the water.

Because he was still here, deep calm filled her.

He would figure something out.

He always did.

For a long time after Eliot died, she'd cried so hard, she'd thought her heart would stop, but it had always carried on, and she'd believed there must be a reason. And when she'd started matchmaking her friends successfully, watched the bloom of interest flower into full, abiding, selfless love, she'd known. She had a calling, a mission. She'd experienced the greatest love, and others deserved to experience it too.

She'd fought her unstoppable feelings for Ciran, but at this critical moment, she rested her faith in him.

He is my one.

"Ciran?" Her voice wobbled. The water rose to her neck. She gasped for air. "Ciran!"

He burst to the surface holding a bottle of water.

No, that wasn't bottled water. That was Sea Opal elixir.

Of course.

See? He always came up with something.

She reached for the bottle.

Ciran held it. "Dannika, you have not pledged to become my mate, but you must—"

"Give it to me."

His brows lifted. "You know this is—"

"Elixir." She sucked in another breath. "And after I drink it, you have to activate it. You have to kiss me, Ciran. I'll become yours."

His gaze smoldered. The iridescent threads in his eyes glimmered with possession.

He uncapped the bottle and tipped it into her mouth just as the seawater rose to her cheeks and flooded in her ears, carrying with it the usual odd muffling and extra loudness that was so unsettling.

She fought the shock reflex. *Swallow*. The order came from inside her mind. She choked.

Ciran's steady gaze mesmerized her.

He had total faith.

She was his one.

He was hers.

Swallow.

She gulped.

Seawater splashed over her head.

The bottle pulled out of her mouth as the water closed over her face, leaving her with cold, dark salt. She coughed. Bubbles erupted in the heavy, viscous blue. Water strangled her, pouring down her throat and into her lungs.

Air.

Spots danced behind her eyes.

Air. Air!

She convulsed.

Trust in me, Dannika. You are transformed. I am your one.

Ciran's strong fingers cupped her cheeks, calming her, and his lips brushed hers in their first kiss.

Her heart stilled, and then the pressure of the water eased. Her chest swelled with warmth, truth, heat.

He was right.

She had transformed.

The spots in her eyes faded. Blackness turned to light, and the sea opened around her.

Ciran appeared first, floating as a warrior. His iridescent coffee-and-green tattoos gleamed, and his unearthly two-tone eyes filled her with dangerous desire.

The darkness beyond him fled to show the whole interior of the plane. Detritus floated, chumming the water with metal and chaos.

The plane rotated, and the tail cracked. The walls bent, and the metal rib released her seat. The weight lifted off her. She slipped out and into Ciran's strong arms.

He crushed her to his chest. His body trembled with feeling. Words thrummed deep in his chest. "Praise the Life Tree."

She "heard" the vibration in her own chest in some sort of echo chamber beneath her sternum.

He was so torn up, so grateful. The wreckage and her unfortunate situation had put him in so much pain.

"I'm sorry."

"Me as well."

They talked but did not talk. The timbre of his vibrations was pleasingly firm, the same as on the surface, yet deeper and richer melodies interlocked with new meaning. Nuanced emotion inflected his vibrations.

He pulled back and stroked her cheeks with his thumbs. Subtle music, pianissimo, infused every touch. "Our first kiss should not have been forced. I wanted you to choose me."

Her heart thudded in her chest.

Because she did choose him. She had.

Dannika pulled him close and pressed her lips to his.

He pulled away in shock.

She clung to him. *I choose you.*

He kissed her back. His mouth explored, questioned, redefined. His upper lip felt thinner and flatter than she'd expected, and his lower lip was thicker and perfect for nibbling. He opened and sought her, chasing and claiming her. She accepted it all, yielding to his embrace, bathed in a hot, fizzy glow of perfect safety, of having found her home, of sanctuary.

Heat swirled into her soul.

He tasted like hope and fury, desperation and renewal, salt and male. Their lips united, and the shock of shifting faded away. Heat and warmth and life kindled within her.

While they kissed, his chest vibrated fiercely, "You are mine."

She was his.

And she also belonged to the ocean.

New exhilaration filled her, just like when she'd survived the plane crash. She laughed with delight. And because she was underwater, her laughter vibrated in her chest. There was no air to bubble within her anymore. The water wrapped around her like an embrace.

Ciran pulled back.

This weightless sensation felt magical. She twirled inside the small compartment, dancing with the debris, an undersea astronaut with perfect form.

Ciran grinned, tired and happy.

He was so adorable. So sweet.

Outside the broken windows, the ocean spread out, lighting up for miles. Ordinary sunlight filtered down from the surface, where the tail of the plane still poked out, but beneath it, a depthless, breathtaking infinity spread in all directions.

Every sea creature, from the tiniest speck of sparkling plankton to the mightiest nova of a humpback whale, appeared in sharp relief. Dannika was a falcon, and the ocean was the shorn grass.

And music flooded in. Beethoven's Fifth Symphony played around her in pieces. Distant whales hummed in a melancholy A minor, and closer, a pair of mako sharks wailed in descending sirens as they darted and interwove. Jellies burbled like happy French horns, schools of tiny silver fish trilled like excited piccolos, massive groupers bellowed like tubas, and swarms of squid jetted across the sea with the low *doot-doot* sounds of the classic contrabassoon in high G.

The fish formed a swarm of glowing musical instruments absent a conductor, and so they played backward, forward, and all at once.

It was chaos, and yet, it was beautiful.

Her fingers suddenly itched to pluck the strings.

She had given up harp after Eliot died. Harp took a short time to sound nice and a lifetime to master. She'd loved playing with her mother so much as a child.

Ciran bumped her shoulder.

Even though her senses had changed to sense lights in the animals, nothing unusual showed on him. Just a broad, powerful chest, lickable abs, a promise of more beneath the Bermuda shorts, and swirling, iridescent tattoos marking him as an honorable warrior.

"Val's raft is drifting." He vibrated in that almost-ticklish way deep inside. "We should surface before the current takes her too far. Can you make your fins?"

Dannika wiggled her human feet. "Not yet."

Bending over made her belly ache. She pulled out the loose caftan bodice. Red welts bruised her abdomen.

The Sea Opal elixir would heal her. It probably had already fixed the worse injuries. She needed to give it time.

Oh, and Val's forehead hadn't looked too good.

"Get some elixir for Val," Dannika said.

"Down here." He kicked through the broken floor into the baggage area.

His broad quads strained the Bermuda shorts and his feet elongated to fins. His shirt floated up, and a series of gills lined his lower back.

Gills!

She must have those too. She pressed the flowing caftan at her lower back, but it was ticklish too.

The tone of the animal symphony changed. Minor keys shifted to majors, and stately adagio sped to frenetic vivace.

That couldn't be good.

Dannika floated to a window.

A heavily tattooed warrior stared back at her.

Adrenaline surged.

She scrambled back. "Ciran!"

Another face poked in through the opposite window.

Ciran zoomed in front of her and brandished the crowbar.

"Undine," the warrior said calmly, identifying the mer city that Ciran had come from. His tattoos were cornflower blue. A long trident rested against his side.

Ciran's grip tightened, and he said the word she most dreaded. "Lusca."

NINE

Ciran hefted the unbalanced human metal rod.

What he wouldn't give for a real weapon. The dinged, bent trident of this Luscan aggressor. His own familiar trident and daggers.

But they rested in safe storage in the reef off Bermuda.

"Can you use your queen powers?" he vibrated to Dannika.

She pinched her fingers together. "No. I'm sorry."

Then it was up to him.

The Luscan warrior watched them. Unusual. Normally, they attacked furiously, without a strategy.

Ciran cast a quick glance around the interior of the plane. He needed more. More information, more time, more distraction. "What do you want, Luscan?"

The Luscan tilted his head. His words were unnaturally calm. "Why is an Undine in a human airplane?"

"Why is a single Luscan investigating?" Ciran tested a feint with the metal rod. "All the cities you have wronged will hunt and execute you."

"I am not your enemy, Undine."

"Oh, no?"

"Father." A plain-faced trainee with almost no markings paddled to the opposite side of the plane and peered in the windows with a second, similar trainee. Stubby coral daggers, more a play weapon for a young fry than a proper weapon for a trainee, hung from his skinny biceps with fraying kelp. "The patrol is coming."

"Inside." The Luscan eyed Ciran and swam in the open door. The two trainees swam at his fin tips. To Ciran, he quieted his vibrations to what would be the surface equivalent of a whisper. "No, I am not your enemy, Undine. They are."

Three tattooed Luscan warriors jetted toward the plane. Sharp tridents gleamed at their sides. Finely honed daggers rested flush against their biceps and thighs.

The warlike leader circled the slowly sinking wreckage.

"What are you looking for, Lieutenant Orike?" one warrior asked.

"Why did the metal bird crash so close to the island of exiles? It is suspicious. Especially since we did not bring it down."

"Any humans inside are dead," one of his warriors said. "The metal bird has flooded. There was a human floating on the surface, though."

"Yes, after we deal with the escaped exiles, we will ensure there are no survivors." The warlike leader raised his vibration to shout at the plane with rage. "Itime? You dared to escape your prison, and now you hide in the human wreck like a coward. The king will shred your traitorous flesh and feed you to the kraken."

The cornflower-blue warrior squinted out the window. "Come and get me, Orike."

"*Lieutenant* Orike!" the other warrior shouted.

"Call me Lieutenant Itime, and I will extend the same honors."

"You lost everything when you turned your back on our noble king, you weak-skulled, toothless coward."

The warriors insulted Itime while their leader, Lieutenant Orike, studied the plane. He apparently considered Itime enough of a challenge not to rush the wreckage, despite their better numbers and weaponry.

Good to know.

Itime glanced over his shoulder at Ciran, his trident never wavering from the threat outside. "Now you understand. We came to rescue you. This is my son, Tulu."

One trainee nodded. He had the same serious eyes as his father. Only one tattoo marked his body: a creature holding a flaming ball in his claws, on a background of trees and scales, drawn with fine lines.

How strange.

"And that is Hadali."

The second youth floated forward, an eager smile breaking over his face. He was perhaps the same age as Tulu but seemed younger, with a similar intricate heart tattoo of a foreign creature and unfamiliar plants. "Hi there. What happened to your plane, anyway?"

"It crashed," Ciran said.

"Sabotage," Dannika said behind him, then shared their names, finishing the introductions. "What do we do?"

"We have to get back to Sanctuary," Hadali said. "You'll be safe. They're not allowed on the island."

"How do we get there?"

"It's that way." He jerked his thumb over his shoulder. "We just have to get past Lieutenant Orike and his warriors first. Oh, and also avoid the rest of the Luscan patrol that we left behind at the island."

Ciran combed through his mental inventory. A fight inside the wreckage was not ideal. "How many Luscan warriors in total?"

"Five," Itime answered. "Three here. Two more circle Sanctuary."

Ciran rotated to Dannika. "Still no powers?"

She flexed her fingers. "Sorry."

"Do not apologize. The first queens developed their powers after weeks of effort. I only ask because you are exceptionally bright."

Her lips quirked to the side, and her soul light brightened in her chest. "And we have an exceptional need."

"You understand."

The plane moaned as it sank into the depths. *Creak.* The sound shivered in the water, a visceral warning.

"Plan quickly, Undine," Itime said, his vibration still as casual as if he were commenting on skipjack migrations. "Before Orike gets bored of this standoff and decides to murder your surface human."

"Dannika, get two bottles of elixir." Ciran remained within the shadows. From here, it was likely that the outside warriors did not know of his existence or Dannika's. They had the element of surprise. "Lieutenant Itime, how fast are you?"

The warrior blinked, then hardened. "They will expect me to fight."

"Then think how upset they will be when they see you escaping with attractive salvage."

Dannika handed Ciran one bottle.

He pushed the bottle into the bag, ensuring the shimmering substance was visible, and passed the bag to the warrior. "Make it look like something you were willing to sacrifice your son for."

Itime took it. "There is nothing I would sacrifice my son for."

Clearly, since he had already given up everything and defied his king. "Do your enemies know that?"

Itime measured him with a long look, then shouldered the bag. To Tulu, he quietly vibrated, "Trust your instincts. I will meet you at the coral."

Tulu nodded solemnly.

"Good luck, Itime," Hadali vibrated. "We'll wait for you."

"You will not need to." He nodded at Ciran and Dannika, squeezed out the window on the opposite side from where the trio of Luscans were still tossing insults, and jetted away, his practiced strokes effortless.

Ciran motioned for the trainees to drop out of sight and remain silent.

"Quiet." Lieutenant Orike's vibration silenced his warriors. "Something is different. Itime?"

The trainees held still. Dannika pinched her fingers, open and shut. Ciran closed his fist over her hands. She relaxed into his firm hold.

"Itime, you are welcome to hide in silence while I send my warriors to destroy another of the surface humans you exiles love so much." Lieutenant Orike's vibrations grew louder as he floated closer to the plane. "Itime?"

His sharp profile appeared over the rim of the windows.

Orange-yellow tattoos, a similar shade to the acidic loquat fruits Ciran had eaten with Indigo's family this afternoon, shone on the lieutenant's skin.

If he peered in the correct direction, he would see Ciran or the trainees. But he fully focused on the last spot where Itime had been. "Itime?"

Hadali tensed. Tulu gripped his coral play daggers.

One of his warriors shouted, "Lieutenant Orike, look. On the other side of the metal bird. The exile flees!"

"Curse it." Lieutenant Orike veered over the plane. "With me, my warriors. He will not escape."

"What of the surface human?"

"She will succumb. Most do."

"Hey, he has something. Look, his arm! He is carrying away human things."

"Itime! Do not evade us. Fight like the warrior you once were. Coward!"

Their voices faded.

Ciran edged above the window, barely moving. The warriors were specks in the distance, and their souls faded to tiny flickers. He peered out, twirling slowly—ocean wildlife, ordinary water, no spies left behind to entrap them —and then circumnavigated the wreckage. They were alone. He returned to the plane.

"Good work," he vibrated at the trainees.

They emerged cautiously from the wreck.

Hadali grinned at Tulu, their souls glowing with accomplishment. "Let's get your friend in the floating thing."

Dannika hung in the doorway. "Ciran, the elixir."

He kicked inside. Debris had settled on top of the elixir cases. He used the crowbar to free it.

The plane groaned and descended.

"Come on," Hadali called from outside. "If the airplane drops, you could get caught in a current that takes you to Lusca."

Dannika tried to help Ciran and winced. "My belly..."

"We need help," he told the trainees. "The human on the raft is injured, and she has a dim soul. We do not know how much elixir we will need to cure her."

The two youths returned. Tulu worked quietly,

focused, and Hadali made small, optimistic comments. "Almost there. Almost... Keep pulling... There. Is this what you want?"

The bottles of elixir gleamed.

Ciran freed one bottle. Dannika reached in for another. The more the better.

Shriek.

The plane's tail separated from its body. Debris shifted like sand, covering the case. Dannika jerked her hand back. Pieces of metal from the flooring had crushed the second bottle.

One would have to suffice for now.

Dannika frowned at her left hand. Her fingers were uninjured, but her soul light fluctuated, darkening to black. She searched through the plane debris.

"Are you hurt?"

She rubbed her bare knuckles. "No..."

"Come," Tulu urged.

Hadali flew after him into the open water.

"We must go now," Ciran told her. "Hurry."

She flicked her fingers and then threw her arms around his neck, holding him tight.

Ah.

"You have done well." He stroked her trembling back. The dress floated around her body like a fluffy halo. "We are not in immediate danger."

She nodded against his shoulder and squeezed him tighter.

All right. She must be feeling the aftereffects of the encounter. How sad that danger had tainted his bride's first experience in the water.

Ciran unwrapped her strangling arms and fitted Dannika to his chest, where she belonged. He kicked them through the gaping wreck, out the open tail, and toward the surface.

She squeezed him tighter. Her body slid, and her feet tangled with his knees.

He slowed to reposition. "Relax. We are safe now."

"Don't I need to breathe out?"

"Why?"

"Because we're rising. The pressure on the air... I don't want to pop a lung."

"You do not have air in your lungs."

She blinked. "Oh. Right."

He skimmed under the surface currents toward Val's raft. It was visible in the distance, and he ought to reach it quickly.

Dannika's grip tightened again.

When a bride swam with his warrior, they usually formed a perfect fit and experienced a boost of speed. But the restrictive human clothing hampered their movement, and Dannika's tight hug put her body at the wrong angle.

He tried to reposition her again.

She clung harder than a limpet, crushing him.

Hadali kicked beside them at an easy pace. "You're a mainland woman, aren't you? Are you his bride?"

"Kind of. Not yet, exactly." She grappled Ciran in a stranglehold. "It's complicated. How—"

"What is complicated?" Ciran interrupted. "You are my bride. You pledged yourself to me."

"Right, but we haven't held the marriage ceremony at the Life Tree of Atlantis, so technically—"

"You are still my bride. You always have been. Now you have accepted my claim. You *are* my bride."

"Right. On the surface, we'd call it a fiancée. That's all I meant."

But her soul light had dimmed. That was *not* all she had meant.

Unease seeped into his heart.

"I know you're hurt." Hadali craned his neck over his shoulder. "But can you hurry? You don't want to run into the patrol on the open water. Trust me."

Ciran kicked harder than ever before, striving to regain his pace when every shock, inside and out, jolted him off rhythm and made him feel like he was churning the water against himself.

"Where are you from?" Hadali asked Dannika. "New York or Florida or China?"

"Maryland," she said. "I have a studio in New York so I can be close to—"

"New York! I have a stepbrother in New York. Maybe you know him?"

Dannika smiled for the first time since the plane was still flying high, and her soul light glowed. All at once, Ciran's kicks smoothed out, and he could finally increase their speed.

"Maybe I do," she said. "What's his name?"

"Hunter."

"Hmm. Well, I know a few Hunters, but no one mentioned being related to a merman."

"You must know him. That's why my mom received a sign and sent us to help. If Lieutenant Orike had gotten to you first, we would have found nothing but chum."

"Your mother received a sign?" Dannika rested her head on Ciran's shoulder, finally relaxing. "That's funny. What kind of sign?"

"We saw your plane go down. Mom said you'd be important."

Tulu shouted. "There, the raft!"

"Oh, good." Hadali veered toward it. "We found it before the Luscans doubled back."

They aimed for the small square dwarfed by the endless ocean.

"You have a mother," Ciran repeated because only a few cities had allowed women to stay on as queens. Lusca, so far as he knew, was not one of those cities.

"Yes, she's a mainland woman like Dannika."

"How does she know us?" Dannika asked.

"She doesn't, but you're going to be important."

"Important for what?"

Hadali and Tulu hovered below the raft. They looked at each other, then at Ciran and Dannika.

"For taking over Lusca, of course," Hadali said.

TEN

Taking over Lusca?

Wait, what?

"What do you mean, taking over Lusca?" Dannika asked the two teens.

"The All-Council tried." Ciran's dark, certain vibration sent ticklish thrills up her spine. "It is impossible."

"Not with you it isn't." Hadali beamed, energetic and hopeful. Tulu nodded. "Our moms will explain."

The two boys seized the edges of the raft and popped out of the water.

Val screamed.

It echoed strangely in Dannika's water-filled ears.

Oops.

Dannika fumbled for the raft. Ciran grabbed the edge and hauled her onto the puffy orange plastic.

The water ran off her skin like peeling gel. It drained out of her mouth and throat. Her chest lightened. She took a familiar breath.

Globs of liquid stuck in her throat like snot in her bronchial tubes.

She coughed and hacked so hard, tears burned her eyes and real snot clogged her throat. She gagged and threw up over the side. A wave slapped her in the face, dousing her. She gasped and choked.

Ciran steadied her.

She collapsed bonelessly in his arms. Everything felt heavy and rough. Her throat filled with grit. Tears streamed down her cheeks.

"Dannika!" Val crawled toward her. Blood crusted on her face, and her skin underneath was green. She patted Dannika's shoulders. "You're alive."

Dannika wheezed. "Barely."

Ciran rested the crowbar at his now-human feet and handed Val the bottle of Sea Opal elixir. "Drink and heal."

She took the elixir. "Are they your friends?"

Hadali and Tulu floated on the other side of the raft. They had jumped in, and Val had screamed. They must have jumped right out again.

"Friends? No, we have just met them," Ciran said.

Val fumbled for Ciran's crowbar.

"They...rescued...us..." Dannika managed between coughs.

"Yes, do not harm them. They may be allies."

"We will take you to Sanctuary," Hadali said.

"Oh, you speak English." Val sighed with relief. "You gave me the biggest scare."

"Sorry."

Tulu dove.

"What's Sanctuary?" Val asked.

"Our island. It's not far. Except we're going the wrong way. Excuse me." Hadali dropped beneath the waves as well.

The raft jerked to the left. The teens pulled it across the

currents, and waves bumped and splashed the fragile plastic.

"Are you well?" Ciran asked Dannika.

Dannika nodded. Her throat burned with salty fire. "I heard shifting was rough."

"Changing back is the hardest." He released her. "I will assist with the raft."

Under the water.

Where the Lusca hunted.

Where he could die.

She grabbed him. "No!"

He sat stiffly.

All the blackest, most awful terrors gushed into her mind, choking out her reason. His elbow poked her bruised belly, but she hugged him even tighter. "Don't go. You're injured. It's dangerous."

"You are injured." He gripped her sore shoulders, gently easing her away from him. "I am capable. And I must help the trainees pilot this raft. If a full patrol attacks in open water, Luscan tridents can easily pierce this plastic."

Logically, it made sense.

But if she let him go…

Disaster. Crisis.

Death.

"Dannika." He pulled her onto his lap once more and hugged her, rocking her gently. "You survived. The Luscans did not harm you. We will evade them. Do not dim your light with tortured thoughts."

His bulging arms tightened with quelling strength.

She was being irrational. No, that wasn't true. She was a hundred percent rational after the sabotage, the plane crash, and the hostile warriors, but dwelling on those fears didn't make her any safer right now.

Ciran was right.

She would do anything to keep him safe in the boat, but that wasn't an option right now.

Dannika tried to force in a shaky breath. Her bronchial tubes constricted and wrenched another torrent of coughs from her beleaguered lungs.

Ugh. She couldn't even breathe deeply as normal because of the gritty shift. She had to learn a fresh way to calm this anxiety attack.

"I'll be okay," she finally managed.

"Of course you will be." He helped her to sit comfortably across from Val in the raft and rested her hands in her lap. "You have a large, selfless heart. If you could change places with me, you would do so without hesitation."

He was right. God, he was so right.

"Harness that frustration so you can develop your queen powers." He brushed her wet hair back from her face. "And then I, a second lieutenant of Atlantis, will shelter under your protection."

Oh. Gosh.

He always knew exactly what to say.

His brow cleared. He stroked her cheek with his broad thumb. "Now your soul is bright. Hold on to this feeling. It gives me strength."

She clasped his taut forearm. "I'll do my best."

"I know you will." He leaned forward.

She lifted her chin for his kiss.

Hadali popped up behind the raft. "Hey, Ciran? We could really use some help down here."

"I am coming now," Ciran promised.

Hadali disappeared again.

Val offered Ciran the crowbar.

"You keep it." He pressed his lips to Dannika.

She melted into his touch.

The comforting kiss was exactly what she needed. His firm jaw did not yield to her fears. His rough male skin grazed her soft cheek.

His scent filled her with warmth and protection. Images flooded her. The way he'd wielded the crowbar, the way he'd never given up. *It is okay to love this male. He will never drown and leave you.*

He pulled back, and a small smile curved his lips. The coffee-and-green tattoos swirled in alternating patterns across his high cheekbones, never quite touching even though they got so close.

Would this be her last view of him? Oh, she had to remember every detail. Her bruised belly tensed again. What if this was their last kiss?

His lips flattened. "Channel your strength. Not your fears."

"You're right." She took a half breath and let it out with only a little cough. "I know. I'll work on it."

Hadali bobbed above the surface again. "Ciran?"

"Yes." He released Dannika's hands in her lap. "Believe in me."

"I do believe in you."

He slipped over the side with barely a splash.

She gripped the side of the raft. The waves reflected the clear afternoon sky and her anxiety. "Come back."

———

BENEATH THE RAFT, Ciran took a position between the trainees. Tulu kicked quietly. Hadali peppered him with questions.

"Have you ever fought a Luscan?"

"Yes," Ciran said. "They sometimes attack Undine."

"And you survived? That's good. Have you ever fought a kraken?"

"No."

"That's not good. Can you really help us take over Lusca?"

"Perhaps." Ciran kicked steadily. He had planned no takeovers since his training days. And even then, the question had been hypothetical. Mer cities were so depleted, they did not have enough warriors to defend their own Life Trees and declare war on another's. "What are your resources?"

"There's us." Hadali gripped the raft with one hand while he counted off on the other. "Me and Tulu. Now you. And Dannika, and the other one."

"Val."

"Right." Hadali lifted his gaze toward the surface as he thought. "Itime, of course. And Konomelu."

Another warrior name. "Your father?"

"No. But his son, Nuno, is the oldest kid on the island now. They distracted the patrol at the beginning and let us sneak out to help you."

He made a mental map. Itime and Tulu, this Konomelu —assumedly another exiled Luscan warrior, like Itime—and Nuno. A third father, most likely, and Hadali.

"And our moms, I guess. But they don't go in the ocean."

Brides who could not transform?

"How unfortunate," Ciran murmured. Three queens once defended Atlantis from the All-Council army and their fiercest, most unstoppable nightmare trench creatures.

And while he had no driving interest in rebattling

Lusca after the All-Council had failed, three queens would have made evading the Luscan patrol and returning Dannika to the mainland much easier.

"I know," Hadali said, and Tulu nodded. "And everybody else is too young. Well, some of Tulu's and Nuno's brothers are getting up to our age. But look at us. We're barely trainees."

"Only because we haven't been allowed to train," Tulu murmured.

"Stupid Lieutenant Orike." Hadali gripped the raft and kicked extra hard. "I hate him. Hate him! Lieutenant Figuara was much nicer. He brought me a swordfish spear on my tenth birthday."

Their raft bumped into a sunfish lounging on its side in the waves.

In the raft above, Dannika's soul dimmed.

A matching coldness seeped into Ciran's joints. His muscles tremored. Weakness threatened to stop him.

He mentally commanded her to channel her strength.

Do not let fear win.

The marine animal flipped over and burbled away, rippling at half the size of the raft.

Three queens who already commanded their powers, secure in their soul-mate bond, and who could teach Dannika to do the same would have been much appreciated.

The raft bumped into another sunfish.

He paid more attention.

Around them, the surface teemed with familiar life. Jellies and blue dragons, copepods, and krill. The silvery fish that shivered like surface leaves, and the long darting needles that sometimes erupted from the water into flight, aggressive groupers and predatory swordfish, and backward-shooting nautilus.

But as they swam into currents that tasted of an island, they floated into thick clouds of squids—and the predators that feasted on them.

Most predators veered out of their way.

The raft bumped over yet another stationary, side-floating sunfish.

Ciran was done. "One of you, guide the raft around the surface predators."

The trainees looked at each other.

"I mean, if you think it will help…" Hadali shrugged.

Tulu moved to the front.

The squid closed around them.

"Why are there so many here?" Ciran asked.

"I don't know. Mom said it used to be called the Forbidden Island, but Tulu's mom said it should have been called Squid Island."

One flew at Ciran's face. It eyed him like a dignified visitor, its tentacles hanging in the front like a tapered nose and its mantle fins fluttering in a rilled pattern.

Then it attached to his elbow, clinging with all eight tentacles, while the two longer clubs squeezed his wrist. A sharp pinch of its beak cut his skin.

"Off." He brushed the annoyance away.

Its brow ridges turned gold, and its central limbs changed to white. It jetted away, leaving behind a cloud of acrid ink.

Then it veered back and latched onto Hadali.

"Hey!" Hadali slapped it. "I live here. Stupid squid. Bite one of the Luscans. Jeez."

The island appeared, and the ocean floor rose in thick

mats of vibrant coral. Jutting up from it was an ancient, dead reef that stretched from the vibrant floor all the way to the surface. It separated the cove from the open ocean.

"The sharp coral will pop the raft," Ciran cautioned.

"That's okay." Hadali kicked steadily. "Once we're inside, we're safe. And Itime will meet us here. We just have to—"

"Shhh." Tulu veered sharply to one side.

Hadali vibrated softly. "What?"

"Don't you hear? My father beat us."

Uh-oh.

Vibrations—war cries—echoed across the open ocean. *"Itime... We will end you..."*

And Tulu was correct.

The cries hadn't come from behind them.

They came from around the far side of the island and grew louder. If Ciran and the trainees continued toward the coral, their enemies would arrive first and cut them off.

Especially since Dannika's soul darkened again, causing that matching weakness in his own body.

"We'll go to the cave." Hadali kicked with new urgency. "It's a low, narrow entrance, but the raft should fit."

A small, agitated squid bumped into Tulu, whirled around, and latched on to his head.

He smacked it off.

It made an indignant blat and squirted ink before fleeing directly into the mouth of a waiting grouper.

Ciran focused on speed.

They rounded the corner of the island, fleeing from the ever-growing shouts.

"Just a little farther," Hadali vibrated, kicking furiously.

New war cries sounded ahead of them.

Was it the rest of the Luscan patrol? The warriors who had remained at the island?

They were racing right into a trap.

———

A LITTLE EARLIER...

CIRAN WAS FINE.

Nothing was wrong.

Dannika repeated that mantra from the moment he disappeared over the side. They'd traveled at least an hour, and they were still in the middle of the ocean.

There was no way the Luscans were surrounding them and tightening like a noose.

No way.

Ciran was fine.

Nothing was wrong.

She lay flat on her back in the moving raft and used her long sleeves to shield her tender face from the sun.

How sharp were tridents?

Sharp, probably. They could do a lot of damage.

How fast could Ciran heal?

A lot slower on the surface, so far from his Life Tree.

Ugh. She should have collected more than one bottle of elixir.

"Dannika?"

She dropped her hands. The late-afternoon sky was a pale blue fading into white. "Yeah?"

Val hunched under a sunshade made from an inside-out duffel bag. She'd rinsed her face. Blood was matted in her curly brown hair. She lofted the bottled Sea Opal elixir. "Is this going to shift me into a mermaid?"

"Not unless your soul mate is a merman."

"You sure?"

"There are only two documented cases of women spontaneously transforming. One turned out to be the daughter of a merman."

"Oh yeah, weren't they supposed to only have sons? And didn't she grow up somewhere landlocked, like Omaha?"

"Yes, so she never swam until she was an adult. It was quite the surprise. The other, I'm actually guilty of matching her with the wrong warrior. She felt something was wrong, but she had transformed. Then, after checking security cameras, we discovered that she'd been exposed to her real soul mate just hours earlier. It was a mess."

"Huh."

"So as I said, as long as your soul mate isn't a merman, you will only receive the healing components of the Sea Opals. You won't transform."

"If my soul mate is a merman, my wife is going to smack me into next Tuesday." Val swigged the elixir. "It tastes like tap water."

"New York's finest."

"And it's supposed to heal me?"

"Ciran can see it shine. I still can't, though."

"Right, they can see all sorts of things we can't, like souls." She swigged again. It really looked like ordinary bottled water refilled from the tap. "Mm. How do I know when I've got enough?"

"I don't know."

Their raft bumped and jolted abruptly.

The Luscans were attacking!

Dannika bolted upright. "Is he okay? Does he need the crowbar?"

Val peered over the side. "Huh?"

"The Luscans. Are we under attack?"

"No, I don't think so. We ran over one of those weird flatfish. You know, the ones that look like they only have half a body?"

Dannika joined her. That side of the raft dipped.

"It's gone," Val said.

Their raft banged over the top of something else.

"Oops, it's back. It's like a fish head with a tail fin glued on, and no middle."

"It's a sunfish." Dannika retreated to her last resting spot. "They like warmth."

"Well, there you go. We're running over fish. Seems to go a lot better for them than it does the armadillos."

"Yeah."

She tried to relax. There was plenty to get upset about, so she shouldn't waste her time worrying over nothing. Ciran was more capable than that. If he were in trouble, she'd know.

But...

Dannika encircled her left hand, testing the scratched, bony knuckle of her ring finger.

It was bare.

For the first time in almost twenty years, her ring was off. It had disappeared during the plane crash or rescue.

It wasn't just that she'd lost the last token of Eliot.

Ciran could disappear just as suddenly. One moment here and the next gone. Warriors' lives were far more dangerous than an upper-class Jewish boy's in Layhill.

She squeezed her fingers.

"Oh, Lordy. I must be feeling better." Val tentatively

touched her forehead, where she'd washed the cut to a reasonable gash. "I'm starting to wonder if I'll ever fly again. I love it so much. But..." She shook her head. Tears glistened in her eyes.

Dannika sat up. "You will. You absolutely will."

Val hiccupped.

Dannika eased to her side of the raft and gave her a hug. "You'll put this behind you. Just think of how great it will feel to get back in the pilot's seat."

Val sniffled and nodded.

"It'll be even better the next time around," Dannika said. As if she would know. Ha. How easy it was to counsel Val to get back on the horse—winged, in this case—when Dannika couldn't handle ten minutes of a second relationship. "But it's also just fine to ease back into it, take your time, and don't worry if it doesn't go well right at the beginning. Just, you know, keep breathing. Sit in the seat. Hold the controls. Soon, you'll be ready to fly once more."

Yeah. That's right.

Fear was natural. She just had to work through it. And Ciran was so understanding. With Ciran's help, she would—

"Huh?" Val pulled back and gave her a funny look. "No, I mean, there's going to be an investigation. They could take away my license. And even if they don't rule against me, I might never get another job. Running out of gas is amateur hour, and here I am, carrying passengers."

Oh.

Dannika patted her arm again. "Wasn't it sabotage?"

"I should have caught it. I should have double-checked." Val touched the scab matting her hair and winced. "You know how some kids get bedtime stories? My pappy read accident reports. Before I took the crop duster up, he made me visualize what to do. 'Pretend somebody's trying to screw you, Val,' he used to say. 'Where would they do it? How?' My commercial instructor said I had the most thorough preflight check he'd ever seen. And then this."

"So how did they screw you?"

"I don't know." She held her forehead. "If I think about it any harder, I'm going to give myself a migraine. Worse than I already have, I mean."

"Don't dwell," Dannika advised. "You have a head injury. And besides, we—"

"I've got it." Val rocked under the sunshade, dislodging one of the poles she was using to keep it in place, and fumbled to fix it to get the precious shade back. "The problem was in the third tank. Because I had to switch tanks, right? On a schedule, to keep the plane balanced. And it was after that third switch, the fuel didn't flow. I couldn't switch back. Something jammed. I cycled everything, as you do, and did my Maydays. Ah." She shook her head again. "This is going to drive me crazy. I just know it."

"Could it have been a regular engine failure?"

"Sure, maybe, except that somebody took out the EPIRB." Val sorted through the emergency supplies floating in the raft's bottom and enumerated everything that was missing, including their emergency locator beacon. "It happened in Bermuda. I did a full check before signing out the plane in New York like I always do. In fact, now that I think about it, the kit was missing a few things in New York. I had to get a different one, and I reported the problem to the company. Then in Bermuda, the same things went missing, only I wasn't out of the plane for longer than two hours. At least they left us the raft."

"So it was sabotage."

"If not attempted murder." A piece of paper fell out of

the upside-down bag and onto Val's shoulder. "Oh, what's this?" Val flipped it over.

A side profile of a Classical-era male with a beard was inside a circle.

Ugh.

Of course.

"Holy Zeus," Val said.

"Hercules." Dannika tapped the page. "That's a side profile. Middle Roman era. You can tell because of the stylized beard. They've gone through a few logos, but that's the current calling card for the Sons of Hercules."

"Terrorists." Val stowed the paper in a waterproof bag for evidence. "I can't wait until we land. I'm going to call it in. My wife's going to be so worried. And we've got to find the saboteur before they hurt your other mermen."

Dannika flexed for her cell phone. Was Hazel in danger? Or Starr? She had no way to warn them. Her phone was somewhere below, in the abyss.

Gone, just like Eliot's ring.

The raft approached an isolated tropical island surrounded by a ring of bleached coral. Was this Sanctuary? She squinted at the foreign land. Getting off the raft, drying out, and contacting Hazel were her top priorities.

The empty shores looked ominous.

The raft drifted to the right. The beach disappeared, and the coral connected to tall cliffs where island birds cooed and cawed. The raft slowed to a stop again, moved against the current, and then hovered.

"They can't decide which way to go." Val uncapped the elixir. Her face seemed paler, as if it wasn't working. "Like me, right before—oh!"

The raft jolted forward. The elixir sloshed out and

splashed Val in the face. She recapped it and huddled in the bottom of the raft.

Around them, the water swirled with danger.

The crowbar rolled toward Dannika. She seized it. The thick metal was heavy and unwieldy, and it felt wrong in her hand. But it was what she had.

She clung to the raft and readied herself to attack.

ELEVEN

Ciran and the trainees kicked hard. The raft flew along the undersea cliffs. The trainees looked over their shoulders.

"I hear warriors ahead," Ciran said.

"If it's at the cave, Konomelu will make sure we get through," Hadali said.

"What about...?" Tulu asked cryptically.

"No, no," Hadali said. "Your brothers wouldn't start a race now. That's irresponsible. They know how important our mission is. They'd stay in the shallows and never get in our way."

Waving lines in the rock cliff led to a cavern entrance. The entrance above the water looked low and narrow. Vines draped into the seawater. Dannika and Val would have to duck.

In the raft above, their souls darkened.

His calves and thighs weakened in response.

Believe in us, Dannika.

Shouts behind them grew louder and then abruptly

went quiet. Ciran's stomach constricted. The silence was much worse. It meant they focused on speed.

The Luscan warriors chasing Itime must have seen the raft and realized that much more was at stake than running after a long-standing nemesis.

He tried to kick harder. The raft bounced on the rough current near the cliffs.

On the other side of the cave, two careless trainees raced each other around the island. Laughing and whooping, they looked over their shoulders at a pursuer—and not at the raft bearing down on them.

"Uh-oh," Tulu said.

"Look out!" Hadali cried.

The trainees faced forward, saw them, and pulled up in shock. They blocked the cave entrance.

"Move!"

The trainees, who were clearly Tulu's brothers, knocked into each other.

Lieutenant Orike's deadly order came from far too close behind Ciran. "Get the Undine."

Itime cut in front of the raft, hooked his sons one with each arm, and zoomed into the cave.

The raft crashed through moments later. The sides wedged on the rocks. Tulu yanked it. *Pop.* The plastic tore, and the raft limped inside.

Hadali and, last, Ciran crossed the threshold into the cavern mouth.

The jagged tip of a trident flickered at Ciran's periphery.

He released the raft and whirled to face the Luscans.

Lieutenant Orike's lips curled in a snarl. His arm drew back, and he thrust the trident at Ciran's bare chest.

Clang.

Another trident, held by a warrior on Ciran's left, parried the thrust.

Ciran kicked deeper into the cave.

Lieutenant Orike jerked his trident free. "Konomelu. How dare you violate the terms of your exile?"

Konomelu, the warrior who had saved Ciran, growled. "How dare you violate the sacred church, Orike?"

"He is Lieutenant," one warrior vibrated from outside.

"Not to me."

The other warriors who had chased the raft stopped outside. Only Orike had entered the cave. He floated now just inside the lip.

"Taking in humans and other exiles violates the agreement." Lieutenant Orike waved his trident at Ciran. "I have every right to slaughter the Undine."

"After you get through me." Konomelu brandished his trident.

"And me." Itime flew to Konomelu's side and they formed a wall defending Ciran from the Luscans. "Spill no blood in the sacred church."

"Or what?" Lieutenant Orike sneered at the cluster of youths, who had doubled or maybe tripled in number and crowded the cavern behind Ciran. "The sacred brides are long dead."

"Ours are—"

"Yours are anathema. Even the weak All-Council would say that. The king should take all your young fry and give them a proper education before you turn them into dim-souled, land-bound humans."

"Try it and die," Konomelu snarled. The furious orange tattoos shimmered on his skin, and his tendons stood out in sharp relief.

"I should." But Lieutenant Orike turned away. "I

cannot wait until you are all dead, and I can serve my king in a noble role that better fits me."

He kicked through a cloud of squid. One bumped into the lieutenant. He sliced it in half with his trident, deflating it like a bubbling human balloon. It dropped in ribbons, and the other squids clustered around the free snack.

One of the older youths pushed past Ciran. "How could you leave us, Orike? You make such a handsome squid herder."

The rest of the youths tittered.

Konomelu patted the youth's shoulder with approval.

Lieutenant Orike stopped and turned back, eyes narrowed. "Nuno. Your true king awaits the day you venture out of shallow waters and realize you are more than a caretaker for young fry."

Nuno's jaw flexed.

Like the other youths, Nuno had mostly bare skin with a tattoo of foreign creatures and plants over his heart. But unlike the others, his chest had broadened into a warrior's, and his daggers were fastened to thighs and biceps that had filled out to an adult's measure.

"Do you never wish to become a warrior?" Lieutenant Orike pushed.

For the shortest moment, a dark longing stole over the male. And then it disappeared. A cocky grin split Nuno's face. "Sure, but then I remember I'd have to look you in the eye and pretend to respect you. I'd rather strap myself to a pair of electric eels."

The youths tittered again.

"So be it." Lieutenant Orike kicked to his warriors. He assigned one to patrol and led the rest into deeper water.

The youths jeered at the Luscans. "Squid-sucking sunfishes! Jelly-for-brains sea slugs!"

Konomelu shooed the taunting youths. "Enough, my trainees, enough."

The youths swam deep into the cavern.

Konomelu and Itime rolled a boulder along a groove. It grated against the stone and sealed the cavern.

Neat, but ultimately useless.

"What two warriors can close, other warriors can open," Ciran said.

"We do not close out the warriors." Konomelu released the boulder and floated to Ciran. "We close out those wretched squids."

Fresh cuts nicked his forearms, but he was surprisingly healthy for an exile.

"I am Konomelu of Sanctuary." He waved a hand at Itime. "You have met my colleague."

Itime nodded.

"Once, we served together as lieutenants of Lusca. Now?" He rotated to take in the shallow cavern lagoon filled with excited young fry and a deflating, sinking raft. "This is our city."

The water level was twice as deep as Ciran was tall, but for a mer, it was the shallowest of pools.

But they had started the formal introductions, so Ciran stiffened and made the salute of Atlantis. "I am Ciran."

"What is an Undine doing with two humans?" Konomelu asked.

"I am formerly Undine."

Their brows lifted. Itime's hand subtly curled around his trident.

A warrior never voluntarily left a city, and only the worst crime resulted in exile.

He pushed through the discomfort. "Now, I am from Atlantis."

"Atlantis?" Konomelu's chin jerked back. "The ancient fable?

The two warriors moved to form a subtle wall, separating Ciran from the rest of their haven. He'd given them two answers they disliked.

The raft fully deflated, and panicked splashing broke the calm lagoon's surface. Their supplies were dispersed, and the crowbar fell to the cavern floor.

"Please let me assist the humans," Ciran said. "Both are injured, and one is not used to shifting."

Konomelu vibrated loudly without looking, "Nuno? Trainees? Help the humans."

The young fry converged on the women.

Konomelu popped his trident out of his elbow and gripped the long rod. "Where are you from, really?"

"I am from Atlantis."

"Why did you tell me Undine?" Itime asked casually, as if he didn't care about the answer.

"On the plane? I did not bother to correct you because there was little time. King Kadir found the ancient wreckage and is rebuilding the platform to unite humans with mer."

Both warriors regarded him skeptically.

The continued splashing wore on Ciran. "Have you listened at no echo points?"

"We do not care about the opinions of the weak All-Council," Konomelu sneered. "Atlantis is a myth. Your honor markings are Undine."

"And? Your honor markings are Luscan."

Konomelu lifted his chin proudly. "We are the only true warriors of Lusca left."

"Be that as it may, if you had listened at any of the echo

points, you would know of Atlantis. We seek mainland brides. Uniting us is Dannika's mission."

"And that is why you were flying in a human's metal bird?" Itime asked. His flat vibrating tone was disinterested.

"Yes."

The splashing sound continued unabated. Through gaps in the crowd of young fry, Val's legs and feet appeared. She treaded water, keeping her head above the surface, but her movements were jerky and weak. Her soul light, already dim, blackened with fear.

She was going to drown. "Will you not let me help my pilot?"

"Trainees?" Konomelu roared without looking. "Help the humans to the land."

They wiggled in aimless motions.

"I know what it sounds like." Ciran rested his empty hands on his chest, the buttoned shirt fabric bunching oddly beneath the water. "Five years ago, I would not have believed it. But the ocean has changed. Atlantis has been founded, queens have returned, and—"

"Queens?" Konomelu's brows and lips twisted, and then he burst out laughing. "You tell us Atlantis has queens? With their impossible powers? Ha-ha! This must be some Undine strategy."

"If your goal is confusion, it works well." The tip of Itime's trident never wavered from Ciran's direction. "Because I cannot fathom why you would make such claims."

"Where were the queens hiding? Did you unearth them in the wreckage? Ha-ha-ha. Did they arise from the black-night sea, or the deepest trench? Ha-ha. Oh, and did the All-Council welcome them?"

"No," Ciran said.

"What is next?" Konomelu ignored him, still chuckling. "Yes. I know. A queen will bear a female mer."

"That has happened."

"While warriors walk among humans. I suppose whales now soar through the night sky and birds swim in the trenches. Ha-ha-ha-ha."

Ciran could float here and debate with them for hours.

But Val was still treading water, and her head dipped below the surface. "Hey, my pilot—"

"Trainees?" Konomelu half turned away from Ciran to vibrate at the young fry. "Why have you not helped the humans?"

"We can't," Hadali vibrated plaintively.

"Huh?" Konomelu turned fully. "What? Why not?"

"Because...I don't know." Hadali pointed at Dannika, who'd shifted and now floated in the middle of their crowd. "She's gone all glowy."

Dannika's eyes were closed. White light glowed from her fingertips, and a see-through, bubble-like glowing shield formed around her and Val. It extended from the surface to beneath their feet and stopped at the rock wall behind them.

Ciran's chest lifted.

It was always awe-inspiring to see a queen use her powers. The light glowed with the energy of the Life Tree, and it reflected Dannika's bright, caring soul.

And to see Dannika use it after just a few hours... It proved that they belonged together. She was a mer. Not just a mer, a queen.

She had tapped into their love, believed in it, and now the power of the Life Tree flowed through her.

His chest ached.

Konomelu and Itime tucked their weapons away and

joined the rest of the young fry encircling the shield, their interrogation forgotten. Ciran paced them.

Val finally hugged the rock wall behind her. She rested with her head above water.

Dannika held the shield steady, a serene expression on her face.

One of the rascally young fry brothers who had caused so much trouble outside the cave entrance backed up. "Watch this."

"Wait," Itime said.

The young fry zoomed forward and bounced off the shield. The water echoed with his giggles. The shield glowed, unperturbed, energy cycling across Dannika's fingers and then out again to the bubble-like shield.

The other young fry eagerly followed suit, and they all bounced off, one after another, laughing and whooping.

Konomelu hesitantly reached out and touched the shield. "What strange magic is this?"

"That," Ciran said, "is a queen's power."

Konomelu's mouth moved, but no vibration or sound emerged. Awe and an aching hope filled his face.

Itime regarded it solemnly, and his soul light brightened. Unlike fluctuating humans, a warrior controlled his soul light, so it rarely changed. It didn't show on his face, but he was deeply moved.

"I am Ciran of Atlantis." He rested his hands on the shield, causing Dannika's eyes to open and fix on him. She released the shield. "And this is my bride, the newest queen of Atlantis, Dannika."

TWELVE

Dannika knew the instant Ciran approached her. When he touched the shield, she felt him in her soul, and his puffed-out chest filled her with the same incredible serenity.

She'd done it.

She'd overcome the fears that had stabbed her with a thousand anxious needles when their raft had surged into the dark cavern and popped, and then the strange shadowy motions not quite seen appeared beneath the sinking raft.

Val had clutched her duffel and elixir to her chest. "I feel like I'm about to be eaten by piranhas. Ciran better come back soon."

But he hadn't come back.

Dannika had sat in the chilly pool of water seeping into their raft, thinking all the worst things.

He might be dead. He might have been attacked. He might be fighting for his life right now.

And that had snapped her out of it. Because if he was fighting for his life, the last thing she'd want to do was distract him. She'd closed her eyes and concentrated on being useful. Strong. Protecting him. Protecting Val.

"We're sinking. Oh, Lord. We're going down. We're going under," Val had cried. "Dannika?"

She'd opened her eyes long enough to say, "It's okay, Val. I'm a mer now. I can breathe underwater."

"Good for you." Val had wiggled toward a distant rocky ledge. "I might...almost...make it if something doesn't get me."

"Okay. I'll protect you from the piranhas."

"What?"

Dannika had released her air, descended into the middle of, well, honestly, it was a lot of thrashing fins and skinny boy limbs, and quite a few squids.

Between their bodies, she caught glimpses of Ciran chatting with Itime and another adult. He'd been explaining something and didn't look concerned. So the danger was over.

And anyway, the kids hadn't seemed to mean her harm, but she'd promised to protect Val. So she'd closed her eyes and focused on protecting.

And a deep, peaceful calm had filled her.

Her chest had filled with Ciran. His presence, his confidence in her, his intense love.

Her fingers had tingled.

"Dannika?" Val's voice had echoed through the water into her ears. "Did you find the flashlight? The water's a little... Hey! Go, uh, toward the rock ledge. I can, uh...*glug*... *cough*...I can almost reach it."

And then she'd heard just the vibrations of the youths until Ciran's announcement. She'd opened her eyes. The awe of two adult warriors and a full soccer team of youths had helped the tingling sensations to drain away, and the light from her fingers had dissipated.

This is my bride, the newest queen of Atlantis.

Which was awesome, but the queens of Atlantis knew how to control their powers. Dannika pinched her fingers together. She'd done it. Somehow. And now her fingers felt ordinary again.

Ciran drew her to his side, and she melted against him. He was whole and vital beneath her fingers. No new scars. Her fears had been for nothing.

"Will you help us?" a fierce orange-tattooed warrior Ciran introduced as Konomelu asked her. "With such a shield, we could fly to Lusca and confront the king himself without harm."

"I'll try." She nestled against Ciran. "First, I really need to call my assistant and let her know I survived."

Konomelu and Itime exchanged glances.

"And then if I could get a shower, maybe a little bite to eat, and a nap, I'll be at my full fighting strength."

"Fighting? You are a warrior?" Konomelu asked.

"No. Sorry. I, um..." *No open-door policy.* "I'll be ready to help, I mean."

"If she could use this power in battle," Konomelu said to Itime and smacked a fist against his palm, "we would be unstoppable."

"A very formidable opponent," the cornflower-blue warrior agreed.

"My queen has requested your help," Ciran reminded them.

Konomelu's enthusiasm calmed, and he vibrated a rueful tone. "We have no ability to contact the mainland. Our brides have tried many times. As to the other things, yes, we can provide them. Come. Meet our brides."

He swam to the rock ledge where Val had disappeared and stopped. Opening his arms and with a twinkling smile, he formally intoned, "Welcome to Sanctuary."

The tingling sensation washed over her body again. Somehow, it was right that she was here. *I am meant to be here.* She brushed her fingertips over her chest and then rested them on Ciran's forearm. He looked down at her in question. Whatever she had sensed, he didn't seem to share it.

Hmm.

He instead lifted her from the water, setting her on the ledge and jumping out. His fins shrank and folded into human feet. His shorts and shirt slapped his body.

Her caftan stretched and dripped. She opened her mouth in case that somehow helped the water drain, waited until she couldn't stand it, and then took a breath.

Water gurgled in her lungs.

She rolled onto her hands and knees and threw it up.

Ugh.

Her body convulsed, and she coughed so hard, she was afraid she'd burst a vessel. Somehow, her second shift was much harder than the first.

Ciran knelt at her side and stroked her hair back from her face. She rested her head on his powerful knee and concentrated on breathing. Air in, droplets out. The other warriors and youths pattered effortlessly around her, already chatting and squealing. Their excited noises echoed in the beautiful lagoon. It was so unfair.

"Hey." A woman about Dannika's age with East Asian features and kind brown eyes offered her a coconut shell half filled with water. "This is going to sound weird, seeing as you just puked out half the lagoon, but I think you should have a drink. It'll make you feel better."

Dannika took the cup and swirled it. There weren't any parasites in Caribbean fresh water, right? Oh, maybe they had a filter. She sipped it.

Ciran grunted in surprise. "You have elixir?"

"Elixir?" the woman repeated.

"Healing elixir. Made with the mating gemstones."

"Hmm, well, something like that." She sat with her feet beneath her, a woven grass dress fastened around her tanned bust and extending over her thighs, and tucked a lock of straight, black hair behind her ear. "I'm Meg. I think you met my husband, Itime, and our oldest son, Tulu."

"Mama, Mama!" A skinny little four-year-old bounced into her arms.

Meg hugged him. "I'm also the mother to this little guy, and three more in between. I heard you met Orike. What a drama queen, am I right?"

Another woman with East Asian features, maybe in her sixties, approached with matronly welcome. She'd tucked her straight black hair into a woven box-shaped hat, and she wore a longer grass dress with fashionable red stripes. "Welcome. I'm Angie, the leader of our little group."

Meg jerked her thumb. "She's my mom."

"My husband, Konomelu, says you two would like to shower and dress before dinner."

Dress before dinner? Angie's accent hinted at upstate New York refined by Ivy League schooling. Meg's was a little more modern, but definitely East Coast.

Dannika coughed out the last of her phlegm and tried to return their greetings. "I'm actually desperate to contact my assistant."

"I understand." Angie clasped her hands. Her nails were surprisingly neat, the edges shaped into classic ovals, although her palms were rough from manual work. "You've been through so much. And I hate to be the bearer of bad news."

"Konomelu said you have no method to contact the mainland," Ciran affirmed.

"That's right. We'd love to contact them. But unfortunately, our engineering wizard hasn't quite gotten the radio working."

Oh, so they were close, actually. "You have a radio?"

Angie pursed her lips as though searching for the right words.

"No," Meg said bluntly. "We have pieces of a radio."

"She's trying her hardest to get it working," Angie said.

"Well, yeah, but saying 'we have a radio' to these guys is like saying Johnny Cash had a Cadillac. It's a slight bit misleading."

"My daughter knows what she's talking about." Angie squeezed Dannika's hand and released her. "We can offer you a refreshing beverage, and then Meg can lead you to the shower. This way."

Dannika used Ciran's help to stand and leaned heavily against him. It always took a couple of minutes to get used to supporting her weight on land again.

They followed Angie through the naked youths and equally nude warriors and passed a carved depression in the wall. Plants and Sea Opals filled it.

Beside it, Val rested against the wall with her head on the cool rock. She'd washed off the blood and looked battered and pale. Hadali handed her a coconut bowl filled with water.

Meg hummed Johnny Cash's *One Piece at a Time* song, in which he stole from the car factory piecemeal across several decades. The end result was not exactly a Cadillac.

"And I'll ask Bex about her progress with the radio," Angie continued.

"I'm sorry." That name was too distinctive to be a coincidence. "Did you say 'Bex'?"

"Hmm? Yes." Angie turned, her grass gown swishing her legs, and raised one hand to wave over the chaos. "Bex?"

Crouched near Hadali and Val, a woman with dirty blonde hair examined Val's tiny cell phone. She wore a short grass bikini and skirt, and she looked up at Angie's call.

"Our new guests are asking after you," Angie said graciously.

"Me?"

"Yes." Dannika went to the curious woman. "Just today, we met one of your relatives."

Hadali rocked on his knees. "Mom, they didn't know Hunter."

Bex nodded cautiously.

"But Dannika lived in New York," Hadali said.

"Yeah, and I'd be shocked if she knew my old cat."

"I don't, I'm sorry. But we just came from Bermuda taking video for our dating profiles, and our videographer was Stevie."

A smile cracked Bex's face. "You know Stevie?"

"Yes! This is so amazing. He's been looking for you all this time, but no one ever talked about Lusca, so he had no luck until just...gosh, today, actually."

"I cannot believe you survived." Such awe filled Ciran's voice, he looked like he was about to poke her to make sure she was real. "No single warrior caught alone survives an attack by the Lusca. I told him you were dead."

"He was undeterred," Dannika assured Bex. "He had total confidence in you."

Bex scratched her nose, still grinning. "He's doing okay?"

"More than okay. He's going to charter a boat. I wish your radio was working. We could direct him here to pick us all up."

Her words wiped the smile off Bex's face.

The other excited youths fell silent, and only a whistle of wind and a drip-drip-drip filled the lagoon.

She looked at the other women and warriors. A silent communication passed between them, then Bex looked back at Dannika. "You better get washed and fed. We'll talk."

THIRTEEN

Angie led them up the back steps, out of the sacred church, and across what must once have been Lusca's sacred island.

The young fry raced around them. The two oldest, Nuno and Tulu, helped Val. Hadali carried her bottle of elixir.

Konomelu and Itime were surprisingly friendly toward Ciran considering he was a foreigner who would usually not be allowed on their ancient lands. They had stowed their tridents somewhere in the cavern lagoon and kept only a dagger strapped to a thigh.

"Perhaps we can strike Lusca much sooner than we hoped," Konomelu crowed, bouncing up the steps behind Ciran. "With an Undine—I mean, an Atlantean who used to be an Undine—we could see resources we had missed or weaknesses to exploit. Warriors we had discounted."

"Patrol patterns we previously missed," Itime agreed calmly.

"How to weaponize the squids!"

Ciran held up a hand. "I am a warrior, not a mystic."

Konomelu flubbed his lips in disagreement. "You have shown us a queen. With powers! There is no limit to the wonders I am prepared to believe."

Ah.

That was understandable but worrisome. If their brides could not develop their own powers, and only Dannika had the abilities, then three warriors and one queen might have a difficult time bringing down an entire city.

And why did their brides have no powers? They had elixir in their cavern.

Strange.

The trail emerged into the sunlight and traveled along a headland that overlooked cliffs. The interior was dense with greenery, and a stone-lined path through grassy hills led to roofed structures at the top of a white sand beach.

They were permanent structures. The warriors had lived on land for some time.

One larger roof covered a work area. A second sheltered smaller tables and baskets. Yet a third one had a raised platform, and the young fry scrambled onto it and sprawled.

Between nearby trees, hammocks stretched out, and lounge chairs made of curved wood were scattered around. The trainees helped Val onto a hammock and covered her with a sunshade.

In the center between the structures, closest to the work area, rested a plank. Bex rotated a crank. Woven ropes lifted the plank like a thick lid, revealing a smoky, blackened firepit.

"You guys rest here." Meg showed them to two lounge chairs. "I'll be right back with your drinks."

Ciran took the seat beside Dannika. The wood was soft and frayed from wear.

Dannika closed her eyes. Dark shadows appeared underneath.

He rested his hand on her knee.

Her lips curved, and her soul light twinkled.

She would be all right.

"Konomelu? Boys?" Angie lifted a woven grass loin skirt —a belt with thigh-length panels covering front and back, with the sides open.

Konomelu's lips swerved to the side. The trainees and young fry made a collective "awwww" of disagreement.

"This is a formal occasion." She pushed the skirt into her husband's arms, then stalked the young fry. The older trainees dutifully donned theirs, and the younger ones raced away nude. Konomelu tightened his, grimacing against what was probably scratchy grass.

Meg returned with two wooden cups carved with chunky designs. "Here's some plum liqueur. It will help with your bruising. Eventually."

Dannika opened her eyes and took it with thanks.

Ciran swirled the liquid. It shimmered with elixir. "You drink this often?"

"Only when we need to feel refreshed."

"But you have drunk it before?"

"Oh, yeah, everybody has."

Ciran tasted the drink. It was sweet and a little acidic.

Everyone drank this...

"It's good." Dannika opened and closed her lips. "Is it loquat? It doesn't taste alcoholic."

"Yes and no. It is loquat, and it's not alcoholic. Did you want the good stuff? We have it, but, you know, we save it for...oh. I guess this is a special occasion. Mom?"

Angie was still chasing the young fry at the far end of the beach.

"I'll ask her when she gets back. The wine is less healing, though. You're much more likely to regret it in the morning." Meg looked over at the far hammock. "Hadali, would you make sure that Val's cup never goes dry?"

"Sure." The eager trainee checked around Val's hammock. "But she's still drinking her special water from the plane. Where did... Mom? You're drinking Val's special water."

Bex choked and lowered the cup. "You poured her water into my cup?"

"Yours was closest. Didn't you see? Her water is shinier than the spring water."

"I can't see the shine."

"Oh. Yeah. Oops."

Bex handed over what was left of the elixir and switched to a different cup.

"So. You know Bex's ex-stepson." Meg rested on the back of the chair. "Small world, am I right? Oh, you're about done with your drink. Did you want another one, or did you want a shower?"

Dannika rubbed her sandy, damp forearms. "A shower, if that's all right."

"Absolutely. Right this way."

Ciran stood. Dannika took a moment longer, but she also rose. He rested a hand on her elbow to guide her, and she leaned into his touch.

"Ciran." Konomelu headed a group of the oldest trainees—cocky Nuno, solemn Tulu, and several others that were younger. Itime waited down by the seashore. "Our trainees invite you to watch their hunt. Witness the prowess of Sanctuary and consider how you would use them in a true battle."

His heart thudded with conflicting desires. "Already?

You invite me to... You honor me."

Konomelu grinned because it was an honor.

"But my mate. Dannika, you—"

"I'll be fine." The smile stretching her lips clashed with the deep shadows beneath her eyes. "I'll take it slow."

"And I'll hang out with you." Meg held out her elbow for Dannika. "We'll get in a little girl time while the big strong men do their guy stuff."

Ciran closed his hand over Dannika's. "Are you sure?"

Her soul glimmered, calm, and she nodded. "Have fun."

Very well. He released her and watched as she strolled slowly up the path with a kindly, attentive Meg.

Perhaps Meg would benefit from close contact with a queen. Dannika could learn why she didn't enter the water. He turned and followed the group of warriors down the beach.

They all dropped their coverings at the edge. Ciran left his damp shorts and shirt there as well.

Angie, who'd been walking back with Meg's smallest young fry squirming in her arms, dropped the excited youth and threw up her hands. "Are you kidding? Nuno. Konomelu. Boys!"

"C'mon, Mom," Nuno said. "It's not like we're not nude all the rest of the time."

"We cannot wear our coverings under the water," Konomelu said. "And we are showing the Undine—I mean, Atlantean—how our trainees hunt."

She crossed her arms, and her soul light dimmed. "Don't go too far."

"We will not need to." Konomelu stamped her lips with a kiss, and her soul brightened. She put her hands on her hips instead and watched them stride into the water.

"Here." Itime handed Ciran a stubby coral dagger.

"Have you used one before?"

He carried it in his hand because he had no sheath. "In training."

"Now, it gets a more extensive test." Itime's expression and tone did not change to reflect his dry words. "You should not need it. But..."

They both looked over the young warriors. Itime and Konomelu were showing him their resources because they were serious about invading Lusca.

Very well.

Ciran clenched the dagger and dove.

Perhaps three warriors, one queen, and a handful of trainees could be enough.

MEG LED Dannika up delightfully terraced steps into a lush, broadleaf forest with multiple trails leading in mysterious directions. Colorful birds chirruped in the fragrant grasses and shrubs.

Had this day really started at sunrise in Bermuda with the sound of peacocks? So much had happened, it felt like a week, and the day wasn't over yet.

Meg peered over her shoulder at the retreating beach. "I hate it when they go hunting. Do you ever feel like when they go in the water and disappear, they might never come out?"

Prickling apprehension needled Dannika's spine. She twitched. "Ciran's just watching."

"Yeah." Meg sighed. "Well, what can you do? Here's the shower."

They descended along a small riverbank and then down a terraced, rocky pathway below the river into a pleasant grotto. A folding screen shielded them from any passersby. Little seashells dangled with a pleasant clinking.

Dannika stepped onto a small platform of dry slatted wood.

"Pull this lever by your head and divert the stream." Meg demonstrated. The river above poured down a spout and showered the slatted wood. "Natural shower."

The cool water soothed her hot, salty skin. Dannika rubbed her hands together under the stream and dampened her sleeves again. "This is wonderful on a hot day."

"It's wonderful every day. Bex is a wizard. She made a tub once, and we used it all the time, but a tropical storm blew it away. Now we always rescue the shower."

A woven basket nearby held an assortment of brushes and sea sponges.

Meg squeezed one. "Natural loofah."

"Ooh, luxury."

"My mom tries to bring a little sophistication to island life." Meg hiked to the screen, then paused. "Hey. Do you really have, you know, superpowers? Like they said? To make a shield to protect yourself?"

"I made a little one." Somehow. "Other women have impressive abilities. They can shield entire armies, deflect underwater gunfire, push away sharks. Anything."

"Wow. Just imagine raising your hands and poof, bye-bye, hurricane."

"Oh, it only works underwater."

"Aw. Well, that's still amazing, though." Meg wrinkled her nose. "Changing back is so awful. Isn't it?"

"It's pretty bad."

The woman brightened. "Right? That's the one thing I don't miss. It feels like you're suffocating and drowning at the same time."

"It really does." Dannika splashed water up to her chest. So soothing and fresh, surrounded by the lush garden and peaceful, wet scents. "Are you saying it doesn't get any easier? I've been banking on it getting easier."

"I don't know. I had to give it up a while ago."

"Your kids shift so well."

"Well." Meg rolled her eyes. "My kids have slapping contests to see who can stand the hardest hit. They're not the highest standard for how much something sucks."

Ah, children.

"But, anyway, I'll let you get your shower." Meg climbed to the other side of the screen. "Toss your clothes over, and I'll put them in the sun to dry."

Dannika rinsed her caftan and underclothes, tossed them over the screen, and then stood under the pleasant falling water. It pulsed gently over her bruised and battered body.

"Ooh, underwear." Meg's voice wasn't quiet, but it also was self-directed, like she was used to talking to herself and not having anyone around her to respond. "I remember wearing underwear. Oh my God, a bra. So people still wear bras."

Rustling sounds emerged from the other side of the screen.

Then Meg called out, "I'm right here. Say something if you need me."

"Okay, thanks."

The birdsong, flower blossoms scattered at her feet, and the cheery tinkle of the shells reminded her of the outdoor showers she'd enjoyed in years past in Bali.

The ordeal was over. The terror begun on the plane had finished. She could relax.

She wet the sponge and scrubbed. Its rough-soft texture

made her skin tingle. The healing elixir had closed the few cuts, and the bruises had faded to a light purple already.

Dannika prodded the bruises.

She was not the same woman who'd awoken today.

Eliot's ring was gone.

A pang of loss flooded her nose, her mouth, her eyes with prickly grief.

She sucked in a deep, trembling breath. Then she clenched her empty hands to her chest and cried.

Like the water washing away the sticky salt from her cheeks, the tears cleared the passages in her heart.

She sobbed for the husband she'd barely had, the life she'd never lived, the memories she'd already forgotten. She grieved for the girl who'd held big dreams and lost all.

A new life awaited her. One she'd already taken a big step into. And that step had loosened the stitches in her neatly tied-up emotions, unbundling hopes and fears, and exposing her raw vulnerabilities for the first time in two decades. She was ready, but the process still hurt.

And then she rinsed her face, streaming away the last of her sticky salt.

To the future.

She closed up the shower and called for Meg, who passed over her clothes. "It dries fast in the sun."

They smelled like the sweet grass, empty and ready for her. She pulled on her undergarments and tied the caftan's belt. The strings were stiff but pliable.

Dannika faced the beach.

She had to be stronger now. Ciran needed a powerful woman. He deserved her showing up, at full force, being her most amazing self.

And so did she.

FOURTEEN

Dannika's soul glowed much brighter as she strode down the twilit path to the beach, even though her eyes were as dark from exhaustion as before, and she looked refreshed. "You're done already?"

"The hunt was faster than I had expected." Ciran gestured at the feast preparations, Bex and the others lowering their prey into the pit behind him. "I was—"

"Oh, no." Dannika snatched the hand he'd used to gesture and traced the red, stinging cuts. "I thought you were just watching."

"The fish did not receive the same instructions."

"Gosh." Her soul light dipped. "What happened?"

He recounted his experience.

Itime had led the group over the shallow reef. The Luscan patrol had moved out to sea. They were just visible from the coral lattice, and so the younger trainees had raced and frolicked with the reef creatures to cause a distraction. Konomelu, Nuno, and Ciran had slipped away, slinking down a secret chute to an exit deep beneath the island.

In the shadows had lurked a deadly striped fish with razor teeth.

Ciran had paused when he'd seen it, and Konomelu had given a slight sign, but Nuno had been looking the other direction and passed right by.

The fish had suddenly darted out, snapping at Nuno's fins.

Ciran had jetted forward and attacked. The fish had swerved to bite him, and his coral knife had broken off in its jaws. It had him pinned to a rock. He'd worked his fist into the gills to trap it. Nuno had returned and buried his knife in its brain.

"I got it!" Nuno had vibrated and swooped around the fish's corpse. "I killed it myself! See, Dad? I *am* ready to join you on the open ocean!"

Konomelu had smiled with tight lips, vibrating subdued congratulations to his son, while he'd yanked the fish off Ciran's fist.

This was a test for a much younger trainee, and as Konomelu had vibrated to Ciran on the return trip while Nuno surfaced with the kill, "They rarely hide so close. They prefer the other side of the island, where we have no chutes to reach them. The previous lieutenant guarding us, Lieutenant Figuara, patrolled different areas on a set schedule. He let our sons train. But Orike does nothing so generous."

He'd called the other trainees in, and they'd paddled past Ciran to the shore. Out beyond the tangle of dead coral separating the sheltered cove from the open ocean, Lieutenant Orike had watched. Even from the vast distance, it had seemed as though his eyes had narrowed.

Ciran finished his story for Dannika. "I think that lieutenant is reaching the end of his good judgment. I would not want to face him with only a coral blade."

She squeezed his hand. Her soul light remained dimmed. "Meg said she hated the hunting, but I thought you'd be safe."

"This is an ordinary wound."

"If these were on your throat, you could have been killed."

"It is a risk the mer take when we hunt. But dying is rare, and mer heal quickly." He scratched the skin around the deep cuts. "These will scab over soon."

Her breathing hitched, and her soul dipped even darker. "I was so dumb."

Tears pooled in her eyes.

"Dannika." He pulled her into his embrace. "Do not injure yourself by dwelling on pasts that have not come true."

"No, I know." She sniffled and hugged him, squeezing his torso and palpitating his shoulder blades, spine, and lower back as though to convince herself he was whole. "I had a bit of a cry in the shower, and I thought it was moving the emotions through me, but it also brings them closer to the surface."

"You cried in the shower?"

"Yeah. It was nothing. Just the stress of today."

He stroked her fluffy black hair. Her soft breasts and hips rubbed against his hard planes, and her soul brightened in his embrace. As it should. He pressed a soft kiss to her forehead. "Meg did not comfort you?"

"I didn't want to bother her. We just met, and she's too lovely a woman to burden with my breakdown."

"I should not have left you."

"You didn't know." Dannika nuzzled his cheek. "What was that you were saying? Don't hurt yourself by dwelling on could-haves or should-haves?"

"Yes." He tucked a lock of windblown hair behind her ear. "Then please remember you can come to me. I will hold you while you release your stresses. You no longer have to cry alone."

Her soul shone. Her chin wrinkled, and she rubbed it with one hand while sniffling again. "It was a little bit about Eliot, though."

"I have no competition with the dead."

"That's generous of you."

"He was an honored male. Your chosen one. Because he was worthy for you, he is also worthy for me. And any time you wish to revisit your sadness at his absence, I will hold and comfort you."

She squeezed her eyes tight and buried her face in his shoulder. "Ah, you really will make me cry again."

He held her, steady as his promise, until her wave of sadness passed. If he could take this pain away from her, he would do so, but even the most powerful queens and talented healers hadn't discovered a way to erase grief.

She sucked a shuddering breath and then lifted her face and brushed his jaw with her lips. "Thank you."

He had done nothing worthy of her thanks, but he understood. This was Dannika's generosity of spirit. He sought her lips for a brief comforting kiss.

She melted against him. Her mouth opened, and she moaned in sweet welcome.

Heat flooded his veins and pulsed into his cock. He had only meant to comfort her, but he stroked her crevices, possessing every inch of her mouth, and his cock hardened against her upper thigh. He needed her now, all of her, completely. Entwined with his body, sobbing his name, in ecstasy from his thrusting cock.

"All right, guys," Meg called out cheerfully behind them. "Ciran? Dannika? Appetizers are ready."

Young fry streamed past them, bumping and jostling.

Ciran pulled back and made a buffer sheltering Dannika from the horde converging on the food tables behind them.

Meg shrieked. "No, no. You guys, wait. Don't cram three in your mouths at once. There will be none left for our guests. Seriously, wait—"

Tweeeeet.

A shrill whistle silenced the trainees. They turned en masse toward Angie, who wielded the glare of the fiercest warrior, and cowered.

She removed her fingers from her mouth. Her chest rose and fell. And then a graceful smile brightened her face. "Thank you so much for your kind attention. If everyone who is eating now would finish, and everyone who accidentally dropped their formalwear please put it on, I'd like to say a few words to commemorate this historic first dinner."

The trainees with bulging cheeks swallowed, and the nude ones tied on their loincloths—including, surreptitiously, Konomelu.

Angie graced him with a pleased nod, and he returned it with a tight smile. She wore even more decorations. Long grasses sprang from her boxy hat, dangling jauntily every time she turned her head, and a large flower adorned the weave above her left breast.

She opened her palms. "First, thank you so much to my son Nuno for providing us with his very first razor-stripe grouper, and to Konomelu and Ciran for helping him bring it home safely, and to Bex for barbecuing it with her inspiring genius. Thank you to my daughter Meg for our wonderful place settings and artful decorations that will make eating so much more enjoyable."

Angie thanked more of the trainees and young fry for their contributions.

"And finally, thank you to our new friends, Ciran and Dannika, who will help us finally swim beyond the coral barrier and return to the mainland, where mermen are now well-known and accepted, and where we can introduce our new families and enroll our sons in a proper school."

Dannika's shoulders dropped. She locked her gaze with Ciran and bit her lip.

"And we can train our sons in the open ocean," Konomelu added.

"And eat real food again," Meg said. "Like cake and ice cream and dim sum."

"And all of that." Angie beamed and clapped twice.

The trainees moved toward the food tables again.

Angie tutted, arresting them, and gestured grandly to Ciran and Dannika. "If you please? Meg, make a little plate for Val."

Meg selected a leaf, scooped the different foods from their trays and carved wooden bowls, and neatly arranged the little clumps.

Dannika did the same, and Ciran mirrored her. As they finished, Angie released the others, and they stormed the table, shoving each other and causing Angie to enforce table etiquette.

The warriors had fashioned tables by mounting planks onto wooden supports. Woven mats were arranged around them on the sand. Dannika sat at one of these and lowered her voice to Ciran, who sat beside her. "I don't know how to tell them they might not be able to bring their families to the mainland. Imagine getting all the way there after years of eking out a living, surviving storms and deprivation as a castaway, and having your husband and children turned away at the shore."

He patted her knee. "Maybe you will not have to."

"Oh, because the government will drop the restrictions?" She brightened and picked up an intricately carved wooden spoon. "Boy, I hope you're right."

He tilted his head. Trust Dannika to focus on the positive.

But the real reason was that he'd seen the fighting prowess of the island now. He nodded at Konomelu, Itime, and the others who took seats at the table around them. By his calculations, the island had two warriors. The rest—humans who did not go in the water and trainees who did not know basic skills—were liabilities.

If this was all they had to combat the Lusca, Dannika's fear about being turned away at the mainland border would never come true.

Because they would never get off the island.

———

THE SUNSET DINNER WAS DELICIOUS.

Dannika crunched seaweed chips, savored grilled pawpaw and crisp green purslane, and filled her belly with finely sliced sashimi drizzled with sweet salsa.

And then the fish came out.

Sizzling with juices, seasoned to perfection. Mmm.

Dannika had imagined they were living in privation, but this was a proper feast.

Val awakened and limped to the table. She lifted Meg's miniature heart-shaped basket loaded with flowers. "I feel like I'm on an episode of *Survivor*. Any second now, the host is going to pop out of the bushes and hand us a challenge."

"What's *Survivor*?" asked Meg.

"A TV show that sticks people on a tropical island and makes them compete for a million dollars."

"We'd definitely win. For one thing... Oh! For the love of—" Meg jumped to her feet and brushed two massive black tarantulas off her lap.

Itime calmly shooed the hairy spiders away.

Her middle sons on the other side started giggling.

She whirled on them. "Kids. How many times do I have to tell you? No pets at the dinner table."

"Sorry, Mom," one said, singsong, and the other echoed it, still giggling.

"Sure you are." Meg rolled her eyes and sat again with a shudder. "You know I hate it when they sneak up on me like that."

Dannika scooted back and peered under the table. The sun had already descended beneath the horizon, and dark shadows hid the recesses of the table, but she only saw crossed legs and feet. No one else reacted. The others continued eating as if it were no big deal.

Val shielded her face. "I did not just see that."

"Are you afraid of spiders?" Angie asked.

"Not yet."

"Don't worry. They only flock to me." Meg patted her chest. "It's my Disney princess power."

"Well, call me a Pixar fan, but I don't remember any Disney princesses with spiders."

"Then they just haven't expanded enough creatively." Meg waved over her shoulder at the hidden tarantulas. "Aside from Alvin and Simon over there, I'm frequently tripped up by iguanas, beetles, birds, you name it."

"Alvin and Simon?" Val peered into the darkness. "What happened to Theodore?"

"We're not a hundred percent sure, because we only came upon the scene after the incident...but we think Alvin ate Theodore."

Val blinked. "I don't remember *that* scene in *The Chipmunk Adventure*."

"Yeah, you probably don't remember them all being hairy brown spiders either."

"Here, Meg." Angie carried over a small clay vessel. "Maybe this will help."

"Ooh, is it the newest wine?" Meg held her cup for her mother to pour. "I'll have a little. It's strong."

Angie lifted the vessel for Dannika. "Can I offer you Sanctuary *grand cru*? It's our finest vintage."

"Our only vintage, you mean."

"Meg." Angie shushed her playfully, and Dannika accepted the offer. Their premier wine tasted of coconut and citrus, sharp and sweet, with a definite kick.

Nuno held out his cup.

Angie snorted at her son. "Have tea."

"But I killed a razor-stripe today."

"Tea is good for warriors."

He grimaced and stabbed his third heaping plate of food. "That would be great if I ever got the training to become a warrior."

Konomelu and Itime exchanged meaningful glances, then both looked at Ciran.

He straightened on the mat beside her and finished his meal.

"I'm surprised you don't know *Survivor*," Val said, filling the quiet gap. "That show's been on forever, it feels like. Hasn't it been on twenty years? Huh."

"Oh!" Meg folded her empty plate, tossed it into the firepit, and rummaged in the raised platform. "Yes. Oh, yes. *The date.*"

"Ah," Itime said.

Konomelu's brow lightened, Angie clapped, and the kids hooted excitedly. Meg dragged out a woven shoulder bag, unrolled a small square of fabric that contained a feather pen, and opened a bound journal. She dipped the quill in a pot of ink and poised over a page. "What is today?"

"Thursday," Val said.

"No, the date. What's the date?"

"January twenty-third," Dannika said.

"Are you sure?"

"The twenty-third," Val agreed. "Is it still the twenty-third? This morning feels like a million years ago."

"The twenty-third..." Meg noted it carefully in swirly, artful script, blew on it to dry, carefully capped the ink, and stowed the quill, and then jumped up. "We were three days off."

The younger kids scrambled to their feet and bounced around the smoky firepit, dancing and shrieking. Konomelu grinned broadly.

Angie waited until Meg collapsed at her seat in a lump. Then she tapped her brow. "Where did it happen? Early on? A leap year?"

"We've had a few surprises. Remember that one hurricane? We lost a week. But." She grinned at Ciran and Dannika. "Now we never have to worry about losing days, because you guys will get us to the mainland."

The warriors focused on Ciran.

Bex kept her gaze on her plate.

Angie smiled graciously, although worry lined her eyes. "I am thankful you've come. We all look forward to returning home after twenty years."

FIFTEEN

Twenty years.

Wow.

Dannika had lost Eliot eighteen years ago. It felt like a lifetime, and yet, these women had been castaways for two years longer.

"It is amazing how wonderful you've made this island," Dannika said, and everyone smiled. "And I do hope we can find a way back to the mainland soon."

"God, yes." Meg squeezed her hands together in a plea. "I miss black forest cheesecake with the passion of a thousand burning suns. And Mom misses dumplings."

"Rice." Angie smiled dreamily. "Hot pot. Beef noodles. Jook."

"Chocolate peanut butter cups or chocolate bars dipped in peanut butter or just a spoonful of peanut butter."

"Noodle soup. Hot and spicy noodles. Hand-pulled noodles."

"Yellow birthday cake with chocolate frosting. And ice cream cake. Also, chocolate. And everything off a dim sum cart. Everything." Meg shook herself and bumped Itime with her shoulder. "But we do what we can, and honestly, it's not so bad. Look at me, tarantula queen. So long as you have your soul mate, you can get used to anything."

Yes, that was true. They were not the traditional castaways stranded in a foreign environment with nothing but their emergency kit. No, they were stranded with natives and magic. Their positive attitudes must help as well.

"What about Val?" one of the ten-year-olds asked plaintively from down the table.

"What about Val?" Meg repeated, scrubbing her woodware in the cleansing sand.

"Where's her soul mate?"

"Oh, baby." Meg glanced at Val and away again. "Her soul mate's not here."

"Yep, she's at home," Val said. "And I'm hoping to get back to her as soon as I can."

They all sobered.

Angie and Konomelu exchanged meaningful looks, and then Angie stood and clapped her hands. "Children? It's time for bed!"

A disappointed chorus answered back.

Itime gathered his children. "Come."

"I'm old enough to hear your plans," Nuno argued.

Konomelu wrestled with the younger twins. "No plans are being shared until after your siblings are in bed."

"Dad!"

"My son." Konomelu lost the twins, then rose and clapped Nuno's shoulder. "Do you think I am not assisting?"

"But..." Nuno gazed at the star-spackled sky. "I want to ask Ciran questions."

"You will."

"And I'm not just a caretaker of young fry. I'm a warrior."

"And a warrior does not argue with his commander."

Nuno thrust his hand at Val and Dannika. "Why do they get to stay?"

"Because they are not related to your brothers. Nuno, your protests are not befitting an honorable warrior. Assist us, or you will not hear the plans."

Nuno stomped after his youngest brothers. He looked older, but Konomelu was right. This behavior resembled that of a whiny teen, not the maturity the other warriors had displayed in front of Dannika.

Hadali and Tulu crowded in. "If Nuno stays, I want to too," Hadali said, and Tulu nodded.

"Actually," Val yawned, "if you don't mind, I'm going to cash in again. I feel a lot better, but I'm almost snoozing. Food was delicious," she told Angie. "Please don't think I'm rude."

"Not at all. Hadali? Tulu, help Val to the hammock." Angie arranged netting and a sunshade for the morning.

Dannika helped store the food into animalproof vessels. Bex stoked the fire and partially replaced the lid to smoke the rest of the fish overnight. The older kids reluctantly put the younger ones to bed, with Itime and Meg supervising, and then they returned with Nuno, Tulu, and Hadali. The adults pulled mats around the curling smoke of the fire just as in eons gone by. A million stars burned overhead.

"Returning to the mainland will not be easy," Konomelu said to Ciran. "When we escaped from the Luscan king with our soul mates, Itime's father, Elder Daka, guaranteed the sanctuary of this island. But it has been impossible to train our young fry in these waters. Lieutenant Figuara, the previous patrol leader, looked the other way for the early tests. Eventually, we reached an impasse."

The fire popped. Its sparks cast a temporary, somber glow on the warriors.

Ciran cleared his throat. "And then?"

Konomelu sighed heavily. "Prince Ankena decided that we must attempt to finish the training."

"Prince Ankena?" Dannika repeated.

Everyone looked at Bex.

Bex poked the fire. "My husband."

Hmm.

Konomelu continued. "As a Luscan, we must also avoid other cities and the All-Council. Prince Ankena took his first son, Lukiyo, to the nearest echo point to hear the news of the ocean and discover the safest route to train. They were captured."

"By Luscan warriors?"

"Yes." Konomelu closed his eyes and grimaced in pain. "I argued that I should go first, alone, before he risked traveling with Luk. But he said it would be a good test, and his father would not kill him outright."

"He was right," Itime said.

"Is what happened any better?" Konomelu slammed his hand to his chest. "It should have been me. I was his original lieutenant. I followed him where no others would go. And yet I failed."

Angie nodded solemnly, supporting her husband, her face reflecting his regret.

"We went to find them." Konomelu indicated himself and Itime. "The king had imprisoned Prince Ankena and was raising Lukiyo as his own. But by the time we arrived, it was too late. Prince Ankena had already attempted an escape and was killed."

Dannika's heart stopped.

Killed.

Oh, no.

No, no, no.

Hot and cold flushed through her body, which was so strange because she was hearing about a tragedy for a stranger that had already happened, but her hands trembled with a mind of their own.

Ripping away a key member had affected the community deeply. A father, a husband, and... She turned to Bex. "Your soul mate?"

Bex nodded.

Sadness welled up and crushed Dannika. It was like hearing about Eliot all over again. "Oh, I'm so sorry. That must have been a terrible day."

Bex nodded again, accepting Dannika's heartfelt condolences with her usual stoicism.

"That day was over three years ago." Konomelu leaned back and rested on his palms. "The king demoted Lieutenant Figuara for failing to contain us. Orike has no value for young fry. He has threatened to kill us and take them many times."

And no one would ever comfort Bex again.

Dannika's chest ached. To lose a soul mate like that... Oh, it was her greatest nightmare.

If she lost Ciran...

Her stomach squeezed.

No, this wasn't time for her grief. She had to be there for others.

"I'm so sorry for your loss," Dannika said again to Bex. "If you ever want to talk about it, I'm here. I've experienced something similar, and I know how devastating it is. I am so, so sorry."

"Thanks, but it's a mistake," Bex said. "He's still alive."

"Oh. Uh..."

The others frowned. Angie regarded Bex with pity.

Meg glanced at Hadali in the shadows with Tulu and Nuno. She grimaced with frustration. "Bex, the guys aren't making it up. They got the intel and they searched. If Prince Ankena was alive, they would never have come home without him."

Bex lifted a shoulder, unconvinced.

Was it denial, then?

Ciran leaned forward. "Why do you believe he is dead?"

"Because the king stabbed him and tossed his body in the trench," Konomelu said.

Angie nudged him. Hadali was listening.

"It is a common punishment for traitors." Konomelu looked unrepentant, as though the trainee deserved to know the truth, but he softened his tone. "He did not suffer long. The trench dwellers ended him before his body could reach the bottom."

Ciran frowned. "First Lieutenant Soren survived a trench."

"Filled with what?" Konomelu snorted. "Fish? Lusca is not planted on solid rock. It perches on a nest of colossal squids. The king barely controls them with the mirror stones."

"It is true," Itime said. "No one ventures into the den of the kraken and survives."

"It is impossible," Konomelu said. "The king himself grieved, and he is the one who ordered the execution."

The silence stretched.

"Ankena was a good man," Meg said.

"The best," Itime agreed quietly.

"His royal legacy will live on in his son." Konomelu glanced up the hill where Hadali would sleep with the other young fry and corrected, "Sons."

"And yet..." Bex shrugged.

"Honey." Angie stood and went to her, then hugged her. She pressed Bex's head into her grass-weave-covered belly. "We all wish he were still alive." She glanced at Hadali, a pale slip in the shadow, and then patted Bex's shoulder. "Maybe it's time to stop saying it aloud at all."

Bex frowned.

"I'm sorry, Bex," Meg said. "I have to agree with Mom on this one. It's not like when you envision a sauna and make it happen. This is life or death here."

So it was denial, then.

Ciran was still studying Bex as though trying to figure out what was wrong. "Did you see his body?"

Konomelu and Itime exchanged glances.

"No," Konomelu said shortly. "We delved into the trench as far as we could. But even if we had searched the full length, we would not have found a body. Trench scavengers leave nothing."

Dannika pressed her hands to her chest. "A sudden loss is so hard. Especially if there's no body. You have to cling to hope. But at a certain point, that hope will hold you back from living your life. And I'm sure Prince Ankena wouldn't have wanted that."

Bex listened.

Honestly, Dannika felt like she was talking to herself again. "Please believe me when I say I know exactly what you're going through. Losing the man you're supposed to spend the rest of your life with is devastating. You'll loop through a lot of emotions. Denial, anger, grief."

Bex's eyes flicked to Ciran's hand resting near Dannika's knee. "Yeah?"

"But when you finally accept and let go of the past, you'll be able to breathe again. And you never know what might be waiting. This is your dark time. But there will be another dawn."

Ciran took Dannika's hand in his warm grip.

She squeezed his fingers.

"Thank you, Dannika." Angie smiled at her warmly, graciously, and squeezed Bex one last time before returning to her seat. "I suppose it is up to you warriors to pool your resources and come up with a strategy to rescue Prince Lukiyo and get us to the mainland."

Mm. Right.

Dannika still had to break the news about the visas.

"Which means attacking Lusca." Konomelu clenched his fist. "Decisive victory. Complete domination."

"You know our resources and our goals." Itime focused on Ciran. "What is your opinion?"

But Ciran squeezed her hand and stood. "You cannot attack Lusca with your current resources. You cannot win."

Konomelu stood as well. "Not even with your queen? Her shield?"

Ciran looked down on her. He hesitated a long moment, and myriad cryptic emotions passed over his face before he settled on his answer. "No."

"You hesitate," Konomelu said.

"Because Dannika could shield us, all of us, once she develops her powers." He focused on the warriors. "But she cannot do so now."

Oh.

Hmm.

That was a little disappointing. Of course, Dannika

agreed. Ciran was one hundred percent right. She might luck into figuring out how to make her shield again, but how could she sustain it to Lusca? And while under attack? No. She couldn't.

"But if we had four queens." Ciran locked gazes with Angie and Meg, who both looked away, and Bex, who held his gaze resolutely. "Then we could most likely do anything we wished. Cross the ocean, retake one city, face off against the kraken itself."

Konomelu crossed his arms. A flicker of interest crossed Itime's usually stoic face, but Meg pursed her lips with concern, and Angie studied her smoothed toenails as though Ciran's words didn't apply to her.

"And we will need to do that, clearly," he continued, holding all their attention in his resolute grip, "because Prince Ankena is still alive, and we must descend into the trench to rescue him."

SIXTEEN

What?

Prince Ankena was alive?

Konomelu turned five shades of red. His iridescent orange tattoos glimmered like sparks of fire on his skin.

And then he exploded.

"We have searched!" Konomelu shouted at Ciran. "To the very rim of the trench. We barely escaped with our lives."

"We never would have left him if we were not certain," Itime said calmly.

"How dare you? You foreign—scheming—insulting Undine. I mean, Atlantean. To say that I, Prince Ankena's most loyal commander, would leave him. *Leave him.* In a trench, injured and alone, to fend for himself against the kraken?"

"Yes," Ciran said, equally unbending.

This was about to become dangerous.

Dannika stood and put a calming hand on his forearm.

Angie did the same to Konomelu.

"What makes you say Prince Ankena's still alive?" Dannika asked quietly. "Do you think their informant lied and he never went into the trench?"

"I do not know," Ciran said.

"So he might have survived this deadly trench?" Dannika asked. "How?"

"I also do not know."

"But then how do you know he's still alive?"

"I do not."

A tense stillness fell over the group as everyone processed his words.

"Well then, why did you say he's still alive if you don't know it?" Dannika demanded.

"Because she does." Ciran gestured at Bex. "Every warrior can sense his bride. He feels their shared resonance in his soul. Do you not sense me? I sensed you for the entire raft journey, our separation during my hunt. Even now, I feel you." He pressed her palm to his chest, hot beneath the shirt. "Here."

A stark silence fell over the group.

Oh.

God.

Everyone was looking at her.

Did she feel him?

"Brides don't see resonance," she reminded him. "We don't see the glowing light."

"But you should still sense something. The other queens of Atlantis do. Not as clearly, perhaps, but they feel dread when their warriors are endangered. You feel nothing?"

"Um...well... It's only been, uh, half a day... I might be feeling a lot of stuff, but it's all overwhelming, and I'm still getting used to it..."

He nodded slowly, clearly disappointed, and focused on the other warriors. "Connections between a warrior and his bride defy distance and time. You know."

"I have never heard of it," Itime said, calm as always.

"Because it is a lie," Konomelu growled.

Ciran's mouth opened and closed. He was genuinely shocked. "Your fathers never spoke of their connection to their sacred brides?"

The two warriors regarded each other with dark silence.

Itime answered. "My father never spoke of his. She died soon after my birth. "

"As did mine," Konomelu said.

"What a terrible coincidence. Or was it?" Konomelu growled.

Angie raised her hand again. Not in warning, but to offer a reminder.

Konomelu grimaced. "It was no coincidence."

"I am... I have no words." Ciran turned to her. "Dannika?"

"Hmm? Oh. Words. God, I am so sorry. That must have been so hard and sad for you and your father. You've done a wonderful job raising your children with both loving parents and developing a supportive community so your children can thrive."

Angie lowered her hand.

Konomelu pursed his lips, swallowed hard, and nodded. "It...was hard... And without Prince Ankena, I have tried my best to lead as he would." He pressed his lips together. His nostrils flared, and he tried to continue, but his voice broke. He turned to Angie. She enfolded him in a hug and stroked his shoulders, looking as surprised as the rest of the watchers and, heck, Dannika herself.

Meg rested her hand on Itime's bicep. "Are you okay?"

"My youth was trying as well, and I am pleased to raise my young fry better."

"That's it?"

He nodded.

She patted him. "Okay."

Ciran shook his head. "But the other warriors, the elders. Who raised the orphaned young fry?"

"The king." Konomelu's voice was muffled over Angie's shoulder. He straightened, cleared his throat, and let out a long breath. She rubbed his back.

"Many young fry come into the city without their parents," Itime said. "Some are taken, like Lukiyo."

Ciran rubbed his forehead. "I would have thought *some* of your young fry were not stolen."

Konomelu pushed back. "We did not steal them. We rescued them."

"From exiles," Itime said flatly. "Even my father spoke against that. He was overruled."

"We liberated them," Konomelu protested.

"We liberated them directly from their parents' arms."

"But we gave them a better life."

"I am sure that is what the king tells Lukiyo."

"Stop it, guys." Meg gestured at Hadali, who was grimacing into the flames. "Both of you. You don't do that anymore, Konomelu. And you've said a hundred times you don't agree with it. Mom?"

"Meg's right." Angie crossed her arms matter-of-factly. "You said it only a few hours ago when that Orike threatened to take Nuno and turn him into a warrior. Because his first act will be to hurt one of us. Me or the boys." She dropped her arms. "It's the Luscan way."

He released a pent-up breath, turned toward Angie, and tapped his cheek.

She slapped him across the face. *Smack.*

He rubbed his cheek, then nodded to her. "As agreed. Thank you."

"I keep my promises." She glared up at him, diminutive against his full height, but just as fierce. "You believed in the laws of Lusca for most of your life. But you *are* a father and a warrior of Sanctuary."

"Yes. And you are my queen."

She twisted her lips to the side. "Well. We'll see."

He bent her over and kissed her passionately.

Nuno looked away.

"Oh my God, Mom." Meg shielded her eyes. "It's been, like, a decade since you guys did the crying-and-slapping thing. Whew."

Itime bumped her shoulder with his. "Do you wish I were more passionate?"

"God, no. You're perfect just the way you are." She waved away her mother and stepfather's display. "I want no part of that drama sandwich. But Ciran, could Prince Ankena really be still alive? Really?"

"I do not sense his connection." Ciran gestured at Bex. "But if you know he is still alive, then, as impossible as it seems, he must still be alive."

Bex's grimace deepened. "Dannika doesn't sense you."

"Her sense should grow with her queen powers."

"I don't have queen powers."

"Shifting is a continuum," Ciran said. "Passive senses, such as seeing underwater and breathing, appear instantly. Queen Elyssa worked for weeks to make her fins and then channel the Life Tree. But Queen Lucy channeled the Life Tree power long before she reliably made her fins."

"You'll show us?" Meg asked Dannika. "Tomorrow? I

totally want to see. Oh, did you have goggles in that emergency kit?"

"You must shift," Ciran said. "The powers are invisible to human eyes, although humans will still feel the effects."

"Ugh. Shifting." Meg dropped her head into her hands. "Never mind."

"You must shift. It is the only way to retake the city."

"Well, there you go. I'm never going to stab anybody." Meg mimed slashing a trident. "I feel bad when I squish a bug."

"I also have a few questions before racing into battle," Angie said.

"You do not have to hurt anyone," Ciran said.

Konomelu threaded his fingers with Angie's. "Your kindness is commendable, but the warriors we fight will not extend you that same mercy. You must be ruthless. A blade that cuts through the swaths of enemies."

She wrinkled her nose. "Mmm. Maybe I will leave the fighting to the experts."

"You must try to develop your powers," Ciran said. "If you are serious about saving your friend and retaking Lusca, it is the only way."

The women shook their heads.

"There has to be another way," Meg said. "Because if it's up to me turning into a warrior, I'm not interested."

"Not even a little bit," Angie said.

"Well, maybe a little bit," Meg said. "But I can't go in the ocean. No way, no how. People die in there! And it's full of giant squid."

"So, what time tomorrow?" Bex asked. "When will Dannika show her queen powers?"

Konomelu looked at Itime, who shrugged. "We should meet in the reef before breakfast. Without the young fry."

"Dannika will inspire you," Ciran promised. "She will show you all."

So, great.

All Dannika had to do was find and develop her powers, convince the others it was worthwhile to develop theirs, and then retake a warlike city ruled by an angry king, rescue a missing prince from a trench infested with the kraken, and all before the city went on the warpath and sank their rescue boats, specifically the one chartered by Bex's stepson, Stevie.

No problem.

Dannika helped stow the mats and disassemble the tables to keep them from blowing over in the sometimes fierce winds. Her mind churned.

She'd interviewed the early queens. Their inner confidence, serenity, and passion had formed her vision of the kind of brides her warriors needed. But she hadn't listened as a student who must one day teach.

"Where do you want to sleep?" Bex glanced at Dannika's bruises in the dwindling firelight. "You can breathe underwater? You should probably have the lagoon for healing."

"Are you...?" Meg asked, letting the question, whatever it was, hang.

Bex shook her head. "Just the lagoon."

Mysterious. They'd been open about so much, but they weren't telling all their secrets.

Bex led Dannika and Ciran up the stone path, over the headland, and back to the cave.

"This path is so nice and bright with the moonlight," Dannika said. "You've done a wonderful job."

"Thanks." Bex glanced over her shoulder. "There's no moonlight."

Dannika stopped.

Stars stretched into infinity, and the waves also stretched in every direction.

She could see in the dark! "I really have changed, haven't I?"

Ciran stood at her shoulder. "You have."

Oh. Wow.

Bex kept strolling at her easy pace, her grass skirt swishing. Dannika hurried to catch up.

The lagoon glimmered with unusual beauty lighting the worn statues. The iridescence was coming from inside the cave. More specifically, inside the water.

She rubbed her eyes.

"This glow coming from the water." Ciran knelt and dipped a fingertip in, swirling. "I did not notice it earlier with so much noise and energy. It is oddly familiar."

Bex shrugged. "It's an old church, so..."

He rubbed the liquid between his fingers.

"Well, tuck in." Bex turned away.

"Wait, you want us to sleep underwater?" Dannika squinted at what she thought was the distant cave entrance, but she couldn't quite see it through the stalactites and vines. "Can't just anyone swim in?"

"A boulder blocks the entrance. Mostly for the squids." Bex lingered in the doorway. "Did Stevie talk about himself?"

"He said you're the reason he became a videographer," Dannika said. "He's the lead at his company and has his pick of jobs."

Bex grinned, then rubbed her face. "Anything else?"

"You'll have to ask him yourself when we get out of here."

Her smile fell. She gazed through the rock, and her eyes got a distant look. "Do you really think we can take Lusca?"

Well...honestly, Dannika had no idea.

"Yes," Ciran said.

Bex faced him. "Even though Angie doesn't think we should and Meg is afraid?"

"You have a new advantage: You know what is possible. And according to the other queens, that was all they needed to bring forth their powers."

Bex nodded slowly, then bid them goodnight and headed up the steps.

Dannika's fingers tingled. "If only you could bottle some of that certainty, I would drink it like the elixir. I can't believe you promised everyone that I'd show off my powers tomorrow. I still have no idea what I did."

"You will."

"Seriously, give me that confidence. I'll drink."

"Your confidence will grow with your mastery. It is the same with any warrior."

That was hard to believe.

"Doubts plague even the most confident warrior when he is tired." Ciran shucked his clothes and strode proudly to the lip, muscles rippling with unrelenting grace. He slipped into the water up to his waist and held out a hand to her. "Rest with me, Dannika. Heal your body and your mind."

Well, he wasn't wrong.

She slipped off her caftan, folded it neatly beside the freshwater bowl, and hooked a finger under her bra strap.

Ciran rested both elbows on the ledge. His hot gaze drifted down her body and back to her face.

Answering heat kindled in her. She was tired, but

excited butterflies awoke in her stomach, and suddenly, sleep was the last thing on her mind.

She forced the underclothing off, angling to disguise her worst flaws. The pooch at her belly that had grown. The wrinkly sag under her arms that made her switch from youthful tank tops to flowing sleeves. She clothed her body well and rarely agonized over the natural changes because she had no one to show.

Then she forced herself to her feet and hurried to the water's edge beside him, covering first her belly and then her arms, and then her belly again, and oh yes, her private areas.

He watched her hands move and tilted his head. "What is wrong?"

"Just thinking." She sat and dropped her feet in, the water cresting her calves, and positioned herself for the best angle. "It's been a long time since a man has seen me naked."

He moved around her and rested one hand on the ledge beside each thigh. His chest bumped gently against her knees, and the iridescent threads in his eyes gleamed. "Lucky me."

The suggestion in his tone made a delicious throb between her legs. Her butterflies flurried. She squeezed her elbows in tight, hugging her breasts and hiding her belly.

He bumped against her. "You will be more comfortable in the water."

"I'll be more comfortable ten years younger."

"Why?"

"Because I wanted you to find a woman with fewer miles on her." She risked reaching out and stroking his earnest, chiseled cheek. "You deserve someone like that."

He caught her hand and pressed a sizzling kiss to her palm. "But I want you."

Her breath hitched.

He'd always said that. And it was too late for them now, anyway. He embraced her. She just had to embrace him back.

He kicked back from the ledge and gently tugged her in.

She entered the water with a splash. It was warm and salty, just as before. She blew bubbles out her nose, and the stillness of the lagoon seemed to chime into her waterlogged ears. She *had* shifted. She just had to release her bubbles and believe it.

Leap of faith.

Again.

Everything about Ciran was a leap of faith.

The protests of hundreds of her dating clients echoed in her mind. *I don't even know why I walked in here. Dating never works. I'm different. I've been trying to meet the man of my dreams for years, and all I do is meet losers. What do you mean* my *attitude is what has to change?*

She breathed in.

Water filled her mouth and hit the back of her throat.

She choked.

There was no way not to feel the wrongness of it. Heavy chill in her lungs, unnatural, promising death...

Ciran whirled over her, rolling her around and making the rocky floor the ceiling, the air above her toes.

The glow brightened as the lagoon opened up around her. Tiny, clear shrimps fluttered like moths. Algae glowed blue, and small anemones suctioned to the underside of rocks dusted with sea stars. Wind chimes from a hundred stained glass windows tinkled in her chest, in her ears. Stalagmites punctured the surface, and it was much deeper at the edge of the ledge than she'd realized. He hadn't been standing on the bottom. No, he'd been floating or kicking those long fins.

"You continue to wish for another bride for me." His chest vibrated as they gently twirled in the lagoon. "But I want you, Dannika. I want your doubts and your miles and your worries and your hesitation. I want the you who is lost and afraid. I want the you who is finding her way again, and who comforts others even when she feels fearful herself. I want the you who works tirelessly for my warriors and cries tears of frustration because she cannot give them an easier life."

He slowed, and his incisive gaze pierced her very soul.

"And I want the you who is cautious with yourself, even though your natural urge is generosity, because you are not sure if you are ready to fully gift yourself to another soul mate."

Her heart ached.

How did he see so much?

She cupped his cheeks. These were the bones of a proud, arrogant warrior. She teased her fingertips along his dark, expressive brows. "I wasn't always like this."

"And you will change again. Because although I want the you who is uncertain, I want even more the woman who knows her desires and claims her destiny." He pressed another kiss to her tender fingertips. "I want to take that journey with you. Let me hold you when you cry. Someday, we will stand together, and you will smile."

Her heart squeezed again.

"I keep thinking I'm going to get over Eliot's death. 'This will be the last time I cry.' But I lost his wedding ring today." She showed him her bare left hand. "I felt a lot of guilt for his death. We were visiting friends on the lake, and one afternoon, I just felt too tired to go out. I'd gotten a sunburn the day before and still had a headache. He didn't want to be rude to our hosts, so he went out on their new boat, and a sudden storm capsized it. Everyone else was fine, but Eliot didn't survive."

He remained respectfully silent.

"A thousand hours of psychotherapy assures me it's not my fault." She closed her left hand into a fist. "But even now, I can't help playing the game of 'What if?'"

"You are not to blame for the death of your first soul mate." He touched her forehead with his. "But there is a different knowing in your body and in your heart."

He was right.

God, he was always right.

The tears, somehow ever-present these days, pricked her eyes. In his comforting embrace, she successfully swallowed them down.

"It's funny. You think grief is like a storm, and when it's over, the sun comes out. But it's really like the waves of the ocean, cresting and falling. Usually, the tide's going out, but every once in a while, a sneaker wave drags me in."

"Then"—his embrace tightened—"I will stand on that shore with you even if the tide rushes over our heads."

She chuckled, but underwater, it was more of an interrupted vibration. "Then we'll both get wet."

He leaned back and cocked a brow. "I am a mer. I am not afraid of wetness."

That's right. He didn't fear drowning. Because no matter how heavy and deep her grief, he would float beside her, supporting her, just breathing.

Because he was her one.

She had loved Eliot wholeheartedly. And now she came

to Ciran with a cracked heart, and he loved her just as she was.

He loved her just as she was.

Tingles filled her veins like starlight.

The water seemed to heat between them. Her bare breasts pressed to his solid chest, her hip tucked to his, and her feet dangled between his ankles. His cock pressed, hard and ready, against her upper thigh.

He pressed a gentle palm to her chest. "You are feeling better. Rest now. I will hold you as you heal, and you will carry this strength into the morning."

"Mm, I have a better idea." She fitted herself more fully to his body.

He cupped her hips. "Better than sleeping?"

"I'm feeling kind of nervous about demonstrating my powers."

"But you have already used them."

"Right." She nuzzled his cheek and nibbled on his inflexible jaw. "You have so much confidence. I want to drink it up."

His chest rumbled with amusement. "I am not a vessel of water."

"Are you sure?" She flicked her tongue against his earlobe.

He shivered and focused on her with new intensity. "I thought you would want to rest."

"Hmm." She rubbed her tightening nipples across his chest. "Suddenly, I'm not tired." She tugged his lobe, causing another delightful shiver in him. "Because of nerves. I could use your advice."

"My advice?" He hunted her mouth and took her lips, questing deep and awakening her senses. While kissing her, he vibrated, "I have dreamed of possessing you for so long,

Dannika."

"Good. Me too. Will that help?"

"I hope." His lips curved into a smile, and he broke from her mouth to kiss her cheek, her forehead, her hair. "But only you can grow your powers. Brighten your soul light so you do not fail."

"You know I can't see my own soul light."

"But you must feel it." He pulled back and kissed her chest, searing her with sudden and unstoppable heat. "Right now. This sensation. You shine."

This sensation?

Ciran cradled her, loved her, worshipped her. His kisses melted her collarbone, nipping teeth that made her feminine core clench. She flexed her fingers to entwine him, but he gently gripped her wrists.

"This sensation, yes." His lips melded to hers, passionate and true, driving in and overwhelming her. "You are a queen, Dannika. Increase our resonance and claim your power. In time, you *will* turn back storms."

She drowned in his sweet insistence. "But if I'm not even there..."

"We will never part."

So much was still unresolved. Hesitation buried deep in her heart.

But she wanted to believe.

She would anchor herself to his certainty.

Because they were soul mates.

And embracing him was the only way she would ever truly live.

His tongue plumbed her depths, into the places she hid, and she welcomed his sensual assault. He wove his fingers into her hair and goaded her to duel, to face him with the same urgency. Heat crackled into her veins. He was the rake unearthing her soil, and she was finally breathing again as she opened herself to his life-giving sunlight.

"You will become confident," he promised. "You will change and grow and flourish. And you will unite your soul more tightly with mine."

Starlight filtered through the overhead caverns and lit the ocean with a beautiful hum.

It penetrated her skin, her chest, her heart.

And so did he.

His eyes gleamed, calculating and watchful. His tongue flicked her dark nipples, teasing her to hard pearls.

Heat streaked to her center, and she moaned with a desperate vibration. Her desire filled the water. It tasted of musk and need, a thousand empty nights, a thousand salt tears of loneliness.

She drew him to her breast, seeking relief for the ache he created, and he resisted, kissing around her hot pearls, stoking her with painful need. He finally closed over her nipple and sucked. Intense relief gave way to new pinnacles of clenching feminine need. All she wanted was him. His driving sex, hard against her thigh, and his certainty. If she could just draw them both inside her, she would never fear losing him again.

He stamped his possession in with every kiss, every nip of teeth, tasting and tormenting her. She clung to him like a buoy in a storm.

And with unstoppable strength, he freed himself from her embrace and lowered between her legs, resting her thighs on his inflexible shoulders.

Her pussy throbbed. Yes, she wanted him there, exactly.

His tender fingers stroked her feminine flower, folding back the petals, and then his tongue explored, soft and gentle, then, as she drew him tighter, firm and commanding.

Some men would never do this, but Ciran was attuned to her every tremble, enjoying and savoring his control. He latched on to her sensitive nub.

She craved more. Now. Faster.

He thwarted her urgings and took his time, persisting at his pace, leading her around the winding road to a peak of gorgeous perfection. He didn't stop at the easy, quick release. No, he led her from a slow-burning ache into an explosive orgasm that made her whole body shatter.

She arched and cried for him. "Ciran!"

He released her and trailed his powerful hands down her shuddering body, gazing at her beautiful ruin with satisfaction.

A soul-deep peace flooded her veins with sleepy promise.

He'd stood against all the times she'd pushed him away. He'd stood against her clinging desperately for more. He was a post, a rock, an anchor point, and he would stand against anything.

And now he held her gently, cradling her tenderly to sleep, completely ignoring his own unsatisfied desire that still prodded her belly.

She curled her hands around his rebar-hard cock.

He tried to disentangle her fingers. "You were sleepy a moment ago. Do you not want to rest?"

"Yes, I do not."

He frowned. "You always give so much. This time, it is okay to receive."

"Same to you."

"Release me, Dannika." He tried to separate them.

She clung on. "No."

Surprise shuddered through his taut body. "I should have known you would not simply accept pleasure."

"You should have. Because you said you want me, even the imperfect me. I'm not ready to believe in forever, but I am ready to try. So if you can wait while I figure this out, I will do my very best to become your queen."

He cupped her cheek. Emotion tightened his jaw. He vibrated for her. "I will."

Heat seeped into her crevices and throbbed with the pleasure she'd just received, readying her for even more.

Because she wanted to spend tonight with this warrior.

And tomorrow, and the night after that.

And then they'd just see.

"Make me believe in us." She snugged him close. "Claim me as your bride."

EIGHTEEN

ake me believe.

M Ciran had tried to convince her from their first meeting.

Only she could believe.

But he would give her all the reasons he could.

And then he just had to hope his devotion carried her the rest of the way.

He bent his head to chase her lips. "You are powerful, Dannika."

She returned his kiss with a sweet push-pull and twirled her hand around his cock. "I want to carry your child. I want us to make a life together."

"And you will forgo MerMatch and live in Atlantis?"

She squeezed his cock. "Don't push your luck."

"But I have a duty to my king, so we must—"

She pulled him in tighter, silencing his vibrations with her hug, entwining him like a strangling vine, and rubbed her soft, sensual female curves against his hardest places. "Reason later. Love me now."

Very well.

He wedged his hand against her hip to stroke her delicate feminine core.

But she pulled him in tighter, melting against him with more compliance, and ensnared his torso with her legs. His cock bobbed between her thighs. She fitted his sensitive head to her channel and tightened her legs around his buttocks, pressing him in.

He buried his cock deep in her channel connecting their bodies for all time.

Dannika's chest glowed.

He shuddered. His very soul throbbed.

She was his bride. They belonged together.

Forever.

Dannika's hands tightened on his shoulders. "Never leave me."

He kissed her taut brow. For the worthy soul mate who had once been forced from her arms. For the uncertain future that made this promise impossible to keep, but which he made anyway because it was what she needed to heal. "Never."

She squeezed him inside so tight. He was gripped by her, and he only wanted more.

He slid out.

She entangled their legs to stop him from leaving her.

He surged, filling her more completely, grinding against her sensitive button.

She moaned. "Ciran, yes."

Her cry caged him, cornered him, drove him. He chased her moans, thrusting again and again, bucking and clashing in a battle for who could give the other the most pleasure. She broke for him, shining in the water as her body trembled, sobbing his name.

Her second release made his groin spasm.

He prevented his own with iron control.

Because he would not let her past dictate her future.

He would not let one shining pleasure be enough. Dannika was too selfless, too generous. She must know that he would never give up on her. He worked his cock in deeper, faster, chasing the hot pleasure erupting within her so she cried harder. Each cry was stronger and more beautiful as the light filled her.

He would make her believe in him. Make her trust in their connection by strengthening it beyond the bounds of human and mer, bride and warrior.

Her inner light glistened. Around them, other light danced. Her powers throbbed. Dannika was a queen. The power was all inside her. She just needed to unlock it.

And he would be her key.

She bucked with release, arching and twirling them slowly as sparkles shuddered through her body, melding their spirits and turning their bodies to liquid.

And then she looked him in the eye and dug her fingernails into his back. "Come with me."

He erupted, burying his seed deep within her womb.

She shuddered, glowing with a third release.

Somewhere across the infinite sea, but so distinct it almost felt like it was in this very lagoon, he heard the chime of a Life Tree.

Odd.

Dannika curled around him.

He tucked her close, floating with her in the quiet lagoon.

She splayed a hand over his pectoral. "I hope I can show my queen powers tomorrow."

"You will."

She snuggled close, and her soul glowed. "I hope the

others can make their own powers too. We'll be unstoppable."

"You alone can stop an army."

"Oh, no, I…" Her soul dimmed, and she wiggled in his arms awkwardly. "I couldn't stop a whole army. Not alone."

"Trust in your power, Dannika."

She laughed without mirth and wiggled again. "I'm trusting in you, Ciran. And I can feel your faith in me. I'm sure that's enough."

Tomorrow, they would find out if she was right.

NINETEEN

Dannika was well and truly satisfied.

She struggled out of the lagoon when Ciran said it was daylight—not that she could tell, floating in a luxurious half daydream on Ciran's chest—and tiny tendons she hadn't felt in her hips for two decades squeaked to announce themselves.

That was after she finished upchucking seawater and regretting her life choices, of course.

She rested on the ledge while Ciran shifted effortlessly and tugged on the Bermuda shorts, sliding them up commando-style over his well-formed buttocks and snugging them around his muscled abdomen.

He left his shirt unbuttoned and ran a hand through his water-slicked hair. Droplets highlighted his muscles from his honed jaw, across his implacable chest, down his rippling abdomen, belly button, and lower.

Dannika did a few yoga stretches to loosen up, then crawled over to her caftan. Did she really need underwear? Meg had been so surprised yesterday, and she was just going to shift...

"Dannika! Ciran!"

A herd of youngsters, all nude, clattered down the back steps and hurtled into the lagoon, then jumped out with playful shrieks and raced up the stairs.

"...breakfast..."

Some wake-up call.

She tied on her caftan and stuffed her undergarments into one pocket. "My morning nude-visitor count is going up. Although I suppose these are shorter."

"For now." Ciran sobered. "I did not want to infringe on your memories of your first soul mate last night. But it is customary for a warrior to give his bride his mating gemstone."

From his pocket, he pulled out an iridescent Sea Opal and rested it in her open palm. He curved her fingers around it. "Please."

It was smooth and heavy in her hand, and so large, she couldn't fully close her hand. Most Sea Opals were white as clouds, but Ciran's had a stormy underbelly. Iridescent white gleamed with streaks of green, blue, and black.

And yet it was him. Solid, comforting, and unbreakable.

He was so earnest, so worthy, so certain. The cry echoed in her, in the deepest recesses of her heart. *I wanted an easier love for you.* But he knew what he was asking. He knew her. And he wanted the struggle, the burden.

He was truly a good man.

She pressed the gem to her chest. "Thank you. I'll treasure it."

He brushed her lips.

These were the lips that had kissed her so thoroughly last night. Her body recognized him, oriented on him, craved him. Desire streaked to her pussy, and she clenched her thighs.

He tilted his head as if he'd only intended to give her a quick kiss and now, her reaction to his slightest touch caused him to deepen the connection. His cock hardened against her thigh.

Maybe they could slip into the lagoon for a few minutes before breakfast...

"Dannika?" Hadali called at the top of the stairs. "Ciran? Do you mind if I get Val some elixir?"

Maybe not.

Ciran leaned back and licked his lips.

She took a deep breath and let it out with a shaky cough. "No, please come down."

He pattered down the stairs and scooped a coconut shell full of water. They returned to the beach structures where they'd had dinner the night before.

Breakfast was mashed sweet pumpkin with coconut milk, smoked fish, and a sharp tea with peppery spices. It wasn't coffee, but her heart hopped.

Val needed help rolling out of the hammock, and she limped to the breakfast table between Hadali and Tulu. One leg had swollen, and bruises almost sealed her eyes shut. She picked up her spoon with a shaky hand. "I know what you're going to say. *Now* I look like I was in a plane crash."

"I'm so sorry." Dannika smoothed her Sea Opal. "You've been drinking the elixir, right?"

"Yeah, so I'd hate to see what I'd look like without the magical potion."

"You would look largely the same." Ciran offered to cut her smoked fish into smaller chunks, and she accepted. "It is a problem with your resonance. I am sorry, Val. You do not have an affinity for the sea."

"Don't I know it." She touched her cut lip and winced.

"I never wanted to go on a cruise. I'd rather go to the mountains than a beach any day. Maybe I'm secretly a dragon. Speaking of dragons, Hadali, is that a Chinese dragon on your chest?"

Hadali looked down at the round tattoo covering the left side of his chest. It did not look like a dragon. It looked like a lion with scales and hooves, but it was shooting flames against a bamboo backdrop.

"It's a qilin." He stroked the center. "It symbolizes protecting the home. And the bamboo means flexibility and endurance. I'm supposed to have a bunch of tattoos already, but we haven't officially started my warrior training, so I'll get more then." He pointed down the table. "Nuno's got a tiger."

Nuno straightened and puffed out his chest. "Courage."

"And the plum blossom means he's unafraid of difficulties," Hadali said.

They went around the breakfast table showing off tattoos. Each child had a central animal surrounded by a floral motif. Tulu had a protective lion and steadfast pine trees, and the others had a mysterious mantis, happy magpie, industrious crab, and more surrounded by a variety of plants.

"Fascinating," Ciran said. "The heart tattoo is normally a personal totem symbol but ours are usually more abstract."

Dannika tapped the curling circles on his pectoral, the green and coffee brown almost like a yin yang. "This has meaning?"

"A feeling." He traced the colors with his index finger. "Reason and emotion. For an effective strategy, both are necessary to understand your enemy and yourself."

Itime and Konomelu had similar abstract tattoos;

Konomelu's meant fierce loyalty and Itime's meant a quiet blade.

"In Sanctuary, Prince Ankena ruled that we would honor the traditions of our brides *and* our warriors," Konomelu said.

"And not a single dragon," Val said.

"I tried." Meg dropped her carved wooden spoon with a clatter, stretched, and sighed. "I used so many squid inks and at least five feather quills. I drew on so many leaves. I just never got it right. No dragons, no chrysanthemums. And nobody wanted a squid. I could draw those in my sleep."

Val shook her head and then winced again. "Maybe I need my eyes checked."

They had to get Val real help. She needed modern medicine.

Being stranded on a deserted island for decades was much worse for an ordinary human than for a bride with access to healing elixir. Meg and Angie and Bex were all healthy and strong, and they barely had wrinkles, much less scars. Dannika's bruises from being whipped by metal had faded to shadowy greens and light purples in a day.

Hopefully, Angie, Meg, and Bex had secret powers up their sleeves.

Even though their island grass dresses were basically sleeveless.

The kids finished their breakfast and ran off to play. Angie called them back to help clean up. Over the chorus of frustrated "aws," Meg stood.

"I have an announcement." She rested her hand on Itime's calm shoulder. "After breakfast, I'm going in the ocean."

The kids all fell silent, eyes wide.

"And I'll need your help. You know why. So, uh, let's be helpful, okay?" She patted Itime's shoulder and sat. "That's all."

Her kids rushed to pack away the food.

The warriors gathered at the top of the flat white beach.

"Why does Meg dread the water?" Ciran asked the warriors.

Tulu answered. "Disney princess powers."

"What does that mean?"

Konomelu exchanged glances with Itime. "It is best if you see for yourself."

Shallow blue water stretched to the coral. Waves stumbled over the ring separating their island sanctuary from the wild, free ocean.

"Gosh, this is beautiful." Val squinted from beneath a sunshade. Meg's youngest played in the sand beside her. "Well, good luck transforming into an unstoppable force."

"Thanks," Dannika said.

Bex sauntered over, then Meg, followed by the biggest cluster of kids, and then Angie, arms crossed, bringing up the rear.

They divested themselves of their clothes. Dannika held on to Ciran's Sea Opal for good luck. The sand was warming up fast, and the damp line where the waves ended soothed her hot toes. The turquoise water—clear and sandy up close—invited her in.

Ciran strode into the low waves.

They had made love yesterday. Her body tingled with his nearness. Her unused muscles twinged in a liquid reminder of how long it had been since a man had filled her.

Ciran's gaze lasered onto hers as the clear surf splashed up her thighs. He sensed her emotions, as always, and amplified her determination with dark promise.

She would succeed today.

The other women would witness her queen powers and develop their own. They would push back the warriors who confined them to this island.

"Okay, guys." Meg squeezed her eyes shut and held out her hands. "Help me in. And get ready."

Tulu walked in front of her. Her younger sons took her hands and led her, cautious and blind, into the shallow surf. She let out her breath in a nervous hiss and talked quietly to herself. "Here we go. Here we go..."

Angie stood back with her arms crossed.

Out at waist level in the gently rocking waves, Tulu asked, "Ready?"

Meg took a deep breath, held it, and nodded. On their cue, they all descended.

Dannika dropped as well. Water closed over her head.

Her eyes adjusted even before she finished sucking in seawater. The sand gave way to spikes of coral, which housed schools of royal-blue tang, curious yellow-and-black butterfly fish, bumbling green, blue, and yellow parrotfish, and, of course, squids.

Big squids, small squids, bumbling squids, inking squids. They floated tentacles first, their mantles pointed downward so they looked like sock puppets with big eyes on the sides. The fins on their mantles fluttered like rivulets trickling down a small stream.

As the ground descended into the deep ocean, the slope reversed. Ancient, bleached coral grew for the surface like a lattice fence. A large coral ridge sheltered them from the Luscan patrol's view.

Nuno and Bex waited below the ridge in a sheltered hollow. Dannika would join them and demonstrate her powers.

Her stomach squeezed.

Behind Meg, Angie's kids splashed into the water and shifted, squealing. The passel of squids rippled colors across their funnels and jetted away, then reversed course and chased after the giggling children, seizing them and pinching with their beaks. The kids shrieked.

"It is strange," Ciran vibrated, floating beside Dannika. "I have never seen squids behave this way."

"Chasing and biting?"

"Usually, they are curious, solemn creatures who would rather trick us into thinking they are a marine hermit crab than draw attention to themselves. Yet these squids swim erratically and attack. It is as though they hear an irritating noise that they cannot escape."

Something drove them mad. But what?

Meg's bubbles ascended for the surface, and she convulsed as she shifted. Her sons floated close to her. She opened her eyes, peered around, and grinned. "I did it!"

"Good job, Mom," her sons chorused.

So, she was happy to submerge. Just getting into the water, though, was a whole operation.

Itime approached Dannika. "Can you shield her?"

"Shield her? Right now?"

He nodded.

Adrenaline flooded her body. Her hands trembled and her heart raced. Dannika clenched the Sea Opal close to her heart in one hand and flexed her fingers on the other. Nothing happened.

"Um, give me a minute." She flicked her fingers like trying to dry-start a lighter. Nothing, nothing, nothing. How frustrating!

Ciran clasped her hand, gently calming her. "Your soul is dimming."

"I know."

He stroked her cheek and pressed a soft kiss to her lips. "You have the power within you. Remember what you did before and let it flow out."

He was right.

She kissed him back, letting his hot, sweet caresses center her. And with new calm, her fingertips tingled with power. Dannika pulled back and turned to Meg, extending her hand to release the power.

But horror transfixed Meg's face. She held up her own hand in a warning gesture. "No. *No.* No!"

The power in Dannika's fingertips drained away.

Hmm?

Doot-doot-doooooot.

The contrabassoon of squids grew from a normal symphonic bass to the insistent rumble of a train grinding into Grand Central Station. Every squid near the reef oriented on Meg, tentacles pointed like arrows, longer arms trailing.

"Your shield," Itime repeated, and his usual calm had an edge.

Oh, right.

Dannika held out her one hand again and willed the calm to return. *Be conscious of Ciran. Don't think about what's happening with Meg. Focus.*

But she hadn't gotten her license in Zen Buddhism yet and hadn't become enlightened enough to hold her meditative state while witnessing a wild squid storm.

Meg turned and kicked her stubby little feet for the shoreline. "Quick, boys. Go, go!"

Tulu floated at the ready, tensed for battle.

Dooot. Dooot. Dooooooot.

The contrabassoon of doom blatted as the squid

converged on Meg and her sons. Tulu bashed the bodies away, waving and kicking. Itime flew to his side, and they tried to ward off the mollusk invasion.

Okay. Okay. Tune it out. Focus.

Shield.

A squid smacked Dannika in the face. Another crawled across her outstretched arms, and a third gnawed on her toes.

What in the heck?

She shook them off.

Ciran battled his own horde. "What is this behavior?"

Meg shrieked and kicked for the surface. She broke free and splashed.

The squid surged after her.

This was not a Disney princess. This was *The Birds*, or in Meg's case, *The Squids*. Plus a few random tangs and parrotfish caught up in the excitement.

The kids helped Meg reach the shore, and Dannika and Ciran stumbled out of the surf with her, fighting through the marine bodies to reach the sand.

Meg crawled and lay facedown on the beach.

Squids flew after her, hurtling through the air and beaching themselves on the hot, white sand.

"Whew!" Val waved from her sunshade. "I've heard of flying fish. I've never heard of flying squids."

Angie shook her head, hands on her grass-dress-clad hips. "We hadn't either."

"There are some species," Konomelu said. "But, yes, this is rare."

The kids frolicked through the mess and tossed beached fish into the surf.

Dannika drained out the last of her water, finished

coughing, and wiped her face. She asked Angie, "Does that happen often?"

"All the time," Angie said.

Bex, sniffling from her shift, nodded.

"This is why, as nice as it would be to discover secret powers, I doubt it will ever be possible because my daughter can't even enter the water."

TWENTY

They tried all morning to get Meg in the shallows, but the squids were too agitated. They even took a lunch break, and at the first attempt in the afternoon, Dannika managed to wade in unmolested and put up her shield. Meg snuck in, and the shield held okay.

Then the squids turned on Dannika, pinching and biting her, and the morning's frustration repeated all over again.

The kids gave up in boredom and went their own ways on the island. Konomelu and Itime retired to a quieter section of the reef to hunt the evening's dinner. The women did beach duty.

Meg collapsed on the white sand, chest heaving, tears and salt water streaming sideways down her face, the flailing corpses of insistent squid suiciders flopping around her.

"Why me?" she asked the cloudless white sky. "What did I ever do to you? Why am I the first seahorseman of the squidocalypse?"

Ciran had remained near. He flipped squids back into

the surf, comfortably nude. "It is a mark of your power. If it was not so strong, you would not call them so fiercely."

"Oh my God. You mean that's my queen power? I can summon a cloud of squids to attack me?"

"No." He snorted. "What an odd power."

"Hey, you're the one telling me. I'm just Meg of the Squids over here."

"Yes. What I meant was that you have a strong resonance. The other queens have an affinity for some sea creatures, but their connection is not as intense as yours. Once you control this and can swim in the water unmolested, we will discover which of the three powers you possess."

"But we can't find out because I can't even get in the water. Argh."

Dannika tossed in another wriggly rubber squid, doing her part to clean the beach. If she could just make a big enough shield to cover herself as well as Meg, this wouldn't happen.

But she needed practice.

A lot of practice.

"Is there somewhere else we can go?" Dannika asked. "Somewhere that's far from prying eyes and tentacles? Where we can get centered and explore our powers without fear?"

The trio of women looked at each other.

Bex stretched and straightened. "There is."

"I'll just stay here with Val and prepare dinner." Angie brushed down her grass dress and retied her fashionable box-shaped hat.

"Mom," Meg said in warning. "If I can brave squids, you can do this."

"Of course, but someone should check on Val."

"I'll be fine." Val waved. "Have fun."

"See?" Meg grabbed Angie's hand. "Come on."

Angie let herself be dragged. "I'll just be in everyone's way."

"Whine, whine, whine. You'd think the island would collapse if you didn't plan four courses."

"Well, I take my hostess duties seriously."

"What about your duty to rescue Prince Ankena and Luk? Come on."

Angie surrendered and walked away from the beach with only a few long-suffering sighs and a small "You can't complain if dinner isn't up to its usual standard..."

"No one will complain if we have to eat squid jerky and sashimi. This is important. Let's go."

Dannika and Ciran followed the group up the headland trail back to the cavern lagoon.

Of course. What a perfect place to practice.

Ciran divested his clothes and dove in with a tiny splash.

Bex dropped her wrap and stepped off the ledge, disappearing into the water with a much bigger crash. Angie and Meg did the same. Meg had no hesitation, which just proved she was afraid of the squids, not the water. Dannika took the longest tugging off her damp clothes, and then she splashed in.

Shifting was rough as ever. Dannika choked through it.

Bex paddled to Ciran. "Did you check the boulder?"

"It is in place."

The women floated, ready to learn.

"The first step in developing your powers is to fully shift into mer." Ciran swam back and forth in front of the four women, his long fins dangling in the quiet, shallow lagoon. "Can you transform?"

"We can make fins?" Angie squinted. "Just like the men?"

"Yes. What is your greatest level of transformation?"

Angie crossed her arms.

"You're looking at it," Meg said.

"Then the first step is to shift your feet into fins."

Ciran flexed below the ankle. His fin snapped back to a human foot. Then he shifted more slowly to a fin. The middle of his foot unfolded and elongated, stretching the skin tight as his bones shifted to a scuba diver's fin. His tattoos stretched, still intricate and beautiful, the coffee-brown and leaf-green patterns always circling each other, never quite touching.

He flexed, and his fin returned into a human foot. "Now, you do it."

"My feet don't fold that way," Angie said flatly. "And I wore a tremendous number of heels."

"No bride has ever failed to transform."

"I might be the first."

"Mom." Meg rolled her eyes. "Don't be a drama queen."

Angie flopped her ankles, wiggling with great irritation, as though under protest.

Bex focused. "Show me again."

Ciran did so, patient as ever. "Partly it is flexing the muscle, and partly it is pushing your soul light to glow. Once you have found your center of power, growing it is a matter of practice. You will conquer any army, destroy any opposition."

Angie frowned.

Ciran gazed at Dannika. His truth burned into her soul.

I believe in you.

Dannika closed her eyes and believed him.

Her toes tingled.

Was that it?

As soon as she wondered, the tingling dissipated. She opened her eyes. Her toes were the same as before. Hmm.

"You shifted," Ciran vibrated, and smiled. "Just a small motion. But your belief is your strength."

Well, his belief was, anyway.

"You shifted?" Meg whirled on her. Little glowing bits stuck to her face, and a cloud of shrimp buzzed around her toes like a subtle beehive. "Oh my God. How?"

"Show me," Bex said.

"Sure, um...it's trickier to do it on command..."

"You will develop this ability," Ciran said. "It is an essential skill of all queens."

No pressure or anything.

The women awaited her answer.

"I just closed my eyes and thought I could." Dannika closed her eyes, but the sensations of everyone staring at her killed the magic. "I'll practice."

"But you feel it. You feel something," Meg pressed.

"Yes."

Everyone tried with renewed determination.

Ciran stopped in front of Angie. "You can never transform when your soul is this dark."

"Mom." Meg rounded on her. "You've got to try."

"I am." She crossed her arms even tighter, then threw them out in a trembling panic. "This warrior stuff isn't for me. What am I even trying to do? Bend a spoon? Or what, levitate?"

"You already levitate in the water. What is your question about spoons?"

"I just—what exactly is the point of all this? What am I supposed to do with these so-called powers?"

"You are supposed to save a warrior and his son," Ciran

said. "And free your family from the Luscan's reign of terror, bringing peace to this territory and harmony to the ocean."

She lowered her shoulders, her expression slowly changing to acceptance, and her lips quirked to the side. "Well, when you put it *that* way, I suppose I could give it another try."

"There we go, Mom." Meg squeezed her arm.

She patted her daughter's hand, then lifted her chin. "What are the three powers again?"

"Pushing, shielding, and healing."

"And how do I know which one I possess?"

"You possess all of them, but you will have an affinity for one over the others. A natural preference."

She flexed her fingers. "Pushing? Shielding... Ladies, do you know yours?"

"Pushing," Bex said.

"I have no idea," Meg said.

"Healing," Bex said.

Angie agreed. "Meg, your power is probably healing."

"Really? Because I could definitely go for shielding myself or pushing those squids away. Oh, Dannika." She reached out and brushed a finger over the ghostly bruises on Dannika's abdomen. "Did you have plum liqueur with lunch? I'll make you a cold wrap with it after dinner. It makes a huge difference. Last year, when Tulu fell out of a tree and broke his leg, I was on twenty-four-hour poultice duty with him, and he was good to fall out of more trees in, like, days."

Her belly tingled where Meg had touched it, and white sparkles filled the pool. Dannika's bruises dissipated.

"I think you just healed me with your touch," Dannika said.

Meg laughed, chest vibrating, and waved her away. "That's just the plankton. They always sparkle when I'm around."

Dannika looked at Ciran and pointed to her belly.

He inspected her. "A very strong power."

Meg argued more but was overruled by the truth.

"Great. So I have healing and squid powers." Meg flicked her fingers to dislodge the plankton, which, for some reason, stuck only to her. "I think pushing or shielding would be more useful."

"At least you know what you are," Angie said placidly.

"What happens after fins?" Bex asked Ciran.

"After? First, you must make your fins, and then—" He made a noise of surprise.

Bex's feet dangled as long fins. Unlike Dannika's brief stretch, they extended all the way.

She'd done it.

Meg exclaimed. "How did you do that?"

Bex shrugged. "I thought maybe I could do it some time ago. This time, I didn't stop myself."

"Amazing..."

Ciran pressed his hands to his chest. "From the same place, channel your power."

"Anywhere?" Bex asked.

"Just point your hands in a direction. Ah." He kicked to the side. "Allow me to stay out of your way."

Bex eyed the nearest stalagmite. Then she lifted her hands. Her fingers glowed.

A band of white zapped out and struck the stalagmite. The rock cracked.

Holy moly.

The tenor of the ocean changed, with sea life speeding up their music and fleeing from the incredible power.

"Very good." Ciran beamed at Bex. "You have excellent control and power."

Bex formed her hands in fists and looked at the other women. "When do we go to Lusca?"

Meg shared a rueful glance with Angie and then Dannika. "Sorry, Bex. We'll work harder, won't we, guys?"

"You will improve faster by increasing your resonance." Ciran kicked to the ledge. "I will collect the warriors."

He kicked and disappeared.

Excitement buzzed in the water.

Dannika squeezed her Sea Opal and focused her energy on it. Her toes tingled. Things were going well.

Maybe they could find their powers right now. They could leave the island, get Val medical help, and she could warn Hazel about the sabotage.

They would work together and get off this island. Because the women had the power, and their loving warriors believed in them.

TWENTY-ONE

"The women have no power," Konomelu said to Ciran when he interrupted the conference with Itime in an isolated area of the coral. "Angie resists. Dannika cannot perform under combat conditions. Meg cannot even enter the ocean."

Itime nodded.

"We cannot rely on them," Konomelu said. "They may use their powers in a calm lagoon. But we must storm a city."

"Bex already showed great power," Ciran argued. "She pushed out great energy and broke a rock."

"Bex has no warrior to protect her," Konomelu said.

"Once the other queens have developed their powers, they will shield her."

"We were both impressed with Dannika's demonstration. But today, we also witnessed its failure. Our brides are not warriors. Distractions, loss of concentration in battle—we struggle with training our young fry in these shallow waters. How can we train a bride in a power we cannot even understand?"

"Dannika will improve with practice," Ciran insisted. "And yes, Bex leaves her back unguarded, but once we ensure her protection, she will be unstoppable."

Itime raised one finger. "Are you willing to stake Bex's life on this?"

Because if their brides went out into the ocean and their powers failed, the warriors would, of course, protect their brides.

Who would protect Bex?

Over on the reef, the trainees were conducting familiar shallow-water exercises. Nuno, Hadali, and Tulu supervised the younger warriors.

Their bare skin stood out.

A warrior's first tattoos were for simple accomplishments such as swimming around the limits of the city's territory alone. Patrols swept the territory clear in advance, but there was always a small element of danger. Next would come joining the hunts for deep ocean fish, crafting weapons from the deep sea beds, and expertise in fighting.

But Nuno, Hadali, and Tulu couldn't receive their first accomplishment-tattoo because they had never swum the length of a city's territory.

They could not.

Because they were stuck in this shallow island reef.

And out beyond the coral lattice floated the patrolling warriors who would never let them escape. Not unless they forced their way to freedom.

"Without a warrior to protect Bex, it is too dangerous to take her into the open ocean," Konomelu said gravely.

"You cannot enter Lusca without the queens," Ciran said.

"We must. And we have figured out a way to do so."

Konomelu puffed out his chest. "I am no Undine, but even I can strategize."

Ciran raised a brow. "Your description of Lusca is of a typical mer city."

"Listen and learn, Undine. I mean, Atlantean."

Konomelu pointed out the various features of the reef, asking him to pretend that a certain coral spire was the Life Tree and another spire was the king's castle. Those rocks were the prisons beneath the city, and this serpentine crevice represented the trench.

"All we must do is slip past the patrols. The king stations city guards here, here, here-here, and here-here-here-here."

"And here." Itime pointed out yet another spot.

That was more guards than in Atlantis and Undine. "That is quite a few guards for a 'typical' mer city."

"They rotate frequently based on the mood of the king. Anyway. Prince Ankena, if he survived the trench, must be near the top."

"Because the kraken lies deep beneath," Itime said.

"The king drops his captives in the center as a demonstration of power. Prince Ankena must have swum to one of these distant outcroppings. He will be just beneath the first ledge, surviving on trench fish he has wrestled with his bare hands. All we must do is avoid their deadly holes and bring him to safety." Konomelu pressed his hands together with pride. "Not bad for an old warrior, right?"

Ciran mentally pushed aside the image of a bare-handed warrior wrestling deadly trench fish that had ended more than a few fully armed warriors. He focused on the knowns. "Just to ensure my proper understanding, Lusca patrols its territory with multiple units *and* nine rotating guards watch the city limits?"

"To prevent warriors from defecting," Konomelu agreed.

"How many warriors does Lusca station in the city?"

"Summer or winter?" Konomelu asked.

"There is a difference?"

"In the summer, there are more hurricanes, and so more warriors fill the city. In the winter, the weather is more conducive to attacking ships, so two teams deploy with the giant squids. They tether the squids to the far side of the trench." Konomelu pointed with his old dagger. "Here."

Right. Okay. "We're still in winter, so that field would be empty..."

"Not necessarily," Itime said. "It depends on the king's mood."

So the way to the trench was guarded by multiple patrols, nine guards, one or two tethered squids, and one or two additional units trained in attacking with them, plus all the warriors normally stationed within the city.

And that assumed Konomelu was right, Prince Ankena awaited them in perfect health on the cliff of the trench, and they could rescue him easily without alerting any guards.

"And we must also rescue Lukiyo," Itime reminded Konomelu.

"Ah, yes. He will be in the king's castle." Konomelu sheathed his dagger and tapped his finger against the worn pommel. "We must draw him out and then capture him before anyone realizes we are there. Yes. Very well. After we rescue Prince Ankena, it will be easier if anyone raises an alarm, because we will have four warriors instead of three."

That sounded like a nightmare.

If any single warrior saw them and raised the alarm, an entire city would pit themselves against four warriors.

Maybe Lotar could attempt it. The city of Syrenka was a cold, dark void in the ocean, and their warriors trained in silence and deception. He'd accomplished many solo missions to gather information, and he had a warrior's affinity for sharks.

But Ciran did not possess those skills.

And Lotar had never tried to rescue someone during his stealth missions. He just gathered information.

"And then after we have rescued Prince Ankena and Lukiyo, how will you retake the city?" Ciran asked.

"We will ask Prince Ankena," Konomelu said confidently, and Itime nodded. "He is a prince. He knows how to do this. We will follow him."

Okay. So, no plan.

"Let us back up." Ciran deliberately turned away from the coral map. "To leave this island, how will we evade the patrol?"

"The same way that we divided them to investigate the plane crash." Konomelu pressed his hand to his chest. "Nuno and I will slip out the chutes and come up beneath the warriors. When they sight and chase us, we will split, dividing their forces. Itime, Tulu, and Hadali will do the same, dividing the remaining patrol. Once they drop off, we will reunite and continue."

"But the patrol nearly caught us. Twice."

Konomelu waved his hand. "Adult warriors will evade them more easily."

"How?"

"Orike is not so clever." Konomelu jutted his chin. "But you supposedly are. If my plan is so bad, Undine—I mean,

Atlantean—then fix it. How can we rescue Prince Ankena and Lukiyo? And retake the city?"

"I see two methods."

"Two?" Konomelu floated back in surprise. "Very well. Explain."

"First, you increase your resonance with your brides and work with them to develop their queen powers. Once they are at combat readiness, we will simply swim past the patrol, glide down to Lusca, float before the Life Tree, and declare ourselves the new rulers. A unit of Luscans will brave the trench to rescue Prince Ankena."

"That is all?" Konomelu squinted. "Just swim past the patrol. Glide into Lusca. Declare ourselves the new kings, overthrowing the existing king and Prince Ankena while we are in the mood."

"Queens hold the power, Lieutenant Konomelu."

He stiffened at his title, but it was a noble stiffness, as though no one had reminded him of it for a long time.

"I have witnessed queens defending their city with my own eyes. They were far more effective than warriors. Lusca has not faced a real adversary before. I doubt they are prepared for the power of our queens."

Itime raised a finger. "And Meg's affliction?"

"She will summon the squids to her side and, if needed, use them in battle."

He lowered his finger.

"How convenient." Konomelu rubbed his brow. "You have an answer for everything. Too bad it depends on brides who have even less experience than our youngest trainees."

"Then we will give them experience," Ciran said.

"How?" Konomelu slammed his palm to his chest. "I cannot give my sons experience. How can I give it to my vulnerable sacred bride?"

Ciran ticked off the ways on his fingers. "Increase her resonance. Give her small tasks. Watch her confidence brighten her soul light. And then? She must face the patrol here."

"Never." Konomelu slashed the water with the flat of his hand. "Never suggest such a thing to me again, Undine. I will cut your tongue out with a blade and feed it to bottle worms."

Heat flashed through Ciran. His heart leaped in his chest. He flexed his fingers.

"We will do my plan." Konomelu turned away.

Ciran gritted his teeth. "Your plan is suicide."

"And what of it?" He whirled back. "I would die a thousand times before my bride goes before that jelly-for-brains Orike. If one warrior even dares to point a trident in her direction. If he even unsheathes a dagger. No."

"You are stronger together."

"Stop this talking." He waved his hand by his ear, even though they communicated by vibrating in their chests. Some surface gestures carried over no matter how long they lived underwater. "I will not hear it."

"You do not know a queen's power."

"I saw all I needed to see when yours failed."

Another hit of fury vibrated in Ciran's veins. "Dannika has only begun to try. Other queens practiced a hundred times before—"

"And our brides have had twenty years to make fins. We cannot rely on them, and I will not hear you."

"Because you have encouraged them to hide their abilities from the patrol. If we encouraged their abilities, they will—"

"When I want your opinion, I will ask for it!" Konomelu roared.

Ciran flexed for a weapon. Trident, dagger, chunk of coral. But his crowbar was on the beach, and he had broken his borrowed coral dagger.

So he lifted his fist—the rudest gesture he could think of —and whirled before any of them could answer. He swam directly for the dead coral lattice.

"Hey," Konomelu called. "Hey!"

The Luscan warriors floated out in the ocean.

"Warriors!" Ciran shouted through the lattice, vibrating hard to carry his hail across the distance. "Luscan warriors!"

The patrol rotated to face him. Lieutenant Orike's sharp eyes narrowed. The patrol bristled with daggers, tridents, bolas, and other weapons. Would they really not cross the coral lattice? In places, it was solid, but in others, an armed male could easily swim through.

"What is it, exile?" the lieutenant asked with irritation.

"I am Ciran of Atlantis. On behalf of my city, which has no war with you, let me and my bride go."

"Atlantis?" Lieutenant Orike lifted his brows. "Ha-ha. This must be an Undine joke. Or has your insane king rechristened your city to match the fable?"

"We are a new city. Is Lusca so sad at being cut off from the ocean it does not even bother to listen at echo points?"

"We do not waste our time with the affairs of the losers."

"How silly. Ignorance kills."

"Yet gullible fools are the first to die." The lieutenant waved to one of his warriors. "Tell our king that Undine insults him. It is time for our giant squid to teach them their place."

"Sir!" The warrior saluted with the slash gesture.

Ciran shook his head. "I warned you."

"And I warn you." The lieutenant kicked to the other

side of the open, barely symbolic marker dividing them. He lowered his trident. It took all Ciran's will not to flinch. "You ventured into our territory. Leave that coward's hole and face me."

Ciran flexed his empty hands. "When a warrior challenges an unarmed male, who is the real coward?"

"That depends on whether or not he is an exile." Lieutenant Orike jabbed the trident at the coral.

Ciran kicked back, out of reach.

Lieutenant Orike's lips curved. He veered away and swam to the ocean leaving behind one warrior to patrol.

Well, that went as successfully as Ciran could have hoped.

He kicked toward the shore. Dannika made excellent progress. She was starting to believe. And if she could make her fins and her shield, they could leave and seek help on their own. They'd have a real chance to...

Itime and Konomelu swam in front of him.

"You waste your time with that squid sucker," Konomelu said.

"You are wrong." Ciran kicked to the side to swim around. "But I will not share my opinion, because you have not asked for it."

Itime paced him. "Wait."

"I will not waste your time either."

"You do not. Stop. Atlantis warrior, I ask you."

Ciran flipped to hang upside down.

"I wish to hear your second plan," Itime said. "And so does Konomelu."

"He has an odd way of showing it."

Itime tilted his head in acknowledgment.

Konomelu rested his palm on his own chest. "I have guarded this island, these young fry, and our brides for twenty years. And for three years, I have done so without my prince. I was not born to rule, but I have. All the brides and young fry under my charge have remained healthy and secure."

"May you succeed another twenty." Ciran turned.

"Wait, you. Listen!" Konomelu darted in front of Ciran.

Ciran rolled right side up and lifted one brow.

Konomelu realized he was listening, and waiting, and he sputtered. "Itime, you explain."

"Atlantis warrior, Lusca has been isolated for a long time. We are not used to the ways of other warriors. In your city, what rank are you?"

"Second lieutenant."

"That is..." Itime trailed off. Both warriors looked surprised. He rallied. "Were you not trained to obey your king without question?"

"I was, but King Kadir listens. He respects my observations and experience. I would not serve him if he forced me to be silent. And that is why I will not be silent now. I had to watch too many avoidable tragedies in Undine. Never again."

"This Atlantis really is different."

"It is. Will you never tell me to be silent?"

Itime turned to Konomelu.

Konomelu gritted his teeth. "I vow it."

Good enough. "Just now, I tried to goad the lieutenant to go to the nearest echo point and brag about my capture. Some are eager to announce their prowess, but it sounds as though he will not."

"No, Orike is too sure of himself for that," Konomelu muttered.

"Then we must go ourselves."

"It is too dangerous." Konomelu shook his head. "A unit

frequently passes by and watches for foreign warriors. They must have caught Prince Ankena and Lukiyo."

So, an echo point occasionally guarded by *one* unit was dangerous, but an entire city guarded by many more warriors was no concern?

But Ciran focused on the point. "The warriors of Atlantis will hear of our plight and send an army to rescue us. They would bring queens who could teach your brides their powers."

And they were back to queens.

The slightest shadow of confusion passed across Itime's normally expressionless face. "Your bride's shield was so small."

"Because it was her first."

"You speak with such confidence. Are queens really so powerful?"

"Like in the myths," Ciran said. "And more."

Both warriors shook their heads in awe.

"And that is why you must help your brides increase their resonance."

"Mine will not even enter the water," Itime said.

"And mine has no wish to learn the skills of a warrior," Konomelu said.

"Whatever the reason, you must change their minds. We have time to do this. You have already endured twenty years on this island. Can you not endure twenty days? Or even two?"

Both warriors looked beyond him at their young fry, the too-old trainees supervising, and the lattice that separated them from their destinies.

"We can wait," Itime said. "But can our sons?"

"They will wait," Konomelu growled, then grimaced. "Very well, Atlantis warrior. We will do what we must, and we will test them slowly. But if your queens cannot perform these powers on command, we must act. Alone."

"I will act. With Dannika."

Konomelu pressed his lips together from the effort of not exploding in protest. Itime blinked, expressionless, and yet he seemed to disagree.

That did not matter.

If these warriors could not resonate with their brides, Ciran would pour all his training into Dannika. He would wait patiently until she was ready. She would shield him, and he would defend her.

And together, they would conquer the enemies that lurked in the ocean.

TWENTY-TWO

Ciran emerged from the water that evening to find the sun setting in the sky, the young fry milling around Val aimlessly searching for food, and the women just returning from the lagoon. When they sauntered into the camp, Dannika gave him a look.

His whole body came to attention.

Power emanated from the glow of her chest.

He drew her to his side. "You have done it."

Dannika grinned. "We're on our way."

The other brides glowed equally strong.

Meg clasped Itime's hands with excitement. "I made my fins!"

He blinked, his usual blankness hinting at surprise. "In the ocean?"

"In the lagoon." She forced his hand up and clapped it in a human high five. "Congratulate me. This is a big step."

"Congratulations," he said placidly, and she preened as if he'd gushed compliments.

Angie put her hands on her hips and posed in front of Konomelu. "And I made mine."

His jaw dropped. "You did? Then, let us go into the ocean now and—"

"No," Angie said.

Konomelu's shoulders lowered. "No?"

"First, this is a moment of celebration."

"Well, yes, but—"

"And second, we have to practice. I have very limited control."

"Ah, then—"

"And third..." She drew up proudly. "It is past dinner-time. Our guests must be starving. I'll live down a lot of things, Konomelu, but never the reputation of being a bad hostess."

"No, you—"

"And I will deserve the reputation if we don't put something on the table right now. Everyone?" Angie clapped her hands twice. "Dress and take your positions. It's time for dinner!"

Everyone sprang into action. The young fry fastened on their loincloth skirts, the older trainees and adults put out the day's leftovers supplemented with stored supplies, and soon, a full meal spread across the reconstructed table. They lit stinky tallow candles, which, to Ciran's nose, had no scent.

And they celebrated.

The dinner was lively, with the women engaged in lighthearted jokes to each other, loving comments to their husbands and children, and laughing. So much laughter filled the small enclave. The doom that had hung over their previous night lifted. The young fry played bois-terous games and the older trainees indulged with them kindly.

Hope infused the sparkling night.

At the end of the night, Konomelu stood. "My fellow warriors, brides, and guests."

He smiled at the young fry to show that he included them in the "warriors" part of his greeting.

"Today, thanks to the help of Second Lieutenant Ciran and Queen Dannika, we have a new way to make war on the warriors who confine us. They are the true traitors. And when we save Prince Ankena, everyone will know."

Angie's smile faded, along with her soul light, and she crossed her arms.

Hmm. Konomelu himself had said he did not feel fit to lead, and this example of a speech did not rouse or inspire the important listeners.

"In one week's time, my bride will demonstrate her powers." He put an arm around Angie's shoulders. "And then she will make Orike flee like the coward he is."

She eyed him skeptically.

"In one week." He squeezed her and straightened again, then raised his arms. "We will crush our opposition, free Prince Ankena, and rule Lusca."

The trainees hooted and cheered, the women politely clapped, and dinner ended swiftly. They cleaned up, and all retired to rest and focus on growing their resonance. Ciran and Dannika strolled back to the lagoon alone, divested their clothing, and sat on the ledge kicking their feet in the calm, glowing water.

Dannika leaned against Ciran. "Why do I feel like Angie's soul light might have dimmed after her husband's speech?"

"Because you are a wise and intuitive queen."

"Queen..." She shivered. "Ooh, goose bumps. Can I really be a queen if we haven't done the ceremony in Atlantis? I haven't pledged myself or anything?"

"You use your powers. You are a queen."

"You were stricter with Indigo."

"Indigo is not my bride." But Dannika was right. "If she makes her powers on Bermuda and not in Atlantis, I will call her a queen."

"Very generous." Dannika nudged him with her elbow. "I'm glad to hear the geographic requirements are off."

"The more defenders we have in Atlantis, the safer we make the city for our young fry. But." He gestured at the vines dangling through the ceiling in this hidden grotto. "We could really help here too. Especially you."

"Everyone here already found their mates."

"You are more than a matchmaker, Dannika." He hooked his arm around her waist and splashed her into the water, and after she had shifted, he nuzzled her gently. "You are my queen."

She glowed.

His own chest ached. She was so beautiful and strong. And for the first time, she had stopped saying she wished he would be with someone else. She was beginning to accept herself and open to him.

Her smile twisted, and she curled her fingers around his hardening cock. "Then make love to me, my warrior."

He eagerly obeyed.

The second time, her body was more familiar, and he knew what she would like and how she would moan. But every touch was still a discovery tinged with newness, and delight fueled their arousal, until their bodies united and their souls combusted with shuddering heat of release.

He held her in the soft stillness of the aftermath, pressing kisses to her forehead and tucking her gently under his protection.

Her soul glowed with steady fire. "Do you think a week is enough to develop our powers?"

"I do not know."

"It feels like it's not enough time, but on the other hand, every hour we delay leaves Hazel and your warriors in danger."

He stroked her cheek with his thumb. "I have seen queens struggle for weeks. And I have seen those same queens come into their full power in an hour. It is not time that will decide your path to developing your powers. It is *you*."

A small smile tugged at lips. "Like how you walk by the same dating agency every day, lamenting that you haven't found love, and then one day, you decide to go in and change your life."

"Yes. This happens to me often on my walks."

She vibrated a laugh at him. "All the walks you take underwater, I'm sure."

"Every day. Twice during festival days."

"Sure." Her smile faded, and she brushed her fingertips over his heart tattoos, green entwined with coffee brown. "Will you watch us train tomorrow? I feel like I've gotten a good start, and Meg knows her power. Bex is ready to storm Lusca. But the one person I can't seem to reach is Angie."

"I will come."

"Thank you."

He hugged her close. She fisted his mating gemstone, pressing it between them like a talisman of strength. He would be that strength for her as long as she needed it. And someday, she would be strong and fearless by herself. Her fractured soul would heal.

And then she would come into her full power, and they would leave this island.

TWENTY-THREE

The warriors joined Ciran and the queens-in-training in the lagoon after breakfast, but quickly it became apparent that they couldn't stay.

First, the young fry splashed and frolicked, moving the boulder, scraping themselves on sharp coral and crying for Meg, and squeezing squids. They reduced the women to vibrating shouts and breaking up disputes, and only Meg practiced her healing power.

Itime and the older trainees herded the younger fry out, especially once it became clear that no one was "sparking off fireworks underwater," and Meg performed a cross-her-heart-and-hope-to-die pledge to call them back right away if anyone did.

Next, the lagoon was much calmer and emptier, and the boulder returned to its place, leaving the women to their practice. Ciran floated at a respectful distance, but Konomelu kicked right up to each of them and barked orders like he was evaluating trainees for the next test.

"Serious face. Why are you smiling? No talking there." The soul lights of the women all diminished as he barked at them, and they flinched away. He reached Angie. "You must focus with all your might."

Angie's soul light flared. She jammed her hands on her hips. "What do you think I'm focusing with?"

He zoomed to her. "When a warrior attacks our sons, will you return with this comment? No. You must attack. Grrr. And parry. Graaah. Then your enemies will know to flee from your blade."

Her soul light dipped. "I don't have a blade."

"Ah, of course." He patted the dagger sheathed on his bicep. "I will supply you with a training knife now. You will take the dagger of the first enemy you defeat."

Her soul light darkened even further. She wrinkled her nose in disgust and pushed away in a warding gesture. "I don't want to carry a dagger. Ick. What if I had to use it?"

"Then you would be grateful to carry one."

"No, no, no." She shuddered and made more warding gestures. "Forget it. You do your warrior stuff. I'll be sure dinner is hot on the table and your sons are neat as a pin."

"Do you want to save Prince Ankena or cower on this island?" he demanded.

"Yes."

"Yes? To which do you say yes?"

"Yes to both. I'll stay here with Val. The rest of you can have fun breaking kneecaps and causing traumatic brain injuries."

"Are you a warrior, or are you afraid?" he roared.

She refused him with her whole body, darker now than Ciran had ever seen her.

This was not working.

Ciran vibrated a soft interruption. "She is not a warrior, Lieutenant Konomelu."

The furious orange warrior stiffened. He seemed still

unused to being addressed by his respectful title. Then he gestured harshly. "I know, and I am trying to make her into one because only a warrior can storm Lusca."

"Actually, you are wrong."

He whirled on Ciran with wide, dangerous eyes. "You dare to disagree with me? *Second lieutenant?*"

"Yes. Because Angie can contribute to rescuing the prince."

"As a warrior! That is my point."

"No, because Angie is not a warrior," Ciran repeated patiently. "And look. Her soul light brightens every time I repeat that phrase. 'Angie is not a warrior.' Do you see it?"

Konomelu whirled and glared at Angie.

She glared right back. "You heard him. I'm not a warrior."

"You must be."

"No," Ciran emphasized, "Angie is not a warrior *because she is a queen.*"

Konomelu blinked. "You...are right. Her soul brightens. But she is fierce like any warrior."

"No, she is fierce like any queen." Ciran nodded at Angie. "Some queens protect their city through battle. But some protect it in other ways. Honor your bride's desires so she can strengthen her powers, and then she will accomplish all that you wish without ever touching a blade."

"But I..." Konomelu shook his head, his hands empty at his sides, lost. "I do not know how to help you in this way."

Her shoulders lowered. "You're trying to help me?"

"Of course. You are a fierce protector. If Second Lieutenant Ciran is correct and the other brides must rescue Prince Ankena, you will not be satisfied by staying behind."

She lifted one hand and brushed a bit of sparkling plankton off his hair. "I might be. For a short time."

"While worrying for the entire time." He clasped her hand. "Passion must flood your soul. You are now, and always have been, a fierce mother and a bold protector of our community."

She floated closer to him, her shorter legs dangling between his long legs extended even longer by the fins. "So are you."

"Of course." He jutted his chin. "That is why we are soul mates."

She kissed him, and he oriented on her with the power of twenty good years of support, kindly meant, no matter how misguided. Her soul light burned bright.

And then she pulled back and patted her husband's broad chest. "Go train with your warriors. You're good at it, and it's something you understand."

He glanced at Ciran and the other women, and then took his leave, kicking his fins and surging out of the water onto the ledge.

Angie turned to Ciran, hands back on her hips, focused again. "I now understand that we are not training as warriors, so how *do* we train?"

"As queens."

She squinted at him as though trying to test if he were joking. "And that means?"

"You must do whatever you need to strengthen your inner core."

Meg lifted one hand. "I've got to agree with Mom here. So are you saying we need to pick up yoga? Or do sit-ups?"

"If that increases your core power, then yes."

The two women looked at each other.

"How do we go from this"—Meg pointed at her partially extended fins, and then jabbed her finger at the other two—"to that?"

Bex floated on the end of their row, flipping around on her fins, in her own world. Dannika listened, but she also practiced quietly, the white light of the shield glowing around her in ghostly outline.

"If Konomelu's training style was wrong, how do we do it right?"

"The base of a warrior's power is his muscles. His tendons. The quickness of his blade." Ciran flicked his wrist as if it held a dagger. "But the base of a queen's power is the Life Tree. So she must open a channel to her Life Tree and let the energy flow through her until it becomes an unstoppable force. And that"—he tapped his chest—"happens here. In your soul. Your resonance."

Angie vibrated an underwater sigh. "I suppose it isn't easy, or else we would have done it before now."

"Perhaps. But you can accomplish anything if you try."

Angie rubbed her temples. "Yoga... This seems so impractical."

"Question." Meg drummed her fingers on her chest. "If I'm summoning the Life Tree, why don't I have to be, like, touching the Life Tree? How is it channeling without, you know, a channel?"

"The queens usually practiced while communing with their Life Tree," he acknowledged. "But that is just to start. The connection is within your soul, and distance does not affect resonance. Once you have felt it, you will know how to channel it again. Without a Life Tree, this is the best we can do."

Meg and Angie both looked at Bex.

Bex shrugged.

Angie traded looks with Meg, then pressed her lips together, shook her head, and released another underwater vibration like a sigh. "Does it really make a difference? Practicing while touching a Life Tree?"

"Since it is the base of your power, I think it will never hurt. But Life Trees do not grow on the surface."

"That..." Angie flexed her fingers and made a pleasant smile. "Isn't entirely true. Bex? Will you show them?"

Bex kicked her fins and zoomed backward—under the rock ledge—and disappeared.

How intriguing.

The other women followed. Dannika wove her fingers with his and paddled her fragile fins. At the back wall, under the stairway, a cave spiraled down and inward like a conch shell. They soared around the coral-lined path until it opened into a small cavern.

A small white Life Tree grew upside down from the ceiling.

This close to the surface?

Impossible.

A Life Tree could only thrive in the deepest corners of the ocean. Above the vents and trenches, obviously, but above a certain depth, it could not germinate. Not in a shallow lagoon only a few feet beneath the surface.

This couldn't be a Life Tree.

Its bare branches stretched for the floor, and it grew from the ceiling with no trunk. All the little speckles of resin drifted down to the floor instead of piling around the base as usual, but otherwise, it cast pure, radiant white light and made subtle, beautiful, tinkling sound.

It *was* a Life Tree.

His heart hammered in his chest. Awe suffused him. "How is this possible?"

The women floated beneath it in the small space. There

was just enough room for their community and no more to cram beneath its healing branches.

"Sorry we didn't tell you earlier." Meg winced in apology. "We talked about it, but... Well, I mean, we just wanted to get to know you a little more before... We don't even let the kids play in here. It's, you know. Sacred."

He knew.

A Life Tree here was impossible. Unimaginable. Yet, here it was. "What human science is this?"

"Not science," Dannika said beside him. "Scientists have tried growing it on the surface before, but even using pressurized chambers, they've never gotten one to sprout. How did you do it?"

"I don't know." Bex drifted between its branches. "The seed cracked, and Ankena thought he was burying it in the cavern floor. But it grew downward into this space."

Its roots hugged a large sphere.

"What is this?" Ciran asked.

"We're not sure," Meg answered. "It's something to do with the sacred brides and fertility, probably."

Bex tapped it. It vibrated at a low ring. "It rang when your plane went down."

Incredible. Even with nowhere to grow, the Life Tree had survived.

"It's so small." Dannika swam around its thin, sparkling tendrils. "But so beautiful."

"I had thought I was finished experiencing wonders." Ciran floated back. "But here is one more. No one would believe me if I told them of this. No one."

"Right?" Meg wiggled her fingers. "Now you know what it feels like when you say we have powers."

"Why doubt?" Angie asked her. "Aren't you a Disney fish princess?"

"Oh my God, Mom. That's totally different."

"Is it?" Angie arched her brows. "Well, it seems I have no powers, Disney inspired or otherwise."

And that had to change.

The small group practiced for a while in the shining light of the Life Tree, but other than noting that their soul lights dimmed with disappointment and frustration when they failed to make progress, Ciran felt like he was interfering rather than helping.

"Will you tell me what to do?" Angie bent in half and touched her toes, then rotated and wriggled in the water. "I've gone through every pose I remember from the yoga studio when all of Howard's work wives were so enthused with Ayurveda. It was uncomfortable then, and it's uncomfortable now."

"You should stop because it is not brightening your soul light."

"All that for nothing?" She shook out her arms and legs, then scrubbed her face. "Maybe I've told myself no so many times, I can't find my way to yes."

"Aw, Mom. Don't be overdramatic. You'll get it."

Angie dropped her hands and cocked a brow. "Overdramatic? You haven't seen drama, Meg. Like what will happen to our trainer if I. Don't. *Get*. This."

Ciran held up a peaceful hand. "You should focus on what is comfortable."

"Nothing is comfortable." Angie shook her head. "Nothing."

"Then perhaps you should start again. You will never develop your powers with a dimmed soul."

Angie glared daggers at him. Dannika rested a hand on his forearm to stop him from responding. Angie flexed her fingers and her toes, then shook herself in frustration.

"She must not continue on her current path," he vibrated quietly to Dannika. "Her efforts exhaust her and only darken her soul. I do not know how to help her."

"Mm. I've seen this before."

"You have?"

"In the dating world. It's common when a well-educated, strongly motivated high achiever fails to find their match. They're so used to accomplishment on the timeline they've given themselves to succeed that any perceived setback threatens their very identity."

Angie glared at him again. "Now am I glowing?"

"No."

She tensed all her muscles, then abruptly relaxed and rubbed her cheeks. "Ah, I'm going to give myself wrinkles."

His presence was definitely hindering rather than helping, and they had no time to waste. He squeezed Dannika's hands. "I will leave this with you."

She clung on. "Can we really be ready in a week?"

The others stopped practicing to listen to his answer.

He hoped so. "The only one who knows that answer is you."

The Life Tree made a cleansing, tinkling sound of hope.

But it was so fragile and unprotected here. No wonder the castaways had avoided showing it to them.

The world outside was hostile. If the Luscans learned of its existence, the king would likely violate the sanctuary just to rip it out by the roots.

Dannika and the other women must develop their powers.

Everything depended on them.

TWENTY-FOUR

C iran kicked out of the little hollow, the gorgeous upside-down snow globe cavern that encased the Life Tree, leaving an encouraging squeeze with Dannika.

It was up to her.

She kicked to Angie. "I'm guessing that you've been phenomenally successful in your life."

The older woman wrinkled her nose. "I used to think so. But it has been a very long time since I practiced yoga."

"The point of yoga is to put yourself into a meditative, focused state and open yourself to possibilities."

"Like the possibility of failure?"

"Mom."

"Any new skill requires a period of learning," Dannika said calmly. "But if yoga doesn't put you into the right mindset, then let's brainstorm different ways you can release your tension and open yourself to the universe. Or the Life Tree."

Angie nodded, her lips pinched, and Dannika tried to

tease out of her the things she did to relax, feel centered, and make decisions.

Meanwhile, Bex zoomed around the small arena, and Meg watched in awe.

"How do you make it look so easy, Bex?" Meg asked.

"Focus on what you want." Bex's human feet elongated and stretched into fins. "And shift."

Dannika closed her eyes.

She had the power. She had the power. She had the power...

Ciran's voice echoed in her head. His words of encouragement, his kisses, his patience.

I believe in you, Dannika. Anchor your faith to me. You can turn back the storm.

Her toes tingled. She stretched and opened her eyes. Her feet flattened out, long and slender, and her polished toenails looked funny spread out at the ends of a scuba diver's flippers.

She could do it.

Angie made a noise of frustration. "You too. I'm the only one who'll never get this."

"Did you flex?" Meg rotated her right ankle, which was half shifted to fin. "Or what?"

"I want to see Ankena and Lukiyo again," Bex said. "And then I thought, 'Let's go.'"

"You thought, 'Let's go,' and your fins went?"

"Yeah. More or less."

"That makes sense," Dannika interjected. "You are in touch with your true desire, and it empowers every movement. Good job."

Bex smiled shyly.

"Okay." Meg closed her eyes and lifted her index fingers. "I want to see Ankena and Lukiyo again. Let's go."

She kicked, and her half fins rolled up into ordinary feet again. She opened her eyes and laughed. "Whoops. Wait, wait. I want to see Itime and Tulu again. ... Mm, apparently, I don't. What do I want?"

"I feel very content," Angie said. "Is that the problem? I'm too able to accept the deprivations of island life?"

"You don't fall asleep dreaming of carrot cake," Meg said.

"No. Maybe my favorite facial cleanser and whitening serum." Angie rubbed her cheek. "You'll swim out of here and leave me behind."

"I'm not going anywhere until I solve the squid problem. How about...I want to have a nice swim without being swarmed by flying squids?" Meg flexed her human feet. "Nope. I thought I wanted that, though. Man, it's a mystery what I want."

They tried on a bunch of "I want" phrases, trying to get clear on their true desires, and even though they didn't make a lot of progress, their uplifting encouragement and jokes and laughter seemed to make the Life Tree glow.

Little sparkles winked on Meg's skin like glitter.

"You're sparkling," Angie told her.

"Oh? Again!" Meg closed her eyes. Her body glowed, and the Life Tree chimed, and the sparkles all floated away. She opened her eyes, the smile breaking over her face as if she were awakening from a wonderful dream, and she shivered. "All gone."

Huh.

"What was that?" Dannika asked. "What did you do just now?"

"Oh, that was just my Disney princess power again." Meg swirled her fingers through the water, and the flecks of glitter twinkled. "At least these guys aren't annoying. Itime said they're little creatures, like plankton, and just like everything else, they're attracted to me. On the shore...well, you saw how it usually is."

"I'm so sorry I couldn't shield you."

Meg waved her apology away. "We're all struggling with these powers. And it didn't use to be so bad. I cruised the coral every day. One day? Attack of the squids."

"And there was no warning?"

"None."

"Hmm. How did you get the plankton to drop away just now?"

"I do this little mantra." Meg closed her eyes and touched her temples. "I think, 'Thanks for coming by, little guys, now scoot' and then *poof*."

The Life Tree glowed.

She opened her eyes and smiled again. "Away they float."

"If you said that to the squid, then you could go in the ocean again."

Her face fell. Little bits of glitter stuck to her again, winking. "That's why I wish pushing stuff was my power. I'd shout at the squids, 'Go on, get out of here! Get off my lawn!' But, no."

The tinkling of the Life Tree sounded sadder and more discouraged.

"At least you know your power." Angie lifted her fingers and teased them through the water. "How do I know?"

Dannika refocused. "At the risk of being annoying, I'd like to point out, Meg, that you shooed away the plankton without pushing them. So you don't have to go against your preference. If anything, I think you should lean into your true desires, which in this case sounds like gratitude. You thanked the plankton for coming by to say hi. Can you do that to the squids?"

Meg bit her lip.

Yeah, Dannika knew what it sounded like. Just stand in front of the squid hurricane and say, *Hey, thanks for coming by, off you go now.* It warranted the skepticism.

But she continued, "And Angie, don't hate me for saying this, but I think if something makes you feel powerful, it's your power."

Angie cocked her brow. "If something makes me feel powerful, it's my power? Have you considered writing motivational speeches or greeting cards?"

She laughed. "I know. I know."

Angie shook her head.

"Dannika's right," Bex said.

"My power is whatever makes me feel powerful?" Angie asked with a wry vibration.

"It's in your mind. I have a *certainty* when I'm doing this." Bex flexed, and her feet snapped out to fins, then snapped back to human feet. "You have to feel it."

Angie put her hands on her hips again.

Bex tapped her forehead. "It's mental. Like babies."

"Like babies?" Dannika repeated.

Bex and Angie both looked at Meg.

"Okay, so, it's just a hypothesis. But." Meg held out her hands in a pause gesture. "We each had an 'I want to have this man's babies' moment and then got pregnant. Like, the next day. And not just once, but with every kid."

Bex nodded.

Angie lifted her brows and her chin in a "a lady never tells" expression, but that basically admitted that she agreed.

"Tulu is closer to Hadali's age than Nuno or Lukiyo.

Why? Because a year after theirs" —Meg indicated Bex and Angie—"I was like, 'We're doing it all the time. What's the holdup?' But subconsciously, I expected to get off the island and go back to grad school, and I always planned to have kids *after* grad school. One day, I was watching baby Nuno play with baby Luk, and I thought, 'Yeah, okay. Maybe we'll never get off this island, maybe I'll never go to grad school. Do I want to be a mom? I guess I'm ready to be a mom.' But I really *felt* it, you know? A day later, I had morning sickness."

They only got pregnant when they wanted to...

It made sense. The mind-body connection of mer, their Life Tree, and healing was so much stronger.

Meg summed it up. "I wanted a kid, I had a kid. I wanted another kid, I had another kid. Etcetera."

"The first set of twins exhausted me," Angie said. "And I was ready to stop. But then Meg had another cutie, and I thought, maybe one more..."

"And that was the same for me," Meg said. "Each time mine passed the baby stage. And now my youngest is four, and after what happened to Luk, I..." She glanced at Bex and quickly away, picking at the sparkles sticking to her fingers. "Well, we're going to leave the island pretty soon. I don't want to move while I'm pregnant, anyway."

Angie also frowned.

Bex shrugged. "I always wanted two."

Angie and Meg both smiled at her gently.

But Dannika also heard what they hadn't said.

Meg's youngest would have been a year old when Lukiyo had been taken.

It was all a mind-body connection.

Meg was calling the sea creatures to her subconsciously, and she used to have it under control...

"Is that when the squids started attacking?" Dannika prodded gently. "Three years ago?"

"Huh? Oh, no. It was...gosh, when Tulu was a baby." Meg scratched at the sparkly plankton sticking to her cheek. "I used to hang out in the coral shallows while waiting for Itime to get back from a hunt. Old Lieutenant Figuara didn't care when the warriors went out. He wanted the babies taken care of, so he always busied himself in another part of the island when he saw the warriors preparing to 'sneak' out."

The plankton built up on her sparkling fingers like paint splatter under a black light.

"This one time, a big old tiger shark dove through the lattice. It grabbed Tulu right in front of me and shook him, and I—well, I *screamed*, you know, like you wouldn't believe —and the shark let him go. Tulu fell like he was dead. Oh, God. He was hurt so bad."

Meg shuddered.

"The shark veered back to get him again, and...and I don't know, but suddenly, these clouds of squids surged up from seemingly everywhere. They flooded the reef, hiding us. I couldn't even swim to the shore in case the shark saw us. They can cut you down in knee-high water, did you know that? I just held Tulu in my arms, and I prayed and prayed and prayed."

Her fingers glowed with the memory, even brighter than the plankton, shining with power.

And then Meg lowered her fingers and shrugged. "My little boy opened his eyes. He was fine. All that praying, and...totally fine. Even the scars healed. He barely had a scratch." She lifted an index finger. "But the squids. The squids never went away."

"They protected you." Well, this was a news story for

the night. Chalk one up for mermaid queens. "That's amazing. Do you think they're still trying to protect you?"

"Well, I don't know. I'm not being attacked by tiger sharks anymore. I don't even go in the shallows without a warrior."

"Why not?"

"The shark moved so fast, and I was so helpless." Meg twitched, obviously still reliving it. "I never want to feel that way again."

"But it sounds like you *are* feeling that way. You feel panic every time you go in the water."

"Not that I *can* go in the water."

"Ciran said affinity to sea creatures is a queen power, and yours is especially strong. You're calling them to you."

"I don't know how." Meg flicked her fingers. The plankton latched on, increasing her glitter. "Sticky little buggers. Oh, look at this, guys. I have a sparkle trail. Gosh, they're aggressive today."

"Because you're feeling upset, probably."

"Gee, reliving the worst day of my life, when I couldn't do anything but cower and cry is upsetting? Ha-ha, I wonder why."

This wasn't getting anywhere.

"Okay, let's reframe this." Dannika mentally reviewed her checklist for reframing trauma. She was no licensed psychologist and had no claims to be, but she'd had a lot of practice trying to help frustrated would-be daters get out of their own way. "You know, since your power is healing, maybe you really saved Tulu's life that day."

Meg flubbed her lips. Little bubbles emerged. "God, I wish."

"But you did wish, didn't you? You wished it so hard. And your power is healing."

"Yeah, but…"

"You summoned the animals to hide you. We all know you did that. But your actual power is healing, which you did when you held baby Tulu in your arms and prayed. And he did get better. He came back to life. And now, even years later, these same animals want to help you because they know you channel the healing energy of the Life Tree."

Meg's gaze rose to fix on Dannika with new intensity. She stopped trying to brush the plankton away, and after a moment, the sparkles drifted off on their own, without her even trying.

"You did something very important that day," Dannika emphasized. "You weren't helpless. You saved your son's life."

Meg studied her fingertips with new eyes. "Do you really think so?"

"Yes."

Meg looked at Angie, who shrugged as if it were possible, and then at Bex, who nodded as if the answer was obvious.

"Okay. Say I did save Tulu." Meg suddenly stopped and swallowed hard. Her eyes reddened, and she scrubbed her cheeks. "Ah, it was a traumatic time. Um, say that I did save him. Say I'm summoning the squidocalypse to this very day. How do I turn it off?"

Great, okay, now they were making progress.

"So, let's reframe the squidocalypse into help. They're all just trying so hard, in their little squid ways, to help you. And maybe you can just thank them for caring, like you did the plankton, and calmly tell them to go."

"Just tell them things are cool? Just…tell them?"

"You have to believe it. You know. Because of the mind-body connection."

"Right. Cool and calm. Channel my inner Itime." Meg dropped her hands again. "If I really saved my son..." She shook her head, her black hair waving under the water. "All this time, I've concentrated on how he almost died while I was watching him, and how Itime should never trust me with any of our kids again. If I actually healed him..."

"You healed him," Bex said.

"You have always been a very sweet, caring child," Angie said.

Meg smiled, a little wobbly, and her eyes reddened. "Thanks, you guys. It means a lot. Oh!" She pointed down.

Her toes unfurled into fins.

"It's happening!" she squealed, and flutter-kicked with her mini fins in a somersault, fists waving. "You guys. You guys! I didn't even think about it that time. I'm a mermaid superhero. Oh my God. My heart is overfilling right now. The drama. Oh my God."

Bex grinned.

Angie smiled, closemouthed, beaming with pride. But her happiness for her daughter was also tinged with sadness.

Did old fears also hold back Angie?

Angie noticed Dannika's eye and composed herself. "Yes? Oh, don't look at me. I'm not the one you should concentrate on."

"Why not?" Dannika asked.

"Because I told you already, I have no interest in storming any city." Angie waved her fingers in dismissal. "I don't know what it's like to be a warrior, and honestly, I don't want to know. I have no opinion on how they posture and shout."

Posture and shout? "That sounds like a strong opinion, actually."

"Well, it's not." Angie kept her pleasant smile in place, but pressed her lips together like a crease cut by a knife. "Konomelu keeps us safe, and I make Sanctuary into a pleasant home."

"Mom, you're not really happy here." Meg stopped kicking. "I mean, you joke about skincare, but you also lamented that none of the kids will ever receive my education."

"Yes, but the solution isn't more violence. If it were up to me, I would forget this war. People will get hurt, and maybe even killed." Angie shook her head and backpedaled. "But what do I know? I've got no opinion. I'll stay home."

The tinkling sounds of the Life Tree punctuated the silence.

"That sounds like a *really* strong opinion," Dannika said.

Meg and Bex chuckled. It dispelled the tension.

Angie's lips curved into a self-deprecating smile. "Oh, I suppose. But it doesn't matter what I think."

"Why not?"

"Because I *don't* know." Angie gazed up at the Life Tree, then shook her head. "I shouldn't tell you this, but when Prince Ankena took Luk to that echo point, Konomelu and I had a huge argument. I knew they shouldn't go, or at least not alone. 'You do not understand,' Konomelu said. 'It is one of the tests. A trainee must fight at the side of his father.' And then they never came back." She shook her head again and hugged her elbows. "I got so mad."

"Because they didn't listen to you?" Dannika asked softly.

"Yes!" She threw up her hands. "And someone *did* get hurt. I'm sorry, Bex. You think Prince Ankena is still alive. I want him to be alive too, but I don't think Konomelu will ever forgive himself for not finding him the first time."

"You don't think this is one time Konomelu would prefer to be wrong?" Dannika asked.

"Yes, I suppose. Oh." Angie pressed her hands to her chest. "This can't be right. I feel worse now than before we started this talk. I'm sorry, ladies. I need to check on the boys, and you know that underwater time dilation is tricky. It seems like we just entered the lagoon, but I have a feeling it's already past dinner."

What a letdown.

Dannika swam after the other women, and they all emerged from the lagoon, where Ciran was waiting for her—and it was just dinnertime after all.

But worry seeped into her.

Bex was ready to storm Lusca. Meg knew what she had to do to control the animals and her powers, and now she needed to do it. But Angie...

Dannika had less than a week to connect with Angie.

And then they'd find out if it had been worthwhile.

Because this time, Dannika would float beside Ciran, the other warriors, and her fellow women.

And if anything happened to them—if anything happened to Ciran—she would never forgive herself.

Never.

TWENTY-FIVE

Six days passed.

Dannika tried her best, and everyone made great progress—except Angie. The night before their big test on the coral, Dannika could barely eat dinner.

But they had to rush. Hazel was still in danger. Everyone thought she and Ciran were dead. Stevie might be sailing into a Luscan trap.

And closer, Val looked worse and worse. Her leg swelled and turned purple, and her face puffed unrecognizably. They elevated her leg, wrapped it in compresses, and tried to set the obviously broken bone, but she seemed so fragile.

Despite her suffering, her attitude never flagged.

"I wish I had a camera." Val tapped her waterlogged broken cell phone against the table at dinner. "Then I could take an amazing 'before' picture for my future memoir, *Crashed and Burned: How One Plucky Jet Pilot Survived on a Hidden Island with Ticklish Tarantulas, Murderous Mermen, and Very Agitated Squids.*"

"That sounds amazing," Meg said.

"I'll send you an autographed copy. Watch for me on *Oprah*. Or whatever daytime show is running now. I'll get you all new cars."

Meg snorted. "Because that's practical on a no-road island."

"Sanctuary." Angie tipped her small wine glass at Val. "And thank you. I look forward to reading your novel. We'll start an island book club."

Meg rolled her eyes. "Yeah, if I ever get my hands on literature, a tome about being stranded on this island is the last thing I'll want to read."

Angie sighed. "And you call me dramatic."

"Well, you are."

A few kids raced up to Val and offered her a wiggly, fuzzy tarantula.

"Oh, another one?" Val only recoiled a little. "Good job, my environmental biologists. Carve it on the survey stick. You're going to impress my wife and her colleagues so much."

They dropped it on the table and scampered off.

"Ooh, you, uh, forgot the specimen," she called.

Tulu picked it up and carried it away from the table for her.

She let out a sigh. "Thank you, hon."

He nodded.

Beside him, Nuno blinked heavily into his cup of nonalcoholic tea, and Hadali drooled with his head on the table. While the women practiced their powers, the warriors upped their routines with the older boys. Val had miraculously taken over the younger ones and, despite her terrible injury, had done an Oscar-worthy performance of keeping them occupied.

They all turned in early.

Dannika followed Ciran into the lagoon. As she shifted back to mer and floated into the familiar water, her veins buzzed.

She *needed* tomorrow to go well.

She needed to let her powers flow through her, she needed to trust the warriors and her fellow women, and she needed to trust herself. For so long, she'd been living a half-life. To free Prince Ankena and Lukiyo and everyone, she needed to be more than she'd ever been before.

She'd really have to turn back the storm.

Ciran swam beside her. "Your soul light is very fragile tonight."

"I am so nervous about tomorrow."

He stroked her cheek. "Show me your power."

She stretched, and her fins unfurled. That part was easy now. She lifted her fingers and *believed*. A shield of white light glowed around Ciran.

"Also shield yourself."

She tried to, but the moment she stretched, the shield dropped away from both of them. "I haven't mastered it."

"Can you not make it bigger? Big enough to encompass both of us?"

She closed her eyes and focused. *Believe. You can shield everyone. You can shield everyone. Your shield is big and bright, and you can shield everyone.*

Except what about Ciran? *If I'm covering myself, doesn't that make him uncovered?*

"Ah, again it dropped." He floated over her. "I tried to stay close. You are an expert at shielding others, but you will not shield yourself."

She rolled on her back to gaze at the rippling surface of the lagoon. "I'm working on it."

"How?"

She told him about her affirmations and the negative echo.

He chuckled softly and drew her against his body. "Queen power is not like a human bedcovering where if you pull the one side, it uncovers the other. You can shelter everyone."

"I know."

"Ah." He nuzzled her. "You know it in your mind, but not in your soul."

He understood her so well. "Yeah."

"Then let us practice. You will shield us." He kissed and teased her, heating the water with a sizzling caress. "I will increase our resonance."

She melted into his kiss.

He delved and teased, filled her with his tongue, and made her beg. Her nipples hardened into points and her pussy squeezed, anticipating his delicious domination. But he refused to progress and withstood her seduction even though his cock hardened encouragingly in her gentle hands. "Shield us."

"Right now?" Her mind whirled with desire, sex, hunger, need. "I don't know if I can make it right now."

"You can."

He was serious. Okay. "Say, 'I believe in you, Dannika.'"

His chest rumbled with heat. "I believe in you, Dannika."

The water tingled as if his vibrations sparked fire.

Her body heated, and she pushed that warmth out her fingertips into light. The shield swirled around them, cinching them together, small and tight.

"Bigger." Ciran turned her, twisting her away from him and pinning her in place. The water flushed over her tingling breasts. "Expand outward to fill this lagoon."

Her derriere brushed his hard cock. His arms caged her. His hands cupped her full breasts, teased the nipples. Pleasure surged in her brain, fighting the fear, and awoke a deep ache in her core.

She moaned with need.

"More power." He nuzzled her ear, tugged the lobe. "Yes, like that. Feel me even when I am not in front of you."

His hand lowered to her feminine curls. He cupped her mons, embraced her, and caressed her slick folds. The ache intensified, and she liquefied for his possession.

She arched to reach him.

He stilled, holding himself taut. "Not yet. You are capable of more than this."

Sure, she was capable...

She closed her eyes and drew a shield around them.

"Ah. Your powers."

The shield shrank in. His cock pressed against her cheeks, and she wiggled him into the proper place against her aching entrance.

He chuckled dangerously. "You are playing with me."

"You asked me to shield us." She undulated her hips in invitation. "I'm shielding us."

"Yes." He nipped her nape, imprinting her with lust. "Feel my reward."

His cock slid between her legs, teasing her with frustratingly close pleasure.

"Ciran." On the surface, she'd pant. She squeezed her thighs together, trapping his hard cock. "Don't ever leave me."

"I will always be with you," he vibrated. "Near or far, our souls are linked. Let me pleasure you a little longer. You are too selfless, and you deserve much more than you take."

She arched her back again. His cock, nestled against her channel, inched in.

He grew taut. "Dannika. Do not..."

She entwined their thighs and eased him deeper.

He shuddered. "Do not rush me."

She trapped his legs, drawing him in until he filled her. Connection ensnared their souls. He held her tight, enfolding her in his embrace, and loved her.

Hard.

His fingers dug into her hips, and he levered his cock in, driving and thrusting, chasing her pleasure. She accepted, rolled with him, took. He thrust faster and faster, and a deep vibration of pleasure strummed through her body, tightening like a string to just the right pitch.

His vibrations changed to unsteady. "You are capable of anything."

"Fill me," she commanded and rocked him all the way to the hilt. Her body contracted, channel clenching his cock, and she felt him shudder all the way through her. "Take me, Ciran."

He lunged, losing control, and plucked that string. A stunning orgasm shattered her to pieces and melted her into a new woman.

Ciran held her tight. They floated, her back to his front. And what started out as a sweet, comforting, protective hug changed as the cooler water seeped between them into cracks where their bodies didn't quite mesh as one.

You will turn back the storm.

Could she, though?

Tomorrow would be the test.

TWENTY-SIX

The energy at the beach was so kinetic, it was almost visible even in the air. Ciran took a deep breath and let it out. Today, the queens demonstrated their powers.

Val sat beneath a sunshade and kept Meg's youngest occupied.

Itime stood in the shallow waves with the trainees.

Ciran reviewed the plan.

Once Meg showed that she could enter the water without causing a surge of squids, the younger trainees would conduct their usual exercises.

The queens would sneak into the hidden area of the reef to demonstrate their powers. The older trainees would monitor and distract the Luscan patrol.

If all went perfectly to plan, the queens would pass Konomelu's tests, emerge from hiding, and, while still safely on the island side of the coral fence, use their powers to drive back the patrol.

Drive them far into the ocean and keep them there.

Once they cleared the way, the warriors and queens

would travel to the echo point and share their information. The currents would take some time to reach Atlantis, but their message would eventually arrive.

They would warn Hazel about the sabotage, tell Ciran's warriors his status, and summon backup from Atlantis. Humans would fly out to heal Val.

The Atlantis queens would teach their queens any needed skills—especially Angie, who, even after a week of practice, had not yet discovered her powers.

And they would all descend in an organized fashion to Lusca, turn aside the enemy units, charm the giant squids, overthrow the king, and rescue everyone.

Easy.

But it all depended on how things went today.

Nuno emerged from the water, shifted to human effortlessly, and gestured at the distant coral. "They're acting weird."

Uh-oh.

Now? Of all times?

Itime looked at Ciran.

Up at the firepit, Konomelu reviewed contingency plans with the queens. What to do if Meg couldn't enter the water. What to do if a predator interrupted their tests. What to do if they felt like they were losing control and might reveal their secret prematurely to the Luscan patrol.

But none of those contingencies had taken in the possibility of the Luscan patrol becoming a problem.

Ciran dropped his fraying human clothes and strode into the waves. "Show us."

Nuno led him and Itime to the center of the reef and pointed. "They're all around the reef today. It's like they know we're doing something."

Out beyond the dead coral lattice, one Luscan warrior

kicked slowly back and forth. He watched more intently than on the other mornings.

A second patroller floated beyond the first.

"They never post more than two warriors in one place on the island," Itime vibrated.

"There's a third." Nuno pointed to the far end of the lattice, closest to the cavern, "and at the other end, a fourth."

Itime stilled.

"Should we cancel the training today? I do not see Lieutenant Orike."

Nuno pointed. "He's there."

The lieutenant was far out enough to see the curve on the island.

"Good eye," Ciran said.

Nuno puffed out his chest.

The whole patrol had gathered to watch their demonstration.

Konomelu kicked to their position, bubbles trailing from his swift dive. "The brides are ready."

"But we are not." Ciran pointed out the odd behavior. "They are planning something."

Konomelu squinted at the patrol. "We altered our schedule. Perhaps they have guessed that *we* are planning something."

"Should we delay?" Itime asked.

Konomelu considered it for a long time. "No. If our brides demonstrate the powers Ciran says they are capable of, they will defeat the patrol as planned. If they do not demonstrate those powers, then they will not engage. The patrol will be none the wiser."

"Unless the patrol comes through the coral barrier," Ciran said.

"They will not violate the agreement." Konomelu nodded to his son. "Prepare the trainees."

Nuno kicked to the younger trainees. "Squid races! Right here, pick your squids."

"Mine is named Lieutenant Ori-idiot!" one of them cried.

"Don't name it that," Nuno jeered. "That name's always a loser. A sore one too."

The patrol drifted closer to the lattice, definitely watching the young fry.

The back of Ciran's neck itched. Would they really respect the coral barrier? It was symbolic, not functional, with its fragile dead lattice and gaping holes. The other warriors shared his unease, but they moved forward with the test.

Squids clustered en masse at the entry point for the women. Tentacles and mantles, long club arms, and the occasional parrotfish squirmed and intermixed. But they weren't as frantic as in times past. Light glimmered within the mass, and then the squids all changed color from agitated to peaceful. They dispersed, their fins fluttering, tentacles first, without a single ink squirt.

Dannika released her glowing shield. It had encased just three women: herself, Meg, and Bex.

Meg opened her eyes with a pleased smile. "It worked. I told them to go away, and they went away."

"Where is Angie?" Konomelu demanded.

Meg's smile slipped. "She, uh, stayed on shore with Val. She still hasn't figured out her powers."

Konomelu set his jaw and glared at the shoreline. "She has never backed down from a challenge."

"That probably makes her failure extra upsetting,"

Dannika said. "Did you want us to wait while you go talk to her?"

He frowned heavily. Again, another long pause, and Konomelu finally ground out his answer. "We will continue. Itime, the first test."

Itime stared at Meg, expressionless.

Konomelu turned to him. "Itime?"

He twitched. "Yes?"

"The first test. Begin."

"Ah. Yes." But he continued to stare.

Meg beamed at the cornflower-blue warrior, then hugged him. "Don't cry."

Itime shook his head, looking very far from crying. "It has been a long time."

"I know. It's exciting to be in the ocean again." She kissed his flat cheek. "This is the first of many swims. Everything's about to change. Today is the beginning."

He nodded.

Meg gave him one last squeeze and resumed her place in line.

Itime swam back and forth before them. "When I give the command, Dannika will raise her shield and everyone else will amplify it. Understand?"

The women focused.

"Now."

They fumbled but got a shield around them, including Dannika. She smiled. Her soul light glowed.

A weight lifted off Ciran's chest. They would succeed today, at least enough to go to the echo point and start everything in motion.

With every successful command the women completed, their confidence bloomed. Konomelu traded a pleased look with Itime, but a wrinkle of stress still ringed his orange-threaded eyes. He worried about his bride.

Nuno left the young fry and flew to the males. "Dad, when you go to the echo point to summon the Atlantis army, I want to go too."

Konomelu's brows descended. "No."

"They can barely make their fins, and I'm a warrior."

"In training."

"Only because I'm always here. I can do this. You have to take me."

"You have a duty to protect the young fry."

Nuno glared. "Orike was right. You'll never let me become a warrior. You'll always keep me in shallow waters."

Konomelu's nostrils flared, and he snarled. "A warrior knows his duty. A warrior obeys his commander. Your task is to distract the patrol, and you have abandoned it. How can I take you on the most dangerous journey of your life if you cannot perform your duty?"

Nuno's eyes reddened, and he swallowed hard, then flew furiously back to the trainees, shouted at them to start a new race—to chase after him—and flew at the lattice.

Hadali and Tulu chased him, and the rest of the young fry scrambled.

The patrol in the deep ocean swam closer.

Nuno zoomed to the nearest patrolling warrior, shifted to toes, and kicked. His feet hit the lattice near the warrior's head. The bleached coral creaked. The warrior rotated to face him.

Nuno dove into the shallow end of the reef.

The young fry wheeled and followed.

Ciran's unease grew.

Itime joined them, giving the women a break. "Bex and

Dannika are strong. Meg's power seems weak in comparison. But her soul burns as bright, if not brighter."

"And Angie cannot use her power at all." Konomelu crossed his arms. "Why?"

The warriors debated the differences. All the women had bright souls. The Life Tree of Sanctuary was strange and stunted, but the Life Tree of Atlantis was small and young.

"Perhaps our elixir is more potent," Ciran said. "Balim makes it with a modern method using something called an Instant Pot."

"Then why is Bex so strong?" Konomelu asked.

The women had floated closer to listen, and Dannika's eyes widened. "Oh, actually, Bex drank that elixir too. Hadali poured the last of Val's bottled elixir into her cup, and she drank it by accident."

Bex shrugged. "Oops."

Could that be the difference?

Nuno left the young fry in the shallows and swam along the lattice again. "Jelly for brains! Squid lover! Nudibranch licker! Shark chum!"

But something was wrong.

The muscled, armed, tattooed warriors paced him on the outside. When Nuno switched directions, a different warrior paced him the opposite way.

Ciran had been taught the same method to hunt cornered prey.

And a warrior in shallow water against a beach was the definition of cornered.

Why were they treating Nuno as prey?

Nuno vibrated insults at the warriors. The patrol sneered right back.

Was this normal?

Each captured the other's full attention.

"They hunt us like cornered fish," Konomelu grumbled. "Again. Always they harass us. Nuno! Ignore them. We have more pressing work. Swim inshore."

He turned away from his son to engage with the training women, clearly more worried about them being hidden from the warriors than about the patrol.

So this was normal.

But Ciran couldn't stop his unease.

Nuno ignored his father's order and slashed his coral knife at the patrolling warrior. "Enter my domain, and I will end you."

"You think to scratch me with that little toy?" The patrolling warrior sniggered. "It would not even penetrate my scales."

"I sharpened it myself!"

The patrolling warrior laughed and glanced back at the two other patrollers ranged behind him. "That is even more reason."

The trio laughed.

"Oh yeah?" Nuno kicked up to the lattice and reached through to slash at the male's arm. "Feel this!"

The patrolling warrior darted forward and grabbed Nuno's arm.

Nuno shouted in rage and fright.

They yanked him against the coral.

Konomelu whirled. "Nuno!"

This was not normal.

The hole was too small to fit Nuno through, but the patrol yanked him hard, twice, to try. He cried again.

"Nuno?" Meg whimpered. "Nuno..."

Squids surged in the water and rushed toward Meg. Ciran arched over the horde and kicked hard.

"Nuno!" Konomelu fought his way through the squids.

"Call them off." Itime dove and shoved the creatures away. "Meg."

Another Luscan darted through a bigger hole and entered the reef. The first warrior released Nuno's arm. The second dragged him, dazed but struggling, through the larger hole and into the ocean, where the first warrior grappled his other arm and forced him away.

It happened in an instant.

Nuno was being kidnapped!

Ciran's heart spiked in his chest. He was unarmed. But he was also closest.

The younger trainees clustered, as they'd been trained to respond to danger, and Tulu and Hadali shepherded them inward to the shoreline. Dannika shielded them and Bex guarded their retreat.

Ciran kicked through the lattice and clashed with the first warrior, who slashed at him. He dove out of the way and kept after the kidnappers. He just had to slow them enough for the other warriors to catch up.

The warriors dragged Nuno to the rest of the unit and secured him in a net.

Lieutenant Orike intercepted Ciran, trident out. "Come to seek your doom, coward?"

Ciran slowed.

Two warriors secured Nuno. The remaining two flanked Lieutenant Orike. Sharp tridents gleamed. Each warrior wore five blades, and their intricate tattoos and scars showed they had all the experience they needed to wield them.

Three against one again.

But he needed to make it five against one.

Because if he could trick all five of the patrol into dropping Nuno and chasing him—Ciran the interloper, the foreign warrior—then Konomelu or Itime could sneak in, cut Nuno free, and they'd have a real chance of escaping.

He just had to think fast and pique the warriors' territorial anger, and Konomelu and Itime had to sneak—

"Orike!" Konomelu flew past Ciran. Itime zoomed on the other side in a coordinated attack. "Give me back my son!"

So much for sneaking.

Lieutenant Orike brandished his trident. The other warriors braced.

Itime parried both flanking warriors.

Konomelu punched the trident out of his way and smashed into the lieutenant, barrel-rolling him backward.

The flanking warriors turned on Itime.

Very good.

Ciran kicked past the fray. The remaining two warriors had Nuno in their net and were dragging him as fast as possible away from the fight. Unencumbered, Ciran was faster. He almost reached them.

They suddenly dove.

A deadly bull shark, siren wailing, bore down on Ciran.

What?

He jackknifed and dove.

The shark veered after him. Squids came at him from either side, and a large, peaceful manta ray emerged from the depths beneath him, flapping its great wings as a barrier.

The patrol escaped with Nuno on the other side.

The bull shark dove after him.

He kicked back. Lotar could calm or redirect the animal, a rare trait in warriors, and Ciran did not have the skill.

The squids latched on to his arms, biting and squeezing.

He shook them off. Frustration pinched him even more than their hard beaks. "You pursue the wrong warrior. Look. Go after those warriors. They are the ones you must stop."

But he was no queen.

The bull shark veered in for another attack.

He retreated, kicking along the bottom. Lobsters and crabs rose from their burrows, clacking warnings, and small fish nipped his fins. Ribbons of eels squiggled after him.

Far in the distance, Lieutenant Orike fought both Konomelu and Itime while the flanking warriors looked on, waiting for their chance to strike. Ciran kicked toward them steadily.

"You will pay for this treason." Konomelu slashed his coral trainee dagger at Lieutenant Orike's chest.

Lieutenant Orike arched over his swing. "It is not treason to kill traitors." He thrust his gleaming, sharp trident at Konomelu's unguarded back.

Itime parried the trident with his coral dagger. It cracked. "You violated the safe area."

"There is no safe area, exile. We have orders to turn your weakened young fry into a warrior. Thank Prince Lukiyo." Lieutenant Orike jabbed his trident at Itime.

Itime parried the blow. His weakened blade broke in half, leaving a jagged end.

"Monster!" Konomelu slammed his shoulder into Lieutenant Orike's back.

The lieutenant grunted, whirled, and thumped Konomelu's gut with the hard, rounded end of his trident.

Konomelu bent over.

Itime moved to defend him, but Lieutenant Orike whirled and drove him back. While Konomelu floated helplessly in the water, the other two warriors moved in.

Ciran led the infuriated squids, wailing bull shark, giant manta ray, and agitated sea life right into the middle of the fight.

The bull shark bashed into the warriors, its razor teeth snapping at their knees. They whirled and danced away from the sudden threat. Squids latched on to their elbows and ankles, the eels vibrated electricity between their legs, and the wash of the manta ray's wings spun them head over fins.

Lieutenant Orike broke off his assault on Itime and scrambled back, slicing away attackers. "What madness is this?"

The bull shark bumped Konomelu, then veered away.

Inside the shallows, Meg had her eyes closed. She was out in the open, Dannika beside her, Bex on the other side.

Itime helped Konomelu through the lattice.

Ciran kicked to swim around the lieutenant and unsettled patrol. They had to regroup. This was a disaster.

The bull shark rushed him, blocking his way. Then the shark veered away, and all the animals dispersed. Dannika or Bex must have told Meg to release them.

Except now he was alone on the wrong side of the lattice with the patrol blocking him from reaching the shallows.

Lieutenant Orike didn't notice what was happening inside the lattice. He watched the dispersal of the animals in shock. "The Undine has an affinity for sharks. He will only cause us irritation." He leveled his trident on Ciran. "Destroy him."

The Luscan warriors charged Ciran.

He arched over them and raced for the largest hole.

Lieutenant Orike shouted. Would Ciran make it through? He was nearly there—

The sharp blades of Lieutenant Orike's trident speared across the hole, blocking him.

Ciran grabbed the handle closest to the blade.

Lieutenant Orike yanked it back, dragging Ciran closer, and then jabbed hard, aiming for his belly.

He forced the blades away.

Lieutenant Orike yanked and thrust again, and a third time. He was strong despite the recent fight.

Ciran's energy drained.

Oh, no.

Dannika, do not fear. Not now. Use your shield.

Feel your power.

"I told you not to enter my territory, exile." The lieutenant yanked his trident out of Ciran's weakening hands. His lips curled into a snarl. "Now feel the wrath of Lusca."

Ciran kicked backward. He would have only one more shot at escape before his strength drained away completely.

The lieutenant darted forward and stabbed.

Ciran arched over the thrust—and kicked through the opening in the lattice.

Now he was in the safe zone.

"Yah!" Lieutenant Orike cried behind him.

Shocking pain pierced his shoulder. The tip of Lieutenant Orike's trident emerged through the front of his upper chest, the fleshy muscle, and the upper arm.

He bellowed in pain.

The lieutenant had leaned through the lattice to hook Ciran. He dragged him back, toward the open ocean.

Ciran struggled against the pull.

From across the shallow reef, Dannika locked eyes with him. Horror contorted her face.

She screamed.

Her scream echoed through the water like a wall of shattering glass.

It reached into Ciran's soul and yanked at the roots. Nausea soared up his throat, and his very heart turned black. He collapsed on the trident.

Lieutenant Orike grunted in pain. "What is that noise?"

And then a white wave of light whipped the coral lattice. It shuddered as though it had been smashed by a giant fist. And then the coral crumbled into pieces and toppled to the reef floor.

TWENTY-SEVEN

The rest of the fight passed in a blur.

Lieutenant Orike flew back empty-handed, leaving his trident embedded in Ciran's shoulder. "What is that?"

Dannika's agonizing scream faded.

Lieutenant Orike searched the shoreline and fixed on Dannika, who was now floating alone. "Your mainland bride..."

Meg and Bex had moved to Konomelu and Itime. Lieutenant Orike's gaze passed over them without stopping. Did he actually see them? He called his other warriors to him and growled, "Do not challenge me again, exiles, or I will see you murdered by your own young fry."

They swam away.

Ciran was dead. He was dead. Oh, God, Dannika had messed it up. She hadn't shielded him in time. Everything was wrong, and he was dead.

She'd been so terrified during the fight, and angry at herself for not having better control to push through and make a shield when she felt like she would throw up, and horrified for him, fighting on bravely and alone while everyone else was safe inside the lattice.

But then he'd escaped through the lattice, and she'd relaxed. It was okay she'd failed this test. She'd have another chance.

And then he'd jolted, horribly, and that warlike lieutenant's trident had stuck out of him. Her horror had ejected in a scream. She hadn't even been able to control it, and all the warriors had flinched.

Then Bex, the real hero, had used her powers to push the lieutenant back.

It had also taken half the coral lattice with it. But at least the lieutenant had abandoned Ciran, and they'd all swum off.

Now Ciran floated on his back with a trident sticking out of his shoulder like a harpoon.

Dannika jetted through the water. Her heart throbbed in her throat. A metallic taste filled her mouth. She couldn't feel anything below her neck.

She reached his side.

"Ciran?" She touched his taut face, stroked his cheek, brushed his scratches and bumps. *Please be alive. Please don't be dead because of me.* "Ciran?"

She delicately probed around the sharp, angry spear points. Blood, his blood, seeped into the water.

He arched his back in agony.

Death throes.

Was that what happened when people died?

Would she have seen this already if she'd been present when Eliot had died?

His lashes fluttered. He moaned.

No, no. There was still hope.

She had powers. Not strong, but Ciran believed in her. She clenched his Sea Opal, her focus during the earlier tests. That was the problem. When she'd been so terrified for him, she hadn't been able to tear her gaze away from the fight to focus on his Sea Opal. Of course she hadn't made the shield.

She held his Sea Opal in front of her and stared into its swirling depths. If she had any healing powers, let it flow now...

Oh, no.

A massive crack fractured the Sea Opal nearly in half.

Her scream. Her terror scream. She'd clenched it too hard and cracked it.

She had no useful powers.

Her chest convulsed. A sob, or throwing up, one of the two.

She had no healing powers. She had nothing.

What was she doing? What was she thinking?

"Meg?" Dannika clutched his uninjured hand and towed him to the shore. "Meg, you have to heal Ciran. Meg!"

———

SOMETHING TICKLED CIRAN'S SHOULDER.

And then a sharp pain jolted him back to awareness. Heat radiated from an agonizing wound in his shoulder. Meg leaned over him, her brow furrowed, her straight black hair floating around her.

"What happened?"

"You got hit." Dannika floated on his other side. Her

eyes were red and her soul light dim as night. "Your shoulder. That's my fault. I'm so sorry. I was so upset—I couldn't focus. I didn't shield you."

"It is okay." He summoned the strength to comfort her and raise her soul light. "You did your best."

"No, I didn't do anything. You were right there. I couldn't stop those warriors. I made you weak and slow, and I...I cracked your Sea Opal."

His strength drained. He wanted to comfort her, reassure her, but his words were all gone. Her sadness was his sadness. His soul reacted to hers and shrank into a dense, protective ball.

Itime gripped the trident still sticking out of his shoulder. "This will hurt." He yanked.

White-hot pain snatched his consciousness.

Then the cool ocean seeped in. Heat seared his shoulder, and the pain eased.

He opened his eyes again.

Meg's glowing hands hovered over his shoulder.

Everyone else hovered over his other side, anxious. The warriors relaxed and eased back. But Dannika looked destroyed.

"Not bad, if I do say so myself." Meg poked his shoulder. "Try it out."

The deep cuts still rubbed and stung, but it no longer felt like his ligaments were severed. He made a fist, dared to move his shoulder back and forth, and shrugged. *Ouch.* Although he had a small range of motion, with his healing rate amplified by Meg's powers, he should be back to full health in a few hours.

"Good." Meg folded her lips in rueful apology. "I so didn't mean to send the animals after you. I directed them after 'the warriors who didn't belong,' which was obviously a mistake. So, oops."

"We all made mistakes," he vibrated.

Dannika's soul light dimmed again. She pressed her palms to her collarbone. Even if she couldn't see soul lights, she must feel the terrible ache.

Konomelu was grim. "We will talk more on the shore."

Where they would have to face the rest of the islanders.

They staggered out of the ocean. The women collapsed as they shifted back to human, coughing out the fluids they hadn't yet learned to expel gracefully. Itime and Konomelu had both been injured, and they limped.

The young fry gathered in a silent crowd by Val at the top of the beach. Angie stood in the front. She took a few steps toward Konomelu. Her gaze raked them and desperately moved past to the ocean, then returned to her husband.

"Nuno?" Her voice broke on the second syllable.

Konomelu shook his head.

A sob burst from her. She covered her mouth, forcing the emotion back in, and then her knees bent. Konomelu caught her before she hit the sand. He held her, silently grieving, while the wind swept across their isolated beach.

Nuno had been taken.

The coral lattice was down.

No one would come to rescue them.

They had to rescue themselves.

After a few minutes, Angie recovered. She stood, dry-eyed, and neatened her hair, straightened her grass dress, and removed the crushed flower on her chest. "You're leaving today?"

"As soon as we are fit." Konomelu touched his bruised abdomen.

"You'll need lunch." She turned and strode through the solemn young fry into the structure, then almost mechanically began pulling out the containers of food to create a meal that nobody felt like eating.

Itime and Konomelu conferenced quietly. They were planning to go to the echo point alone, just themselves. If the Luscan patrol was busy kidnapping Nuno, no one would stop the Sanctuary warriors from leaving the island. They should escape quickly for the echo point.

But it was not a great plan.

Hadali hugged Bex. "They took Nuno on Lukiyo's order. Didn't they?"

"Yes, it seems Lukiyo has embraced the ideals of his grandfather," Konomelu said heavily. "He has forgotten Prince Ankena, us, and you."

Hadali hugged his mom tighter. "What can we do?"

"Here? Stay on your guard. We will return as quickly as possible."

Bex jerked her chin at the waves. "Can I come with you?"

Hadali sniffed. "Me too?"

"And me," Tulu said.

"No," Konomelu snapped, and Itime also shook his head. "It is too dangerous."

Bex's eyes narrowed. "Not for me."

"For the young fry," Konomelu clarified. "The barrier has collapsed. You must guard them. And when the patrol returns, only you can drive them back."

Bex grimaced.

"It is now clear to me and Itime that Ciran was right. Queen powers are the key. Bex's push attack and Dannika's war cry were both highly effective, even though they were undirected. You two must gain control. And, because we need more queens, we will go to the crash site of the airplane to retrieve the potent elixir. Meg and Angie must gain the same effectiveness."

Angie turned on her heel. "Didn't you say the crash site is near Lusca?"

"Yes, because of the currents. But do not fear. We have snuck into the city before, such as when we searched for Prince Ankena. We will exercise caution."

"Don't take too long." She slapped one platter down with more force than it needed. "Not on account of me."

"You have not experienced the true effectiveness of the queen powers. It is worth the delay. And we must summon the Atlantis queens. The king will try to convert Nuno to his allegiance. We have time."

Angie fell silent, focused on her work. Meg and Bex helped her, and the two warriors debated the finer points of their strategy. Ciran heard the gist, but it was largely what they'd already discussed, and he was so tired.

He collapsed in a seat and closed his eyes. His body felt heavy. Dannika's grief or just the injury? He forced his eyes open and beckoned to Dannika, who lingered at the outside of the solemn group. "Sit with me."

She stopped at his knee. "Here?"

He looped her wrist and tugged her to his lap. His shoulder complained, but everything was better with her in his arms. She'd taken the time to dress, and her damp fabric clung to her skin.

She sat stiffly. "I don't want to hurt you."

He squeezed her close. "Having you in my arms outweighs any discomfort."

Her chin wobbled. "Don't say that."

"But it is true."

"All I do is make your life harder."

"Only one part." He nuzzled her suggestively. "And you like when that is hard."

An unwilling ghost of a smile lightened her. She melted against him, finally accepting the comfort he offered, and he hugged her, taking his own comfort in return.

She was soft and feminine and all he wanted, forever. He wanted her in her dark moments and in her bright moments. All her moments. And obviously, this was a dark moment. His heart hurt for what she'd witnessed. After losing one soul mate, the threat of a second loss always weighed on her. If Lieutenant Orike's thrust had been more central, in Ciran's spine instead of his fleshy shoulder, Dannika's worst fear could have come true.

Ciran well understood her fears and recriminations. He would bear any pain if it would ease her regret. But he couldn't, and so all he could do was snug her close and try, try, try to help her heal. "I want you to swim with me to the echo point."

She sucked in a sad breath. "I nearly got you killed."

"Today was not your fault." He stroked her bare biceps. "The warriors invaded our reef before you finished the tests. We were disorganized and unprepared. You did very well, all of you."

"Getting you stabbed and Nuno kidnapped was a good job?"

"You secured the young fry, as we trained you. You worked with Bex and Meg."

"They did things. I did nothing."

"Because, as you said, you lost focus. The next time you face them, your powers will flow."

"Or I'll mess up again and you'll die right in front of me."

This encouragement wasn't working. "Every trainee makes mistakes."

"Does every trainee's mistakes get people stabbed and kidnapped?"

He sighed. "Not often."

"Tell me something honestly." She snorted to herself. "Sorry. Everything you say is honest. I don't know why I said that. But tell me. Our souls are linked, right? When my soul dims, it makes yours dim, and that makes you weak."

Was there any way to answer her question without increasing her burden of guilt? "I am strong when you are confident, yes."

"And the opposite is also true. So when I watched you evade the lieutenant, my fear made you slow and weak."

"That is a risk."

She shook her head. "I *am* going to get you killed."

"No." He gripped her. "You are angry at yourself, but this will pass. You will recover your confidence. And I will be there to cheer you on."

"What if it never comes? What if this is as good as I will ever be?"

"Then I will still be here, holding you, like this." He tried to burn his truth into her soul. "Someday, we will swim the open ocean as one. I promised to embrace you until you were strong enough to believe in yourself. And I will."

"I can't let you." She pulled back. Agony reflected in her dark, sincere eyes, in the tremble of her lips, in her soul light. "I told you a hundred times, you should find another woman. One who wasn't so broken. But I never thought that loving me would endanger your life."

"You still need time—"

"How much time?" She swallowed and held up his

mating gem. "I broke your gemstone. I saw you jolt when the trident hit you, but I also saw you spasm when I screamed. And I couldn't stop. What if I scream again in the middle of a battle? Or when another shark attacks?"

"We will conquer this together."

"I can't." She traced the crack, then pushed it at him. "Just take it."

His heart contracted.

Dannika didn't think he was worthy. She didn't think he was strong enough to bear her grief, help her to her feet after she stumbled. She didn't want to enter a new life with him by her side. Her selflessness showed again. She would deny herself happiness and live the rest of her life alone to keep him safe.

Long ago, back in Undine, he'd dreamed of a bride who would desire his honesty, treasure their union, and hunger for the truth. Dannika did that.

But his truth did not give her comfort.

His throat tightened. He tried to clear the lump, but it choked him. He tried several times and finally forced words through. Closing her fingers around the cracked gemstone, he pushed it back to her chest.

"I gifted it to you. Our souls *are* linked now. So, you cannot give it back."

Her chin trembled. "I don't want to hurt you."

"While I am gone, practice believing in us. In yourself. Hold this cracked gemstone and think your most powerful thoughts at me. Banish the fears. What is your dating phrase? 'Reframe your fears into belief.' You will give me the strength I need to return."

She closed her eyes and nodded.

"Ciran, Dannika." Angie summoned everyone to the table for a last meal. "Lunch is served."

Dannika rose, and Ciran clambered unsteadily to his feet. But he was already stronger. Meg's healing was powerful.

While Dannika remained here, he would consider how to remake himself.

He either had to become the warrior she needed, or he had to accept that he would never be good enough and return to Atlantis alone.

And this time, he would accept her rejection.

Forever.

TWENTY-EIGHT

The warriors left at dusk.

Everyone gathered at the shoreline. Without the barrier of the coral, the waves rolled up to the shore and crashed more violently. The spray misted Dannika even though she was farther back.

Ciran kissed her one last time. "You are a powerful queen. Focus on your strength. One crack is not the end of us. Believe."

Sure. Right. Okay. "I'll do my best."

Sadness shimmered in his vibrant irises. He stroked her cheek, joined the other warriors at the shoreline, and looked back one final time.

Dannika waved and pasted on a smile. Why, though? He could sense her true feelings.

Then again, she wasn't trying to fool him that everything was fine. No, she was still trying to fool herself.

Except it wasn't fine.

Her bones felt like glass tubes filled with helium. Her heart was squeezed in a wire cage. Everything was wrong, and she was sending Ciran into danger, and she had to be strong for him when her soul cried out in protest. *I am killing you.* She pressed the cracked Sea Opal to her chest and blinked back tears.

Ciran didn't smile as he turned and disappeared into the crashing waves. The other warriors disappeared as well.

They left the women and children behind on the forlorn shore.

Bex glared at the horizon.

Val leaned on the staff Bex had made for her. "We're as cheerful as a funeral."

Angie and Meg snorted.

Then everyone dispersed.

Dannika sat by the firepit staring at the sand until darkness fell. Bex asked her, "You going to sleep in the lagoon tonight?"

Without Ciran? The wires around Dannika's heart tightened. "I don't know if I could bear it."

"I felt that way." Bex hung two hammocks by Val and patted one for Dannika. "I'll be on the other side if you need me."

The wires loosened. Dannika sniffled and rubbed her nose. "Um, thanks. That's really kind."

Bex nodded shyly.

Dannika helped her tidy up, then clambered in the hammock. The routine and noise of the women putting their children to bed elsewhere on the island faded away. The stars spackled the night sky, and a breeze flushed away the stinging insects.

She pressed the cracked Sea Opal to her chest.

This was wrong. Ciran should be here. She should have been stronger.

Sending him away was just like when she'd sent off

Eliot. She'd made a mistake. She should have gone with him.

But then he might have died in front of you. Because of you.

Now he might die out of sight. She might never see him again.

Her bones ached, and the anxiety lifted her out of the hammock, forcing her to toss and turn.

She'd made a mistake. She *knew* she'd made a mistake.

But it was too late.

It was far, far too late.

———

THE WARRIORS SWAM in standard V formation with Konomelu in the lead. He and Itime had sheathed old daggers to their biceps and thighs. Chipped tridents rested in the crooks of their arms.

Ciran carried a shiny new trident. Lieutenant Orike's was well balanced and finely wrought, with the points twisted into tentacles. It was not what he would have chosen—his trident was solid, plain, and forthright—but it was much better than the human crowbar or a trainee's coral dagger.

This would have been a perfect test for the women and their budding powers.

Dannika. Have faith. I am strong enough to be your warrior. When I successfully return, please, please finally believe.

His heart beat out of order.

He forced his mind to clear.

Unlike the tumultuous trip to the island, the sea life no longer agitated their currents. Squids rilled past him peacefully. Sharks emitted their warning sirens with territorial swagger and faded away as the warriors passed out of their territory again. The off-tune yodeling of faraway giant cave guardians, utterly absent from around the island, marked their distance.

"Two more songs," Itime vibrated for Ciran's benefit. "Then we will drop beneath the echo point. That is where the current patrols like to hide and ambush unwary travelers."

They passed two more giant cave guardians, which the humans called giant octopi. In surface time, each giant cave guardian lived a day's swim apart, but under the water, time had little meaning. Unlike the circadian dictates of the surface, Ciran could swim for weeks without food or rest. There was only current, fish, and ocean.

His strength flagged and flourished on a rhythm. Was Dannika thinking of him? *I feel you. I believe in you. I am healed. You too can heal.*

Konomelu dove, and he and Itime followed. They entered a slower current and coasted to the vortex that carried vibrations across the oceans. Konomelu suddenly veered into a reverse current and held up a hand.

They both joined him. Ciran readied his trident.

"...come here? ... attack...exiles will not pass. Undine thinks...do...Atlantis..."

Five or six voices sounded too close.

Itime drew his thumb across his throat. Luscans.

Konomelu nodded and tapped his index and thumb together five times, hesitated, and another five times. Two patrols of five.

This was an ambush.

Curse it.

Ciran's attempt to get Lieutenant Orike to brag into the

echo point about having beached him had backfired. He might slip past one patrol, but as soon as he spoke a word, they would hear and capture him. Two patrols? He would never reach the echo point.

Konomelu raised his fist at the echo point—silently insulting the patrols with an obscene gesture—and then kicked into a fast current flowing away from the echo point.

When they were at a safer distance, he vibrated his change of plan. "We cannot reach the echo point. The queens must make their powers first. We will take the elixir to Angie and Meg, train them in the lagoon until they have the same force as Bex and Dannika, and then we will conquer the echo point."

"Agreed," Itime vibrated. "Ciran?"

They could descend for the elixir, or they could return early to the island. Five surface days would have passed by now. If Dannika had been practicing, she might have overcome her doubts.

I can't risk you.

If he was wrong, then they would have wasted more days. The patrol might return in full force and block their escape.

It felt like the wrong answer, but it also felt like the only answer he could give. "Agreed."

The trio descended to the barren, rocky seafloor. Great spires thrust upward amid mountain ranges and vents. Schools of fish and flashes of coral showed that they were closing on a mer city.

A giant ray lifted off and ruffled its wings like a whooshing ghost. It followed the warriors for too long before flying off on its own deep, melodious flight.

Konomelu held up his hand.

They kicked to a stop.

Juvenile squids fled big-mouth predators and swarmed silver prey.

Ciran couldn't hear anything.

Itime shook his head.

Konomelu frowned and continued cautiously over the rise.

Beneath, the tail of the wreck lay embedded in the seafloor.

Finally!

The tail had separated near the surface. The body must be close.

They fanned out, leaving sight distance between them. Itime winked in and out from behind the passing squids.

Konomelu pointed up.

Above them, on a tall spire, the main wreck teetered.

The tube was mangled. All the windows had broken or fallen out. Something had wedged the door closed, and debris filled the middle aisle.

Konomelu drifted above the wreck as a lookout.

Ciran wedged Lieutenant Orike's trident in the gap and forced the door open.

Metal shrieked.

Konomelu's eyes widened. Itime grimaced.

Ciran pushed and squeezed inside.

"Where is the elixir?" Itime vibrated quietly.

"It was in the lower compartment." Ciran sifted through the wreckage. Dannika's folders were strewn across the mangled seats. Her pen balanced on the broken table, as though she would lean over and take notes.

She had been so much brighter then. Bright and confident, and he had known she was ready to heal. Ready to embrace a new life. Ready to accept her second chance at true happiness.

That memory, like the plane, was now a hollow wreck.

"It has taken too long to find this." Itime peered through the holes. "I do not see a lower compartment. Has it sheared off?"

Ciran gathered the folders. A massive crab side-stepped from a dark corner. Ciran jumped. The crab clacked its claws, then crawled out the window and disappeared.

Where was the elixir?

Ciran pushed over the broken seat. The pen drifted down and bounce off a cracked, empty plastic bottle.

Uh-oh.

He waved off the dust. Cases of cracked bottles greeted him with jagged, empty smiles.

Heaviness filled his limbs. "I found it."

Itime flew beside him. "Where? Oh."

"The elixir has leaked out."

Itime studied the broken plastic, impassive.

They had risked so much, searched so long, pinned so many hopes on this moment.

For nothing.

"Every crab outgrows its shell," Itime murmured.

"Hm?"

"Sanctuary. It has sheltered us, but now it is our trap." Itime lifted the bottles one by one, seeking any shining droplets in the bottom. "I enjoyed seeing Meg in the ocean, joyful and fierce, as she was when we met. To think that she must retreat once more hurts my soul."

"Meg does not have to retreat. She made her power. You know, I do not think she is weaker than the others. Her powers are different. She is not a warrior, but my injury is almost healed, and no weak queen would summon a bull shark to her side."

"But she cannot shield herself or push enemies away. She is too vulnerable to battle at my side."

There, he was right.

But Ciran was from Undine, wasn't he? He kicked to the door. "This is a problem they trained me to overcome. How far are we from Lusca?"

"About a day." Itime kicked after him. "Why?"

"We should go there first, review the security, and gather information." Ciran squeezed out the plane door. "I will form a complete strategy for how to take over Lusca."

"Take over Lusca?" Lieutenant Orike's sharp voice repeated. "Not likely, Undine exile."

Ciran's veins froze to arctic ice.

The lieutenant floated overhead with a double patrol of brutally armed warriors. Konomelu thrashed in a net, his chest and limbs already bound.

Warriors descended around him and Itime, cutting them off from the plane or any other escape.

"I thought you would go to the echo point. But when you did not, I knew you would come here." Lieutenant Orike smirked. "Your bride has a strange power."

Ciran evaluated their attackers for weakness. "She is a queen."

"Of course a warrior who claimed to come from the mythic city would say that. But do you know what I learned? Your new Atlantis is made of exiles. Not even your weak All-Council will help you now."

"I do not need their help."

"You poisoned your bride with a strange human concoction. We destroyed it before you could poison the other brides." Lieutenant Orike curled his lip. "And after we imprison you, we will liberate all the young fry from the weak humans and train them to be proud Luscan warriors."

Help me, Dannika. I must defeat this patrol and escape to warn you. Think strong thoughts.

Itime rotated his trident, as did Ciran, clearly seeking the weakest warrior to make his best chance for an escape. "Only traitors violate the sanctuary of the brides' island."

"You violated it first. The Undine must suffer for his arrogance."

Ciran picked out his best chance, then pointed the trident at Lieutenant Orike. "Come and get me, then."

Lieutenant Orike's eyes narrowed. "Did you enjoy using a real weapon, exile?"

"Greatly. I used it to lever the wreckage apart."

His nostrils flared. "You did not."

Ciran nodded, never removing his eyes from the weakest warrior.

"He did," Itime said calmly. "I saw him."

Lieutenant Orike gritted his teeth. "Patrol? Do not kill these warriors. The king wants them alive. But he does not care about the condition in which they arrive." Lieutenant Orike lowered his backup trident at Ciran. "And I am going to enjoy beating you."

TWENTY-NINE

Two weeks after the warriors had left, Dannika awoke in a sweating panic.

Something was wrong. Very wrong.

The night sky faded into dawn. Stars winked out on the horizon, and the sky turned a pale white like the inside of an egg. A cool breeze rustled through the coconut palms and shivered through the long island grass. It chilled Dannika's sweat-dampened skin. She hugged herself.

The nightmare slowly faded.

Someone had locked her in a tiny coral-lined room, her body aching as though she'd been beaten nearly to death. Ciran's voice had echoed. *I am sorry, Dannika. I was not the warrior you needed.* And then a warrior she didn't recognize, an older guy with a massive scar running down his face through his left eye, appeared in the window to the coral prison and vibrated, *"Feed him to the kraken."*

And she'd jolted awake.

It was just a dream.

Just a dream.

She hugged Ciran's Sea Opal to her chest. Even though

it had cracked inside, the outside was smooth. It held together, fractured but whole.

Dannika touched it to her forehead. *Be safe. Be strong. I'm thinking of you.*

And then, with a lump in her throat, *You are the warrior I needed. You're my soul mate. Come back, Ciran. Please come back.*

The boulder crushing her chest rolled off, just for a little while, and she breathed deeply. Could she go back to sleep as she had the past three mornings? ... No. Even though she felt better, uncertain dread lingered on the periphery of her consciousness.

Dannika rolled out of the hammock, folded the scratchy grass blanket protecting her from tarantulas and who knew what else, and sauntered to the main structure.

Angie was already chopping a green pumpkin for breakfast. "You're up early again."

Come to think of it, Dannika hadn't slept in since she'd left New York. And compared to the nightmares, she'd much prefer to be awoken by nude warriors, tall or small. "Do you need any help?"

"I couldn't ask a guest." Angie smiled at her. Lines around her eyes showed just how hard she worked to stay in pleasant denial of their situation.

"I know." Dannika sat beside her on the mat. "I need to do something with my hands."

"Well, in that case." Angie passed over a pumpkin and a coral knife. "You can peel."

Dannika sat with the older woman and peeled pumpkins into a woven basket.

Early morning bugs skittered in and out. The seabirds cawed. Out on the shore, Bex stood alone at the water's edge, gazing in the direction the warriors had gone.

Meg stumbled to the preparation mat, yawning and rubbing her eyes. She blinked and peered at the piled-high basket of peeled, chopped pumpkins. "Mom, you made too much again."

"Did I?" Angie dropped her knife and sighed. "We'll save them or use them up one way or another."

"That's what you said after Luk and Prince Ankena disappeared." Meg collapsed on the mat. "Do you remember how much we threw away?"

"This is fruit. I'll make a wine."

Everyone fell silent.

The island, which had seemed like a paradise when she'd arrived, now closed in on Dannika. She'd walked its beaches and trails every day, searched for seashells or pretty rocks—or a passing ship she could signal—but her gaze kept turning inward.

She felt Ciran's presence more than ever.

His phantom arms wrapped around her. His soft voice murmured on the wind. *Believe in yourself, Dannika.*

Was this how Bex felt?

In her dreams, Ciran was in trouble, but alive.

And she just wanted to save him. Somehow.

But the dreams were only reflections of her inner turmoil. Any good psychologist would say that.

Bex walked to the firepit, winched it open, and stoked the fire.

"Any sign of the warriors?" Dannika asked, even though it was a stupid question. If they had sighted the warriors, everyone would have screamed and danced, even stoic Bex.

Bex shook her head.

"They could come back today." Meg penned a note in her squid-ink journal. "In a few hours, we could be chugging elixir on our lounge chairs while the Atlantis army destroys Lusca. We'd get Prince Ankena and Luk back and never even break a nail."

Dannika studied her ragged fingernails.

Bex chewed a hangnail.

Val limped to the table, rested the new crutch Bex had made against the wood, and settled into her seat with a yawn. Her split lip had healed to a scratch, and most of her bruises had faded to a ghostly greenish-yellow. "Oh my. I used to think I was a morning person, and here you all are."

"Not me. I never get up early," Meg said. "This is out of character. I had a bad dream."

What?

"Me too," Dannika said. "For three nights now."

"Oh my God, me too." Meg's eyes widened. "In mine, I'm trapped in a prison cell, and the king of Lusca is glaring in at me, making threats."

"Well, that is creepy." Val helped herself to a sliced papaya. "You've met the king of Lusca?"

"Oh yeah, he showed up to sink Mom's yacht. He's this terrifying old guy with gray eyes. Or, one eye. The other one has this long scar through it."

An unholy shiver traveled up Dannika's spine. "Meg, were the threats in your dream 'Feed him to the kraken'?"

Angie stopped chopping.

Meg gaped at Dannika. "What? Get out of my head. How did you know that?"

"I've been having the same dream, except I didn't know who it was. It's really more of a nightmare."

"Oh my God." Meg rubbed her arms. "Look at that. Goose bumps. Bex, have you had that dream?"

She shook her head. "No king. I'm trapped in tunnels, and it's getting dark out."

Meg shuddered. "No, thanks. Mom?"

Angie rested her knife on the cutting board, wiped her hands on a neatly woven mat, and then smoothed her eyebrows and neatened her hair.

"Mom?"

She stood abruptly. "I don't want to talk about it." She strode down to the shore, careful of the more aggressive waves.

Meg bit her lip, stood, and hurried after her mother.

Val made the *Twilight Zone* theme music and helped herself to another slice of fruit. "That's probably not a dream, in my opinion. Not that I'm a dream interpreter, but I'm just guessing."

"How long have you been dreaming about being trapped in tunnels?" Dannika asked Bex.

"A long time."

"Three years?"

She shrugged one shoulder. "Maybe."

Meg brought Angie back on the promise they wouldn't talk about it anymore, but Meg whispered that it meant Angie had had the same dream and was afraid to get too emotional.

She finished preparing breakfast just in time. The kids woke from their various hammocks on the island and crowded the food table—cranky and sniping from the unspoken tension. Why was breakfast always sweet pumpkin and coconut mash? Did they have to eat smoked fish? What did Meg mean, no pets at the breakfast table? Aw, she was so mean.

The same tension vibrated under Dannika's skin like a hot wire.

Angie clapped her hands. "If you can't say anything nice, don't speak."

The kids grumbled.

"Mom's right. When I was a kid, I was expected to be seen and not heard," Meg said.

One of her middle children rolled his eyes. "You were *never* a kid."

She leveled a slice of papaya at him. "Sometimes, it feels like it."

They ate a subdued breakfast. The kids haphazardly finished their chores and then spilled down to the sand, but the fighting and crying didn't let up.

"Mom, Squiddy washed up on the beach." One of Meg's younger sons waved a floppy, very deceased squid. "Can you fix him?"

Meg pursed her lips. "Again? Oh…"

The squid hung cross-eyed and upside down, was missing one long arm and several smaller tentacles, and was coated in sand.

He was an ex-squid.

"I think it might be his time," Val said from the breakfast table.

The child shrieked hysterically. "It's not his time! He's coming back! Just like Dad!"

Oh, no.

Meg headed down the beach and hugged her sobbing child.

Dannika's heart ached for both of them. Because honestly, her son's cry echoed what they were all feeling.

Silently begging the warriors to come back, fearing they never would, promising herself that she just had to be patient one more hour and then Ciran would climb out of the sea triumphantly leading a whole army to rescue them. She had to cling to that fantasy.

Because if it didn't happen, then she'd never know.

They'd wait on, suspended between hope and terror, day after day. Like Bex had been for three years.

Dannika shuddered and hugged the cracked Sea Opal.

You are all right. You are fine. You are my soul mate.

Come back.

Meg carried Squiddy down to the beach and disappeared with him into the rough waves.

After just a few minutes, Angie joined the heartbroken boy. She scowled out at the ocean. Any warrior who saw her right now would turn around. But without the barrier, they couldn't feel safe.

Not that they ever had been safe. As Nuno's abduction proved, the coral barrier was illusory.

"You know, if Meg's smart, she's out there hunting for another squid missing a long arm and a few tentacles." Val munched on a snack of smoked fish. "You all are going through a tough time. The kids don't need more trauma. But how can she keep bringing it back? That squid was a little too ripe for calamari, if you know what I mean."

Dannika did.

Meg eventually emerged and waved at the water. Her child pranced happily. Angie descended beneath the waves. Despite the missing barrier, they didn't want to totally take away the familiar play area. Their current safety system was to let the children play in the shallowest section of the reef with an adult or older teen always present.

"Did you bring that squid back?" Val asked Meg. "Or was it an honorable burial at sea?"

"No, I did something. I don't know if you'd call it *healing* at this point, but yeah, he scooted off with a new, probably temporary, lease on undersea life." Meg slumped on the bench and dropped her wet face in her hands. "Ugh."

"All hail Lazarus," Val muttered.

"That's amazing," Dannika agreed. "I mean, the squid was dead this time. Really dead."

"Argh!" Meg straightened and lifted her hands to the sky. "Why? Why don't I have a useful power like shielding or pushing? Then we could've stormed off with the warriors, and *I* could have shielded them." She glanced at Dannika. "I'm sorry."

"No, I know." Dannika stroked the Sea Opal. "I'm the one to blame."

Meg stood abruptly. "This isn't helping. I have to do something. Something!"

Her kids screamed. "Mom. He started it. Mom!"

"Okay, that's not what I meant." Meg sighed heavily. "I'll be right back."

Sick pets were followed by broken toys. Everything went wrong. Everything was a crisis. And when the youngest kids cried to their mothers for comfort, they got hugs but left after mere moments, unsatisfied, and started wailing yet again.

Bex spent the morning hunched beside a salt-scummed, waterlogged, sun-bleached radio box.

Val stretched out her leg. It might be Dannika's imagination, but the swelling had finally seemed to go down. "Any luck with the radio?"

"Not yet."

"Did that whole caboodle wash up on shore?"

Bex shook her head. "Itime's dad, Elder Daka, brought us stuff. He said he was negotiating peace. He did always tell Ankena to go back to his dad and mend the rift, but Ankena said his dad was beyond hearing it." She shrugged. "Ankena was right."

"It's a marine radio?"

"Yep." She scratched off a speck of rust. "If I get it working, the range will be tiny. Someone will have to sail past, and you might as well light a signal fire. But." She shrugged again. "It's something."

And they all needed something.

Especially Val, who couldn't transform. If the warriors didn't come back, the women would wait for the kids to grow up, and then they could try something crazy, like swimming to Miami or Nassau. But Val couldn't do that. She was stuck.

"I hope we get lucky," Val said.

"Yeah." Bex blew air out of her mouth and worked on the wires again. "Could use some luck."

The morning passed into lunchtime. Tulu and Hadali traded places with Angie supervising the beach, one in the water and one on the sand, watching two fronts for danger. Angie returned to the firepit to start lunch.

"Everyone's snappish," Val said from her usual spot. "Maybe the air pressure's down. Hurricane's on the move."

"Good," Bex said.

"You want a hurricane? Here?"

"The Luscans only attack in clear weather," she said.

And Stevie might be crossing back and forth, in a grid pattern, exposing himself over and over to the danger.

They ate an uncomfortable lunch, and then the kids fought on the shore. Something was rising, and it wasn't just their impatience.

"Okay." Dannika addressed the adults together. "Let's just be honest. We all feel bad right now. And Bex?"

Bex looked up from the radio she was tuning from static to static.

"I'm sorry for doubting you," Dannika said. "You must have been living with this feeling for a long time."

"What feeling?"

"Like something is wrong," Meg said. "Like Itime's imprisoned and helpless, alive, but he can't get out. He's trapped. That's how it feels."

Angie crossed her arms. "I thought we weren't talking about this."

"We have to talk about it, Mom. Dannika's right. Bottling it up isn't helping."

"It's helped for the last twenty years."

"Okay, well, that's what you said when Dad filed for divorce, married his best friend, and gave you the yacht as the 'sorry I convinced you to live a lie, I guess I couldn't really do it after all' for also, if I recall, twenty years."

Angie flattened her lips into a white line.

"It doesn't matter how long you push the feelings down. They're going to come fizzing back up in the most dramatic, day-drinking, 'I'm not an alcoholic because I don't drink at night—because I pass out at four p.m.' drama queen bull hockey. And this time, Konomelu's not here to tell you to let it out."

"Language," Angie said.

"You want language?" Meg snapped her fingers. "I can tell you exactly what I think in Latin or Cantonese."

Mother and daughter glared at each other.

Bex turned to Dannika as if no one had interrupted. "Yeah, I've been feeling this way for three years. So, thanks. I'm glad you believe me."

Meg's shoulders dropped, and she opened her arms to Bex. "Oh, God. I'm so sorry. I believe you now. Hugs."

Bex accepted her hug with her usual stoicism, but her blonde brows lightened.

Angie smoothed her grass skirt, which today had a hibiscus corsage, and put on a pleasant smile for Val. "I'm so sorry you had to see that. Normally, we disagree with more grace."

"Don't worry about me." Val snacked on a strip of roasted seaweed. "This stuff is better than popcorn."

They all took a seat around the table and broke into the snacks and wine. It really felt better to discuss her dread in the open, and so once they'd all had a few sips, Dannika continued her facilitator role.

"Okay, so we all feel like our warriors are trapped. What do we do?"

"There's nothing we can do, which is why I refuse to dwell on the negative," Angie said. "Why upset ourselves for no reason?"

"Now, can I ask you something?" Val held out her hand. "Did you know your husband was gay when you married him?"

Angie sighed. "Yes. Of course I did."

"You didn't mind?"

"Well, I wanted to have children, and he was from a good family. Besides, I wasn't in love with him either. He was a kind man and great with the kids. It was a different time." Her eyes narrowed. "And then along came that Ellen, who came out on TV and convinced him it was okay, and ruined everything." Angie took a bigger gulp.

Meg rolled her eyes. "And then along came Konomelu and five more children. Hello?"

Angie nodded, unable to argue.

Meg shook her head at the other women. "I told you. Such a drama queen. But still, she's right. Even if the warriors are in trouble, we're stuck. We become true castaways. Nobody knows we're here. We're on our own."

That was true.

But was it really?

Could she reframe this the way she reframed the laments of new clients who insisted they would never find love?

"We're all feeling bad," Dannika said. "Let's honor our bad feelings."

The women looked at her skeptically.

"Honor them?" Meg repeated. "Like, honor them how?"

"We have to feel them. Really lean into the badness. We're all afraid of ending up isolated and alone. Let's honor that."

Meg set down her cup and rubbed her hands together. "Okay. Are we supposed to, like, close our eyes and hold hands?"

Angie pursed her lips.

"No, let's just be quiet inside and listen to that bad feeling. What's it saying?"

They all fell quiet. The wind rustled the palms, and the waves crashed on the shore. Insects buzzed and iguanas hissed.

Val crunched a seaweed chip.

Hmm. Well, maybe this had been a dud activity...

"Get out." Meg opened her eyes. "It's saying to get out."

Oh. It had worked?

"Get out?" Dannika repeated. "Of the trap?"

Angie opened her eyes. "Of the water."

At the same moment, Meg also said, "Get out of the water."

They looked at each other, eyes wide.

"That's a little odd." Angie tapped her lip with her index finger. "I suppose we are mother and daughter."

"Yeah, we're on the same wavelength." Meg laughed uncomfortably.

Val crunched another seaweed chip. "I thought the old reef was safe."

"I know, it is." Meg flubbed her lips. "That's so weird. Whatever. Ignore me."

Dannika hadn't had any warning when Eliot had died. The storm hadn't even made landfall, dissipating long before it reached her guest cottage as a mild gust of wind and a nasty black cloud. She'd had no idea that he'd already been ripped away from her forever.

But now she was a mer. She'd drunk the elixir and accepted Ciran's Sea Opal. Dannika rubbed the sphere in her caftan pocket. She felt him.

And the mind-body connection was real.

It was the source of her power.

She'd pushed it away. She'd filled her heart with fears. So many fears, like the squid crowding Meg until she suffocated.

Dannika opened her mouth to say something.

Bex did it first. "Maybe it's not safe."

Everyone stared at her.

"Maybe you're feeling a message." Bex touched her chest. "Maybe you should hear it."

"Oh, no. The children can't lose another familiar comfort," Angie said. "Besides, I'm used to this anxiety. Ask me how I was when I used to plan my husband's big soirees."

"When you were living a lie," Bex said. "And ignoring the truth in your heart."

Angie stopped smiling. "Yes, well... I don't want to *scare* them..."

"Kids!" Meg screamed, running for the shore. "Get out of the water!"

THIRTY

Angie watched Meg race down to the shore screaming. Her brows lifted. "So much for not scaring anyone."

The kids hustled out of the water.

Hadali went to Bex. "What is it, Mom?"

She put an arm around him. "Keep everybody up here by Val."

"Why?" Tulu carried his youngest brother with him while the others staggered, wet and dripping, behind them. "What happened?"

"Call it a bad feeling." Meg touching each of the children as if to count they were all present. "Mother's intuition."

They milled uncertainly.

"Hey, kids." Val summoned them to her side of the table. "You know what we can do on the interior of the island? A pirate treasure hunt!"

"Pirate treasure hunt?" the younger kids chorused.

"How it works is, I make a map with my fellow pirate leaders." She winked at Hadali and Tulu. "And we make a list of the island's secret treasures. Then you go and find them, and whoever gets them all first is the winner!"

Val was the true treasure.

And the amazing thing was how she kept coming up with new ideas to entertain the children.

"Are you sure you weren't a preschool teacher instead of a pilot?" Meg asked while the kids got together and decided on teams.

"Camp counselor." Val rubbed her ragged collar. "Ten years. I've got all my badges. This is just the top of my Mary Poppins carpetbag."

"Entertaining the kids will save our lives."

"Well, I hope it helps, seeing as there's not much else I can do but sit by this radio and hope somebody stumbles upon our island."

The radio crackled.

"Warn them about the reef," Bex said. "I destroyed the big part, but there are still fragments. They can bottom out."

The kids gathered around Val in their pirate treasure teams.

"We're ready for the pirate treasure hunt," Hadali announced.

"Well then, the first thing we need to find is ten seashells. Let's—"

"Shouldn't our hunt start at Cock-and-Balls Crater?" Hadali interrupted. "Everything always starts there."

Val blinked. "Where?"

"Cock-and-Balls Crater."

"Uh..."

"All our secrets are coming out today, ha-ha." Meg cleared her throat. "Why don't you show Val?"

"Can we?" the kids chorused.

"Sure," Meg said.

"I'm a little curious myself," Dannika said.

The younger kids skipped ahead.

"It's at the top of the crater." Hadali brought over Val's crutch. "You will need your staff."

Val grabbed his hand, oofed to her feet, and leaned on the crutch. Up the hill, past the shower, and deep into the interior, they completed a short, sharp hike to the tallest point of the island.

The Bahamas were not volcanic islands, so weather or something else must have sculpted the "crater" from the ancient limestone. Vines trailed over the sides. Inside, at the bottom in a lake, a massive, weathered phallic statue thrust from between two boulders. It did indeed resemble short, squat, somewhat deflated male genitalia.

"Huh." Val panted and leaned on her crutch. "Cock-and-Balls, you say..."

"It's, ah, not the most poetic name." Meg laughed awkwardly. "But this *was* the island of the sacred brides, so they would have fertility symbols, and once you see it, you can't unsee it, you know?"

"That's funny, because I see more of a giant squid. Those bulges on the sides look like eyes. Those ridges are tentacles climbing the walls."

Huh.

Actually, when Val said that, the boulders *did* resemble eyes, and the triangular flaps on the sides were more like fins.

Meg laughed in disbelief. "Okay. We've been living here twenty years and I have never once thought it was a giant squid. But you're right. That's what it is. Is that crazy?"

"It happens." Val grinned. "You just needed an outside perspective. Can we get down and check it out?"

"There is a way down." Bex pointed out a narrow, vine-strewn ledge.

"I wouldn't, though. Not with your leg. You have to hang off the cliff a little," Meg said.

A strange tone echoed in the crater, resonant and deep, like an ancient bell.

"What is that?" Dannika asked. "I keep hearing it."

Meg answered. "The, um, tentacles are clutching a bell. Like the Life Tree one, only bigger."

"It sounds familiar."

"We can go look at it. Actually, for us, there's an easier route from the lagoon. It's how we first discovered it."

They left Val with the children starting the pirate treasure hunt. Val promised to keep the teams together and inland until the women returned.

Bex led them to the lagoon. They undressed, and Dannika folded her stretched, fraying caftan. Pretty soon, she would have to weave some scratchy grass or give up and go naked.

Bex stopped them at the ledge. "Wait here." She dove into the water.

Her splash was bigger than the warriors, who disappeared with barely a ripple.

She emerged a moment later, head up, on the far side. "Boulder's in place."

Dannika hadn't even thought of it.

"Oh, good," Meg said, also making an oops face.

"Yeah. Come on." Bex dove.

The women hopped feetfirst into the water. Dannika let the water flow into her, heavy and wet and honest. Her throat closed. Her lungs convulsed.

You are changing, Dannika. No one can believe this for you. You must believe in yourself.

Ciran's voice said it, but her heart repeated it.

She had to believe it in herself.

Bex floated in front, her fins unfurled. "You ready for this?"

Nerves quickened with excitement.

Angie and Meg also unfurled their fins.

Bex kicked away from the ledge where they usually descended to practice by the Life Tree, toward a different wall.

Another tunnel hid behind artfully positioned coral. It was secret, all right. And narrow. A sudden current tried to pull them back to the lagoon. Dannika squeezed through, barely kicking as the tunnel enclosed them.

Worn carvings lined the tunnel curving down, down, down, and then up, up, up. Then the surface wavered overhead. They emerged in the crater.

Bex clambered onto a wide stone ledge, coughed, and gagged as she shifted back. Angie and Meg did the same, but less gracefully. Dannika was in good company as she hacked up seawater. Her nose ran and tears streamed from her eyes, but she survived.

Dannika sucked in a breath and coughed it out, then again, and she was better. "Oh, I hope this is worth it."

Bex grinned and lifted her hand.

The massive squid loomed over them.

It had the elongated triangle mantle, two side-mounted eyes, and indeed, the tentacles. Two long ones quested up the walls, but the smaller eight clutched a big round ball. A series of flat stones, kind of like seats, were scattered around it. Their surfaces were cracked and broken.

Strange symbols surrounded the base.

"Are those words?" Dannika asked.

"If they are, the warriors couldn't read them," Meg answered. "Ugh. I feel so dumb."

"What? Why?"

"Because Itime even told me that when the sacred brides were in trouble, they could summon the kraken with a giant bell. This is clearly the squid bell. Like, I always thought it was a little bell-like, but I've never needed to summon a kraken."

"They must have made the bell before the sacred brides were taken." Dannika walked around it on the narrow, plant-broken path. "The kraken used to be their protector. It wasn't always a destructive force."

"You're right. Huh, I never thought about the original purpose."

"These are the mirror stones." Bex tapped the flat, cracked rocks. "Yep. Giant squid."

Angie leaned over the big ball. "How do you suppose the bell rings?"

"Do you need to summon the kraken, Mom?" Meg teased.

"A lady is always prepared."

They all laughed. It was nice to explore rather than sit around and feel dread.

Bex paddled to the bell and rapped on it.

Nothing happened.

"I swear it makes noise sometimes," Meg said. "Maybe it's clogged. Or the ringer's under the water."

"We've looked before," Bex said.

"But that's when we were looking for cocks and balls," Meg reminded her. "We haven't looked for baby squid ringers."

"Ringers?" Angie glanced at her highly educated daughter. "Is that the official term?"

"Clappers." Dannika waded into the lake again. "My first husband repaired church organs. I got to know the terms for some of the other instruments."

They descended, shifting again. Dannika forced the water back into her beleaguered lungs and rotated to tease her fingers along the wavering surface. Shifting wasn't great, but floating as if the rippling surface was her floor and the seafloor was her ceiling? Redefining her world like that was amazing.

They clustered around the base.

"We discovered this statue when a tropical storm struck for, like, three weeks," Meg said. "We hid in the lagoon. And then we lost baby Luk. Mom doesn't like to talk about it."

"I have never lost a child before or since." Angie's arch declaration faded into quiet sadness as she, and then they, all realized that she had lost Nuno, although she hadn't even been in the water, so it wasn't her fault.

Meg broke the uncomfortable silence. "That was a crazy storm. Lieutenant Figuara was so worried about us, he brought in a fifty-pound snapper, in secret, and made his patrol think he'd eaten the whole thing himself."

Bex smiled.

"He was a nice man. It's really too bad about his replacement." Angie peered into the bell. "I wonder how it works."

Meg trailed her fingers along the base of the bell structure. "Look at this mud. The maid will never work in this town again."

"Isn't the maid us?" Angie scooped out a handful of silt.

"We'll never work in this town again," Dannika joked, and even Bex smiled.

They cleaned off the statue, tossing out vines that had fallen in and rotted, and scraping away to bare rock.

"Lieutenant Figuara was a gentleman." Angie reached up to her elbow into the base of the statue and forced out centuries' worth of muck. "But that Lieutenant Orike sounds like a confused little boy. No mother, no father. No grandparents."

"What do you mean, Mom?"

"Aren't the Luscan warriors stolen? The younger generation, I mean. Not Itime and Prince Ankena's generation. They knew their fathers. But that Lieutenant Orike and the others in his patrol, I'm sure I heard none of them had parents, and how can they be raised right? But warriors have to fight." She blew out a long stream of water, making her dark hair flutter over her forehead. "They need a stern talking-to, not death. And now poor Lukiyo is caught up in it. He was such a sweet child. I could never use any 'queen' power against him."

Wait.

Wait, wait, wait.

"That's it," Dannika said.

"Hmm?" Angie flicked muck off her fingers and it drifted down in the cloudy water. "What is it?"

"Your powers." Dannika floated back, and everyone turned to look at her. "You're afraid to use your powers."

Angie pooh-poohed her elegantly despite being elbow-deep in the mud. "What powers?"

"You're afraid to find out, but you can use your powers for good. To give that stern talk and stop those warriors from hurting each other."

"I don't see how." Angie flexed her fingers. "I know healing isn't my forte. And I refuse to make all the mess like a certain engineer who knocked down our coral and exposed the reef."

Bex twisted her lips to the side.

"Then don't. Use your power to hold back the people who would try to fight each other. Stop their attacks. Shield your sons and their enemies so they can all sit down and talk out their differences."

Angie leveled a skeptical eye at her. "I know I'm asking a lot, but I'm not entirely delusional. These are warriors, you know. They solve things by fighting it out."

"And you're not a warrior. Which means that you can show them another way. A way of peaceful disagreement."

"That's an oxymoron."

"But it doesn't have to be. You can have amazing power, Angie. You just have to believe."

And yes, Dannika knew exactly how hypocritical she sounded urging Angie to believe in herself when all Dannika's problems stemmed from being unable to focus.

"Just think about it," Dannika said.

"Shield." The tips of Angie's fingers glowed. She studied them thoughtfully. "I suppose I could stop fights. That would be ideal, really."

Bex made a noise. "Ah."

Everyone clustered around her.

"Ah?" Meg repeated. "What did you find?"

She rapped a long pipe with her knuckle. "The ringer."

"You mean clapper," Angie said.

"If it's outside the bell, I think it's a mallet," Dannika said.

Meg rolled her eyes. "Whatever it's called, let's gong it."

Bex eased the long pipe through the water. It tapped the bell.

The bell resonated in Dannika's chest like loud bass at a rock concert. "Whoa." She rubbed her chest.

The others mirrored her, equally affected.

The echo reverberated in a high G contrabassoon. Just like the squids' *doot-doot-doot* noises.

Because of course it did. It was a squid bell.

"It's a little flat," Dannika said.

"How can you tell?" Meg asked, startled, and everyone stared.

"Because it doesn't sound like a squid yet. Let's clear off the rest of the muck."

Somehow, this must be the key they needed.

The key to save Ciran.

And themselves.

THIRTY-ONE

Voices vibrated above the tiny coral-lined cell of Ciran's prison.

He peered up through the gaps in the coral.

The Life Tree of Lusca floated overhead. Spiked plates of coral armor covered its thick stalk to deter any destructive squids. They regularly emerged from the massive trench on the other side of Ciran's prison. Squares of red mirror stones pointed at the trench, keeping the kraken confined beneath. They emitted a constant high-pitched whine.

That was where they had thrown Prince Ankena.

And where he, Konomelu, and Itime would also be thrown.

Soon.

A strange angry scream reverberated through the city, momentarily silencing the voices.

Ciran floated to the wall of his prison closest to the trench. "What was that?"

"It is howling." Konomelu's vibration came weakly from the far cell. He hunched, favoring his ribs. "As we rage at the surface humans for taking our sacred brides, the kraken rages at us for taking her young fry."

"Her young fry?"

"The ones the king lets out to harness for his attacks. They chain only one in the field. See?"

Across the distant trench, a few tentacles moved, but the coral mostly obscured Ciran's view.

The howl died out.

A low musical tone hummed. The same vibration had sounded when Bex had destroyed the coral barrier, only much fainter. "What is that?"

"The warning bell. The Life Tree roots around it." Konomelu fell silent, then summoned the strength to continue. "When the bell tolls, the sacred brides are in danger. The kraken must rise. But in their hour of greatest need, the bell never sounded, and so the kraken never rose to save them. I long wondered why, but now that I am imprisoned, I see. Someone muffled the bell."

Ciran peered through. Was that a curve? "Dead coral has fallen on it."

"And slabs of curved wood, like the kind humans use for their hulls, packed with mud. The mud is a red color found in distant fields. It was brought here deliberately."

"Why did they muffle the bell?"

"Perhaps it was inconvenient. Perhaps the kraken arose even when the bell was not rung and caused damage. Perhaps..."

"Why muffle the bell if the mirror stone controls the kraken? Or does the bell overcome mirror stone?" He waited. "Lieutenant Konomelu?"

"I do not know."

Itime groaned from his cell and then fell silent again.

The voices sounded louder again.

"Someone is coming. Not the king." Konomelu wheezed urgently. "You escape. I will...I will make a distraction. Prepare to fight."

"Your drive to free me, while admirable, is doomed to fail. Rest yourself, Lieutenant."

Konomelu, and Itime in the cell between them, had barely survived the beating. The warriors had attacked them with rage pent-up over years of hate.

Ciran was in better shape, but he could not escape the city alone.

"You will see the truth in time," a confident young male declared as he floated down to the prison. "Lusca is unstoppable. No warrior stands against us, no human dares to hunt us, and we follow no rules but our own. Pledge yourself to our king and become a true warrior."

The speaker floated in front of Ciran's cell.

He was an older Hadali with darker brown hair, a fiercer expression, and a filled-out, adult body. Luscan tattoos crossed his torso and shoulders, the markings of having completed the first levels of training and becoming a warrior.

But on his chest, over his heart, a different style of tattoo was still just visible.

It was a phoenix.

"Lukiyo," Ciran murmured.

The young male turned imperiously. "That is Prince Lukiyo to you, Undine!"

Konomelu rose with a groan. "Luk?"

Behind him Nuno floated, defiant and scared.

"Nuno," Konomelu exclaimed hoarsely.

"Dad!" Nuno strained toward the cell. "Dad, I'm so sorry, I—"

"Silence!" Prince Lukiyo slashed a trident in Nuno's

face. Nuno jerked back. "Do not apologize to this traitor. He turned his back on his duty. On his king. It is a mistake you should not repeat."

Nuno glared at Prince Lukiyo. "Don't be crazy. This is my dad. You grew up with him. He was your first trainer, your—"

"Do not call me crazy. I am your prince."

"They got inside your head. You even sound like them now."

"Because it is my heritage. Thanks to my king, I have found my true purpose as prince and future ruler of Lusca."

Nuno shook his head. "You've lost it."

"I have gained everything. Their cowardice kept us on the land. Feelings weakened my father, and I am ruled by honor. Look at me." He gestured at his tattoos. "A warrior. You will become one too. It is what we always wanted."

"Not like this."

"Free your mind, Nuno. The traitors no longer trap you inside the coral."

"Mom and Dad didn't keep me inside the coral. Your king did."

"Because our fathers violated—"

"And they went inside the coral to snatch me. So they violated the rules too."

Prince Lukiyo scoffed at him. "My warriors would not do that."

"Ask them."

"No, no. I knew you would tire of being pent up on the island. Someday, you would break free, and when that happened, I would teach you. You would become a warrior with me. And it happened just as soon as I conveyed the order to Lieutenant Orike."

"As soon as he got the okay to swoop in and steal me."

Nuno jutted his chin. "And if you thought I would ever worship an insane, bloodthirsty maniac like your king, you never really knew me at all."

Prince Lukiyo crossed his arms. "Don't be stupid, Nuno. Living so long on the surface has baked your brain."

"Now you sound normal again."

Prince Lukiyo straightened and lifted his chin. His vibrations lowered to a deeper, more royal tone. "Return to my castle. Enjoy my fruits, my steaks, my bounty. But beware. If you do not pledge yourself to my king, you will join the traitors in feeding the kraken."

Prince Lukiyo called over two warriors who took Nuno away. He swam in front of the cells, glaring at Ciran, a still-prone Itime, and Konomelu.

Konomelu watched soberly.

Prince Lukiyo sneered at him. "You used to say I would never belong here. But look at me. I am a true prince."

Konomelu vibrated softly. "I regret that I was wrong."

"Well, I regret nothing." He slammed his palm on the bars. "You are the ones who should regret. Regret turning against my king! And you'll get what you deserve, just like my father."

Itime's vibrations emerged, calm and placid as always, but with a more ragged edge of pain from his prone position in his cell. "Prince Ankena fell in love with your mother. They were soul mates. It is an undeniable bond. Your grandfather ordered him to kill her."

"That is the past. You could have crawled back and begged his forgiveness. He would have taken us in and trained us as warriors."

"We would have stranded your mother."

"She served her purpose. And now she ruins Hadali,

weakening him the same way Angie coddled and weakened Nuno."

"If Bex heard your words, she would cry," Konomelu said.

"What are you saying? My mother would never cry. And anyway, she never thinks of me."

The warriors were silent. Some warriors stopped a conversation when more words were only noise.

Ciran was not one of those warriors.

"Actually," Ciran said, "Bex wanted to rescue you years ago."

The prince flew to his cell. "Oh, really, foreign warrior? Then where is she?"

"They stopped her." He indicated Konomelu and Itime. "Because they feared what your warriors would do if they caught her. And I think you're afraid too."

"Ridiculous. I never think of her."

"Is that why you told no one about her abilities?"

Prince Lukiyo frowned darkly and glanced over his shoulders, but they were alone. "I do not care. But if you care, do not say it aloud again."

The lieutenant and the other warriors hadn't realized anyone besides Dannika could breathe beneath the water, but all the young fry knew their mothers could breathe underwater as mer. Lukiyo surely knew. Which meant he'd kept it a secret all this time.

"Prince Lukiyo," Ciran said, "most mer have unresolved feelings about our mothers. Mine gave me up as part of the ancient covenant. She bore me, gifted me to my father, and returned to the air world. But yours did not. They took you from her. She has not forgotten."

Prince Lukiyo shook his head and kicked back. "Well, she should. I do not need her here. I do not care about her."

"That is a pity, because she still cares about you."

"She loves you," Konomelu said.

"Very much," Itime said.

"And she was waiting for us to return. Unless you do something, she will come for you."

"She will never come here." He laughed, but the vibrations sounded harsh and forced. "You are so stupid, Ciran of Undine, or wherever you are from. So stupid. I have heard all about your plans from Nuno. Atlantis queens, and other fables. If you are so wise, then why are you in my prison?"

That was a really good question.

And it was one that Ciran had been thinking about for some time.

Like his plans to escape—which currently relied on the miraculous appearance of a friendly outside force, since he could not succeed on his own—he had reviewed every aspect of Nuno's kidnapping.

He'd gone the wrong way.

Dannika was stronger with him. She needed him, relied on him. He kept telling her to have faith in her abilities, and he'd promised over and over that he would be her rock, her anchor, her pillar of support until she was ready to let that go and fly on her own.

And then, at the very first test, he'd turned away from her.

That moment when the patrol had dragged Nuno through the coral, Ciran should not have pursued them bare-handed.

No.

He should have turned and flown directly into Dannika's arms. Where she could see, feel, touch, and taste him. He should have helped her steady her power until her shield was impenetrable. With her total confidence and powerful shield, they should have gone after the warriors together.

Itime should have taken Meg. Konomelu should have taken...well, he should have guarded Bex.

Meg would have made the shark attack the kidnappers. Bex would have pushed anyone who tried to attack. And Dannika would have shielded them just in case.

They would have rescued Nuno.

Yes, his problem was that he'd said he'd believed in Dannika, but he had dropped his faith at the moment it mattered most.

And now it was too late.

"You will regret underestimating our king." Prince Lukiyo snarled at the prisoners. "You will regret it when we welcome new recruits and feed you to the kraken."

He kicked away, leaving the prisoners alone with the howl of the kraken screaming for her lost young.

THE WOMEN WORKED STEADILY on the base of the statue, occasionally trying the mallet again with softer taps. Bex traced the mechanism up and out of the water and peeled off vines. They could operate it above or below water. As they worked, the sound mellowed, then sharpened to a nice, solid high G.

Suddenly, Meg gasped. "Oh my God, guys." Meg held out both hands, eyes wide. "We've been ringing this thing all afternoon. Did we just summon the kraken?"

Oh.

Uh... "The sound wasn't quite right until the end..." Dannika matched the winces of the other women.

"No." Bex gave a final soft tap. "If the mirror stones are in place, the kraken won't rise."

"Oh yeah. Hey, do you think that's why it didn't rise when the island got attacked by the conquistadors? The mirror stones were in place?"

Bex shrugged.

"Itime said they used to ring the bell at an annual festival." Meg studied it. "His great-great-grandfather attended the last one. The kraken swam freely in the sea, and the warriors all got out and celebrated where it was safe on the land. After the kraken descended again, the warriors had to clean up after her. Of course, they stopped that festival after the brides were taken, so..."

"Does that mean she's been trapped since the time of the conquistadors?" Dannika asked.

Bex shrugged again.

"I know, right?" Meg shook her head and gazed up at the base of the statue from the clean lower depths. "And I thought twenty years was a long time to be stranded. I hope it's a big trench."

They took turns swimming around and under the bell.

"Is there a secret here that can save my husband?" Angie tutted. "I feel silly looking for an answer in an ancient gong. But..." She closed her eyes and opened her palms. "Answer me, oh sacred brides. Ancestors, spirits. What inner strength do I need to rescue my husband?"

"The sacred brides wouldn't know," Meg said practically. "They were enslaved, victimized, killed. Modern history doesn't know who they are. They were wiped out."

"Just like the mer," Bex said.

"But not even in legend, right? They're voiceless. Gone, forgotten beside a historian's footnote guestimating how many might have been lost in the carnage."

"Goodness, Meg." Angie fanned herself. "How depressing."

"It just means we probably can't rely on the past," Meg said. "Because if we do, we're just repeating history. And I don't know about you, but what happened to them is not what I want to happen to me. Or my kids."

Bex nodded.

"Yes, I know." Angie sighed and flexed her fingers. "I'm starting to acknowledge a sensation—I don't know if I would call it power, per se, but a definite tingle—and I simply don't know how to access it. I suppose neither did they, which is unfortunate because they certainly could have used some defenses."

Angie was right.

The power was within Dannika too. Bex controlled hers, but the rest of them struggled. Were they doomed to repeat the past?

"But the brides of the past didn't know their own power," Dannika said slowly. "We do."

"Hm?" Angie turned to her. "What was that?"

"The brides of the past didn't know they could wield power. Just like Bex never tried to transform, even though she felt like it might be possible. But she knows now. We know. We're not like the brides of the past. We're already different."

Dannika couldn't have saved Eliot. Even if she'd been with him on the boat. He might have died in front of her, or she might have died herself.

Ciran was still alive. She had the power.

She could save Ciran.

"I have the power," Dannika said. "We all do."

Her confidence glowed in her fingertips. A matching

glow kindled in Bex, then Meg. It lit up the bell and the undersea lake.

And then it lit Angie too.

"We have the power to change this," Meg agreed, wiggling her fingers. "But...is this enough?"

"Feel your power," Dannika urged. "Let out all your feelings. I'm sure that's the way. Angie, how do you feel?"

"I'm so flustered about the Luscans who've trapped us here." Angie made glowing fists. "I'm vexed they took Nuno and Lukiyo, and I'm also cross that they sank my yacht. I liked that yacht, even if I bottomed out on Bex's reef once or twice. Hmm, anger isn't really my best look."

"It's okay to be angry," Dannika said. "Anger is energizing."

"The Luscans are angry too. And their anger is destructive."

"But it doesn't have to be. We must use the energy to build, to save, to love. Not to destroy, but to create."

Everyone soaked in the light, and the bell resonated with their power, gently, peacefully.

"Well, that did feel better." Angie stretched her hands, focusing the energy into a glowing ball—a shield—around her body. "Meg, you try it."

"Okay. Um...yeah, I still want to go to grad school, even though I've missed twenty years of application deadlines, and the Luscans owe me at least twenty years' worth of birthday cakes. But I'll still heal them, because that's who I am." She shook her shoulders. "That's right. Bex, it's you. Go."

"Feels powerful." Bex flexed her sparkling fingertips, careful not to aim at anything, just bouncing the energy in place. "You know, I wanted to go with the warriors. They didn't want me to. I shouldn't have let them tell me no."

"You never let anyone tell you anything," Meg said.

"Yeah. I've been compromising for three years. It was the right thing to do until you came." Bex nodded at Dannika. "And then it was the wrong thing. Maybe I was scared to change."

"You know." Angie bit her lip, and her glowing shield flickered. "I wouldn't normally admit this, but I'm worried we may have to take this rescuing business into our own hands."

"Oh, me too, like, two weeks ago. Oops." Meg's light went out. She flicked her fingers, and the light returned. "Good. Oh, how funny. I couldn't shift for the longest time, but now I just know how to get it back."

Ciran had tried to be Dannika's strength, and she had only feared losing him, but she hadn't ever considered the other possibility—that she could lose him and then go take him back.

That's what she had to do now.

Wherever he was, she would find him. She would save him. And she would love him.

Because she was his soul mate.

Warmth blossomed in her chest and flowed down her fingers as if she'd taken a deep gulp of hot cocoa. It radiated through her body with whipped cream happiness. She opened her eyes, and the light glowed from her fingers too.

She reached out to Angie on one side and Bex on the other.

They reached back. Angie and Meg touched fingers on the other side.

The light danced between their fingertips, brighter and brighter. A subtle vibration shook the bell. Loose dirt and pebbles cascaded from hidden places, and the metal glowed. It sounded a pure, clear, bright tone.

Like the tinkling of the Life Tree, the sound felt holy, but unlike the Life Tree, the vibrations could also do damage. Its duality tingled in her fingers. This bell was anger, and anger could create or destroy.

The brides of the past had experienced tragedy.

The warriors had lived on twisted by their grief, closed off to future brides, unable to seek new soul mates.

Dannika had almost done the same. Rejecting the devotion of Ciran, she'd preferred her solitary, stunted, upside-down life.

But now she embraced Ciran.

She took his strength, and she gave him her strength.

Wherever you are, my love, feel me. I am coming for you.

Hope welled in her like a bubbling fountain.

She was coming for him.

Dannika opened her eyes and lowered her hands. In unison, the other women did the same, each blinking and flexing their still-bright fingers.

"Well, I don't know about you, but I'm ready to kick some fins." Meg cracked her knuckles. "Lovingly, of course."

"You must be my daughter." Angie smiled at her beatifically. "Because I feel exactly the same way."

Bex grinned.

A discordant noise echoed into the lake. Something was very wrong.

Bex turned toward the lagoon entrance.

Meg gasped. "Did you hear that?"

Angie stiffened and pressed a hand to her chest. "I'm sure it's... Hmm."

A panicked scream echoed down the tunnel from the lagoon. *"Mom!"*

Hadali.

Oh, no.

Bex's fins erupted, and she dove for the underwater tunnel, flying faster than Dannika had ever seen a mer move. The others followed.

Dannika's heart pounded. Dread reverberated in her chest. Her fins bashed the inside of the narrow tunnel. She'd unfurled them without thinking.

Dannika burst after the other women into the lagoon.

The boulder had moved.

Bex darted into the open ocean, heedless of danger.

The ocean was empty of mer, but filled, absolutely filled, with squid.

She shoved one derpy squid out of her path. "Hadali? Hadali!"

Angie and Meg floated behind her, calling for their sons too.

But wherever their children were, they weren't calling back.

Bex put out maximum power, vibrating to fill the ocean. "Hadali!"

No one answered.

The women swam into the cavern, not because they had any doubt about where their children were, but because they had to know why.

They had to know everything.

Dannika upchucked water to shift as quickly as possible. Bex staggered to her feet first, forcing herself to move as she threw up.

Val lay collapsed on the cavern floor, rocking and crying. She saw them and tried to get up without her crutch. Her leg gave way. She fell back with a cry.

Bex helped her to sit upright. "What happened?"

"I'm so sorry," Val sobbed. "I thought we'd be safe here. I thought we'd be safe."

"Val."

"We were up on the headland, searching for seabirds, and Tulu saw them. They were in that shallow water where you usually let the kids play. Then one of them walked onto the land. We hid in this cave. It was supposed to be holy ground."

"It's okay," Bex said.

"It's not okay!" Val sucked in a choking breath. "They came up from the lagoon, like you three just now, with weapons, screaming. The one big one said, 'The males are all gone, and females cannot protect the young fry on land, alone,' so they had to take the kids for their own protection. And I had my staff, but I just froze. I was so scared. I didn't know what to do. They took the children, and I—I did nothing. Oh, no." Val shook, horrified at her own inaction.

"It's really okay," Bex repeated.

"But I let them take—"

"Val, we know these warriors." Angie rested a calming hand on her shoulder, gentle but inflexible. "Bex means you did the right thing. If you'd interfered, they would have hurt you."

"I did nothing—"

"You've told us what happened."

"But I let them go. I let them all go."

"Val."

"I'm sorry. I'm so, so, so—"

"*Val.*"

"Sorry." She blinked and focused on Angie. "Sorry?"

"We need you."

She shook her head, confused.

"We'll have to leave you for a little while." Angie knelt and bowed. "You know how to operate the radio?"

"I mean, as much as we can operate it, sure."

"Then you must remain ready with the radio to tell our story."

"Tell? Story?"

"Val, we need you," Meg repeated Angie's earlier statement, and it finally seemed to sink in.

She calmed down, sniffled, and wiped her cheeks. "Okay. I can be here. I can tell your story for you. If it takes ten years before a ship crashes on that reef, I'll tell your story. I'll, uh, woman the radio and, uh, eat your squid jerky."

After all these weeks, Val knew how to get fresh water, how to shelter from storms, how to stoke the fire, and how to access the stores of food. She would be fine for a few weeks.

Bex held out her arms to form a huddle with Angie and Meg, and they motioned to Dannika to enter the huddle as well. Val rested with her back to the wall several feet away. The queens discussed their options.

"Feelings." Bex nodded at Dannika. "You said it. It's the diesel for our engine. So I'm angry. Angie?"

"Well, I'm highly displeased." Angie sucked in a deep breath and let it out with a glare that personified trouble. "No, I am angry. I'm slow to anger, but they managed it. Oh, yes, they actually did."

"Mom's angry now," Meg said. "Watch out."

"You?" Bex prodded Meg.

"Oh, me? I'm way beyond anger. I'm one safety violation away from an explosion at the fireworks factory."

Yes, that summarized Dannika's feelings nicely.

"They took our husbands," Bex pointed out. "Invaded Sanctuary. Violated their own sacred church."

"They violated everything," Meg said.

Angie said what they were all thinking. "This cannot go on."

And now it was time to do something about it.

"Can we lean into this feeling?" Dannika asked. "We're angry but focused. Sort of a calm rage."

"Isn't that an oxymoron?" Meg asked. "But you're right. That's exactly what's going on inside."

"Yes, I am enraged, and I'm also calm." Angie seemed to be feeling her way into acceptance for the strong emotions. "Because this will not stand. We will not allow them to take our husbands, take our children. We will go to Lusca, and we will get them back."

Everyone nodded.

Bex released the huddle and stood. "Right now."

They started in unison toward the water.

"I hate to just invade a neighboring city without warning. That's like attending a sit-down wedding dinner after you've neglected to RSVP." Angie pulled back her shoulders and straightened her spine. "But it is what it is. We don't always get what we want."

Dannika stopped. "Why not??

"Hmm?"

"Why can't we have everything we want?"

"Well." Angie frowned. "Because there's no way to send a warning that we're coming, is there?"

Meg and Bex both turned to Dannika. Realization dawned on their faces. It broke over Angie's a moment later. "Oh."

Dannika nodded. "The bell."

"Yeah..." Bex mused. "'Red skies at morning, sailors take warning.' That's their thing. 'Bell of the brides...'"

"Better run and hide?" Meg tried to finish her rhyme.

"Join our cause with pride," Angie said.

"That works too," Meg said.

War or peace. The bell had both meanings.

"But we can't ring it too soon." Angie tapped her index finger against her chin. "If we ring it now and show up a week later, they might not realize it's linked."

"True," Meg said. "Oh, but we can ask Val. It'll be a struggle, but she can do it."

"What are you all talking about?" Val asked, still shaky. "You're on your own mystical wavelength over there. I mean, whatever you want, I'll do it."

Bex returned to Val. "When we've been gone...a week. Ankena said it takes a week to reach Lusca. We're not experienced travelers..."

"But we'll go fast." Meg flexed her ankles, shifting from feet to fins and back again. "At least as fast as the warriors. We've got superpowers."

Bex considered it, then sketched out the plan for Val. "Seven days from now, exactly, go down into the crater and shove the long pipe. You'll see it. That will ring the bell."

"Okay." Val sniffed. "You want me to ring the bell?"

"As hard as you can." Bex nodded to Dannika. "It will warn the Luscans we're coming. It has two meanings. They can decide which one they want. A celebration of peace—"

"And they're welcome to join us." Angie opened her palms in invitation. "They really are."

"Right." Bex hardened. "Because the second meaning is a declaration of war."

THIRTY-TWO

Something was happening.

Ciran peered up through the coral prison.

The tone of the patrols sounded different. Anticipating. The first lieutenant of the city flew from unit to unit overhead.

Both teams with squids had left some time ago. They were continuing their reign of violence, sinking ships on the surface, and it was too soon for either team to return.

This was something different.

He flexed his hands.

They moved easily. He'd been feeling stronger and healthier for some time. Ever since he'd realized his mistake at the island kidnapping, he'd sensed Dannika in his soul, filling his body, flooding him with strength. Konomelu and Itime, in the other cells, had also healed—and more than he would have expected, given the normal rates of healing for the mer.

This was different.

"What do you think it is?" Itime asked calmly in the cell beside his. "Atlantis warriors discovered you imprisoned?"

"These are not military cries." Konomelu rested a hand on his cell door and rattled it, as he did occasionally, although it never opened. "They are bloodthirsty, predatory... Ah. New recruits have arrived. They will soon bring us out for display. And sacrifice."

Now. It was happening now.

A group of warriors descended from the Life Tree toward the prison.

"Remember the plan," Ciran murmured, floating back from the door.

"Of course I remember," Konomelu growled and hunched his shoulders weakly, trying to look as incapacitated as he had days ago. "It is all I have thought about since you told us. Although it is insane. Our actions will only hasten our deaths."

"Then I will see you in the blacknight sea," Itime vibrated calmly. "Second Lieutenant, it has been an honor."

"We will survive."

The unit gathered outside the prison.

One warrior opened Ciran's cell. "Out, Undine exile."

He floated out obediently and held out his wrists.

The warrior eyed him like he was crazy while he opened the other cells. "What?"

"You will not bind me?"

"No, weakling scholar. I hope you will resist." He grinned and thumped the base of his trident against Ciran's scarred shoulder. "The kraken likes her meat tenderized."

Konomelu and Itime exited and received more blows—because they were Luscan betrayers, whereas Ciran was just an ordinary enemy combatant. They directed the prisoners to fly up the armored stalk of the Life Tree to the central dais where the rest of the city had gathered.

As they rose, the odd territory of Lusca spread out beneath them.

Ciran tried to take in as much of the landscape as possible.

His plan depended on it.

The Life Tree of Lusca was old and venerable, and its nurturing radiance filled the normally barren seafloor with vibrant life. Healthy coral forests teemed with fish. The thick stalks of the mer castles punctured the seafloor, and the massive green spheres floated level with the Life Tree dais.

A mer castle grew a new layer of rooms every few years. Ciran had grown accustomed to Atlantis's young Life Tree and its small, whale-sized castles. Lusca's were the size of Undine's, colossal and magnificent.

But the city was lopsided, and there lay the key to Ciran's plan.

The forest and castles fanned outward from the yawning chasm. Lusca's Life Tree teetered on the edge. The slightest quake could slide it, castles and all, into the abyss.

Itime and Konomelu had described in detail what would happen next.

To sacrifice them, the king would change the orientation of the mirror stones. The kraken would loft a few tentacles and scare the new recruits into pledging their obedience to the king. For good measure, the king would sacrifice his enemies by tying a great stone weight to their wrists. They would fall into the trench, into the kraken's arms. Then the king would reposition the mirror stones to drive the kraken back, deep into the trench.

He had done the same to Prince Ankena. In fact, he had

even stabbed Prince Ankena as insurance. But Prince Ankena had somehow survived.

Ciran's plan was more ambitious.

Searching for Prince Ankena would be much easier if the trench were empty.

They would raise the kraken.

"We must trick the warriors into dropping us prematurely," Ciran had detailed. "As close as possible to the Life Tree. Then do not fight against the stone. Use it to swing closer to the stalk. The best would be to break the mirror stones closest to the trench. But as a backup, we will unmuffle the bell."

Because of the tentacles, no one would chase after them. They would have a precious few moments to move the coral, wood, and mud. But as soon as the bell cleared, the Luscans would have a different problem to worry about.

He hoped.

"We will have the same problem," Konomelu had growled. "And a kraken to avoid. Itime, reason with the Undine. I mean, Atlantean. This is madness."

"I approve."

Konomelu had frowned.

"We are past the point of reason." Itime had rotated his healing wrists. "It is time to fight madness with madness."

Now the Luscans led them up the stalk of the Life Tree and over the lip of the dais. There, in the center, rested the massive white Life Tree. Like all the old trees of the ocean, it sat on a mountain of unclaimed mating gemstones. Holy radiance bathed them with pure welcome.

Tinkling chimes soothed Ciran's jangling nerves and quieted his pounding heart. Large droplets of resin coagulated and rolled through the barren branches to drop at its base.

This was not his Life Tree, but he was a mer, and its radiance would always affect him, even if he drew healing from the sap of another.

The city's warriors clustered near the Life Tree. Two small boulders rested on the dais, causing the whole dais to slightly tilt. Gemstones tinkled as they rolled against the trunk.

Three warriors carried a third stone and rested it beside the others. The dais tilted further. Stones rolled and clinked.

The trio easily bore its weight, but a single warrior could not.

Hmm.

The stones were heavier than Ciran had calculated. If they were dropped from the center of the chasm, it would be impossible to swing or angle back to the land.

Itime and Konomelu looked at him.

He held out his wrists.

Again, their guard laughed. "You think to face your death with dignity? Oh, no. We will drag you to it screaming like the coward you are."

The Luscan guards bound the stones to their ankles.

Now they had a much bigger problem.

With ankles bound, they had no maneuverability. They would fall where they were dropped.

Konomelu and Itime looked to him for guidance.

"We must go." Ciran indicated straight down.

They nodded their understanding.

The Luscan warrior thumped Ciran's chest with the hard base of his trident. Pain echoed in his chest. "No talking."

He rubbed the spot.

Their guards floated out of grappling range, but close

enough to stab if they detected resistance. And the prisoners could not afford to get stabbed.

Ciran would time their moment of resistance. The other two subtly nodded, reassured.

Around the Life Tree, the rest of the Luscan warriors straightened and turned toward the largest castle. The vivid green bulb was so colossal that the grand entrance—which could fit six warriors swimming across—looked like a tiny pinprick.

The king emerged and led his entourage to the Life Tree.

The Luscans watched in taut, respectful silence.

His single gray eye glared at them out of his scarred visage. The sheaths for his ceremonial daggers hung from his thin arms, and he clenched his trident in his bony knuckles.

He was by far the oldest mer in Lusca, having outlived all the elders who had once caused him so much pain, and the skin around his face was unusually tight around his skull. He had no extra weight, and he was frail, but he'd continued to live on through sheer force of will.

Or of hate.

He shifted his fins to human feet and touched down on the dais beside a long lever.

Prince Lukiyo floated behind him, pale and noble. The sheaths on his arms and thighs were tight and strong, and he carried his trident correctly in his elbow. He took his place to the left of his grandfather.

Another warrior dragged a bound, defiant Nuno. The warrior handed the rope to the king.

Nuno rotated in the water until he locked gazes with his father.

Konomelu clenched his fists behind his back.

"Those cowards have chosen their fates. Face me." The king yanked Nuno's rope until the young male obeyed. "Serve me or die."

Nuno sneered. "Die."

Prince Lukiyo swam forward. "Nuno. Do not speak so recklessly. This is your last chance. Swear you will follow your king."

"I'll follow him into the kraken trench and kick his fins."

The king pulled a long dagger from its sheath, gripped Nuno's forearm, and rested the blade under his chin. "You will feed the kraken. Perhaps in chunks."

Nuno tilted his chin away from the blade, fighting back his horror.

"Grandfather, no, please." Prince Lukiyo floated in front of Nuno. "I can still reason with him. I beg you—"

The king turned his blade on Prince Lukiyo. The point flicked, scarring his cheek. Prince Lukiyo jerked back.

The king's good eye narrowed. "A warrior of Lusca does not flinch."

Prince Lukiyo stiffened.

"And he never begs." The king turned the blade on Nuno and swam him to the stone weights. "Remember your place, Lukiyo. Do not let the weakness of your birth doom you to death."

Prince Lukiyo flexed his fingers helplessly.

The king eyed Ciran. "Why is he in shackles?"

The guard whitened. "He is an enemy, my king."

"I have plans for him." The king gestured with the knife to release Ciran. "Make sure he has a good view."

Two guards directed him at trident point to a spot apart from the Luscans ringing the Life Tree. Konomelu and Itime watched him until the guards shackled Nuno to his stone and floated into place, blocking the prisoners from Ciran.

Curse it.

The plan was going more and more awry.

The king returned to the dais and dug out the mating gemstones that had rolled and piled around his lever.

The Luscans must frequently wait for their ceremonies to begin. The younger ones flicked their fins restlessly. The adults remained in stiff battle-ready formation with full weapons and tridents.

Konomelu rolled the rock, testing it.

Prince Lukiyo paced in front of Nuno. "Why did you not pledge? You could have trained with me. We would have commanded armies."

"You're not commanding anyone," Nuno snapped. "You're just licking the king's fin. Look at him. He's insane. If you flinch wrong, you'll end up here."

"I am his prince."

"So? He'll turn against you. Just like he turned against your dad."

"My father turned against him first. And he would never turn against me. I am his last heir."

"That's not true." Nuno snorted. "There's always Hadali."

Prince Lukiyo blanched. Then he snarled. "Hadali is nothing. I am ten times the warrior. He is too soft, too weak. He belongs on the shore."

"Yeah? Well, I doubt your insane grandfather cares."

Prince Lukiyo's chin wobbled.

An older warrior floated close. "Prince Lukiyo. Chin up."

"Quiet, Warrior Figuara. Do not talk to me." He kicked back to his place of honor and gripped his trident.

The former lieutenant, who'd watched over the island kindly before his demotion, floated closer to the tied warriors. "It pains me to see you here, Nuno."

"Well, then, do something about it." Nuno held out his hand for a weapon.

The guard slammed Nuno in the gut, causing him to bend over, and shooed Figuara away. He turned the pointed end of the trident on Konomelu. "No more games. You will feel its weight soon enough."

Konomelu winced to play up his preexisting injuries, hate burning in his eyes.

The king unearthed his lever and conferenced with his city lieutenant. The gist of their conversation drifted to Ciran.

Everything would start once the recruits arrived.

Hopefully, the new recruits would be older. Trainees taken from an unlucky traveling party or a raid.

A shout heralded their arrival. The city warriors parted to make an entry path. Lieutenant Orike led his patrol. He released a net. Inside floated out a mixed crowd of trainees, some very small.

Ciran's heart sank.

The youths saw Itime, Konomelu, and Nuno. "Father! Dad! Father! Dadaaaaa!"

Konomelu roared and struggled in his bonds.

Itime fisted his shackles, no less emotional, but outwardly calm.

The guards battered both of them. They curled into defensive balls. Konomelu realized his mistake and cut off his fury before they injured him.

The young fry screamed.

"Silence the new recruits," the king ordered.

The patrol jostled the young fry. The older ones obediently quieted, but the youngest wailed.

The king lifted his trident. "Silence him."

His captors jostled and shook the skinny young fry, but his cry elevated to a piercing shriek.

The king lowered his trident. "Must I do it myself?"

"My king." Figuara floated forward. "He is too young. He has had no training to obey your orders."

"No one is too young for punishment." The king twitched his trident at the nearest captor. "You silence him, or I will. And my method will leave us down a recruit."

The warrior's nostrils flared and pity flashed across his face before hardened obedience replaced it. He raised the base of his trident to slam it into the wailing young fry's skull.

Tulu darted in front and took the blow on his shoulder with a grunt.

Hadali pushed through the other trainees and yanked the wailing young fry into his arms. He rocked and shushed him desperately. The young fry's cry grew muffled.

Prince Lukiyo flew to his brother. "What are you doing here? How could you leave the island?"

"I didn't." Hadali bounced the young fry to quiet him. "They came onto land. Lieutenant Orike broke into the sacred church."

Shocked murmurs echoed through the city.

So that sanctuary had been as much an illusion as the coral barrier.

Ciran's stomach squeezed. Why had he been feeling stronger and healthier? These armed, deadly warriors must have terrified the women.

The king floated forward, trident upright, and silence fell instantly. "Lieutenant Orike?"

Lieutenant Orike bowed to the king. "We carried out your orders and rescued the young fry."

"Grandfather?" Prince Lukiyo floated in front of the young fry he'd grown up with. "You ordered him to break the treaty negotiated by my father and Elder Daka?"

"Lukiyo." The king hardened into obsidian. "Your place. Now."

"But Grandfather, the island is sacred ground."

The king's bloodless lips curled back from his teeth. His chest vibrated. "*Now.*"

Prince Lukiyo's brow knitted with worry. He kicked to his respectful position, straightened, and stared into the distance.

His brother and the others watched him. Betrayal mixed with fear, hurt, anger.

How could they unleash the kraken with the young fry here?

Ciran needed to think.

But there was no time.

"Ciran of Atlantis." The king waved him forward. "Watch carefully. Today, you witness the might of Lusca."

Did he dare to still summon the kraken? This position was perfect to make eye contact with Itime and Konomelu.

"You claim that your city is the only one besides Lusca that has the will to stand against the All-Council."

Nuno hunched, groaning. Konomelu would have to push his and Nuno's rocks at once, then explain on the dive. Was he strong enough?

"So it will be a pity when they come to rescue you and are wiped out. It has been too long since Lusca destroyed an army. Lieutenant Orike, go to the city's echo point and transmit that we are holding this Ciran."

Lieutenant Orike made the slashing salute, gathered his warriors, and flew from the ceremony.

"When we have wiped out the army, I will give you the privilege of being sacrificed to the kraken with what remains of your best warriors. Perhaps, if your city is as arrogant and stupid as you, they will even send their king."

How could Ciran save this? *Think.*

"Now, witness what happens to those who defy me." The king returned to the dais and pulled the lever.

Cranks turned with clicking and clanking. Below, the mirror stones rotated away from the trench.

The kraken howls changed tone. Tentacles writhed like a nest of blood-red worms in the shadows within the trench. They slithered out, not eight or ten, but fifty, a hundred, and probed the coral forest, invading and crushing the prison cell he had just vacated. Longer tendrils pushed on the bell, and the very longest wrapped around the stalk of the Life Tree.

Too late.

Too late, too late, too late.

Visceral fear stabbed Ciran. Ancestral dread of the kraken flowed in the darkest tunnels of his blood.

The king pushed the lever past its starting point. The mirror stones rotated back toward the trench.

Tentacles shied away from the Life Tree and retreated into the trench.

How could Ciran possibly release that?

The king pulled the lever into the middle, its starting position, and the mirror stones stopped rotating. The kraken writhed at the lip of the trench, its tentacles just emerging like a questing mouth.

"No one defies Lusca," the king intoned to his horror-stricken audience of warriors and recruits. "I control the kraken, the mightiest beast ever to roam the seas. No one will stop me. Whoever tries will die."

Any moment now, the king would order his warriors to drag the rocks out to the middle of the trench and drop them.

He needed another plan. One that protected the young fry.

But how?

He needed...

Doot-doot-doot.

A small reef squid jetted past, its skin flickering with multicolored sparks, signaling in a code only another squid could understand.

That was odd. They rarely left their surface reefs. For the length of his imprisonment, Ciran hadn't seen a reef squid. Why would one dive this deep?

Another reef squid motored over his shoulder, and a third one torpedoed down over his head.

Ah.

Relief flooded his bones. He rotated his shoulders. His chest lifted, buoyed with squid-shaped threads of hope.

And a new plan snapped into place.

He tried to catch the eye of Itime or Konomelu, but they were fixed on the kraken with horror, just like everyone else.

He tried to vibrate a message just to them. "Hey. *Hey.*"

The king looked up. "Atlantean, are you trying to beg for your life? Or the future lives of your unfortunate city? Do not bother. Surface humans stole Lusca's mercy along with our sacred brides."

"I do not need mercy." Ciran needed time. He straightened, stretched, and rolled his neck, loosening into a ready stance. "No Atlantis warriors will ever be thrown into this trench."

"What a pity. Lieutenant Orike assured me you thought they would try to rescue you."

"I do not need rescue. But you do."

The king's eyes narrowed. He had not reached this age by underestimating his enemies. He glanced at Itime and Konomelu, who still focused on the kraken tentacles as though unable to tear their mesmerized gazes away, and then to the young fry. But Ciran was a lone warrior, unarmed—again—surrounded by a city larger than Atlantis, and facing down a mythical beast that the king controlled. All these calculations played out across the king's face, and he finally allowed himself a small smile.

"I am in danger? Now?"

"Very much so."

The king's eyes narrowed again. "How mysterious, Undine exile. You have a plan, then?"

Ciran nodded. How funny that the terror of the kraken had momentarily blinded him to the deep inner knowledge. Just like Dannika's terror at thinking she'd lost him had momentarily blinded her. But now that he was focusing again, the soul-deep knowledge grew.

She was coming.

"I should not reward your arrogance, but it has been a long time since anyone has provided a proper entertainment." The king rested on his trident. "Enlighten me. How will you defeat me?"

"I will not defeat you."

The king nodded, irritated by the blather.

"But I promise you that in a short time, the attacks on humans will cease. The young fry you have trapped and terrorized will return to their fathers. The Lusca you have created will no longer exist. And you will not rule on the Life Tree dais."

"Ah. Will the new king be you?"

Ciran shook his head. "The warrior who takes your place and commands the city will be its rightful ruler: Prince Ankena."

The king jolted with shock.

Prince Lukiyo tore his gaze away from the kraken. "My father is alive?"

"Do not feed his delusion," the king snapped. "If he manipulates you so easily, perhaps you should share Nuno's shackles and find out for yourself how he died."

Prince Lukiyo clenched his trident.

The king turned his attention back to Ciran. "These traitors have fed you just enough information to construct an impressive fantasy. But I do not swallow such trickery. No one will overhear this lie and come to your aid. My warriors have swept the ocean clean. No rebels or exiles remain."

"Except for the most important ones. And they do not need to hear my words because they already know. Your actions have summoned them. They are coming, and you cannot stop their quest for justice."

The king frowned and glanced around. A few of his warriors appeared to listen, but most still watched the kraken.

"I am speaking, of course, of the ones you betrayed." Ciran pointed up, where two more reef squids fluttered past. "The sacred brides."

Itime and Konomelu looked up and locked eyes with him.

"The sacred brides?" The king shook his head. "Ridiculous."

"My king." Warrior Figuara floated forward apologetically. "We should not have entered the sacred church."

"It is long empty."

"But, my king, our sacred brides—"

"Lusca has no sacred brides, and Lusca needs no sacred brides. They are a weakness. What do we need of sacred brides when we can steal recruits whenever we want?" The king waved at the young fry who had clustered into a tight, defensive ball.

Perfect.

"Yes, my king, but we still have a duty to protect the island. Our ancestors promised, and—"

"Silence, Figuara, or you will join the other traitors."

Figuara twisted his trident in his hands, worrying the worn metal. He had certainly lost favor with the king. His trident was old and dinged. But it was functional, and the older warriors listened to him.

The king changed tack. "This Atlantis warrior speaks what you most want to hear. But we all know Ankena is dead. The sacred brides are gone. We had to take these young fry for their own protection. How could they be raised by humans? They would become shrimp lurking in holes."

The Luscans settled. Figuara studied the young fry with pity.

Ciran laughed. "Humans? What humans are you talking about? Humans did not raise these young fry. They were raised by brides. Brides on your sacred island. Brides that my mate taught how to become queens."

Another murmur spread through the warriors.

He held the king's gaze, mirth still bubbling in his chest. "Queens that are coming here to reclaim their young fry and their husbands. Reclaim what you took. Right now."

THIRTY-THREE

It was a good speech.

It riveted the Luscans. A deep frown wrinkled Figuara's brow. He looked back at the older warriors and then at Itime and Konomelu, who were both sharing Ciran's arch smile. They had to feel their brides coming too.

But it was a little premature.

There was a long, silent pause.

The king cracked a smile. "What a clever Undine joke. 'The brides are coming, and they are mythic queens with unimaginable powers.' Paugh. There is no such thing as queens, and no brides are coming here, because Lusca has none." He shooed Figuara back. "Do not forget your place. Or the next traitor I sacrifice will be you."

Figuara kicked away from the dais, but he did not return to his former drifting location. He straightened and gestured. The older warriors he had just acknowledged subtly moved behind him.

"Now." The king gripped the lever. "Witness my might."

Wong.

A strange vibration filled the city. A low, resonant hum grew and faded on a rhythm.

The mirror stones creaked in their fittings.

The king hesitated.

"What was that?" One of Ciran's guard whirled, seeking the source of the noise. "Some strange animal?"

"Distance could distort an animal's call," the other guard said. "I hear an echo. Coming from..." He looked down. "The trench?"

Ong...ong...ong...ng...g...

No, not the trench.

The king slowly looked up and stared right in Ciran's eyes.

He knew.

They both knew.

Warrior Figuara announced it. "It is the bell. The bell of the sacred brides."

Now.

"It is not the sacred brides," the king argued. "It is another trick of the Undine."

Ciran signaled Itime and Konomelu. While their guards were distracted also looking for the source of the bell, Itime hugged his stone and rolled off the dais. No one even noticed he'd fallen. Konomelu shifted his toes to human, dug in, and pushed off Nuno's rock.

Nuno exclaimed. "Dad? Agh!" The stone dragged him ankles first for the bottom.

The guards turned. "Stop!"

Konomelu rolled off and descended too quickly for them to arrest him.

The king watched them fall with annoyance. "What do

they think they are doing? There is no escape. The kraken will pick them off the ledge as easily as from the middle of the trench." He pulled the lever.

The mirror stones rotated.

Prince Lukiyo swam to his brother and turned, brandishing his trident at the rising kraken and preparing to defend the young fry from whatever might be coming.

Itime had dropped to the coral beside one of the mirror stones. He hauled the stone in his arms toward the Life Tree stalk. Nuno landed in roughly the same place, disoriented, and sat there. But Konomelu hit one of the rotating mirror stones with a sharp *crack*. The mirror stone remained undamaged.

Hmm.

He rolled off, urged Nuno up, and together they struggled toward the base of the Life Tree.

Tentacles rose from the trench like a twitching nightmare.

"See?" The king's lips stretched into a satisfied smile. "There is no escape."

Itime stopped at the bell and dropped his stone. The dead coral crumbled. Konomelu and Nuno put their shoulders to the planks of wood and levered them off. Itime tore at the mud.

The king stopped smiling. "You. Guards who failed me. Go collect them."

The guards who'd lost the prisoners looked at each other, then the king. The leader spoke. "I thought there was no escape from the kraken."

"They are not trying to escape the kraken. They are trying to free her."

"Free her? But you control her."

"I control the mirror stones, which they are trying to break. Stop them."

The guards kicked back and forth. "But they did not break the stone. Not even when they landed on—"

"I need not explain myself to you." The king aimed his trident. "Descend and stop them, now, or I will tie a stone to your fins and drop you in."

The guards descended very unwillingly.

Midway down the stalk, the kraken's tentacles jerked in their direction.

They fell over each other scrambling away and zoomed away from the city.

The king swore and pushed the lever to force the kraken to descend. While the mirror stones turned, he pointed to the next closest guards, which happened to be Ciran's. "There, cowards. I have turned the stones. In a few moments, it will force the beast back into its hole. Now, you do what the others could not."

They hovered, watching the prisoners energetically uncover the bell while the tentacles slowly, far too slowly, receded.

"What are you waiting for?" the king demanded. "The beast will not attack."

"We could wait for the kraken to fully disappear," one of Ciran's guards said. "Why not?"

"Because if the prisoners break the mirror stones, the monster will never recede again."

The guards lingered.

The king chased them away, slashing his trident. They moved more aggressively toward the prisoners.

And now Ciran floated without guards—unarmed, as usual—before the Luscan king.

Everything was going according to plan.

Finally.

The king's panicked gaze caught on his smirk and stopped. His eyes narrowed. He lifted his trident to Ciran's chin. "You are enjoying this too much. Should I gut you now?"

The king was deadly serious.

But Ciran did not flinch. Meg was a very skilled healer.

And all he needed was a little more time.

So he engaged the king. "Your city crumbles around you. This is your last chance to let the young fry go. Will you waste it instead on a foreigner?"

The king lowered his vibration so only Ciran would hear. "Even if what you say is true and those heretical mainlanders have transformed, they will find nothing here but death. Theirs."

"Were you that certain the last time you faced them in battle? And they defeated you?"

"They did not defeat me. I let them go."

Ciran stopped himself from vibrating the quick retort. *How merciful.* Because as much as he trusted Meg's skill, he did not want to distract from what was about to become a very real fight.

The king studied him as if he knew what Ciran had not said and was debating whether or not to make him pay for it.

Bong...ong...ong...ng...g...

A deep, resonant knell filled the city. Although it had originated on the sacred island, the city's bell now amplified it.

Konomelu, Nuno, and Itime had done it.

They floated back from the bell, still tethered by their ankles, and hugged their chests.

"It *is* the sacred brides." Figuara lifted his trident. "They call for our aid, and I, for one, will answer."

The older warriors who must have trained under Elder Daka mustered their weapons and flew into a formation behind Figuara.

The younger warriors, orphaned and trained only under the king, milled in confusion.

"No sacred brides call to us. It is some disrespectful humans who figured out how to bang a pot like the land monkeys they are." The king gestured at the two distant guards beneath the Life Tree. "Forget the prisoners. Muffle that bell. Warriors! Ah, I am surrounded by incompetence."

The two guards did not notice the king's change of orders. They tried to drag the prisoners away from the trench, but the rocks were too heavy. They cut the stone tethers. The prisoners immediately turned on the guards and wrestled for their weapons.

Kraken tentacles quested along the ledge, a creeping backdrop to their struggle.

The king pushed the lever. The mechanism made a grating sound and resisted.

Bong...ong...ong...ng...g...

A third strike reverberated across the city.

Crack.

The mirror stone closest to the Life Tree fell in two pieces.

More tentacles emerged. A new current forced the Life Tree away from the trench. The dais tilted, and mating gemstones spilled off, falling like iridescent raindrops for the coral below. The spiked armor around its stalk creaked in a warning.

Still, the king wrestled with the lever.

Lieutenant Orike returned to the center of the city with

his warriors. "My king, a strange mass of sea creatures drifts this way."

The king ignored him. "I must fix this mechanism."

"The mass is urgent. It is... I cannot describe it. It is organized, directed. I have never seen sea creatures behave this way."

"The sacred brides." Figuara faced off to him. "They summon us with the bell and now the very ocean."

"It is not a summons." Lieutenant Orike frowned at him like he was crazy. "It is an army. Mindless animals, and yet, they storm the city as though guided by a master. We must assemble and fight."

"Fight our own sacred brides?" Figuara lifted his chin. "I would rather fight the water I breathe."

"What are you babbling about, old male? I have walked all over that island. The other females fled. None live there now but a dim-souled human with an injured leg."

"You angered them. You did this. Their ghosts have arisen. We must answer or face their vengeance."

"How do you propose to entreat a ghost?" Lieutenant Orike shook his head in disgust. "While we debate, an unnatural mass descends on our city. Look!"

A sperm whale drifted over the city, not at its usual distance, but just above the tops of the castles. With it, bumping against the castles, soared an entire school of tuna.

"There are your ghosts," Lieutenant Orike said.

Figuara and the others gaped. "They obey the sacred brides."

"For the last time." The king released the lever and aimed his trident at the arguing warriors. "There are no sacred brides!"

Bong...ong...ng...ng...g.

"Then who rings the bell?" Figuara asked softly. "Who summons the kraken?"

Crack. Crack-crack. Crack.

More mirror stones fell. The dreaded tentacles rose level with the midpoint of the Life Tree stalk. It was so massive, the tentacles looked like the fingertips of the beast clawing at the edge of its crypt.

Bong...ong...ong...ng...g...

The rest of the mirror stones collapsed.

Ciran kicked back from the trench. Would their rescue arrive in time?

"There!" A warrior at the back of the assembly pointed. "Ghosts!"

The four women linked hands inside an impenetrable white shield, a bubble enclosing them safely while the animals Meg had summoned surged around them. Dannika floated at the far left. Energy surged out of her fingers and reinforced the bubble. On the far right, Angie did the same. They both had shielding powers. Meg and Bex, in the middle, amplified their power the way the two bells amplified each other.

Dannika locked gazes with him.

She had done it. She had found her power.

And nothing would ever make her doubt again.

He swelled with pride.

The king gaped at the women, then lowered his trident at Ciran. "This is your fault."

"Guilty." He grinned at the king and raised his fist.

The king's jaw dropped. And then rage crunched his face.

How satisfying.

Ciran did what he should have done in the shallow reef

long ago. He turned away from his enemies and raced toward Dannika with all his might.

"Warriors of Lusca," the king snarled. "Annihilate the invaders."

The Luscans who were still loyal to the king oriented on Ciran and charged.

THIRTY-FOUR

A few moments earlier...

The journey across the sea had been amazing, and now they'd arrived.

"I can't believe it." Meg shook her head. "Can you, guys? I mean, we never even asked directions."

Dannika and the other women had swum intuitively toward where they sensed their soul mates. They might not have taken the most efficient currents, but when the barren seafloor finally gave away to coral spires and then a whole forest, they'd celebrated.

The city was also amazing.

The Life Tree floated like a white flower shooting up from the ocean floor. It had a long green stalk, a circular platform for the petals, and the tree itself was like a white stamen.

Much larger mer castles bobbed around it on their own

stalks. The greenish bulbs glimmered with inner lights, but the Life Tree glowed the brightest of all.

"But that is definitely it. Huh. It's a chandelier," Meg said. "Well, half a chandelier."

Because the castles only radiated from one side. The city was situated on a huge canyon. From inside the canyon, a red mass rose, and tentacles twitched and squiggled. The unnatural motions set her stomach on edge.

"Is that the kraken?" Meg asked. "Ugh. It's freakier than I imagined."

"Don't be unkind," Angie said. "She can't help what she is. Even if that display is a little, ah, unsettling."

Most of the warriors clustered around the Life Tree. The closer they got, the larger the tree itself loomed. It was like a mighty, barren oak. Its white branches stretched for the sky, and masses of Sea Opals piled around its trunk.

And next to the kraken, it looked like a weed.

Hopefully, it would be as hardy.

"Well, we're here." Angie looked at Bex. "What next?"

Bex looked at Dannika.

Everyone looked at Dannika.

"We find Ciran. He always knows what to do." Something drew her eye to a figure floating a little apart from the others. "Ciran!"

He beamed at her.

And then the elderly warrior floating by the Life Tree pointed his trident at Ciran. Oh, Dannika recognized the scar. It was the king.

Ciran bolted for them as if he'd heard the starting shot of a sprint.

A flock of warriors darted after him.

He had a good lead. Dannika probed herself for doubts,

fears, worries—but they were gone. He looked healthy, strong, and pumped the water.

Meg eyed the warriors bearing down on them. "How many armies did Prince Ankena say attacked Lusca and failed?"

"Every army," Bex said.

"Oh. Good."

"But we're going to succeed," Dannika assured her.

"How do you know?" Meg asked.

"I can just feel it." She opened her arms to accept Ciran into her shield.

He flew at her full force.

One guard pulled his trident back and launched it at Ciran's unguarded back.

She dropped the shield at the last moment.

Ciran tackled her and they rotated in the water.

The trident flew harmlessly over his shoulder.

She lifted the shield. Hers united with Angie's, and their potent bubble expanded outward. Ciran's pursuers slammed into the white puffy shelter and flew backward, tumbling out of control. Their tridents bounced off it harmlessly.

Dannika hugged Ciran.

Her heart, her mind, her body filled with him. He was alive.

"You have done it." He pressed urgent kisses to her jaw, her cheek, her lips all while vibrating tender thanks and appreciation. "You have found your full power."

She had.

Energy flowed through her arms, lighting Dannika from within, wrapping around her with certainty. The certainty she'd craved from Ciran, she now made all on her own.

"Okay, lovebirds, I hate to interrupt, but I'm on a timeline." Meg rested her shoulder against Dannika's and eyed Ciran. "Dannika said you always had a plan."

"I do. And you have already executed your part flawlessly."

Bong...ong...ng...g...

"The last mirror stones have broken. I..." He frowned. "If you are here, who rings the bell on Sanctuary?"

"Val."

"Ah. Of course." He blinked rapidly as though mentally recalculating and then focused on Angie. "Your power is shielding? Konomelu, Itime, and Nuno need it now. They were cut off, along with two other warriors, beneath the city. As soon as we reach the young fry, you will break off, descend to find them, and extend your shield."

Angie pressed her fingertips together as though she'd heard a note she agreed with.

Ciran focused on Dannika. "You shield the young fry. Meg, prepare to heal the warriors, who will certainly need your services."

"You betcha."

"Bex." He sobered. "You are powerful. I only pray to the Life Tree that you are powerful enough. When the time comes, you must push back the kraken."

She nodded.

They swam toward the cowering children and unsettled warriors. Ciran entwined Dannika, and everything felt better. They were meant to swim as a pair.

A few Luscans led by Lieutenant Orike tried to make a stand, but Dannika and Angie's shield rolled over them like a marshmallow over scattered pebbles.

"Wait." Meg held up a finger as her long fins stroked steadily to keep pace with them. "Bex pushing the kraken might piss her off. Why don't I just ask her not to hurt us?"

Ciran blinked rapidly again. "You can do that?"

"Why not? I'm a Disney princess, and she kind of resembles the tarantulas I've been putting up with ever since my kids were old enough to carry them into my hammock. I can at least try, right?"

"Ah, yes, that would be incredible. Descend with Angie to push through these warriors."

Angie released Bex's hand and took Meg's. "Ladies, it's been a pleasure. I hope to be back shortly. If not, I—"

"Oh, let's just go, Mom." Meg tugged her hand. "They know you love us. We all know."

She blinked, then poked Meg in the belly. "Some of you are easier to love than others, I must admit."

"Please." Meg rolled her eyes.

Her mother grinned and descended, pulling a smaller bubble around her and Meg.

Lieutenant Orike brandished his trident. "By the order of the king, I command you to stop."

"And I command you to stop commanding me." Angie lifted her nose. "Respect your elders. Or did your king teach you nothing?"

He whacked her shield, but his trident bounced off with an equal force, and he fumbled it. The women descended through the scattered warriors.

"Stop fighting," Meg vibrated and also mouthed at them for emphasis. "We're trying to help you."

Dannika, Bex, and Ciran centered on the kids.

A line of older warriors protected them.

The king raged at the leader. "Obey me, Figuara. We have to distract the kraken."

The old warrior Figuara stood firm.

"Lieutenant Orike." The king searched the water and found him ascending from the fruitless altercation with

Meg and Angie. "You are on the unprotected side. Kill the young fry."

Lieutenant Orike frowned deeply. "What?"

"Throw their bodies in the trench. The fate of the city depends on it."

Lieutenant Orike rotated to face the kids.

A warrior floating beside Hadali gripped his trident. "Do not touch my family."

The king growled. "Prince Lukiyo. How dare you betray me?"

"I am sorry, Grandfather." He faced down Lieutenant Orike. "But I cannot let you sacrifice your new recruits."

Lieutenant Orike shook his head. Apparently, he did have some morals after all. He turned on Figuara. "You are acting above your position, old male. Obey your king or face my wrath."

Figuara parried his first blow. Lieutenant Orike's warriors rallied to him, and the battle was on.

The king kicked forward.

Prince Lukiyo met his trident with a clash.

"Now," Ciran said.

Dannika expanded her shield around the kids. Hadali hugged Bex. She returned his hug, but her gaze rested on the fight beyond their shelter. Prince Lukiyo was stranded outside.

The king held up his trident. "How dare you raise your trident to me? After all I have done for you?"

Prince Lukiyo lowered his trident. "I'm sorry, Grandfather. I just couldn't let you hurt my family."

"I am disappointed."

Bex released Hadali and darted out of the shield. She wove between the fighting warriors with lithe grace.

Prince Lukiyo hung his head. "Please forgive me."

"I will." The king lifted his trident and launched it at Prince Lukiyo's unguarded heart.

Bex thrust out her palm. "Stop."

The trident flew away from Prince Lukiyo. It whipped around and around and disappeared beneath the city.

The king glared. "You. Again."

Lukiyo straightened. "Mom?"

The king withdrew a jagged dagger from his arm sheath. "You have defied me for too long. First you turned my son against me. Now you weaken the will of my grandson."

"You shouldn't have sunk my sailboat." She dove back, keeping his gaze on her and away from the children. "Me and Ankena never would have met. You turned him against you all by yourself."

The king roared and slashed at her.

She kicked back toward the abyss.

"Grandfather, please." The dark-haired young prince flew after him. "Don't hurt my mom."

"Of all the betrayals, Lukiyo, yours hurts the worst of all." He grabbed the prince and put a knife to Prince Lukiyo's throat.

Lukiyo swallowed. "Please."

The king's blade pressed hard enough to draw a red line. "A Luscan never begs."

Uh-oh.

A light glowed beneath them. Angie, shielding Konomelu and Itime and Nuno, ascended and joined their bubble. Joyful cries filled the bubble as the children embraced their parents.

Hadali watched the standoff with pale fear.

"What can we do?" Dannika vibrated to Ciran quietly.

"This is all we can do. Prep Meg's healing powers and pray."

But Meg wasn't here. She was still below, alone and unshielded, trying to commune with a storybook creature.

"Let my son go," Bex said quietly.

The bell knelled through the city once more, vibrating in a deep, penetrating call.

The king tightened his grip. "As you destroy what I love, I will destroy what you love."

Meg fluttered her fins until she rose level with the Life Tree. "Okay, guys, relax. I did my magic. I am a Disney princess."

The kraken arose.

She was a mountain emerging from volcanic clouds, unfathomably vast like the Grand Canyon, an Easter Island statue from the perspective of an ant.

Lieutenant Orike and Figuara stopped fighting and gaped. Dannika hugged Ciran. He hugged her back.

The kraken's hundreds of tentacles fanned like a great unholy starfish. Each one jerked with its own intelligence. Six long feeding tentacles caressed the seafloor. Three beaks clacked beneath her fan.

She was a monster, hungry and free.

"Let Lukiyo go," Bex said. "The kraken will leave you alone."

"Your promise is empty. No mortal controls her!"

"You can't because we broke all your mirror stones. But Meg can."

"I can communicate," Meg said. "Control is the wrong word. And I'm probably not the only one who can. You guys really have to get over your issues with brides. If the kraken's roaming about, you'll need somebody here twenty-four seven to remind her not to snack on anything important."

"Lusca will never have brides," the king growled.

"Join MerMatch," Meg suggested. "Dannika will help you find your soul mate."

"My soul mate is gone." He whirled to face Dannika, dragging a pale, stiff Lukiyo with him. "When I was a young prince, my 'wise' elders convinced my father to force her from my arms. They prevented me from going to her. She died on the surface alone."

Oh, no.

"My father regretted his part in that decision," Itime vibrated to the king.

"I thanked him. Because I realized that exposing myself to a bride made me weak, just as in the Lusca of old, the sacred brides made our city weak. That is why none of my warriors will ever woo brides. We will swim the seas taking whatever we want. No soul connection will ever cloud our minds."

Ciran squeezed Dannika.

Yes, she understood. If it was possible to empathize with the king, to reach him even now, this was her time.

Dannika released Ciran and kicked out of the shield, parting the warriors to float in front of the scarred, angry old king. "I also lost my soul mate. That devastation leaves a deep and permanent wound."

He focused on her. His good eye narrowed.

"But look at what is possible from letting brides return to your city." She pointed at the kraken quietly twitching like a disturbing mountain landscape, the shields that she and Angie had made, and the huge family of island children. "Your wound will never disappear. But it is possible to let it scar over so you can move on."

"You think I am injuring my warriors? No. I am saving them." The king jutted his chin at Lieutenant Orike and the younger warriors he'd stolen and trained. "They will never know the pain I endured. They will only know anger."

"Anger can empower, but you have passed into destruction. And we will not let you torture your warriors anymore." Dannika opened her palms. "There *is* a future for Lusca. It includes friendship with the kraken and peace with the surface."

His eye narrowed.

"You are still the most feared warriors in the sea." Ciran emerged from the shield to support Dannika. "No one will rule over Lusca. Not even the All-Council."

"But you have to end your war." Dannika took Ciran's hand. "Instead of sinking ships, you could help the ones that have gotten into trouble."

The king recoiled. "We are no brainless dolphins. We are warriors. I decide who dies. My orders are absolute. No one will ever rule over me again!"

"Ah," Meg winced. "Don't shout. It upsets her."

One tentacle curled around the king's castle and tore it free the way a child plucks a daisy.

The Life Tree shrieked.

A throb of pain echoed in Dannika's chest. She was no mer, but even she could sense the fear of the Luscan warriors soaking the ocean.

The kraken tossed the castle across the trench. It landed on the empty field and exploded.

Ciran tugged her back. With him, she hustled into the shield and reinforced its strength.

"I decide," the king shouted, immune to suffering and fear because he already marinated in those emotions constantly. "I will tear Lusca from the ground before I take orders from a female. The kraken obeys my mirror stones. Her squids are my mercenaries. I take them, I use them, and I kill them!"

More tentacles tore at the ground, undeterred by the sharp coral and the armored spines.

The Life Tree shrieked again. The bell echoed with alarm.

"The time of sacred brides has passed," the king snarled. "We take what we need. No one will stop us. I am the king!"

The king dropped Lukiyo, turned, and raised his dagger at the kraken. "For Lusca!"

Bex dragged Lukiyo inside the shield.

Ancient castles collapsed around them.

Angie opened her arms to the frantic Luscans. "Get in. Come. Hurry."

Everyone, friend and foe alike, huddled close as their world ended. The collapsed walls of the ancient castles crashed on the shield with the force of a hundred terrifying plane accidents...and then casually slid off, as the shield held up perfectly, impenetrable and safe.

"Dannika? Ciran?" Meg clung to Itime. "I lost it. Backup plan?"

"Summon the kraken," Ciran said, hugging Dannika.

"I thought I did. We did, I mean."

"We must ring the bell."

Oh.

No time.

Backup plan?

"Ommmmm," Dannika hummed.

"Um, what are you—"

"High G," she said. "Ommmmm."

"Yeah, but—"

Angie interrupted, matching Dannika's tone. "Ommmmmm."

Meg shrugged and tried it, and a moment later, Bex chimed in. "Ommmmmmm."

Their tones couldn't possibly compete with the crashing city.

But... The kraken's tentacles lowered. She heard something.

Bong...ong...ng...ng...g...

A little sharp?

Dannika modulated her tone to match the bell. Her musical training came in handy.

The kraken turned away from the city.

Thank goodness.

Whoa!

Her movement caused a massive current as if an entire mountain range changed orientation. The Life Tree and the remaining castles were laid flat against the seafloor.

"You will not defeat me!" the king screamed, hanging from one of its red tentacles. "I will never be defeated!"

Almost as an afterthought, the tentacle rolled up, wrapping around the king like a fist closing over a gnat.

His shouts went silent.

The kraken flew away.

———

IT WAS OVER.

Ciran held Dannika. Her soft body melded perfectly to his. Her chest and fingertips glowed. The shield was white, but each woman's corner glowed with her own slight tint. They swirled together to make the shield.

She was magnificent with her power.

And so were the other queens.

They ranged equidistant around the sphere, like four lights of hope in a dark ocean. The remaining warriors of the city and the young fry sheltered inside. Across the crowd, Angie nestled against Konomelu, and in the other corner, Meg snuggled in Itime's arms. Bex glowed fiercely in front of Hadali and Prince Lukiyo, her hands up and ready to ward off any danger.

But as the harsh current tore by them, they floated in place, untouched. For a long time after the kraken had left, they bobbed gently, alone with only each other, in the empty ocean.

The Luscans remained quiet. Warring factions pressed too close to each other to fight. They were all united by survival.

In time, the bedraggled Life Tree righted itself, but it had a deadly kink. One castle shakily rose. Animals, mostly smaller squids and fish, flew past their shelter.

Dannika and Angie lowered the shield.

The groups spread out, gaining cautious distance from each other to evaluate their new positions.

Itime stroked Meg's hair. "You communicated with the kraken?"

Meg preened. "What can I say? I've got the Disney princess touch."

Dannika and the other women laughed. Bex smiled.

The young fry hugged their parents in a happy reunion.

Hadali hugged Prince Lukiyo. "I missed you so much. When you turned on us, I thought..."

Prince Lukiyo pushed him away and floated back from the families. His eyes reddened, and he swallowed hard. But most tellingly, his soul light dimmed.

In a mer, this was extremely rare.

Bex put her arm around Hadali's slender shoulders.

Prince Lukiyo regained control. "Grandfather...he just died. It was so sudden."

"He was awful to you." Hadali frowned in confusion. "Evil. He killed Dad."

Prince Lukiyo bowed his head. "I killed Dad."

"What do you mean?"

Prince Lukiyo choked.

The other young fry gathered around. Hadali tried to swim to his brother. Bex held him back.

"I'm the reason Dad died." Prince Lukiyo hugged his torso. "Grandfather promised to forgive everything if I pledged myself to him. I'd train to be a warrior. We could all be warriors just like we dreamed. So when Dad broke in to rescue me, I didn't leave. We argued, and then the king caught him and...and it's my fault they executed him."

Bex held Prince Lukiyo's gaze. "It's not your fault."

"But I wasn't ready to go. And I couldn't convince Grandfather—I wasn't a warrior. I was weak. I begged for Dad's life when I should have been strong. He had to execute Dad to...to kill the weakness."

"You were a child. He manipulated you. "

Prince Lukiyo shook his head. "He trained me. He tried to make me strong. He wasn't all bad."

"He was pretty bad, though." Nuno rubbed the cuts and bruises Meg had healed, and the other young fry agreed. "Your dad said he'd lost it. And he did. Way before he tried to take on the kraken."

Prince Lukiyo frowned.

Dannika tapped Ciran's chest. He released her, and she swam to Prince Lukiyo. "I'm not an expert, but I do know something about relationships. Abusers are never all bad, and trauma bonds are still bonds." Dannika pressed Prince

Lukiyo's hands gently. "It's okay to grieve for your loss. It'll take time, but you will heal."

Prince Lukiyo remained quiet, but his soul light brightened and stabilized. These were the words he needed to hear.

Bex nodded to Dannika in thanks.

Dannika let go of his hands and swam back to Ciran.

Prince Lukiyo wiped his face, then looked up and frowned. "Who are you?"

The other young fry laughed and gave him an abridged version. They were in great spirits, squealing and darting.

But Prince Lukiyo did not crack a smile. He surveyed the destroyed city. The Luscans had given up on their disagreements and now searched the wreckage for trapped survivors. Now that the king was dead, responsibility for the city fell on his shoulders.

Bex floated quietly next to him. "You can do this."

"I wish I didn't have to." Prince Lukiyo gripped his trident. "It should really be Dad."

"Then let's go get him." Bex held out her hand.

"He's alive?" Prince Lukiyo frowned at her hand, and at the rest of the queens and their husbands gathering around. "The Atlantean said so, but I thought he was lying."

"Second Lieutenant Ciran does not lie," Konomelu promised. Itime nodded.

"Your father is alive." Bex nodded at Ciran. He was the first to believe in her, and his belief had started their rebellion. "I feel it."

The rest of their island family surrounded Lukiyo—Itime and Meg, Konomelu and Angie, and even his old lieutenant Figuara—and their faith moved Prince Lukiyo.

"Come on, Luk." Hadali grabbed his other hand and tugged him toward the trench. "He's waiting."

Prince Lukiyo took Bex's outstretched hand and let his family pull him over the edge. "How can Dad be alive after all this time?"

Everyone turned to Bex.

She shrugged. "We'll have to ask him."

Ciran had never in his life imagined he would willingly descend into a trench—with his bride and multiple energetic, untrained young fry, no less—but Dannika and Angie remade their shield, and they voyaged into the depths like a mystical, glowing human submersible.

In the absence of the apex predator, all the lesser predators could safely come out.

Trench fish burst from hidden holes and gnawed on their shield. Colossal squids tried to entangle them with feeder tentacles, but the suckers slid off. Strange creatures had survived around the kraken, and all wanted a bite of the pliable but impenetrable bubble.

They wended beneath cliffs, descended into pits, and twisted into endless caverns deep beneath the city. Figuara ended up being particularly helpful. His skill at foreseeing which wily young fry thought it hilarious to dangle an arm out of the shield, into a fanged mouth, saved Meg from multiple healings.

Their journey felt aimless, but Bex flew unerringly onward, until at last, they pushed through a veritable forest of trench worms waving deadly pincers. Beyond the turn, Bex stopped.

A group of weakened, half-starved warriors were making their final stand. Worm corpses piled around their feet. More worms hissed, forcing them against the rock.

Bex blasted the worms with a brief, powerful burst. The corpses tumbled like piled leaves before a strong gust, and the living worms wriggled away furtively into deep tunnels.

The exhausted warriors turned to their saviors with shock.

Bex flew into the center and entwined an injured warrior with fiery red tattoos.

"Bex. My love, my dream. Here you are." The warrior pressed his bleeding forehead to hers. "I never gave up hope. I knew I would see you again."

"Prince Ankena," Angie breathed.

"He really is alive," Meg said. "Barely. Ugh. Look at those bruises."

"Dad!" Hadali crushed him in a hug.

He moved Bex to one arm and hugged his son with the other. "Hadali. You have grown so tall and strong."

Prince Lukiyo held back.

"My prince." Konomelu stumbled forward. "Forgive me. I thought you could not have survived. I failed you."

"I as well," Itime said calmly.

Prince Ankena straightened, Bex suctioned to one side and Hadali to the other. "My lieutenants, the kraken does not eat warriors. She is so large that she sometimes accidentally squishes them. But you could not have known this." He squeezed Konomelu's shoulder. "Once I reached a place of safety, her bulk prevented our exit. Until now. We had started to fight our way free when these infernal creatures cornered us. Where is Luk?"

The crowd parted to reveal his older son.

Prince Lukiyo flinched.

Prince Ankena regarded him as one warrior to another, gratitude filling his face. "Luk. Many hours I feared to come upon you in this trench. Seeing you this way fills me with pride."

Luk winced and shook his head.

"Do not hang your head in shame. I know your grandfather. Your survival is a triumph. I know what you must have done to survive."

He swallowed hard, emotion wrinkling his chin. "Dad. You can't."

"But I can." Prince Ankena held out his arm. "I know because I performed the same shameful actions to serve him when it was my time."

Prince Lukiyo flew into his arms, nearly knocking him over, and squeezed him so tight, he winced. "I'm sorry, Dad. You warned me. I'm so sorry."

"No, my son. I know. He was my father. And for all his faults, he has shaped you into a warrior. I am proud."

They hugged.

Ciran's chest swelled. He'd had a fraught relationship with his father. Both had tried to protect the other from the unreasonable Undine king, and their situation had caused moments of frustration and resentment. But he'd always known that his father had cared deeply. Now, Prince Ankena showed the same care for Prince Lukiyo. He helped his son to overcome his shame for past mistakes and flourish into an honorable warrior.

Dannika touched her chest and swallowed, then rested her head against Ciran's cheek. "You will be a wonderful father."

He stroked her shoulder. "I have not said a word."

"I know. I just...know."

He kissed Dannika. She tilted up her chin and wrapped him in her loving, heartfelt, soulful embrace.

———

THE REUNION with Prince Ankena was just adorable.

After he so touchingly greeted his family and close

friends, Figuara moved forward, waiting patiently but eagerly for his turn.

"Lieutenant Figuara." Prince Ankena nodded at the warrior while still surrounded by his wife and sons. "I will never forget your assistance today."

"I am the least of your rescuers, my king. What is this?" Figuara pinched a slender white dagger strapped to one of Prince Ankena's scratched biceps, and a curved, pink blade hanging from a thigh. "And this?"

"This dagger I fashioned from whalebone, and the other from squid beak."

"Squid beak! Such ingenuity."

"I had no weapon, and I thought, 'What would my bride do?' The result impressed even me." Prince Ankena tossed a regal smile at Bex.

She ducked her head and smiled quietly.

Which just made Dannika's heart squeeze. Oh, she loved well-matched couples.

Meg pushed forward. "I'm sorry, Prince Ankena. I just have to do this."

He tilted his head. "Do what?"

"Hold still." She touched Prince Ankena's brow. The bleeding gash closed. She traced bite marks on his chest, then rested her palms like the two paddles of a defibrillator. Meg closed her eyes and hummed a little elevator tune. His skin glowed, and injuries all over his body filled out, sealed up, and went down.

"Bing!" Meg opened her eyes and patted his chest. "Okay. You're brought back to life now."

Prince Ankena touched his scar-rippled tattoos. "Thank you, Meg. What was that?"

"A little something called 'queen powers.' You can thank Dannika and Ciran."

He smiled pleasantly, but with undeniable confusion. "Ah. Thanks to them. Yes."

"They are the reason we are here before you," Konomelu said, and Itime nodded.

"They've been an immense help," Angie agreed.

"Total lifesavers." Meg wiggled her fingers at the other survivors. "These are hot. Who's next?"

Prince Ankena's gaze sought them, and he extended his hearty thanks for the rescue—which he clearly did not understand—then accepted the guidance of his warriors and friends. After all, today was a day of miracles.

The other survivors were also rebels, exiles from Lusca, or unlucky passersby caught in the brutal patrols. With Prince Ankena's weapon inventions, vigilance at rescuing them after the initial fall, and constant encouragement, they'd banded together to survive.

And many were fathers who'd lost their children to the Luscan king. Once Meg finished her emergency healing, the whole group swiftly ascended to the city. Once more, joyful cries filled the ocean. Fathers reunited with sons, exiles greeted old friends, and happy tears mixed with wonder at the mythical events they had all survived.

The city itself was in shambles.

Sure, the Life Tree had survived—if it could recover from the kink in the middle—but only two of the bulb-shaped castles floated.

Figuara's warriors eagerly embraced Prince Ankena—now King Ankena—as the rightful ruler. They were desperate for leadership, and he stepped into the role as if he'd never left.

"Lieutenant Figuara, secure the city borders. I will not give predators an easy meal or let the All-Council think now is a time to strike."

Lieutenant Figuara straightened with the promotion to his previous rank. He summoned his warriors and formed units, then released them to the king. His most trusted warriors fanned out.

King Ankena pointed to the next unit. "Fly the patrol routes. Go to the surface and recall the teams that lead the squid. They must stop their attacks immediately. Collect any remaining warriors of Lusca and inform them of the change."

That unit soared out of the city, streaking for the surface.

King Ankena turned to the third. "Go to the echo point. Warn the ocean about the kraken. Not just Luscan warriors. Everyone. She goes where she will, and the mer world must know."

All the units dispersed, and then the king turned to the remaining warriors—kids, Konomelu and Itime, and others —to pull away the wreckage and rebuild.

Dannika floated with Ciran near the edge of the women and children. "Aren't you going to advise him?"

"There is no need." Clear admiration was stamped on his face. "He listens, like King Kadir, and reacts as I would. He is doing all he needs to do and more."

Fiery red tattoos covered King Ankena's now-healed broad shoulders and tapered waist. Aqua eyes with small iridescent red threads gleamed as he issued his orders.

Hadali rushed around, mirroring his father, organizing the kids to play training games to free up the adults to do the work. But poor Lukiyo floated in the shadows. He bit a hangnail, which was reminiscent of Hazel biting her nails.

Bex floated quietly beside him, just being present and listening.

"I'm the heir," Lukiyo finally said to Bex, but loudly

enough to vibrate to Dannika and Ciran. "And I accepted Grandfather's offer to teach me because I wanted to become a worthy warrior like Dad. But..."

He rubbed the tattoos over his heart. Luscan tattoos had overwritten Meg's phoenix, but the outlines of talons clinging to a willow branch lingered underneath. It symbolized the ability to bend and not break.

"I feel like everything Grandfather taught me was wrong. I shouldn't have listened. Maybe I'll never be fit to rule."

Bex shrugged one shoulder. "You always saw both sides."

"I'm sorry."

"No." She turned to face him. "I mean, yeah, regret your mistakes. Apologize, make amends. But don't get stuck on one 'right.' Your grandfather was stuck. Your dad almost got stuck too, but then he met me. People can be wrong but still get things right. Don't be afraid of your ability to see."

His chin wobbled.

She offered her arm.

He hugged her. They held each other. Suppressed tears made their eyes turn red, but neither one of them cried.

Aw. God. Dannika touched the corners of her eyes, even though she was underwater, so it wasn't like she had to worry about dripping tears.

Ciran squeezed her. "You will be a mother with true empathy."

Her throat closed.

Good thing she was vibrating her chest to speak. "You are so sweet. We must be soul mates."

Bong...ong...ong...ng...g...

The bell rang.

Again.

The kraken was long gone, but giant squid emerged from the trench and fought around the base of the sad Life Tree. They scattered the neatly organized piles of debris and chased the warriors.

Meg kicked down and successfully dispersed them.

Then the bell rang again.

Rinse and repeat.

The third time it happened, Meg called for a conference. Angie and Bex joined her, Dannika, and Ciran. "I guess we should have given Val a stopping point. How long do you think she's been ringing it? An hour?"

"In surface time?" Ciran calculated. "Five days."

"Days? Oh, her arm must be so sore. We'll have to do something super nice for her."

"A tasteful gift basket," Angie suggested. "Perhaps something pilot related. Or a rare mer delicacy."

"Oh? What's the specialty down here?" Meg's lips twitched. "Segmented trench worm?"

"That is no delicacy," Ciran said. "It is tough as the string you lace on your human shoes."

"Never mind. But we should surface fast before the bell undoes all the warriors' work cleaning up the city."

The bell rang again, and the contrabassoon *doot-doot-doots* grew in volume. Meg rolled her eyes. "Okay, you tell King Ankena. I'll be down managing the tentacled crowd."

She descended.

Angie kicked off to inform Konomelu and Itime that they were leaving. Bex floated toward King Ankena.

Lieutenant Figuara got there first.

His warriors brought a bloodied, bound Lieutenant Orike before King Ankena. "This warrior was escaping, my king. What should we do with him?"

The kids swirled around him. "Fish brains! Squid guts! Stupid urchin!"

"Young fry. Do not taunt a captured warrior. It is not honorable." King Ankena shooed them away.

They quieted and floated back to a respectful distance.

King Ankena crossed his arms. "Well, Orike. What do you want?"

Lieutenant Orike hunched in like a crab seeking a chance to swipe. "What do I want?"

"Yes, that is what I asked. Should I punish you or free you?"

His eyes narrowed. "What is this trick?"

"There is no trick. Do you wish to remain in the city of Lusca? Or do you wish to seek your destiny elsewhere?"

Orike slowly straightened. His hands closed on his empty sheaths, and his fingers curled. "Why do you ask me?"

"You are only a little older than Nuno, and my father trained you as he tried to train Lukiyo. Kidnapped, hating the surface, and despising sacred brides. I would wish mercy for Lukiyo if he was captured by my enemies, so I extend the same to you now."

"You can't let that jerk go," Nuno protested. "He beat my father and Itime. And he violated the island and the sacred church."

"Yes, I have conferenced with my lieutenants. He has learned none of the noble history I tried to impart to you and the other trainees. Study that, Orike, and I will hold you to a higher standard."

Orike floated back, freed from his bonds, his nose scrunched with disbelief. "All is forgiven?"

"It is not forgiven, but it is understood. You obeyed

orders. From now on, you are your own warrior. Join the new Lusca or do not. You have your freedom."

King Ankena saw a future in Lieutenant Orike that he didn't see himself.

He lingered, uncertain.

"Return his daggers and his trident," King Ankena ordered Lieutenant Figuara. "And extend the same mercy to any warrior who wishes to serve the new Lusca. We need all the warriors we can get to rebuild."

"Is it wise, my king?" Konomelu floated with Angie, and Itime lingered behind. "You do not know the character of the warriors you are so mercifully forgiving."

"I will learn. And I have the wisdom of Bex and the experience of my sons." He smiled at Hadali and Lukiyo. "Once we stabilize the city, we will begin an exchange. The trainees of the surface are behind in learning how to become warriors of the sea, and the warriors of Lusca are behind in learning about their noble heritage on the surface. And many must seek their brides."

"I'll host." Angie tapped her chin. "Dannika, how many of your girls would be interested in visiting Sanctuary to meet a merman? I must make more place settings."

"Ooh, you definitely will." Meg nudged Dannika's elbow. "Send as many candidates as you want. The price of lodging is one black forest cheesecake. Tarantula visits are free."

Using the island as an interim meeting spot might be perfect. "We'll work out a safe route from the mainland."

King Ankena smiled, then frowned. "Who are you again?"

Ciran snugged Dannika to his side. "She is my soul mate."

"Ah." King Ankena's frown deepened. "And you are?"

"He is my husband." Dannika squeezed him, teasing.

King Ankena tilted his head. "And you both are?"

"Friends," Itime said. "Bex will tell you. You must cover three years."

"Yeah, and the way Bex rambles on, you'll get the whole update in five minutes." Meg grinned at Bex.

Bex shrugged.

"You're concise," Dannika said. "It's a rare skill."

"Was I missing for three whole years?" King Ankena murmured, drawing his wife into his arms and nestling a kiss on her head, amid her floating hair. "Yes, there is much to learn."

"Oh, you'll be floored." Meg cackled. "Cell phones are tiny now. They made a whole TV show about castaways. And everybody knows about mermen."

"The surface world knows? Mainland humans learned of the mer? Impossible."

The bell knelled again.

"One of those impossible humans is right now ringing your bell." Meg raced down to disperse the rising squids, then raced back and snugged up to Itime. "Bex, catch King Ankena up before you ascend in all your royal glory, okay? I'll be waiting with the chocolate cake, and Mom will serve the noodles."

"Beef noodles," Angie intoned, hugging Konomelu. "Ginger noodles. Hand pulled. Mmm."

King Ankena flew with the ascending families to the edge of the destroyed city and waved farewell to their massed, shielded, thriving families.

It was not a farewell, but a see-you-soon.

As it should be.

Itime gathered his family, and Konomelu gathered his.

Dannika hugged Ciran. "Do you have a plan to get us home?"

"Of course." His lips quirked, and he pressed a kiss to her lips. "Not that anyone would dare attack this envoy, but just in case, you and Angie will shield us, and Meg will prepare her healing for the trainees who stick their arms out of the shield and poke the sea creatures that should not be poked."

Yeah, that sounded about right.

Dannika grinned at Meg and Angie. "Ready?"

"Yes, indeed," Angie said.

"Let's hit it," Meg said.

They flew through the undersea world, free and fulfilled, warriors and families.

Ciran kicked steadily, his powerful strokes propelling them forward. He tightened his arms around her.

Once they reached the island, she and Ciran would visit the echo point, put in a call to his warriors, and then continue to the mainland.

What a different world they swam into.

Any Luscan warriors would offer help instead of harm.

She melted against Ciran. His kicks were strong and steady and faster than ever before.

And possible futures surrounded them. Children darted happily. Fathers called them close, and mothers drew them into a protective circle.

She wanted that future for herself.

A family, a husband, a child.

It had been denied her and Eliot. She'd accepted she would never get what she really wanted.

But Ciran had always been beside her.

He'd had faith in her. Showed her life wasn't over. Insisted she deserved true happiness.

And she'd believed him.

More than believed him, she'd believed in herself.

Ciran squeezed her, knowing her thoughts without needing to say anything.

They rushed for the surface to embrace her second chance at her best, most loving, and most loved-filled life.

DANNIKA'S DINNER PARTY

"And so you arrived back at the island, my darling, and you were rescued?" Dannika's friend Frederik asked as he poured another serving of wine for his dinner guests.

Dannika sipped sparkling nonalcoholic cranberry juice. Her wine-colored sleeves pooled around her elbows, and the loose silk flowed over her growing curves. "That's right."

Ciran loosened the stiff collar of his formal black suit and leaned forward. "Actually..."

"Yes, I'm wrong." She beamed and clinked their glasses. Her eyes sparkled, unlike the similarly named bubbling water in her inaccurately described wineglass, and her chest glowed. "You're right. Technically, it was another, what, three weeks?"

"Correct."

"Three weeks before we actually headed home. Because..."

The guests listened to her adventurous recital, spellbound.

"I have to back up. The morning Val was supposed to ring the bell for us, she woke to red skies."

"The sign of the squid." Frederik sat beside his wife and wiggled his fingers in a spooky gesture.

"Right, and she'd planned to ring the bell in the afternoon, exactly the time we had left for Lusca. But she was so worried the Luscans might be sinking a ship that she braved the crater early."

"And was a ship being sunk?"

Dannika nodded. "Stevie's. Her first ring not only summoned the kraken, it also summoned that squid and saved his charter boat."

Val's ringing had been loud enough to reach Stevie's boat—and many others. Human equipment had pinpointed the island, and in a short time, she'd had more rescuers than she knew what to do with.

Ciran shared a smile with Dannika. He enjoyed hearing about this no matter how many times she retold the story.

———

Oh, yes, Val had really saved them.

While Ciran listened, his eyes glowing on her with love, Dannika shared the aftermath of returning to surface, finding the island occupied with all sorts of new people, and hearing Val's tale of, well, valor in the extreme.

They'd surfaced triumphant from defeating Lusca at Sanctuary and greeted Val with happy hugs. And they'd also met a few more new friends—but the story had come out in full that night, when they'd held a great feast around Bex's firepit. Val had shared her ordeal.

"You were right, Meg. That path down was treacherous." Val stretched out her sprained ankle, which, thanks to the new visitors, was now encased in a supportive first aid boot. "It took me a long time to get down, and at the bottom, I slipped and almost broke my other ankle."

Everyone gasped and shook their heads.

"And that bell is not easy to ring. Bex made it seem so straightforward. 'Push on a stick.' She neglected to mention the stick was suspended over the middle of the lake."

"Bex makes everything sound easier than it is." Meg patted Val's uninjured knee. "She's lovable but weird."

"I had to wrap the vines around my waist and lean all the way out with my crutch. It rang softly at first. I wondered if anybody could even hear it.

"But then I thought, everyone else got to be mer and I never would be, and that was okay because I'm devoted to those kids and you ladies, and I was going to help you the only way I could. I rang that bell so hard, the island practically shook down around me. I rang like I was going to tumble into the ocean. I rang it and rang it and rang it."

"You did ring it," Itime agreed calmly.

"And then the red skies cleared. I took a lunch break, rang it until the sun went down, and somehow I made it out of the crater without breaking my neck. The next morning, red skies again, so I went back up into the crater. For five days, I battled the red skies, and on the sixth morning, they cleared. And on the seventh day, who hails me on Bex's broken radio?"

Stevie raised his hand. He sat on a mat at the firepit. The crew of his chartered boat sat beside him, enjoying

Angie's island wine. They'd contributed johnnycake, crisps, and a tub of chocolate ice cream for Meg.

"It was loud," Stevie agreed. "And suddenly, our equipment started working."

"What about your anti-squid devices?" Dannika asked.

"Oh, they got retired. It turns out I'm a videographer, not an expert in battling megafauna."

"And so that was that." Val brushed her hands together and kissed her fingertips "I did something useful without meaning to. The end."

The women rushed to thank her.

"You saved us," Meg assured her. "You thought you didn't, but you did."

"Your ringing came at the most opportune time," Ciran affirmed. "I had run out of ways to delay the king. The bell pushed any undecided warriors to join our side."

"Yeah? Well, all righty, then." She sighed happily.

Stevie's pocket rang. He took his cell phone out and handed it to Val. "For you. Again."

"Oops, that's my wife." She put it to her ear. "Hey there, love. You caught me telling stories around the campfire. Yep, tooting my own horn again." She grinned at them, then staggered to her feet and limped on her thick metal-lined boot to give herself privacy.

"But Bex is below, ruling the oceans, huh?" Stevie sighed ruefully. "She always was doing something."

How unfortunate that his twenty-year search should end so close to his goal. The families talked it over after the crew retired, and Konomelu sent secret word down to Lusca. Dannika and Ciran delayed their departure long enough to receive an answer: Bex was on her way up. And so Stevie waited and finally saw her.

When she finally saw him and learned about his enduring rescue efforts, Bex was touched and overwhelmed.

She expressed it in her usual way. "Wow. I can't believe it."

"Believe it." He grinned and took her under his arm. "Here's a video of my wife. I met her on my second assignment, which I got, by the way, because I'd spent so much time studying the oceans thinking about you. She's a marine biologist. That there is our daughter."

Bex had shaken her head. "She looks happy."

"She is. We're a cheerful bunch." He faced her seriously. "I know you're surprised I'm here."

Bex shrugged. "You were always a good kid."

"Right, but I know you were only married to my dad for a couple of years, and I was already in high school. But you knew my parents. My mom was obsessed with revenge, my dad was obsessed with his image, and all their 'friends' were like them. But you didn't care about any of that. You pursued your own interests, rebuilt your dad's sailboat, and didn't care what others thought. You were the only normal person in my life."

Meg waved from the shelter to tease Bex. "I'm marking it in the journal. Today someone called you normal."

Bex grinned.

Stevie laughed. "So now you know how messed up my childhood was."

They spent the rest of their brief visit catching up on people they'd both known.

Stevie's father, who'd once threatened Bex's life to avoid a messy divorce, had finally gotten his comeuppance. He'd threatened a colleague who outperformed him. Instead of looking the other way, new management had taken the colleague's side, and Stevie's father had finally lost his all-important job.

And then he'd really lost it.

He'd never been charged with threatening Bex's life, but after a year of increasingly maniacal plots to get his job back, they finally arrested him on suspicion of conspiracy to commit murder. They had captured him trying to flee the country, and he'd died in jail.

"He died of a broken heart," Bex mused.

"Broken ego," Stevie corrected. "The heart died, well...I don't remember ever seeing it."

Meanwhile, Bex's cat had lived to a ripe old age with her lawyer friend. Hunter S. Thomcat had dined on the finest Meow Chow while Bex had been stuck on the island with more basic fare.

Bex's lawyer friend, in addition to caring for her cat, had held her portion of the divorce in trust for Stevie.

"So besides being the only normal person in my life and the reason I met my wife and had my daughter, you're also the reason I made a successful career in film today." He put his arm around her and focused the camera on them. "Say something meaningful to my wife and daughter."

Bex stared into the camera, then tucked a lock of dirty-blonde hair behind her ear. "Um, hi."

"Perfect." He grinned.

They parted with many tears—on Stevie's side, as "Bex has the emotional fortitude of a rock" according to Meg—and Dannika and Ciran returned to the mainland in the comfort of Stevie's chartered boat.

Meg and Angie stayed with their families on Sanctuary. They issued multiple takeout orders, and Dannika organized a regular delivery of chocolate, cake, and other essentials.

"Luscan warriors escorted us all the way to the main-land." Dannika wrapped up the story for the listeners at Frederik's dinner party. "We delivered a generator on our last trip, along with the first dating candidates, sponsored by MerMatch. We've had to institute a lottery system. It turns out that everyone is interested in a free vacation to a tropical island, and we don't want economic reasons to stop any match."

"You're a busy bee." Frederik raised his glass in admiration.

"And you're so sweet. Receiving this invitation to dinner delighted me. Especially since I thought you didn't want to reschedule." She turned down the long table and found the one listener who'd never smiled. "Senator."

The senator kept his hands folded in front of his mouth. Now he dropped them and crafted a frown. "Don't you think you're skipping a part?"

"Oh? Let's see." Dannika searched her memory. "You're right. As soon as we emerged and saw Stevie, I begged him for the use of his boat's satellite phone."

Hazel had been nearly inconsolable, sobbing incoher-ently for half the call and promising to stay extra safe for the other half. Someone had broken into the office to delete files during Dannika's absence. A clue must exist inside Starr's data backups, but they hadn't found it yet.

"A member of the Sons of Hercules had infiltrated the ground crew at the Bermuda airport," Dannika offered. "The government arrested three others on charges of terror-ism. Unfortunately, they couldn't trace it to any higher level of leadership."

Sometimes the way the Sons of Hercules operated, it seemed like there *was* no higher level. But someone was pulling the strings. Disorganization still had elements of organization.

And she had a list of the thousands of volunteers and donors from the charity celebration. It would take time, but Dannika continued to meet with them one on one, hoping someone would spark her memory.

It would happen. She would find the leader, and the violence against the warriors would stop.

"So we're still waiting on justice for the men who crashed our plane and nearly killed us." Dannika pressed her hand to her heart. "Thank you so much, Senator, for caring about our well-being."

His lids dropped to half-closed, and he stared at them, stone-faced. "Not that part."

"No?" She sipped her juice. "Hmm. Which part do you mean?"

"The part where you knowingly released a massive undersea cryptid into the ocean. One that is partial to wrecking our underwater assets."

"Mm. Gosh. Well, you know she's been cooped up for centuries. She used to get out every year. She's got a lot of energy to expend."

"And a lot of our military installations to break."

"Certain noises aggravate her."

"Yes, and she shrugs off sonar strong enough to break apart a man. Does she even feel it?"

Ciran tapped his fingertips against the table. "I would guess not, Senator."

"And that's your two's fault. What are you going to do about it?"

"The kraken will return to her trench when she is ready," Ciran promised. "As Dannika said, she must reacquaint herself with the modern ocean and tire of its stimulation. Then she will sleep."

"And in the meantime, American servicemen are risking their lives. And losing."

"Stop tilting at windmills." Dannika rested her hand on Ciran's. "Lieutenant Orike is leading the warriors of Lusca to follow her and help any ships or 'installations' she might have damaged. But they can't help if active sonar will blow them apart. Can they?"

His gaze narrowed.

"Well, I think it was a lovely story." Frederik took his wife's hands. "Brimming with romance, heroism, and a unique brand of underwater justice. And I also think it's lovely to see those reformed young men swimming alongside the sloops, returning lost hats and toys."

"Or beer bottles," one of the other guests said.

The others laughed.

Yes, the warriors had returned quite a few things to the sailing boats.

"And," Frederik sobered, "we have all lost a good friend to the tragedy of drowning. Perhaps these warriors will prevent such a sad loss from darkening our lives ever again."

———

Ciran watched Dannika's reaction, but the mention of her first soul mate did not cause her pain as it once had. She thanked the host sincerely for his kind words. Her soul glowed steadily.

And even though some of the guests had earlier looked at Ciran with concern, focusing on the tattoos crossing his cheeks and hands, they all smiled warmly at him now. Even the humans with no affinity for the water kindled a little glow in their dim chests.

Dannika had been right to attend this party.

She glowed and sparkled and connected with the other guests. Except for the senator, they glowed in response. Someday, she would turn the tide of public opinion, and the United States would offer new visas to the mer. It would be from these small interactions. The connections Dannika made every day just being herself.

She was a wonder.

Sometimes, even now, he ached for her.

He would wake in the night thinking she hadn't become his. Or he would have a dream that he was still in Atlantis having given up on wooing her. Or worse, that he had never escaped Undine, and remained silent as their king spouted hatred and lies.

But she always woke with him, turned, and linked their hands. And the glow in her chest was real, natural, and full of love.

His heart ached with love too.

After the dinner ended, the guests gathered in the den. Dannika made her farewells.

"You really must stay." Frederik walked them to the door. "We haven't seen you in so long, and with your dual marine-human lifestyle, who knows when we'll see you again?"

"Oh, thank you. I feel so welcome." She hugged Frederik, then linked her hands with Ciran's. "But we have a date."

Date? He didn't remember that.

She smiled at him, her chest glowing, and he moved easily to her side. With a sparkling, secretive look like that, she captivated him. He looked forward to this date.

The senator followed them and harrumphed. "Your little PR story? About the violent murderers returning toy ducks to toddlers? That was cute. But let's not forget that these warriors crave our women, and any day now, they're going to flip a switch. Instead of returning a toy duck, they're going to drag Mommy and little sister into the deep. That's why they're never setting one flipper in my country." He glared at Ciran. "Don't get comfortable."

Ciran tugged his too-tight collar. "I will not."

"Senator." Dannika unbuttoned Ciran's top button, and the strangling sensation eased. "You misunderstand."

"No, you're the one who misunderstands. I'll stake my career on never letting them touch my vulnerable, impressionable daughter."

"I meant about us needing to enter the United States." She smoothed Ciran's collar. "The only mer who want to enter the country have already partnered with US citizens. They, of course, want to meet their wives' families and introduce their children. But the rest?"

She shook her head and ticked off their alternate options on one hand.

"We have almost built our mid-Atlantic platform. The mer have multiple abandoned sacred islands. And other countries are very interested in the mer's Sea Opals and untapped ocean resources. If the US doesn't want to partner with the mer, that's your choice. But countries who do will reap the benefits."

He ignored Dannika and raised a warning finger at Ciran. "You'll never control my country like you control the water. Your light tricks don't work in the air. You might stop our depth charges with one of your shields, but on land, your game is over."

Ciran? Controlling light and shields? He laughed out loud.

The senator's brows rose in surprise.

Dannika patted Ciran's shoulder, suppressing her smile.

"I do not know how you rule the land," Ciran gasped between chuckles. "But warriors do not have these powers."

"That's what I'm saying. On land, you're helpless. Don't forget it."

"And under the ocean, warriors do not channel the Life Tree. We support and amplify the ones who do: our queens."

"Who come from the surface." Dannika shook her head at the senator. "And if you don't want US citizens to partner with warriors and control these amazing powers, so be it."

He frowned darkly. "This is another trick."

"Think about it. But if you really don't want US citizens to find mer soul mates, you'd better stop interocean travel and close all beaches. Because if the right people meet, you'll find you can't separate soul mates. The king of Lusca tried. And when it comes to the future of your children..." She rested her hand on her rounded, six months' pregnant belly. "I care about the future of mine too."

The senator flapped his lips.

Dannika turned on her heel, wished her friend good night, and pulled Ciran into the darkening night. Dannika's driver conveyed them away from the grand house.

"Will the senator change his mind?" Ciran threaded his fingers with hers and rested them on the rumbling car seat. "It is unfortunate that Angie's and Meg's children could not visit their homeland."

"I doubt it. I can only connect with people who are seeking the truth, and that senator made up his mind ages ago. But that's okay."

The car stopped in front of a small house. They exited, and she bid farewell to the driver, then led Ciran down the starlit path. "I used to think it was my responsibility to change the senator's mind. But some, like the Luscan king, can't hear others' pain. They're too focused on their own. And while I have empathy for their situation, I can't change them. I can only live in my truth."

Ciran followed her inside the human structure. Big windows showed the beach, sands, and grasses of Florida.

"This is a good view," he noted. "For the air world."

"It was my parents' winter house."

She released his hand and strolled around the lower floor. White cloths covered the furniture. She trailed her fingers along the ghostly shapes.

"I spent the first year after Eliot's death here, staring at the ocean, trying to understand my loss. I asked the sky and the surf, why had my dreams been taken from me? Why had I lost my husband, my chance for a child, my life? It's funny that when I was asking these impossible questions, I was already staring out at my future. I just couldn't see it."

Her chest burned with inner starlight. Matching warmth kindled in his body.

He was still sad on her behalf. She suffered so much after losing her soul mate, and there were still times he wished that he could somehow trade places with that male so she would not have had to endure the pain.

But her life had not ended.

She was here with him now.

He turned her in his arms.

She met his lowering lips with her upturned mouth. They knew each other's body movements now by heart.

Their kiss seared a heat deep inside, their souls glowing as the beautiful light surrounded them inside and out.

She led him up the stairs to a bedroom, opened the big windows to let in the sound of the crashing ocean, and unbuttoned her flowing maternity dress.

"It's funny that you look at me like that in the bedroom." She lifted one brow and paused at the button just above her full breasts. "In the ocean, we're nude all the time."

"It is different above the water."

Dannika's lips curved, and she released the button. The dress parted. Silk caressed her curves and dips, shimmering and seductive.

His mating gemstone, encased in wire, hung from a silver chain.

A crack still fractured the gemstone, but Dannika said she liked it even more now. Despite looking as though it would break at any moment, it had withstood the pressure and survived.

She peeled off her silk undercoverings and lay back on the bed. Her flowing curves, pliable as an anemone, undulated on the bed, and her hair fanned out.

She crooked her finger. "Come to me, husband."

He set his feet, unbuckled his belt, and hooked his fingers in the loops of his trousers. He pulled them over his hard cock.

She touched her lip with the tip of her wet tongue.

He shouldered out of his dress shirt and sauntered to the bed naked and proud, hard and ready.

She opened her arms in welcome.

He kissed her lips and, before she could get too heated, rolled her away from him.

"Ciran," she protested.

He rested his palms on her lower back. "Where do you need me to release your tension?"

She melted against him. "Oh, everywhere."

He kneaded her back and shoulders, then paid special attention to her feet and her ankles. She had earlier mentioned that these areas swelled along with her belly from the pressure of carrying his young fry. She moaned in heartfelt relief.

He rolled her over and stroked her belly.

She watched him.

He smoothed her cheeks, the lines by her eyes. She closed her eyes, then snagged his fingers in her teeth.

"You have caught me." He nuzzled her pointed nose, soft cheeks, lush black hair. "Now what are you going to do with me?"

She released his fingers and wound her arms around his neck. "Love you. Forever."

"I accept."

He claimed her mouth, driving in his tongue, and they surged together like the waves of the sea. She scissored him, catching his bent knee, and centered his cock on her soft entrance. She was already dripping for him, and the slippery sensation made him one hundred times harder. But he must take care not to put pressure on her belly. He rested on his heels, turned her on her side, and eased his cock in to the hilt.

She shivered, and her chest glowed. "Yes."

He rocked her gently, thrusting in and out, tightly encased in her wet heat.

She matched his rhythm, and he listened for the delicate sounds of her building release. Sometimes, in her need to connect, she tried to please him so much, she ignored her own pleasure. She was too selfless.

He chased her relentlessly, thrusting and bucking until she arched and cried out. Her channel gripped his cock. She shuddered, and her very soul glowed with deep, well-fulfilled satisfaction.

She was his past and his future, all he had ever wanted, and all he ever would want. And her pleasure carried him into his release. The world turned white. All he saw was her.

When his peripheral vision returned, her eyes were closed and she was smiling with bliss.

After such a long time of watching her struggle with happiness, this tableau made his heart clench.

He slid out to care for her, then settled her into the bed and made a shelter with his body. Above the ocean or below, he would always be her pillar, her hope, her strength.

She traced the worry lines on his cheeks. "You once said that you wanted to make yourself worthy of me. I hope you know that you are, and always have been, just exactly what I need."

He kissed her palm and pressed his forehead to hers. "It is nice to hear."

"And I've also decided to leave New York."

"You will leave MerMatch?"

"The office." She stroked his cheek. "You've long wanted to return to Atlantis and support King Kadir. I'm already dividing my time between New York and Sanctuary Island. So why not the platform over Atlantis?"

"What about the brides?" Journeying to the treacherous mid-Atlantic was much more complicated than journeying to an island equidistant between Bermuda and the Bahamas.

"This is kind of funny, but after we complete the plat-form, Hazel thinks we should hold a giant welcome party. Bring all the warring cities together and show them poten-tial brides, former brides, and what partnering with modern brides means. It doesn't solve the Sons of Hercules problem, but at least we could get the underwater world to understand our side."

"I think they already know."

"Right, but it's one thing to say you don't want to break an ancient covenant. It's another to look into the face of your mom or your future soul mate and tell them they don't belong."

He rested on an elbow. "I seem to recall being told—to my face—that my soul mate would never become my bride."

She covered his face with a pillow.

He tickled her, and she yielded.

"Agh. I know. And you left." She squeezed her eyes shut and shuddered. "I always knew you were mine, but I was afraid of what that would mean. And you came back, and literally, a few hours later, we got together. Here we are."

Yes. He rested his palm on her belly, where often in the night, he could feel his young fry move and kick. Here they were.

"You're right, though. Just inviting everyone to a big party is probably a little too simplistic." She closed her eyes with a big yawn. "I'll tell Hazel tomorrow when we return to New York."

He agreed.

But his mind stayed awake.

Could Hazel's giant party actually work?

Was it so unreasonable?

King Kadir always listened to his warriors' ideas. Queen Elyssa welcomed all visitors, even their supposed enemies, into the city to observe.

Some Atlantis warriors might return to their origin cities. Capable warriors, such as Lotar, could bypass the dangerous cities to deliver a message. Then, knowing potential brides, or past mothers, were searching for warriors might just be enough to pique their interest...

Warriors acted tough, as Prince Lukiyo had at the Luscan prison. But he had also secretly protected his mother and then broken down when actually faced with Bex.

The All-Council would stand against them. The Sons of Hercules would certainly attempt sabotage.

But it was a good idea.

And why was he surprised? His Dannika had shared it because it was intriguing. She was intuitive and wise about forming connections.

His young fry turned and pushed on her belly.

How wonderful to be born in an era when one could be treasured and loved by both parents.

If warriors came to Atlantis and saw the families, that too would be a powerful image to change their minds.

And any warrior could make a new choice.

Just look at Lieutenant Orike.

"Oh, well." Dannika snuggled against him. "I need to table it and sleep. Why think about all the details now? Go to sleep, brain. I'm so sleepy."

Yes, his queen *did* need her sleep. They could talk in the morning.

And yet...

She opened her eyes. Sensing, through her connection, that something was amiss. "What? You think it's a silly idea too, right? I mean, it's impractical. There's a kraken on the loose, and the ocean already has its share of dangers. Who would willingly expose themselves? What a fool's errand."

She squeezed his hand and settled once more into sleep.

But it was not a crazy idea.

And Ciran was not the kind of warrior to ignore a misunderstanding.

Ciran took a deep breath. "Actually, I think it will work. We just need to resolve a few small details. But I already know several warriors who would be perfect."

She rolled over and kissed him long and hard. "I can't wait to hear your strategy."

Because he always had one.

And as his soul mate, his one and only, the heart of his heart and mother of his young fry, Dannika understood.

Instead of sleeping like good, responsible future parents, they stayed up giggling under the covers and dreaming up a future where everything went perfectly to plan.

Dear Reader,

Thanks so much for reading!

Did you miss the first book in the series? Pick up *Seduced by the Sea Lord.*

The next book in the series is *Saved by the Sea Lord* starring Hazel and Lotar.

Would you like more mer shifter goodness? Join my newsletter and receive supersecret bonus epilogues full of yummy mer warriors + the women who tame them. It's like the happy ending to the happy ending.

Subscribe here: http://smarturl.it/StarlaNewsletter

See you next time!

Sincerely,

Starla

ABOUT THE AUTHOR

USA Today bestselling author Starla Night was born on a hot July at midnight. She hikes, scuba dives, and swims naked in the ocean. She writes about smokin' hot dragons and tattooed mermen at StarlaNight.com.